SILENT PLAYGROUNDS

The path through the park runs from the centre of the city into the wilds of the countryside, winding through old woodland and past the ruins of the mills that used the river to power the trip-hammers and grinding wheels of steel industry. Now it is a weekend playground for children and walkers, but on weekdays it is silent and deserted.

What starts as a routine missing-child report, when six-year-old Lucy gets lost, ends in the death of a young woman. Lucy tries to warn the people she cares about of the danger: she knows that there are monsters lurking in the rambling park, and she knows that they are getting closer, threatening to overlap into the lives of others.

Suzanne lives next door to Lucy, and she finds that her work as a researcher at a centre for young offenders pulls her life and her past into the web surrounding the young woman's death. As a potential witness to the crime, she inadvertently directs police attention to one of the offenders, Ashley Reid, but he mysteriously disappears before the police can question him.

What seems at first to be a straightforward crime turns into something darker, nastier and much more complex. DI Steve McCarthy has to find his way through a maze that involves drugs, lies, evasions and confrontations with the past. There are many questions thrown into his path, including the most puzzling: Why is Suzanne lying to him? But if he is to prevent the escalation towards tragedy, he must find some answers, and he doesn't have much time . . .

A dark psychological thriller that will hold the reader in its grip from beginning to end, *Silent Playgrounds* is the stunning follow-up to Danuta's Reah's highly praised debut, *Only Darkness*.

SILENT PLAYGROUNDS

Danuta Reah

HarperCollins*Publishers*

This novel is entirely a work of fiction. The names, characters and incidents portrayed in it are the work of the author's imagination. Any resemblance to actual persons, living or dead, events or localities is entirely coincidental.

Collins Crime
An imprint of HarperCollins*Publishers*
77–85 Fulham Palace Road, London W6 8JB

First published in Great Britain
in 2000 by Collins Crime

1 3 5 7 9 10 8 6 4 2

Copyright © Danuta Reah 2000

Extract from 'Silent Playgrounds' by Penny Grubb
reprinted by permission of the author

Danuta Reah asserts the moral right to
be identified as the author of this work

A catalogue record for this book
is available from the British Library

ISBN 0 00 232683 3

Set in Meridien and Bodoni

Printed and bound in Great Britain by
Omnia Books Limited, Glasgow

In memory of my father,
Jan Kot,
architect and artist
1913–1995

Przechodniu I powiedz Polsce, że padliśmy tu, służąc jej wiernie.
(Memorial to the Polish Parachute Brigade at Arnhem)

With many thanks to the people who gave me help when I was writing this book. I would particularly like to thank the e-mail writers' group, Sue and Penny, for their invaluable critical advice; Superintendent Steve Hicks for helping me again with details about police procedure; Professor Green for his clarification of details of forensic pathology, and for not laughing too loudly at some of my more off-the-wall ideas; to Richard Wood for his time and his advice about tracing missing people; to the staff at Kelham Island museum for answering my questions about Shepherd Wheel; to Teresa for all her support; to Julia whose editing makes all the difference; to Alex, and, of course, to Ken for seeing this book through with me from start to finish.

People who know Sheffield will recognize many of the locations in this book – Endcliffe Park, Bingham Park, Hunters Bar, Sheffield University. Green Park flats, however, exist only in my imagination, and though I have used the university campus as a setting, the university that is described in the book exists, again, only in my imagination. The coffee in the Students' Union is excellent, though.

I often walk through Endcliffe Park and Bingham Park, through the woods, following the route taken by Suzanne. These are just two of the many parks in Sheffield that are gradually succumbing to vandalism and neglect. Sheffield is enriched by the wild places that run almost into the centre of the city. It is sad that the people who hold the purse strings of the city do not value these places the way the people of Sheffield do. They are irreplaceable.

Only the blue delphiniums show
That these were gardens, long ago . . .

(from *Silent Playgrounds*, Penny Grubb)

1

It was dark now, the blackness pressing close, concealing the high roof spaces, the far corners, the heavy, shrouded shapes. Water ran behind the shuttered window, *drip . . . drip . . . dripdripdrip . . . drip.* The only light came from the glowing coals. Under the grate, the ashes whispered down onto the hearth. The warmth of the fire was fading, but even at its height, it hadn't pushed the shadows back far. The flagstones of the floor were damp; the timbers were rotting and crumbling. The metal of the grate was rusty. But the metal in front of him was bright, its edge catching the firelight, imprisoning it in the brightness of the steel, turning it a deep glowing red. The voices in his head:

When?
Soon, Ashley, soon.
How soon?
Now.

TAKE CARE IF WALKING ALONE BY ALLOTMENTS
The words were written in red felt tip on a piece of lined A4. The paper was attached to the bottom of the notice in the entrance to the park, DOGS MUST BE ON A LEAD. The writing was unformed, the hand, perhaps, of a child. The paper gleamed white in the sun. It had rained in the night, but the paper wasn't wet or smeared. The rain had stopped about five in the morning. At six, on that particular day, the contractors took their cleaning truck through the park, emptied the bins, collected the litter and the broken glass. A newspaper girl saw the paper as she cut through the park on the way to the next block of houses on her

1

round. She stopped to read it, shrugged, then went on her way.

It was still there when Suzanne passed shortly after ten. She had set herself the task of jogging through the two parks that formed a finger of green into the city, close to the street of red-brick terraces where she lived. There and back, it was probably about two miles, and yesterday she had almost managed it without a break. Today she would do it, and then look to extending her run further through the woods. She reviewed her plan for the day as she ran. Friday. A lot to do. It was her weekend to have Michael, and she liked to have those weekends carefully planned, filled with places to go and people to spend time with.

The notice caught her eye, and she stopped to read it.

Strange. What had happened to make someone put up a warning notice? She looked along the main path which ran on past the smooth grass and the carefully planted flower beds, narrowing and darkening as it disappeared into the shadows under the trees. About a year ago, a woman had been attacked in these woods. She looked round her. The park was deserted at this time in the morning, but the bright sun of early summer, the flowers and the fresh green of the new leaves made the woods look gentle and benign. Why the allotments? They were on the other side of the river.

She shouldn't have stopped. She was feeling tired now and she was cooling down. She could have gone on for ages if she hadn't stopped. Her eyes went back to the piece of paper, and she felt a touch of unease at the thought of the lonely path through the woods, so busy at the weekends when families followed the route to the old dam, so deserted during the week when the children were at school and their parents at work. *Stop it!*

She set off again at a brisk walk, watching the shadows as she passed out of the sun and under the trees. There was no wind, and the path was dappled and still. The park seemed empty. The early dog walkers had gone, and the late dog walkers weren't out yet.

The path forked. She could cross the river here and walk on the other side where the track was narrow and muddy.

2

The Porter Brook ran through woods and parks now, but its banks used to house the small mills and workshops that harnessed the strength of the river to power the trip-hammers and grinding wheels of the nascent steel industry. You could still see the remains of the old works – places where the river was diverted with goits and weirs, the old dams that were abandoned, silted up or turned into play-grounds. At weekends or on holidays, people walked by the dams and fed the water-birds that inhabited them now, or sailed model boats or fished.

Suzanne paused for a moment, then followed the path across the bridge to the narrow track that ran by the allot-ments. She picked her way round puddles formed where the mud had been churned up by the passage of mountain bikes. The path was still in the shadow of the trees, but the allot-ments were in full sun. She looked across at them. Some were carefully tended, neat rows of green, raked, weeded, staked; but most were neglected or abandoned, bushes and brambles and wild raspberries growing among and through old sheds and allotment huts. It was quiet. An elderly couple in jerseys and wellies were working on a patch near the stream, but the other allotments were empty. She could see a thin curl of smoke from a chimney protruding from the roof of a hut. She wondered if she should ask the couple about the notice. *Take care . . .*

She frowned, then realized that her walk had slowed almost to a standstill. She speeded up her pace, and headed determinedly along the path. She began to alter her step to a jog again. Jog six, walk six, jog six, walk six. It was peaceful in the park, away from the demands of work and home. She could let her mind roam in a loose, unfocused way, watching the patterns of light on the path, the way the water swirled and eddied round rocks and banks. It was like the library, almost. A place where she could just be, with no thoughts ahead, and no thoughts behind.

She got some of her best ideas in the library and the park. Suzanne's life – now – was focused on her research into young offenders, young men who had a bleak and persistent history of crime, waste and violence. Young men like her brother, Adam. She had put together a proposal that gave substance to her intuition that many of these young men had problems with language, with communication. She wanted to see if she could quantify what she had previously only observed. Months of work in the library poring over journals, phone calls and discussions with other researchers and people who worked with young offenders had paid off and she had been accepted to start a research M.Sc. She had managed to get a small grant, and was now attached to a young offenders' programme, the Alpha Project. If she could prove herself – and she could – she would get more funding and be able to go on to complete a Ph.D.

She was at Shepherd Wheel now, one of the old workshops that had been restored in wealthier, more optimistic times. There used to be regular working days here, when the water was released from the dam to power the wheel and the wheel turned the gears and belts that worked the grinding stones. But the cuts had put paid to that piece of heritage frivolity, and now the building was closed, locked and shuttered, the water-wheel decaying. She slowed again and, on an impulse, walked along the path past the workshop and up the steps, through the gate that led to the yard behind the mill.

The wheel lurked low down in a narrow pit. She could see the bucket boards that caught the water and turned it – empty now. She leaned over the wall and peered down into the darkness that housed the wheel. The sluice that held back the water was above her, and below her was damp stone and moss. An opaque reflection gleamed back at her. She waved, and her reflection waved back. A smell of stagnant water drifted up. She shivered. It had the darkness of a place that never got the sun.

She turned back to the path, following it along the side of the dam. Just a few weeks ago, it had been like a lake almost, with fish and water-birds. Now with the dryness of the summer, it was a stream running through channels of thick mud. Suzanne looked at the prints where birds had walked, already filling with water and fading. Closer to the bank, the mud had been disturbed, the green moss that covered it churned up, as though someone had been digging there. The stone

4

walls of the dam were crevassed and cracked with years of neglect. She walked on, coming out at the end of the park where the woods proper started. She almost crossed the road in a mood of defiance, but the sense of work to be done, work undone, made her pause and turn back. She quickened her pace into a jog again. The run back was all downhill. She could manage that.

As she passed Shepherd Wheel for the second time, she saw a man slip out from behind the building, from the court-yard that housed the wheel where she'd been herself a short while before. Her heart jumped, and for a moment she felt a chill. *Take care.* . . Then, for a moment, she thought she recognized him: one of the young men from the Alpha Pro-ject, Ashley Reid. She got a glimpse of his face, white under his dark hair. She was about to smile and wave when she realized it was a stranger, another pale, dark-eyed young man. She looked away quickly, aware that she had been staring.

Lucy sat on the swing and pushed it as far back as her legs would allow. She lifted her feet off the ground and pulled herself into the seat. Lean *back* and push, lean *back* and push. She hadn't been able to swing herself at the beginning of the summer. Now she could swing herself far higher than Emma would push her. Lean *back* and push. She'd escaped from Emma. Emma would be *pissed off* – Mum's favourite word. 'Wait in the playground,' Emma had said. She meant the small playground, but Lucy didn't want to do that. She liked the big playground better, even if it did mean a long walk. She'd been waiting in the small playground, feeling cross and upset. It wasn't fair! Then suddenly he was there – 'Come on, Lucy. Quick!' – and they were off on a magic ride to the big playground through the woods, across the big road she wasn't allowed to cross by herself.

Emma would know where to find her. First the swings, then the big slide, then an ice cream. If Emma wasn't too pissed off. Lean *back* and push. The swing soared up. She thought she might be able to touch the leaves on the trees if she didn't have to hold on. She closed her eyes and let the light flicker against her eyelids. Lean *back* and push. She worked the swing hard now, flying higher and higher, feeling the chain clank and jerk at the top of each swing. High enough! She let the swing swoop her down and up, and for a moment it seemed as though she was sitting still and the playground was a swinging blur around her. The swing dropped and lifted, dropped and lifted, a little less each time, and she began to scrape her shoes along the ground, catching each time the seat swung through its lowest point. Scuff. Scuff. She brought the swing to a stop and sat there, swaying gently, looking up. She had begun to twist the seat round and round, to give herself a twirly, when she saw that someone was watching her. He was standing by the bench at the edge of the playground, where the woods started. It was the Ash Man. She turned the swing again, and tried to twist the chain higher, to make it twirl faster. As she twirled round – chain swings were really not as good as the one her friend Lauren had in her garden, because they went *jerk, jerk* – she wondered where Emma was.

'Emma's gone.' She looked round. He was standing behind her and was looking down at her. 'We've lost Emma,' he said. Lucy sat very still. She didn't like the Ash Man. He went on watching her. He got hold of the chains of the swing, twisting them so much that Lucy's feet were right off the ground. The twirly rocked her dizzy. He looked down at her. 'We've lost Emma,' he said again.

Lucy looked up at him. His face had a shadow on it from his hair. He'd said it twice. 'I *know*,' she said.

It was after half past ten by the time Suzanne got back to the park gates. The traffic on Hunters Bar roundabout was heavy, and the air tasted hot and metallic after the freshness of the park. She walked up Brocco Bank and turned up Carleton Road, the short steep road where she lived. It was a typical Sheffield street, red-brick terraces climbing up the side of the hill, the pavement a mix of flagstones and asphalt, weeds and grass growing in the cracks and against the walls.

She saw her friend and neighbour, Jane, sitting on her front step with a sketch pad on her lap and bottles of ink on the step beside her. Jane was an illustrator and most of her work appeared in children's books. She smiled when she saw Suzanne. 'Have you been in the park?' Suzanne nodded, and paused to talk, leaning on the wall. She looked at the sketch pad. 'It's these shadows,' Jane said. 'I want to get the red of the brick and the black of the shadows while the sun's just right. They want "a combination of the everyday and the eerie".' She looked at her painting for a moment, then rested her brush on the edge of the ink bottle. 'What were you doing last night? That was a rather flashy Range Rover that dropped you off.'

Suzanne sighed. Jane was currently on a campaign to spice up Suzanne's life. The women had been friends since shortly after Michael's birth six years ago. They had met in the park where Jane was throwing bread to the ducks for the entertainment of six-month-old Lucy. To Suzanne, her family life in chaos, struggling with post-natal depression, Jane's Madonna-like calm had seemed like a haven.

'It was just Richard Kean from the Alpha Project,' Suzanne said now. Richard was one of the centre's psychologists, and one of the few people there who seemed to have any real interest in Suzanne's work.

'Richard? He's the tall one with dark hair, isn't he? So what was he doing dropping you off in the middle of the night?'

'It was half past nine,' Suzanne retorted, goaded.

'That is the middle of the night for you,' Jane said reasonably. She didn't approve of Suzanne's monastic life.

'Mm.' Suzanne was non-committal. There was nothing to tell. She had attended an evening session at the Alpha Project and Richard had dropped her off on his way home. She wanted to get Jane off the subject, so she said, 'I saw something when I was in the park—'

Jane interrupted her. 'Did you see Em and Lucy there?'

'Is Em back?' Emma, Jane's babysitter, had been away for the past week, and Jane had had to juggle her timetable and call in favours to cope with a rapidly approaching deadline. Jane had coped as she always did, wrapped in a hazy cocoon of abstraction.

7

'Yes. She just turned up this morning out of the blue.' Jane frowned and ran her finger along a sweep of pencil on her page. 'No phone call or anything. Actually, it was quite useful.' She looked at the drawing again, still frowning, still dissatisfied. 'I can't get this right. I don't know what I want.' She looked up at Suzanne. 'Lucy's got a hospital appointment. She didn't want to go, so I said she could have an hour in the park with Em, *and* an ice cream afterwards.' Suzanne shrugged in sympathy. Lucy suffered from bad asthma, and hated her regular trips to the hospital. The ice cream was a big concession. Jane was a health freak.

Jane had been backtracking on the conversation. 'You didn't see them? They went to the playground.' Suzanne had run past the playground. It had been empty. Jane frowned, pulling her attention away from her drawing. Her look of vague abstraction sharpened into focus. 'They should have been there. I *told* Em not to take her to the café . . . You know, I'm not happy – Oh, it's nothing serious,' she added. 'It isn't so much the not turning up, it's just . . .'

For the past month, Emma had looked after Lucy for a few hours each week. Before that, Jane had had Sophie, a first-year undergraduate who rented a bed-sit in the student house next door to Jane. She'd turned up on the doorstep just before the start of term and introduced herself, offering her services as a childminder. Jane, after contacting Sophie's parents, smallholders on the east coast, was happy to take up her offer, and the arrangement had worked well. Sophie was inexperienced and unsophisticated, but she was bright and sensible and fun. Jane liked her, Lucy adored her, she was just next door and could fit in with Jane's elastic schedule. But then, quite suddenly, she'd dropped out of her course and left.

Emma was a fellow student. She had been one of the regular visitors at the student house – a house with a lot of coming and going – but Jane and Suzanne hadn't met her properly until after Christmas when Sophie had introduced her: 'Do you mind if Emma comes with me and Lucy?' And she had, imperceptibly, drifted into their lives, a quiet, rather serious young woman, a contrast to Sophie's vivacity. She

8

had moved in to the student house in March, and had rather diffidently offered herself as a replacement when Sophie left. Jane had been pleased at first, especially to have someone whom she and Lucy both knew, but she was starting to have second thoughts. Emma was younger than Sophie, and, Suzanne was beginning to realize, a lot less responsible. She listened with increasing unease as Jane expressed her doubts. Since Sophie had left, Emma had become moody and unreliable. Lucy had started having nightmares, nightmares about monsters, about 'the Ash Man', Jane said, about Emma being chased by monsters. Sometimes she'd come back from the park with the smell of tobacco smoke lingering on her clothes. 'I know Em smokes,' Jane said. 'Her lungs are her business. But she knows not to smoke near Lucy.'

'What did she say?'

'Oh, she said she thought it wouldn't matter in the open air. I suppose . . . I don't know . . . I don't want Lucy to have another upheaval. She likes Emma. It's just . . .'

'The monsters?'

'Yes . . .' Jane frowned at her painting, brushing away a tiny spider that was running on the surface. 'No.' She looked up at Suzanne. 'I've decided. I'm not letting Emma look after her again. I'll find someone else.'

By the time Suzanne had finished talking to Jane, it was nearly eleven. She let herself in through the back door and stepped over the pile of shoes on the doormat. The breakfast dishes were in the sink and the worktops were a mess of toast crumbs, butter and a congealing pool of spilt milk and sugar where she had eaten breakfast. A fly was exploring this, and she aimed a swat at it. It flew up, its drone filling the air for a moment, then stopping as it settled again.

She walked through the middle room to the side door to collect the post. Three brown envelopes lay on the mat. She picked them up and flicked through them. Bills, but not red ones. She put them into the in-tray she kept on the dining table. The new additions caused a minor landslide, and she had to scoop up a pile of envelopes from the floor and cram them back.

She needed to go and do some work.

Upstairs in her study, she closed the door behind her and felt a sense of peace. Her study was in the small attic room under the roof. It had a dormer window, high and narrow, that opened at just the right height for her to lean her arms on the sill and look out across the rooftops. She did that now, enjoying the high, cloudless sky and the gleam of the sunlight off the wet roofs that tumbled up the other side of the valley. In front of her, the slates of her own roof sloped down into the guttering, concealing the drop down to the road below. If she craned her neck, she could just see Jane still sitting on her front step, her head bent intently over her drawing.

But she had work to do. Inside, the study was cool and shadowed. Her desk stood in the light from the window. Further back into the room, the walls were lined with shelves of books, all sorted by subject and author. A filing cabinet, functional metallic grey, stood against one wall, and an easy chair, a splash of colour, fire-engine red, occupied one corner under a small reading lamp. Shelves at the side of her desk held her set of audio tapes, the start of her research project.

If she wanted to study the way the young men on the Alpha Project communicated, she had to record them, study their language, to see if they employed all the strategies and skills of conversation that researchers had identified over the years. When the negotiation degenerated into violence, was it because they wanted to fight, to assert themselves, to establish their dominance, or was it because they couldn't read those subtle signals of language that meant I am being polite, I don't like what you are saying, I am asking you to do something? When they looked blank and nodded in vague agreement to something they hadn't heard, or hadn't understood, was it because they didn't want to hear, or was it because they didn't know they hadn't understood, or didn't know how to say they hadn't understood? And did the resulting frustration boil over into anti-social behaviour?

As a first step, she'd been recording quite formal interviews with some of the young men on the programme. She'd asked for, and been given, the ones with the most serious or the most persistent records. One frustrating thing was that she didn't actually know what they had done, and might never if they themselves didn't volunteer the information. The Alpha management had been grudging with their permission, and draconian about confidentiality.

She took the tapes of the individual interviews out of her bag. She wasn't supposed to have them here. They were supposed to be kept secure at the university. She'd interviewed three of the young offenders so far. Dean – seventeen, and on the programme as a condition of his parole – she was sure could be violent. He had been monosyllabic, sullen, occasionally aggressive; then she'd interviewed Lee – also seventeen, bright, lively and endlessly in trouble. He'd shown flashes of insight when he forgot his manic clowning. And Ashley. That interview had been odd. She knew Ashley better than any of the others, and yet he had been halting, incoherent, illogical. She had listened to the tape several times in the four weeks since she had actually carried out the interview, and she still had trouble making sense of it.

Q. *Tell me about your family, Ashley.*
A. Er . . . It's not . . .
Q. *Sorry, you don't have to tell me if you'd rather not.*
A. Yes.
Q. *You want to tell me?*
A. Brothers and sisters?
Q. *If . . .*
A. (Laughs.) Brothers and sisters.
Q. *Sorry, Ashley, I don't understand.*
A. Er . . . So . . . em . . . loose . . .
Q. *What?*
A. Simon.
Q. *Simon is your brother?*
A. Yes.
Q. *Tell me about Simon.*
A. (Laughs.) Simon says . . .
Q. *Yes?*
A. Not much. (Laughs.)

At the time, she had kept thinking, Odd, odd. He had become increasingly uncomfortable and, in the end, he'd cut the interview short. She wondered if he would let her tape him again. He might be the first one who could provide her with data that would support her theory. Ironically, she had been doubtful about his suitability for her research, as he was classified as having 'learning difficulties', and she wasn't sure if that would skew her results. She needed more background on Ashley before she could trust her analysis. She thought about the new insights her work would give into the dark world of youth crime, which might lead to better ways of helping boys like Adam, before . . . *Daydreaming!* She pulled herself back to the work in hand.

At twelve-thirty, she packed her recording equipment away. She needed to go to the university. She rewound the tape, noting the counter number, and put it back in her briefcase. She felt buoyant and optimistic. She tested the mood, and the feeling of lightness stayed with her. It was as if something heavy and dark, something she hadn't been aware of, had been lifted off her recently, and she was just now understanding how heavy and constricting it had been. She thought about Michael's weekend, and instead of the chest-tightening anxiety she was accustomed to feeling, she realized she was almost looking forward to it.

Maybe she could cope with the responsibility. Maybe there was no reason to dread something awful happening. Maybe all mothers worried about their children. Maybe, dare she say it, maybe she was normal. She ran a comb through her hair and tied it back, thought about putting on some make-up and decided against it. Maybe Jane was right. Maybe it was time to come out of her shell. She picked up her briefcase and ran down the stairs. She grabbed her bag and keys and headed out. As she locked the door behind her, she saw Jane standing at her gate, looking anxiously down the road. 'Hi,' Suzanne greeted her on a note of query. 'Is something wrong?'

Jane pushed her hair back off her face. 'I don't know,' she said. 'Emma and Lucy are late.' She looked at her watch.

'When should they have been back?' Suzanne asked.

Jane looked at her watch. 'Over an hour ago. Lucy's appointment was at quarter to twelve.'

Suzanne remembered their earlier conversation, and felt a stirring of unease. Monsters . . . She tried to be reassuring. 'I shouldn't worry,' she said. 'Lucy will have run off and be hiding, and poor old Em will be frantic. We could go and look.' Both women were familiar with Lucy's disappearing stunts.

Jane's face was tense. 'I've just come back. I went right through both parks. They weren't there. I tried the café. They hadn't been in. Then I thought they might have come back . . . I don't know what to do.'

Suzanne thought. 'Em knows about Lucy hiding, doesn't she?'

'Oh yes. She's helped Sophie deal with it. I gave her the phone. Just in case.' She looked at Suzanne and shook her head. 'I've been ringing and ringing, but there's no reply.'

That made Suzanne pause. There didn't seem a good explanation for that. 'Maybe the battery's run down. Or she's buried it in her bag and it's turned itself off. Maybe it's been stolen . . .' Her ideas sounded lame and she could see Jane starting to form an objection, so she hurried on. 'But I think you ought to call someone anyway. Just in case. Maybe there's been an accident.'

Jane began to look panicked. 'I don't know . . .' she said.

Suzanne felt out of her depth. She was usually the one who got stressed and upset, and Jane was the one who maintained an air of imperturbable calm. 'Come on,' she said. 'It'll be nothing. You'll end up the morning mad as hell with Lucy and wondering why you got in such a state, but let's play safe. When we've phoned, I'll go back to the park and look.'

'You've been through the park.' Jane's eyes were wide and frightened. 'And you didn't see them either, did you?'

Suzanne shook her head. 'No, but I wasn't looking.'

'If Em had seen you, if Lucy had run off, she would have told you, she would have asked you to help. We've both looked. They're not there.'

Suzanne was guiding Jane back into the house now,

towards the phone. 'Yes, they are,' she said. 'We just didn't see them. It's a big park. Do you want me to phone?' Jane looked at her in blank panic. Suzanne hesitated. She wasn't sure which number to ring. They needed to contact the police. As she thought about the situation, she was beginning to feel more worried. It was true that the park was big, but it was narrow for most of the way, and she knew the places that Em and Lucy went. If they had been there, she would have seen them, or they would have seen her. Lucy would probably have lain low under the circumstances, but Em would have been pleased, relieved to see her if Lucy had pulled one of her hiding stunts. She thought about Lucy, her thread-limbed fragility, her will of iron. She picked up the receiver and tried the number of Jane's mobile. She let it ring. There was no reply. Then she dialled 999. This was either nothing, or a very serious emergency.

The mill at Shepherd Wheel was dark under the trees. The doors were padlocked, the bright metal of the hasps gleaming. The windows were shuttered and bolted. The trees stirred as a breeze blew, sending shadows dancing across the water, across the mossy roof. And it began again, faintly, just audible over the sound of the river, just audible to someone standing close to the shuttered windows, just audible to someone with sharp ears, someone who was listening. The ringing of a phone.

2

Suzanne was familiar with crisis. Crisis was something you moved through with cold detachment, an observer of your own life. Crisis was something that held you, panicked and terrified, behind a frozen façade. Crisis left you drained and wrecked once it had moved on. Crisis for Suzanne was Adam, her younger brother, dead these past six years, and it was her father's thin, precise features, and his voice: *I hold you responsible for this, Suzanne!*

She listened to the policewoman telling Jane that children often went missing, that the most reliable teenager in the world could get distracted, and wanted to fast-forward the day to the time when the crisis would be over, one way or another.

Two officers had arrived in response to Suzanne's call, with commendable but alarming rapidity. A man and a woman. The woman had introduced herself, calm, sympathetic, professional, 'I'm Hazel Austen. I'm here about your daughter. Lucy, isn't it?' With a few quick questions she had the gist of the situation, and was now talking Jane through Emma's and Lucy's planned route and routine. '. . . going through the park right now, but I just need you to tell me . . .'

To distract herself from the knot of tension inside her, Suzanne let her eyes wander round the familiar room. There were pictures: framed prints, some of Jane's paintings, Lucy's pictures Blu-tacked erratically to the walls and door. Her toys and books were piled into one corner and tumbled on the slatted shelves that stood by the window. A photograph of Lucy with her father, Joel, was pinned to the shelves by a single drawing pin. That was new. It looked like one of Jane's photos, and the size and curling edges suggested it was one she had developed herself. The faces, both serious, looked out from a background of blurred lights, Lucy's fair hair tangled against the darker hair of her father. Lucy's drawings were stuck to the wall at the height of a child's head, slightly rumpled, slightly uneven. They were captioned in Lucy's words and Jane's writing, each letter carefully copied in different colours by Lucy.

The pictures were part of Lucy's fantasy world. *Flossy my cat in the park*, a picture of a stripy animal with rather a lot of teeth; *Me and my sisters in the park*, a small, fair-haired figure with two taller figures, one fair, one dark; *My mum and dad*, two tall figures, both with yellow hair like Lucy; *The Ash Man's brother in the park*, a dark-haired, smiling figure. Lucy's invented family had a resident father – unlike the absent, peripatetic Joel – had cats and dogs, had sisters and sometimes brothers. The rest of her world was peopled with stranger characters, like her imaginary friend, Tamby, and the sinister Ash Man – and now, apparently, with monsters.

Suzanne and Jane had shared a bottle of wine in this room the night before, talking among the haphazard clutter while Lucy sat at the table drawing. It had seemed warm and inviting then, with Jane's vague irrelevancies and Lucy's intermittent chatter. Now the clutter no longer looked homely and comforting, it looked disrupted, as though a high wind had taken the room apart and let things settle where they would.

'. . . cup of tea.' Suzanne brought herself back sharply. Hazel was speaking to her. Seeing Suzanne's blank gaze, she said again, 'I think Jane would like a cup of tea.'

For a moment, the words meant nothing, then Suzanne said, 'Oh. Yes, of course.' She brought tea and biscuits from her own house, nipping across the shared yard to her back door. She went back into the room, carrying the tray, and occupied herself setting out cups, pouring tea, putting biscuits on a plate.

'She's very independent, and she knows about, you know, not talking to strangers . . . She wouldn't go off with anyone.' Jane was whistling in the dark, as if convincing Hazel could make it true, make it be all right. It was true that Lucy was resourceful and streetwise, Suzanne thought, but she was only six.

She passed Jane a cup of tea, and offered her support. 'Lucy's very sensible,' she said to Hazel, and Jane looked at her gratefully.

Lucy's colouring book and crayons were on the table and Suzanne moved them to one side. She tried not to look at the picture Lucy had been drawing, but it pulled at her attention and she found herself staring at it as she listened to Hazel telling Jane again that it was still early days, that most missing children turned up safe and sound. It was a typical child's drawing, a blue sky across the top of the page, and green grass across the bottom. Two figures, a tall one and a small one, stood on the grass. Their arms came out of the sides of their bodies, each finger carefully drawn. They were holding hands. Lucy and Jane. Suzanne looked more closely. No, the taller figure had brown hair. Lucy and Sophie? She could picture Lucy sitting at the table, hunched intently over the paper, her face serious, talking her way through the picture, partly to herself, partly to her mother and Suzanne. *And they're in the park and they're walking on the big field and also they're holding hands and they're smiling, look . . .* But these faces weren't smiling, she noticed. The mouths were turned down, grim.

She looked up and saw Jane's eyes fall on the book. She should have put it out of sight. Jane picked it up. 'She did this,' she said, her focus wavering between the two women. 'She did this last night. She's good at . . .' Her voice died away and she swallowed.

The man had now come back. He looked to where Jane and Hazel were talking, and then he signalled to Suzanne with his eyes. She went over, and he led her out of the room. Jane looked up as she went out, but only for a moment. The man was waiting by the phone in the hallway. 'You said you phoned the mobile the babysitter has?'

'Yes. There was no reply.'

He looked at her. 'But it was turned on?'

Suzanne shook her head. She'd never had a mobile and

didn't know much about them. 'I don't know. How can you tell?'

In answer, he dialled the number and held the phone out to her. She heard the static before connection, then a recorded voice: 'This number is currently unavailable. Please try later.' Suzanne looked at him and shook her head. 'No. It just rang last time.'

'And that was . . . ?'

'Half an hour ago? Just before I phoned you.' He didn't say anything, so Suzanne pushed. 'What does that mean?'

'It's nothing. It's not likely to be important.'

She wasn't going to be fobbed off. 'But it might be. So what does it mean?'

He shrugged. 'It probably means that the battery's run down. Or that someone switched the phone off since you last rang the number.'

Lucy had been in the park. They found traces of her, far away from where her mother said she had been going. About a mile through the woods, there was a playground close to Forge Dam, the last dam. In the café by the playground at the end of the woods, the owner came out into the sunshine for a cigarette, and said, 'Yes, little girl, fair-haired, yes, she was here earlier this morning, around tenish. She bought an ice cream.' He thought for a bit. 'And a piece of cake. I asked her if it was for the ducks. I've seen her up here before and her mum buys cake for the ducks.'

'Is this her?' The officer showed him a picture and he nodded.

'That's the one. Has anything . . . ?'

'Was anyone with her?' The radio on the man's jacket crackled and said something the café owner couldn't catch. The policeman spoke briefly and quietly into the radio, then returned to his question.

'Yes . . . Well, I think so.'

'Who was it? Could you describe the person who was with her?'

Feeling more uneasy now, the café owner thought back. He hadn't really seen, now he came to think of it. She'd come to the side window of the café twice, once for ice cream and once for cake and a drink. He hadn't actually seen anyone. 'I don't know,' he said, slowly. 'I just assumed . . . I didn't see anyone.'

It had been a quiet morning, a quiet day. Some walkers had passed through earlier, shortly after nine, and had stopped for a cup of tea. He'd seen people go past on their way up to the dam or beyond. The path formed part of the Sheffield Round Walk, and also offered a walkers' route into the Derbyshire Peak District. It was a busy path. Some of the passers-by might have stopped at the dam, spent the day fishing, he didn't know. He'd kept an eye on the café – quiet as he'd said – done his books, had the telly on for some of the time. The officer, making notes, realized gloomily that if this became a real inquiry, someone would have the job of tracking these people down, asking them what they had seen, trying to find out if there was anyone who'd been through that way who hadn't come forward, and if that person hadn't come forward was it because he knew all too well what had happened to the missing child.

Suzanne knew that something had made the police more concerned now. The arrival of a man in civilian clothes, a detective, made the knot in her stomach tighten. She felt uneasy around the police. She had too many memories of Adam, the voice on the phone. *I'm afraid we've got Adam here again. He's been . . .* And her father. *You deal with it, Suzanne. This is your responsibility.* She'd trusted them then, listened to them, done what they'd said. She could still hear the woman's voice. *Just tell us where Adam is. We want to help the lad, Suzanne.*

The man introduced himself as Detective Inspector Steve McCarthy. He checked quickly through the same things Hazel had done, asking one or two more questions as he went. Suzanne was impressed by his efficiency, but found him brusque and cold. Then he began asking about Emma – how well Jane knew her, what she did, where she lived. Jane's face went whiter as he told her that Emma wasn't a student, and had never been an official tenant at number fourteen.

Suzanne hadn't realized before how much they had taken Emma on trust, because they knew her – or thought they did. This was why the police were so concerned. There was something wrong with Emma. She moved to sit on the arm of Jane's chair. She put her arm round Jane and said, 'We know Emma well. We both do. She's Sophie's friend.' He raised an eyebrow at her in query, and she realized what a thin recommendation it sounded.

She told him about Sophie, about her parents, her tutor, the course she had been doing. 'That's how we got to know Emma,' she explained. When he said nothing, she asked, 'What's wrong? There's something about Emma, isn't there?'

'We just need some background,' he said. He'd evaded her question. His face was expressionless as he made some notes, then he moved on to ask about Lucy's father. 'Where does he live? Does he see Lucy often? Would Lucy go round there?'

Jane shook her head. Suzanne couldn't stay quiet. 'Lucy always saw Joel here.' Suzanne wouldn't refer to Joel as Lucy's dad. He didn't deserve the title. He was hardly ever there. He devoted his time, as far as she could tell, to his undefined business interests around clubs and warehouse parties. When he did see Lucy, he took all the icing for a while – bringing presents sometimes, playing with her sometimes, but never consistent, never there when she needed him. When he let Lucy down – which he always did, in the end, forgetting her birthday: *It's only a date on the calendar. Loosen up, Jane*; promising to come to her party and not turning up: *I can't stand an afternoon of screeching kids*; saying, 'Of course I'll come and see you in the play, sweetheart,' and never arriving, so Lucy cried and refused to perform and said, 'We can't start yet, my daddy's not here': *Look, something cropped up. Stop nagging, Jane* – when he let Lucy down, Jane always made excuses for him, always made him look good in Lucy's eyes. But how to explain it? She tried to sum it up briefly and thought she saw a glimmer of amusement in the man's eyes. 'Joel wouldn't kidnap Lucy,' she added. 'He'd pay a ransom for someone to take her off his hands.'

Jane put her face in her hands, then looked up. 'Joel

doesn't live in Sheffield,' she said wearily. 'Lucy won't be there.' Suzanne intercepted a quick look between DI McCarthy and Hazel Austen. She flushed. She could have told them that straight away. Jane forestalled the next question. 'Leeds,' she said. 'He lives in Leeds. And he's in London at the moment, working.' Her face, normally pale, was white, and she looked exhausted. The words were beginning to spill out as though this was her last defence, and when the words were gone there would be nothing left. 'She'll be hungry. She hasn't had any lunch. She's small – it's the asthma. She's very brave, Lucy, but she does get frightened in the dark. She's got to be back before it gets dark. She'll be frightened on her own.' She looked at the man who was listening impassively to her words. 'I need to go and find her.'

McCarthy looked at Jane for a moment and seemed to relent. His voice was gentler. 'There are people out now looking for her.' Suzanne caught his eye for a second, and read there his belief that Lucy was one of the few. She felt a terrible sense of helplessness.

Lucy crept round the bushes and listened. The sounds were changing. There had been footsteps before, soft on the old leaves, backwards and forwards in the bushes. She'd stayed quiet as anything. She'd heard the *whoosh* of a bike on the muddy path, but she hadn't looked. She'd run away from the Ash Man, but there were monsters in the woods.

She'd found places between the stones, places where she could hide and no one would find her. She'd heard someone calling once: 'Lucy! Lucy!' But it wasn't a voice she knew, so she'd kept quiet, *like a mouse*, she'd whispered to Tamby in her head. But now she could hear children calling in the playground. Maybe it was safe now. She scrambled through the bushes and found her way down to the path again. She didn't go to the playground. She wanted to go home. She wasn't supposed to walk through the woods by herself, and most of all she wasn't supposed to cross the roads. She wished that Sophie was there. Sophie knew what to do.

She hopped down the shallow steps that led to the stream and balanced on the stones that marked the edge of the path.

She jumped from one stone to the next, from one foot to the other, moving quickly before she lost her balance. Then she was at the place where the path divided, and she climbed quickly up to the dam. Sometimes people were there fishing, and Lucy and Sophie used to watch them. Lucy liked to look at the boxes with wriggling maggots in. Once, Lucy saw one of the fishermen eating them, but Sophie said that was *disgusting*. 'He really was,' Lucy had said. 'Really. I saw them in his mouth.' *Disgusting*. Lucy looked round. Emma wasn't there. There were no fishermen. There was no one at the dam, no one anywhere. She wanted Sophie. She wanted her mum. She wanted to go home. Her chest felt sore, and she didn't have her medicine. Emma had her medicine. She walked further along the path to the end of the dam. She was *tired*, as well. She was at the cottages now and the long steps that led back down to the stream. She scrambled down them, being careful to step on each step just once, and not put her foot on the cracks. If you weren't careful like that, the monsters would get you.

Suzanne looked at her watch and realized with a jolt of guilt that she should be at the school waiting for Michael. She should have been there watching him singing in his class concert. She'd promised. And she'd promised Dave. She looked at Jane. She didn't want to talk about collecting children from school, remind Jane that she should have been collecting Lucy now. 'I'll be back soon,' she said.

She ran down the hill to the school gates, fortunately only five minutes away. She thought about Michael waiting on his own in the playground, maybe setting off by himself to find her. It could happen so easily, one slip, one moment of inattention and . . . *I hold you responsible for this, Suzanne!* She was suddenly aware of the air she was breathing, feeling it insubstantial in her lungs as though all the oxygen had been leached out of it. Her face and hands were tingling and she had stabbing pains in her chest. She was in the playground now, outside the pre-fab that housed Michael's class. She made herself stop, leant against the low wall and concentrated on getting her breathing under control.

22

It used to happen all the time. As soon as she found herself alone and responsible for Michael she would panic. She remembered Dave's look, first of sympathy, then concern and finally exasperation and anger. 'Post-natal depression,' her doctor had said, airily. But it had never got any better.

All her earlier sense of well-being had vanished into a black pit of fear and guilt and tension. She realized that she couldn't do it. Not now, not with Lucy gone, not with all the things that the weekend might bring. That decision helped her to calm down, and she was able to step through the classroom door and be there for the end of the concert.

She waved to Michael whose face brightened when he saw her. Lisa Boyden, Michael's teacher, slipped across to her with a whispered query about Lucy. Of course, the police would have checked the school. She shook her head to indicate that there was no news, and waited impatiently for the concert to finish.

It was gone four by the time she got Michael out of the school gates. He was full of chatter, pleased to see her, looking forward to his weekend, full of his day, full of the concert, ready to forgive her lateness as she had turned up in the end. She smiled, though her face felt frozen. She said, 'Did you?' and 'Did they?' and 'That's good,' as they walked up the road, concentrating on keeping her breathing under control, not hearing a word he said. She felt his talk fading away as he became aware of her inattention, saw his face go puzzled and unhappy. She wanted to pick him up and hug him and tell him she was sorry. Instead, she said, 'We're going to Dad's first.' He looked at her and nodded, a resignation on his face that hurt because it seemed a little too worldly, a little too knowing. *Responsible!*

Dave lived on the other side of the park and, preoccupied, she turned them both through the park gates. 'Look at all the policemen!' Michael was suddenly delighted. 'There's been a robber,' he said.

Suzanne looked around her. There were two patrol cars parked by the playing field, and men in uniform were talking to people, showing them pictures. There was a van, a police van, with dark lettering underneath its standard insignia.

23

She screwed up her eyes to read it. UNDERWATER SEARCH. The dams. Her chest tightened. 'Yes, I expect they've caught him,' she said, trying to keep her voice under control. 'Come on, let's get to Dad's. Let's see what he's doing.'

'I want to watch. I want to stay.' Michael began to force tears into his voice, dragging on her hand. He could tell she was in a hurry.

She swallowed her impatience. They had to get out of the park before . . . 'Come on, Michael.' Her panic came out as anger and she hated herself for it. He subsided and came, showing rebellion with scuffing shoes and intermittent draggings.

As they approached Dave's house, Suzanne could hear the sound of music pouring out of the stereo, the discordant rhythms of the modern composers that she hated and Dave loved. At least he was in. She pressed the bell, remembered that it didn't work and knocked on the door. 'Dad won't hear that,' Michael observed practically, and hammered on the door with his fists.

'All right. I heard you.' Dave's truculent expression softened when he saw Michael, then changed back as he looked at Suzanne. He swung his son up to his shoulder in greeting. 'Hi, Mike the tyke. Come home early?'

'Can I watch cartoons?' He'd forgotten Suzanne, forgotten the burglar in the park – he was just glad to be home, Suzanne saw with a stab of pain.

'Go on, Mike. I'll join you in a minute,' Dave said, still looking at Suzanne, still unfriendly. He knew why she was here. 'Well?' He was making no concessions. 'Can't you even manage . . .' He looked at her more closely, and his face showed exasperation and impatience.

'I'm sorry,' she said. Getting the words out round her uneven breathing, she told him about Lucy, about the escalating build-up to what seemed an inevitable ending. 'I don't want Michael around if . . . I don't think he should be near that.' It would have sounded sensible and practical if she could have said it coherently.

'Does Mike understand that? Christ, Suze, I can see the problem . . .' Which, of course, he could. 'But how often does

Mike get to spend time with you?' Suzanne felt the guilt twist in her. Dave was right.

'It's been hours now,' she said. 'And there's something the police aren't telling us. I think something's happened.' He looked at her and nodded, recognizing her assessment of the situation. 'If I'm wrong, Michael can come back tomorrow, he can have his weekend . . .'

Dave shook his head. 'He's not a bloody pet, Suze. If he comes home tonight, he stays home. You can have him next weekend instead. I'm going away, and it'll be easier without Mike.' Was this the new girlfriend she'd heard about? Michael had talked about her before – what was the name? Carol? *Carol does eggs with faces on* . . . She felt confused, disorientated, with a sense of everything suddenly out of her control. 'If you're so worried about Jane,' he went on, his impatience making him cruel, 'you'd better get yourself sorted out.'

Jane. And Lucy. She'd been gone nearly an hour. Anything could have happened. She tried a conciliatory goodbye to Dave, but his face remained unforgiving. Michael was watching cartoons and shrugged her off impatiently when she tried to kiss him.

Her head was pounding. Dave was right. She needed to get herself under control before she went back. She decided to walk back through the park, and went on up the road to come in at a gate further into the woods. She couldn't help Jane any more. What could she do or say? There was nothing to do or say. That detective had understood that, she realized. He knew that words were useless. It was what you did that counted.

She turned in to the park. She'd taken Michael by the road after they'd seen the searching police. Now she wanted to look, to see what was going on in the further reaches. Uneasily, she thought about that odd notice – it had been pushed out of her mind by later events. She should have told someone. She'd have to tell them as soon as she got back. But it couldn't have anything to do with this. Lucy and Emma had gone to the playground in the first park. There was a main road and a long path between there and here. She looked round. There were no police. No patrol car, no one looking through the bushes – this part of the park was deserted. It was as if they had given up and gone home.

The sun was low in the sky now, the shadows of the trees slanting across the path. Suzanne walked slowly, letting the quiet ease her tension and letting the park take over her senses. She could see the pattern of light and shadow on the path. She could feel the early evening sun on her arms. She stood there under the trees, listening to the sound of children playing in the distance, the sound of the birds on the dam, the sound . . . That was new, different. A rhythmic, creaking sound that she didn't recognize, and water, churning, running fast under pressure. She looked round trying to locate the source. Sound could be deceptive down in the park – it bounced off walls, off trees, deceived you into looking for it in the wrong directions and the wrong places. She realized that she'd been hearing the sound for a while. Her eyes moved round to Shepherd Wheel on the other side of the stream. That was it, that was where it was coming from. It took a moment before she could identify the noise, and then she wasn't sure. It was – surely – the sound of the water-wheel turning.

She almost walked on, but why was the wheel working at this time of day? Why was the wheel working at all? The council had closed the place down, oh, years ago. Slowly she turned and crossed the bridge over the stream. As she walked towards the building she looked for a way in. The doors and windows were closed and shuttered. She followed the path round to the yard. The gate was padlocked. She frowned. She could hear the wheel clearly now: *creak, creak*. She shook the gate. The lock rattled. She went back and tried the door. It was bolted solid, the padlock bright and polished.

The events of the day coalesced into a picture she didn't want to see. Lucy. The strange young man. The turning wheel. The gate was high metal bars, with a line of spikes at the top: the fence was the same, but it was overgrown with ivy and she was able to hook her foot into a branch and hoist herself up to grip the top of the fence. The branch snapped and she scraped her leg as she slipped, but she managed to keep her hold, to haul herself up further, her foot feeling for another hold in the ivy. There! Now she had her knee on the bar at the top of the fence. That would support her as she edged over the rusty spikes. God knows what she would do if she slipped and impaled herself. Now she had a foot on the other side of the fence. Awkwardly crouched over, she pulled herself across and, holding onto the spikes, lowered herself into the yard.

Her arms ached and her leg smarted where she had scraped it. It had occurred to her as she dropped into the yard that she would be in trouble if there were drunks or vandals, because she had no easy way out, but the lack of voices, of human sound, had reassured her, and she was right. There was no one there, just the wheel, turning and turning, the sluice open, the water falling onto the blades, the wheel turning down, down into the shadows, darker under the trees now that the sun was lower. The water cascaded, throwing out a spray of droplets that shone in rainbow colours where the sun caught them. As she watched, the flood of water narrowed, became a trickle, the rainbow lights faded and the wheel slowed, slowed and stopped. She moved closer to the railing and looked over the edge, down into the darkness where the wheel had turned.

Flowers in the water. Someone had scattered blue flowers that swirled in the turbulence left by the wheel, and the rays of the sun came through the canopy of the trees and turned the surface of the water into patterns of silver and blue, light and flowers, water and forget-me-nots. The bright light dimmed as a cloud crossed the sun, and the water was suddenly transparent, the stones on the wall beneath the water a soft yellow, the fronds of the fern dancing where they dipped below the surface. There was her reflection again, staring up at her from deep down, down beneath the wheel, down in the shadows, in the darkness. But the face was a bleached white, the eyes blank, staring, and the hair waving in the current was pale gold.

She didn't remember climbing back out of the yard. She didn't remember stopping the cyclist on the path. She just remembered sitting on the dry and stony ground, her back pressed against the wall as the feet ran past her.

Lucy. Lucy in the water under the churning wheel.

3

The body of the young woman had been pulled partly into the conduit that took the water back into the stream. A diver had gone down into the narrow space to free her from the grip of the water, so that they could, slowly and carefully, lift her out. The forget-me-nots caught in her hair and stuck to her face as she came out of the water. There were red marks around her mouth and, as her head lolled back against the man lifting her, a trickle of bloodstained water ran down her face. *Suspicious death.* She was young: seventeen, eighteen? She was wearing a T-shirt, nothing on her feet.

Detective Inspector Steve McCarthy looked away, at the scene around him. The wheel was still and silent. There was a smell of damp stone and wood in the air, of weed and stagnant water. The yard was fading into shadows as the sun sank lower behind the trees. A breeze blew, and the trees sighed and rustled, sending the shadows chasing across the flagstones. The flagstones of the yard were mossy and overgrown. The scene-of-crime team were already going over the ground and the wheel, looking for traces of the person or the people who had dumped the girl in the water, who had set the mechanisms going. McCarthy frowned. He couldn't understand the turning wheel. It had attracted attention to the place.

As the team lowered the body onto the stretcher, the senior investigating officer, Detective Superintendent Tom Brooke, passed his quick, professional eye over it and looked at the pathologist. She shrugged her shoulders. 'I can't tell you anything at the moment. She doesn't look as though she's been in the water for long, but I don't know what that current will have done to any evidence.'

28

'What do you think, Steve?'

'Some kind of freak accident?' McCarthy, observing beside Brooke, very much wanted it to have been an accident. He had just left a murder inquiry, one that had dragged on for several weeks without so much as the identity of the victim – a vagrant, an old man someone had kicked and then slashed to death with a broken whisky bottle – being found out. He'd planned to take some leave. Another murder inquiry would put paid to that straight away.

'I've no idea.' The pathologist looked at McCarthy with dislike. She thought he was a cold fish. 'I can't tell you anything until I've done the PM.' They watched as the stretcher was wheeled out of the yard to the waiting ambulance.

The pathologist's refusal to give an opinion didn't bother McCarthy. He'd known before he asked the question that this was no accident. When he'd first seen the face in the water, he'd thought, Kids messing about. The park was a playground for the local teenagers in the evenings and at night. They played interesting games. From the road after dark, you could see firelight in the woods. In the mornings, the litter of broken bottles, used condoms, empty cans, told their own stories. Needles in the old toilets, graffiti on the buildings and even on the trees. *Girls and boys come out to play . . .* She could have been a member of one of the gangs, could have been messing around, got the wheel started, fallen in and drowned. Poetic justice in McCarthy's mind. But he knew that theory was unlikely.

The pathologist had finished packing her things together. McCarthy walked back to her car with her. 'Do you know who she is?' she asked.

'We've got a seventeen-year-old answers the description, Emma Allan. We haven't got an official identification yet. But the woman who found the body says it's her. It's all tied up with the missing-child case from earlier on.' He caught the pathologist's glance. 'No, the child turned up safe and well.'

'The woman who found her,' the pathologist persisted, 'can't she make it official?'

'She said it was the child at first,' McCarthy replied

29

remembering the woman's white-faced incoherence. 'She didn't know she'd been found.' He anticipated the next comment. 'It was understandable, but we don't need an identification from someone who sees what she expects to see, rather than what's there.'

The pathologist looked at him for a moment and shrugged. 'I'll get back then,' she said, pulling off her gloves.

McCarthy looked at the long expanse of the park stretching away west towards the countryside and east back into the city. He'd already worked out that the park was almost impossible to seal off. The gates at either end were blocked; he'd arranged for the path closer to Shepherd Wheel to be closed, but access from the woods, the allotments, across the fields – the park was wide open. They needed to complete the searches of the scene quickly. They needed to get the yard checked, and the wheel. They still needed to find the place where the woman had been killed.

At first, McCarthy's money had been on the yard behind the mill, secluded and shielded from observers by trees. But there was no evidence of anything on those mossy stones. One of the SOCOs had found traces of blood on the wall of the mill, the wall that ran straight down into the water, forming one side of the wheel pit. There was a small, dark window in that wall, a few feet above the water. Brooke thought they'd find the evidence they wanted inside the locked-up mill. That scene was secure, and he was content to wait until they had more daylight to work by.

They'd had trouble contacting a key-holder. They'd had to break open the padlock on the yard gate, but the workshop itself could wait. That reminded McCarthy of something else he needed to do. He went back to the old bridge to talk to the woman who'd found the dead girl. He'd recognized her as soon as he'd arrived. It was the woman with the wary eyes, who had watched him from her seat beside Jane Fielding, as though she was defending her friend from him. She'd said very little apart from giving him a vivid thumbnail sketch of Lucy's father that McCarthy would have found entertaining under other circumstances.

She had been sitting on the ground by the old workshop,

her knees drawn up, her head resting on her arms. He had gone up to her, and she'd lifted her head and looked at him with shocked, blank eyes, her face drained so that the wash of colour from the sun looked almost yellow. She hadn't seemed to take it in when he'd said to her, 'It isn't Lucy. Lucy's safe. It isn't a child.' He'd knelt down beside her to make sure she'd understood him, and she'd stiffened as though she found his presence threatening. She'd muttered something about *responsible* or *responsibility*, and tried to stand up, weaving a little as the shock took her. He'd held her arm, and waved one of the WPCs over. 'Look after . . .' He paused.

'Milner,' she'd said. 'Suzanne Milner. I'm fine. I just stood up too quickly. I'm fine.'

'OK, Mrs Milner, but I'll need to talk to you before you go.' He'd given the officer some instructions, and then gone to where Brooke was waiting, watching the men working in the wheel yard. Now, as he headed back to the woman, he wondered who to get to interview her. He ran his mind over the things she might have seen and not seen, the things he needed to get her to remember. He thought about her story of the wheel slowing and stopping as she watched it. Who had stopped it?

What did he know about her? Nothing, except she had some connection with the Fielding woman. It had all seemed like a rather arty, new-age set up – not McCarthy's kind of thing at all. Her story puzzled him. She'd apparently climbed the gate to look in the wheel yard – a climb that McCarthy wouldn't have liked to tackle, not with those spikes threatening vulnerable bits. He wondered what she'd expected to find.

It was midnight. Suzanne sat at her desk, her head in her hands. She couldn't sleep. She kept seeing that face in the water, and it kept being Lucy. There was something unreal, dreamlike, about the whole thing. The detective – what was his name? McCarthy, that was it – had told her: *It isn't Lucy. Lucy's safe. It isn't a child*, but she couldn't get that picture of Lucy's face out of her mind. She'd gone round to Jane's as soon as they told her she could go but the house was locked

31

up and empty. She'd come back home and wandered list-lessly round, picking up discarded books, shoes, cups and putting them down again. The shards of her weekend lay around her. She bit her thumbnail until a sudden pain warned her that she'd bitten it below the quick. She won-dered about phoning Dave, but that would give him a chance to say those things again: *Can't you even . . . ? He's not a bloody pet, Suze . . . !*

She sorted through some of the papers that were in her Monday's to-do pile, ordering them by size, large on the top, small on the bottom, then reversing the order. They wouldn't make a neat pyramid either way, because they were different shapes and sizes. She went and stood by the window, looking out into the now dark street.

Q. *But, you haven't told me. Where do you go in the evenings? You know, going out, seeing your friends, things like that.*
A. Simon's got somewhere.
Q. *Simon? Is that your brother?*
A. Er . . . not . . . I can't . . . (Pause 5 seconds.)
Q. *In the evenings, Ashley. You said that Simon's got somewhere. Is that where you go?*
A. Yes.
Q. *Where is it?*
A. It's . . . I can't . . . em . . . It's . . . you go down by the garage, where Lee's name is.
Q. *Lee? Do you see Lee in the evenings?*
A. Not . . . It's so and . . . em . . . they said it was all going to be different. I don't know, I didn't know . . .
Q. *What? I'm sorry, Ashley, I don't follow you.*
A. Doesn't matter.

The tape ran on. Her mind, in the way that it did when she was tired, drifted away from her. She was in the office at the Alpha Project, talking to Richard Kean, the Alpha psychologist. He'd made the rules clear. 'You can't have access to the confidential records,' he'd said. 'And that includes their police records, I'm afraid. Not at this stage. They all have the kinds of profile you were looking for:

persistent, destructive criminal behaviour.' She'd nodded in agreement. She wasn't about to argue after the weeks of careful negotiation it had taken her to get through the door of the centre. She'd . . . The machine clicked, and she realized that the tape had run on to its end. Maybe she ought to go to bed. She wasn't concentrating. She pressed the REWIND button and watched as the numbers on the counter reversed themselves. Then she pressed PLAY.

Q. Tell me about your family, Ashley.
A. Er . . . It's not . . .
Q. Sorry, you don't have to tell me if you'd rather not.
A. Yes.
Q. You want to tell me?
A. Brothers and sisters?
Q. If . . .
A. (Laughs.) Brothers and sisters.
Q. Sorry, Ashley, I don't understand.
A. Er . . . So . . . em . . . loose . . .
Q. What?
A. Simon.
Q. Simon is your brother?
A. Yes.

She'd asked Richard about that, after she'd taped Ashley. 'Ashley says he has a brother. I'd got the impression he was an only child.'

Richard had pulled at his lip, thinking. 'Well, if he's been talking to you . . . It isn't confidential as such. Ashley's background is very disrupted. He has a brother who went into care years ago. He was autistic; the family couldn't cope. Then when they found out Ashley had problems, that was when he went into care as well.' He was more forthcoming these days, more inclined to treat her like another professional. 'That's the root of Ashley's problem, I think. No one wanted him. He's never had anyone who really cared about him. That's hard to cope with.'

The tape ran on. *Never had anyone who loved him.* Suzanne had loved Adam, but that hadn't been enough. Her mind was too tired to resist the images. The wet stone had sprouted weeds and ferns, a lush growth that flourished away from the light. The stones were green with lichen. Far down, the water was racing, smooth and strong. Someone was looking up at her from under the water, but she couldn't make out the features, the current was too fast. Then it cleared, and the eyes opened and looked at her with fear and panic and pleading. Adam's face, looking up at her from under the water.

Lucy lay in bed, the covers pulled up to her chin. It was late. She was tired, but she didn't want to go to sleep. Not yet. She'd been to a place with her mum, and talked about the park to Alicia. Alicia said she was a policeman, but she wasn't a proper one, in a uniform, with a hat. There were voices downstairs – Mum and Dad talking. Her daddy had come all the way from *London* on his motor bike. She heard Daddy's voice getting louder. He was cross with Mum.

She turned over in bed. She hadn't told. She'd kept the secret, but she didn't know what to do now. She wished Sophie was there. Sophie would know. She turned over again. Her bed wouldn't get comfortable. She looked at the window. It was dark outside. She couldn't see it because the curtains were drawn, but she knew the dark was there. It was OK, though. Tamby would be watching. *Chasing. . .* Sophie would say, *monsters. . .* But Tamby would watch. *All safe*, she told him in her head.

She heard Daddy's voice: 'For fuck's sake, Jane, what did she say?' and then his voice got quieter. She knew what they were talking about. They thought she didn't know, but she did. They were talking about Emma. The monsters had got Emma, Lucy knew that. Emma was the grown-up and Lucy was the little girl, but Lucy knew about monsters. She'd tried to tell Emma, but Emma wouldn't listen. Emma thought it was safe to play with the monsters, but Lucy knew. You play with the monsters one, two, three times, and they get you. Lucy sighed. She had tried to look out for Emma, she really had.

Daddy's voice, loud again. 'I want to know what she said!'

She looked at the curtain. It was moving, just a bit, just the way it did when it was *draughty*. It's just the draught, Mum said. Lucy didn't know where to watch, and the dark made it harder. It was like that game they played in the yard at school, Grandmother's Footsteps. You turned your back and they all came for you, moving so quietly you couldn't hear them. You turned really quickly, but they were still as anything. You never saw them move, but each time you turned, they were in a different place, nearer and nearer. But they couldn't move as long as you were looking at them.

She was only six, but she knew about the monsters.

4

When Suzanne finally fell asleep, she dreamt. It was the familiar dream, the one she had thought she was free of, of Adam, calling to her: *Look at me, Suzanne! Listen to me, Suzanne!* And her father: *I hold you responsible for this, Suzanne!* She pulled herself out of sleep in panic, gasping, disorientated. She sat up, trying to see the clock face. The sky outside was beginning to lighten. It was nearly five. Her nightdress felt damp, and her legs were tangled up in the sheets. Adam's face stayed with her, bringing the familiar cold lump in her stomach. She pushed the image away. *Over. Gone.*

The relief she'd felt faded as the events of the evening before came back into her head. She tried to shut the memory of Emma firmly out of her mind, but she couldn't stop herself from thinking about what it would be like to be held under the water as the wheel churned above you, or to feel someone's cold hands on you with killing intent, to ... The pictures in her mind were spinning out of control now. *Look at me ... Listen to me ...*

She needed to get up, do something. It was five to five. She'd go and work on the tapes again for a couple of hours, then have breakfast.

They searched the workshop at Shepherd Wheel at first light the next morning. The roads were empty as McCarthy drove from his flat towards the park. He left his car in the entrance to the park and walked the few hundred yards to Shepherd Wheel, enjoying the silence, broken by the birdsong, the emptiness, and the stillness of the morning. Shepherd Wheel looked tranquil in the early sun, the moss-covered roof glow-

36

ing a warm yellow, the walls and path dappled with shadow.

A key-holder from the museums department was there to open up the workshops for them, a young woman who, McCarthy noticed, looked anything but put out at her out-of-hours excursion. If anything, she looked excited. He guessed she was in her late twenties. She had short chestnut hair in untidy curls, her face slightly flushed, eyes shining as she took in the scene. She smiled and held out her hand. 'Liz Delaney. Hello.'

He shook her hand. 'Steve McCarthy.' Yesterday's search had found very little in the yard. Now they needed to look inside the workshops themselves. There were two doors, painted municipal green, with heavy hasps for the padlocks that kept the building closed and secure. He took the keys that Liz Delaney was holding out to him. 'How long is it since someone was last in there?' he asked her.

'I don't know exactly,' she said. 'Someone comes up here and checks it regularly.' She smiled up at him.

McCarthy thought, tossing the keys in his hand. 'How long since it's been open to the public?'

She frowned slightly and shrugged. McCarthy kept looking at her. 'Oh, a few months, I think.' She waited out McCarthy's silence for a moment. 'It's not really my job. It was closed before I ever worked for this department.'

Actually, McCarthy knew, she was wrong. Shepherd Wheel had been open for public access at the beginning of May, just five weeks before. Before that, it had been open for European Heritage Day, or some such crap that people seemed determined to spend McCarthy's hard-earned taxes on. But someone had had access to the place since then.

The first door opened into a small workshop with barred windows in the whitewashed walls. It was light, the window facing the early morning sun. A central aisle ran between protective barriers of wood and mesh, to keep visitors away from the grindstones. A layer of dust lay over the machines. The air smelt dry and closed in. Dead leaves lay in the aisle, where they had blown in under the door. Wheels, plates, oil cans were stacked around the room, on window sills and against the walls. Above his head, a shaft ran across the ceiling and through a hole in the wall to the next workshop. It would have carried the power from the water-wheel to the stones on either side of the aisle.

To McCarthy's eye, the place looked untouched, abandoned. He doubted if the surreptitious visitor to Shepherd Wheel had been in here.

The second door led into a larger workshop. McCarthy pushed the door open and stepped inside. A sour, organic smell hit him in the face, very different from the dry, dusty smell of the first workshop. This room was darker, the windows that lit it still shuttered and shadowed by the trees. The air was damp, chilly after the warmth outside. The sound of water, a dripping, trickling noise, cut into the silence. Shapes lumped in the dark corners, light from the windows catching the teeth of a gear wheel, reflecting off a belt. The dust lay thick in this room too. McCarthy looked round. Behind him he could make out a fireplace in the wall. He shone his torch at it. The bars of the grate were rusty. There were ashes in the grate and in the ash bucket and on the hearth below. The dust in front of the fire was scuffed, disturbed.

He directed the light from his torch along the flagstoned floor and up the wall. There were dark stains where the dust was disturbed, something long and trailing caught on the bars of the grate – threads? Hair? McCarthy stood back as the scene-of-crime team moved in to work. He had already observed the bundle of cloth by the old fire, the drag marks in the dust, and, as he looked more closely, the glint of tinfoil, partly blackened, in the grate. He knew it would take time to comb the workshops, test the forensic samples, continue the hunt for the murder weapon that, so far, was proving elusive. There was a clatter as the shutters swung back, and a dull light filled the room.

A. There's nowhere to go.
Q. *Oh? How do you mean?*
A. There's nowhere to go.
Q. *Do you mean – in your spare time, things like that?*
A. Sometimes.

Q. *So what do you like to do then? In your spare time?*
A. So . . . ?
Q. *What do you do?*
A. I thought we were together.
Q. *What? Sorry, Ashley, I didn't get that.*
A. So, I'm sorry.
Q. *Ashley, do you want to do this? Only . . .*
A. I'm telling you!

Suzanne clicked off the recorder and glanced at the clock. Half past seven. Time for a break. She determinedly kept her mind focused on her work. She could get up to the university, put in some useful hours at the library. She could start doing some serious analysis of the tape, have something to show Maggie Lewis, her supervisor, on Wednesday when they next met. She stretched. She had showered, but hadn't bothered to get dressed, and now she couldn't decide whether to put some clothes on, or to have breakfast first. She had an appointment at police HQ in town. What to wear probably required a bit more thought than usual. Breakfast first, then a bit of power dressing, something to boost her morale.

She was standing in the kitchen making toast when there was a knock on the door. Before she could say anything, it was pushed half open and Joel Severini, Lucy's father, slid round it with his slow smile. 'How are you?' he said, with that slight, characteristic emphasis on the 'you'. He was wearing jeans and an unbuttoned shirt. His feet were bare.

'Joel.' Suzanne stopped in the kitchen doorway, suddenly aware of her thin dressing gown. She hadn't expected to see Joel, though he had been around more often recently, now that she came to think about it. 'What are you doing here?' It came out more coldly than she'd intended, but she didn't soften it with any further comment. Why bother? She didn't like Joel, and he didn't like her. There was no secret about that.

His eyes narrowed slightly, but he took this as an invitation to come right in, and stood opposite her, leaning his shoulder against the wall. He kept his eyes on her for a beat or two before he answered. 'Lucy. She went missing.'

'Yes, I know.' Suzanne shrugged herself deeper into her dressing gown. His gaze made her uncomfortable. *So?* she wanted to add.

'Well, then.' His tone implied that her question was unnecessary. Maybe she was being unfair. Jane always insisted that Joel cared about Lucy. *In his way.* And he clearly had come straight over as soon as he'd heard.

'How is she? Lucy? And Jane?'

'They're OK. Panic over. They're both still asleep. Look, have you got a decent cup of tea over here?' He looked across the yard to Jane's back door. 'Only it's all flowers and herbs over there, know what I mean?'

She indicated the cupboard. 'Help yourself.' Maybe then he'd go.

He crossed over to the cooker and checked the kettle for water. 'You having one?' Suzanne shook her head. She had expected him to take some teabags and leave. She didn't want him in her house. She waited as he made himself a drink, watching him as he moved around the room. His jeans fitted low round his narrow hips, and she could see the smooth arrow of hair on his stomach. When she had first met him, what, nearly six years ago, she had liked him. In the middle of the chaos that surrounded Michael's birth and the sudden and unstoppable disintegration of her marriage, he had seemed gentle and sympathetic. When Dave, who was working long hours, got impatient with her, Joel would say, 'Loosen up, Dave,' and give her that slow smile. Sometimes when she was on her own because Dave had a gig that took him away overnight, he would drop in with some beer and spend an hour or so talking to her. It had been a seduction – or, more accurately, a non-seduction – of the most humiliating kind.

He listened, encouraging her to talk about Adam, about Michael, and said the comforting things that her father had never said to her. When she blamed herself for the way she and Dave were falling apart, he reluctantly (it seemed) criticized Dave for his lack of support, reluctantly told her about the women Dave saw when he played a gig, gradually progressing their relationship from the soothing hand on

40

her hair, the arm round the shoulder into an (apparently unacknowledged) desire. And yes, OK, she had wanted him, even though he was Jane's partner, even though he was Dave's friend.

And he'd known and he'd made his move one evening when she and Dave had had a particularly vicious row. She'd managed to stop herself, even though fantasies about an encounter with him had kept her going through some of the blacker moments. He'd laughed at her – not a sympathetic laugh for her foolish scruples, or even a feigned humour disguising his anger. It had been contempt. 'It's called a sympathy fuck, Suzie. You won't get too many offers coming your way. Look at you,' he'd said. He hadn't wanted her – the casual contempt of his words confirmed that – but he'd wanted to know he could have her. And then he'd gone, and she really had no one to blame but herself.

The *drip, drip* of poison that Joel had fed into her ears about Dave, he had fed into Dave's ears about her. She couldn't blame Joel for the break-up of her marriage, but he'd been a factor, something that had tipped a fragile balance at a crucial moment. She had never told Jane what had happened. She was too ashamed.

Dave had changed, got older, more serious, but Joel seemed no different to her now than he had six years ago. She realized with a shock that he must be over forty. He looked up suddenly and caught her looking at him. His smile widened slightly, not reaching his eyes. 'So what happened yesterday?' His question was unexpected, but more, it was the masked concern in his voice that surprised her. She began to tell him about the morning, about realizing that Lucy and Emma were missing, but he interrupted her. 'No. I got all that from Jane. About fifty times. What happened after Lucy came back?'

She shook her head. 'I don't know anything. Jane and Lucy were gone by the time I got home.'

He drank some tea, staring out of the window, his eyes narrowed in speculation. 'They interviewed Lucy. Jane let them. She wasn't even allowed to sit in on it. "Oh, Lucy was fine about it," she says.' He looked angry.

'I suppose Jane thought – if it helps find . . . I mean, Emma was – killed, wasn't she? It wasn't an accident?'

Joel shrugged. 'It was too soon for them to be going after Lucy. They don't have a clue. Look, Jane listens to you. You tell her. Tell her to make them leave Lucy alone.' He emptied his cup into the sink, his face hard.

'Jane knows what's best for Lucy,' she said. She wasn't listening to any criticisms from Joel.

His eyes met hers. 'You'd know, would you, Suzie?' Her eyes dropped. He was right. How would she know? 'I phoned Dave,' he went on. 'He's mightily pissed off with you.' He was still smiling. 'Just think. If you'd brought Mike straight here, Lucy would have been home, and you'd never have got involved.' She didn't say anything. He put the empty cup down, not taking his eyes off her. He had to pass her on his way to the door. He put his hand lightly on her shoulder and she flinched, shaking him off. His eyes brightened. 'Be sure your sins will find you out, hey, Suzie?' he said. She heard him laughing as she slammed the door shut behind him.

The incident room was set up. Brooke was just finishing the first briefing of the inquiry, and the various teams were organizing their specific tasks. Tina Barraclough assessed the situation and waited to see what was going to happen. This was her first major inquiry since she had been promoted to detective constable, and she wanted to do a good job, make her mark. She looked at the people she would be working most closely with. Steve McCarthy she knew. She'd worked with him before. She'd have to keep on her toes because she remembered him as impatient and autocratic. Pete Corvin, her sergeant, was an unknown quantity. He was a heavy-set, red-faced man who looked more like a bouncer than a detective sergeant. Mark Griffith and Liam Martin, the other two DCs, she knew well enough. She'd worked with Mark when he was in uniform, and knew them both from the pub.

Emma Allan had died of asphyxiation. There were cuts inside her mouth and throat, knife wounds, the pathologist said, as though someone had thrust the blade hard into the girl's mouth in a moment of rage. She had choked on the blood. The absence of defence injuries suggested that she had, up to the moment of the attack, trusted her assailant. There were needle marks on her arm. Tinfoil found in the grate had been used for cooking heroin, but they found no further evidence of drugs use there – no needles, no syringes, no wraps.

Steve McCarthy filled in the background. He ran through the events of the day before when Lucy Fielding had gone missing. It had looked at first like a crossed wires thing, something they were all familiar with, where a mother thought a child should be in one place, the person with the child thought they should be somewhere else. But a routine check had made the alarm bells ring.

Emma Allan, seventeen, had already come to police attention. At fourteen, she had been a persistent truant, involved in shoplifting and petty crime. She had run away from home twice before her fifteenth birthday, but after that had seemed to settle her differences with her parents, until recently. She had been reported missing by her father in March, after her mother's death. She had a recent caution for possession, and had been picked up at the house of a known heroin user who funded his habit by dealing. 'She gave the Fielding woman false information. She was passing herself off as a student, but she'd never registered at the university. She was too young, anyway,' McCarthy said.

The picture of Emma's recent life was unclear. Her father claimed not to have seen his daughter since the last time she left home. 'Did he try? Did he look?' Barraclough had problems with parents who didn't look out for their children.

'He said he did.' McCarthy was adding a note to the sheet of paper he held. He looked at the team. 'So far, we know that Emma was friendly with a student, Sophie Dutton. She looked after the Fielding child until about a month ago. Dutton lived at 14, Carleton Road, next door to Jane Fielding. It's a student house. It's empty now. We don't know how well she knew the other tenants – that's something that needs checking. But according to Fielding, and the other woman' – he checked his notes again – 'Milner, Emma Allan and Sophie Dutton were together a lot.'

'Has Dutton got a record?' Corvin was making the obvious connection.

McCarthy shrugged. 'There's nothing on file. According to Fielding, Dutton is driven snow. Doesn't smoke, doesn't drink, comes from a country village on the east coast.' His unspoken scepticism was shared by the group. The clean-living Sophie Dutton sketched by McCarthy was an unlikely close friend for someone with Emma Allan's interests and background.

'How did they come to be friends? University students are pretty cliquey.' Barraclough knew about the divide that existed between town and gown. McCarthy shook his head. They didn't have that information.

'We need to talk to the Dutton woman urgently,' Brooke told the team. 'We need to find out more about Emma's recent background, find out where she was living, what she was doing, and who she was doing it with.' He polished his glasses, his face looking strangely unfocused without them. 'When did Dutton leave? She went back to her parents, is that right?'

McCarthy nodded. 'According to the Fielding woman, she left in May. We're trying to contact her at her parents' now.'

Emma's missing clothes had been found in a bundle by the hearth: blue jeans, pants and sandals. They weren't torn or damaged in any way. There was no evidence of sexual assault. The pathologist was less certain about sexual activity. There had been no evidence, but the water would probably have destroyed it.

Brooke was winding up now. 'OK. Any questions?'

'One thing I can't understand.' Barraclough was reading through her notes. 'I can understand why he might have dumped her under the water-wheel. He just had to push her through that back window – the yard is well screened. It might have been days – weeks – before she was found. But why set the wheel going? Did he want us to find her?'

Nobody had a good answer to that. 'Someone a few bricks short of a load?' Corvin suggested.

McCarthy nodded. 'It could be. There's been a flasher in that park recently, and there was the attack in those woods a couple of miles along the path, at Wire Mill Dam. That was twelve months ago. The case is still open.'

A random killer. They couldn't exclude that possibility, Barraclough knew. A Peeping Tom in the park, someone who had been watching Emma, watched her having sex with her boyfriend, got his own ideas about what he wanted to do. If Emma had gone to Shepherd Wheel willingly . . . she looked back through copies of the witness statements they'd managed to get so far. A dog walker had seen a woman answering Emma's description walking towards Shepherd Wheel at around ten-thirty the morning of her death – Barraclough still couldn't understand it as a rendezvous, a place to have sex. It seemed dark and uninviting. 'Sticks a knife in her instead of his dick,' Corvin said.

'Someone who felt guilty – wants to be caught?' Barraclough didn't like the idea of a random killer – none of them did. These were the most difficult cases, and often the most high profile.

'What about the father?' Corvin made the logical follow-up to Barraclough's point.

Brooke stepped in again. 'Dennis Allan. Nothing recent, no social services reports. But he did time in 1982. Drink-driving conviction. Killed a kid; he got a year. We talked to him last night, just a preliminary. He's coming in first thing. Steve, you do that interview. We need to know exactly why she left home.' He paused for a moment, then answered the unspoken question. 'He's not in the clear, not by a long chalk.'

'What happened to Emma's mum?' Corvin again.

Brooke looked at the team for a moment. His glasses caught the light, masking his expression. 'She took an overdose. Died. The verdict was accidental death.' A murmur ran round the room.

'Guilt,' Barraclough said.

Emma's father was a small man in his early fifties. He was very unlike his pretty, fair-haired daughter. What hair he had was gingerish, streaked with grey. His face was puffy, the broken veins on his cheeks standing out against his pallor. He looked unhealthy and uncomfortable. He didn't look, to

45

McCarthy, like a bereaved parent. Emma's record told a story that McCarthy didn't like. Something had gone seriously wrong in her life, long before these events, long before her mother's death. Emma wasn't simply a teenager traumatized by bereavement.

They had gone through the formalities and had already established that Allan had no alibi for the previous morning. 'What was I doing?' he said, apparently surprised at the question. 'I worked night shift. Came home and went to bed.' No one had seen him, apart from the newsagent at about eight. He'd nipped in to the shop for a paper and some cigarettes. He began to look uneasy as the implications of McCarthy's questions dawned on him. His face got more colour and his eyes went pinker round the lids. McCarthy waited to see if he would object, but he said nothing, just twisted his hands nervously.

'Can we go back a few weeks, Mr Allan?' McCarthy decided it was time for him to build up the pressure a bit. 'I understand you lost your wife . . .'

'In March, end of March.' The man seemed pathetically eager to tell him.

McCarthy had the date in front of him. March 29. Dennis Allan had come off his shift at six that morning and found his wife dead. 'I'm sorry.' A necessary formality. 'Could you tell me what happened? In your own time, Mr Allan.'

The man's eyes got pinker, and he blinked. 'Sandy, my wife, she . . .' He seemed to be having trouble putting the words together. 'She was ill, see, you know, in her mind. All through our marriage it was a problem. She was on pills, but they didn't always work – made her dopey, so she'd stop them, and then . . .' He looked down at his hands, twisting them together. McCarthy steepled his fingers against his mouth and nodded. Dennis Allan looked at him. 'She was always, I mean she . . .' He swallowed. 'She used to try and harm herself, you know?' McCarthy nodded again. 'She didn't mean it, not like that, not really, but when things got on top of her, she'd take her pills, you know . . .' His eyes sought out Tina Barraclough's, then McCarthy's, looking for their understanding.

'She'd take an overdose?' Barraclough prompted.

46

He looked grateful. 'She didn't mean it,' he said.

'But this time?' McCarthy watched the wash of colour that flooded the man's face.

'She took a lot of pills. And with some drink. She did it while I was at work. She . . .' He put his head in his hands. A display of grief, natural for a man talking about such a recent bereavement, a man doubly bereaved. McCarthy wondered why he wasn't convinced. He waited, aware that Barraclough was hovering on the brink of saying something to the distressed man. He shook his head slightly, and she sat back. McCarthy could detect disapproval in her set face. After a minute, Allan spoke again. 'I found her. When I came back from work. I don't know if she meant it.'

'And Emma?' McCarthy prompted quietly.

'Emma just . . . She packed her bags that same day. Wouldn't speak to me.' He looked at the two officers, trying to gauge their understanding. 'She just left. I tried to contact her at the college, but they said she'd never enrolled. Didn't even come to her own mother's funeral.' His voice was bewildered.

The search for Lucy the day before had identified witnesses who remembered seeing Emma in the park, round about the time Jane Fielding said that she and Lucy had left. A woman walking back from delivering her daughter to school saw Emma and Lucy in the playground near the gate, and had wondered why Lucy wasn't at school. There was a dog walker who remembered a young woman answering Emma's description on the path to Shepherd Wheel, walking fast: 'I noticed her because she looked a bit anxious.' She had been alone. He was quite certain she had had no child with her. So what had happened to Lucy? McCarthy hoped the key would lie in the interview that the child protection team had recorded the evening before, shortly after a tired but otherwise unharmed Lucy had turned up in the woods half a mile above Shepherd Wheel.

But Lucy's story was confusing and inconclusive. She was very young – just six – and fantasized and wove the things that happened to her into stories and daydreams. The child protection officer, Alicia Hamilton, was able to clarify some of the more puzzling aspects of her story. 'It could be some-thing or nothing,' she had said as she discussed the tape of Lucy's interview with the team, 'but it seems that Emma invented this game of chasing the monsters. But there's a bit more to it than that.' *Then Emma went to chase the monsters and I went to the swings. Well, she did but I ran away.*

'That bit's interesting.' Hamilton had stopped the tape. 'It takes a while to sort out – you'll see in a minute – but it looks as though Emma had a bit of a scam going. According to Lucy, Emma would go and chase off the monsters, and Lucy would stay in the playground. Then, as long as she was good, Emma would get her an ice cream.' Lucy's story was clear to this point, even to the point of knowing that what-ever Emma was doing, it was dangerous.

I told her. One time, two times, three times. Then they get you.

But later on in the tape, the child's fantasies became impenetrable.

Why did you go into the woods, Lucy?
Because the monsters. Because the Ash Man . . .
Tell me about the Ash Man, Lucy.
He's Tamby's friend. Only not really. Tamby's my friend.
Who's Tamby, Lucy?
He's my friend.
What about the Ash Man?
The Ash Man . . . the Ash Man is Emma's friend.
Tell me about him.
I said. He's Emma's friend. And Tamby is, too.

'Her mother says that these are characters in her stories. "Tamby" is someone she pretends to play with in the garden and in the park. This "Ash Man" is some kind of giant or ogre . . .' McCarthy felt his head begin to ache. Hamilton went on. 'It isn't all fantasy. There was *someone* – someone must have taken her up to the Forge Dam playground. It's too far for a little thing like that to walk to by herself. And someone gave her money to buy ice cream. But who it was, Lucy can't – or won't – tell us.'

*   *   *

48

Suzanne waited until she heard the engine of Joel's bike, the roar of subdued power from a machine far too expensive for someone who claimed he couldn't afford to support his child, so that she was sure he had left. She slipped across the yard and knocked on Jane's door, pushing it open as she did so. Jane was at the kitchen table, a mug in her hands, staring into space. Her sketch pad was in front of her. She stood up when Suzanne came in and gave her a quick hug. 'I heard,' she said by way of greeting. 'You were the one who found her.'

Suzanne returned her hug. 'How is she? Is she all right?'

Jane nodded, sitting down at the table again. 'Yes. She's a bit quiet, but she's coming round. The police took me straight across to this place where they interview children.' Jane reached across for the teapot and poured Suzanne a cup of pale tea. The smell of camomile drifted into the room.

'What happened? Did anyone . . . ?' Jane's serene manner could be deceptive, Suzanne knew.

'Emma just left her, just like that, and she wandered off by herself.' Her normally gentle face was hard. 'Apparently Emma made a habit of dumping Lucy and going off. Bribing her to stick around. And Lucy wouldn't, not with a hospital appointment looming. The police think that someone was with her in the playground, but Lucy says not. She said she was hiding from the monsters. But she always does these days. And she said that Tamby helped her, and there was something about the Ash Man.' Suzanne recognized the names from the times she sat with Lucy and listened to her stories. 'I talked to her last night, and again this morning. I think she was on her own. She knows the way to Forge Dam. We've walked up there together often enough. I go cold when I think of her walking through those woods. And the roads.' Her hands tightened round her cup, then she looked at Suzanne. 'I feel so awful. I can't believe I just let Emma . . .'

Suzanne knew all about guilt. 'You thought you knew her. We both did.'

Jane wasn't prepared to let herself off the hook. 'I knew Sophie,' she said. Suzanne waited, and after a moment, Jane

49

went on. 'Whoever . . . did it must have got Emma after she left Lucy, thank God. I don't think she saw anything. Joel said I shouldn't have let them interview her, but . . .' Jane gave her a cautionary look as they heard footsteps on the stairs. She began leafing through her sketch book. 'I did some drawings while I was waiting,' she said.

Lucy came in, carrying the peacock feather, a present from Sophie that was one of her treasures. 'Hello, Lucy,' Suzanne said, then, unable to help herself, gave the little girl a hug.

Lucy wriggled impatiently. 'I'm *busy*,' she said.

'I know, I'm sorry, Lucy. What are you doing?'

Lucy compressed her lips, then relented. 'I'm playing. Tamby's chasing the monsters.' She looked at the two women. 'I didn't talk to the real police. I told Alicia about the monsters.'

'The child protection officer,' Jane said. 'The one who interviewed her.'

Suzanne felt cold. 'I know.' *We want to help the lad.*

'I'm going in the garden now,' Lucy said.

Jane watched her as she went out into the back yard, the feather held carefully in one hand as she negotiated the step. 'Still the monsters,' she said. Suzanne kept her mind carefully focused on Jane as she leafed through her sketch book until she came to the page she wanted. 'I finally got it right,' she said. 'I did these yesterday while I was waiting for them to interview Lucy.'

Suzanne looked at the familiar scene: the terraced houses; the wheelie bins at the entrances; the tiny front gardens, narrow strips separating the houses from the road, some cared for and blooming, some overgrown with shrubs, weeds and discarded rubbish. It was the scene she saw every day from her bedroom window, made oddly new by Jane's pencil. The drawings caught the contrasts of light and shade, the places where the sun shone brilliantly, the places where the shadows were black and impenetrable. There was something about the drawings that made Suzanne feel uneasy. She looked more closely. There was a suggestion of something – something larger than human, something menacing – lurking in the shadows of an entrance. A hand, oversized with long nails, reached out from under the lid of a wheelie bin. An eye – an avian eye? – watched with keen intent from behind a curtain. The curtain was held back by a claw. Suzanne realized that everywhere she looked, strange things looked back, half hidden, almost completely hidden, but there. Among and around them walked people, happy, smiling, oblivious. She looked at Jane.

Jane was still looking at the drawings. 'Monsters,' she said.

The trees were in full leaf now, the heavy canopy hanging over the paths that wound through the woods, following the path of the Porter, down through the Mayfield Valley to the silted-up dam at Old Forge, past the café and the playground, and down into the depths of the woods, past Wire Mill Dam where the white water-lilies bloomed, down the old weirs and channels, down into the parks and down past the dark silence of Shepherd Wheel Dam. Here, houses backed onto the park, big stone houses, three storeys in the front, four in the back where the land dropped away to the river. The trees shadowed the gardens of these houses. Their roots undermined the foundations. Conifers and laurel grew close against the walls. The basements opened onto small back gardens, separated from the park by low walls.

The garden behind the first house was derelict and overgrown. The leaves of autumn were still rotting on the ground where the daisies and the dandelions pushed through. A wheelie bin lay on its side, the contents spilt on the asphalt, trodden into the mud and the moss. The foxes and the rodents had taken the edible stuff, had pulled and torn the rubbish and strewn it around the ground. A small patch of earth had been cleared, the edges cut with surgical precision. Seedlings had been planted, nasturtiums and forget-me-nots. The soil was dry, and they were wilting slightly.

The basement window was dark. The back of the house didn't get the sun. The trees blocked it out. Through the window, the white of the walls glimmered faintly in the darkness. Drawings were taped onto the walls, each one a rectangle of white, each one with a drawing carefully placed in the very centre. The drawing was tight, small, meticulous in detail. This

51

one, a fair-haired teenager; this one, a dark-eyed youth; this one, a young woman, laughing. Here, a child peers watchfully through tangled hair; and here, the child again, this time crouched intently over some game, not depicted in the drawing. Her hands play with the white emptiness.

Each sheet is the same size, the space between each sheet exactly measured. At first, the pictures are carefully sequenced: first, the teenage girl, next, the youth, next, the woman, next, the child; the girl, the youth, the woman, the child. But then the pictures begin to run out of sequence: the girl, the child, the youth; the girl, the child, the youth; the child, the youth; the child, the youth . . . and the sequence stops in the middle of the wall.

Suzanne recognized the man who was interviewing her. It was the detective who had been at Jane's the day before, the man who had talked to her after she'd found Emma in the water. Detective Inspector McCarthy. She had dressed carefully for the interview, putting on her best suit – well, her only suit. She'd put on make-up and blow-dried her hair until the fine curls turned into a sleek bob. But despite all her careful preparations, her chest was tight and she felt panicky. She hadn't been in a police station since that last time with Adam, the last of the many visits when Adam sat in sullen silence, until, eventually, the scared child that Suzanne could see underneath the façade of bravado would emerge. They'd always left the police stations, the youth courts, together, until the last time, when she'd had to leave alone, hearing Adam's voice behind her. *Listen to me, Suzanne!*

She pulled herself back to the present. She needed to be alert, she realized as she looked into the cold eyes of the man on the other side of the table. She'd answered questions the night before about finding Emma, but he went over those again, clearly unhappy with parts of her story. Suzanne found she couldn't account for her decision to investigate the wheel. To her, it was as obvious as looking round if someone shouted *Watch out!* but he seemed unable to understand or accept this.

'So it wasn't easy to get into the yard,' he was saying again.

'No, I had to climb over the fence.'

'Over those railings? That's a dangerous climb.'

That was true, it had been. Suzanne wondered why she hadn't thought about that before she climbed – she'd just done it. McCarthy hadn't actually asked her a question, so she said nothing. After a moment, he said, 'What I'm trying to establish, Mrs Milner—'

'Ms,' Suzanne interrupted. She saw his eyes appraise her briefly, dismissively. She remembered Joel watching her in the kitchen that morning.

'*Ms* Milner, is why you went to all that trouble unless you had a reason to think something was wrong.'

'Do you always know why you do things?' She regretted the question as soon as she'd asked it. It made her sound defensive. He had a habit, she noticed, of not replying, of not acknowledging something that was said. He was leaning back in his chair, staring Suzanne in the eye, as though he expected something else from her. She could feel her breathing start to get uneven, and tried to distract herself, to make herself relax. She studied her hands. Her nails were OK apart from the one she'd bitten down yesterday. There was some dirt caught under her thumb, and she tried to scratch it out. She was glad she'd taken the time to put some varnish on. It made her feel more confident for some reason. Her breathing steadied, but she was still unable to think of an answer to his question. 'I don't know . . .' she said in the end, in the absence of anything else to say. She saw his face harden slightly, and reinforced her answer. 'I *don't* know. You know what was happening. Maybe I thought it was something to do with Lucy.'

'Did you think that?'

'I don't know.' Impasse. He waited in silence. She felt the pressure building up again. She half expected to see, across the desk, the woman who had talked to her, that last time, about Adam. *We want to help the lad, Suzanne.* She deliberately began a mental review of the scale for testing communication that she'd been adapting for use at the Alpha Project. You asked a series of questions that had fairly obvious answers, then tested the responses you actually got against a checklist: *No response. Contextually inappropriate response* – like Ashley when she was asking about his family . . . It was strange, the way Ashley had reacted in the interview. She tried to remember if he'd shown any signs of those odd responses when she'd been talking to him in the coffee bar . . .

'. . . in the yard, Ms Milner?'

'Sorry. Could you just . . .'

Again that slight hardening of the face, which she could understand this time. She should have been paying attention. It made him seem a bit more human. 'Did you see anything that might have made you think something was wrong in the yard?'

'Right. Sorry. I'm a bit tired.' She tried a smile. There was no reason to be antagonistic, she told herself. This wasn't to do with Adam. He didn't respond, but waited for her to answer. *But not that human.* 'Well, not that evening, I mean apart from, you know . . .' *Oh, for Christ's sake get on with it, Suzanne!* 'I mean . . . are you asking about the evening, or the morning?'

'You were in the park yesterday morning?' She realized then that she hadn't told them. She'd let them think that her evening visit was her only visit to the park that day. His voice was neutral, but she thought she could detect exasperation underlying it. She felt stupid, but she felt angry as well. Didn't he understand? Was he so used to violence, to sudden death, that he just went on like an automaton, and expected everyone else to be the same?

'Yes.' There didn't seem to be anything else to say.

'What time?'

Suzanne thought. 'I went into the park about half past nine, and I got home at around ten-thirty. I go running. Jogging. I went through Endcliffe Park, and then I crossed over the main road and went on through Bingham Park.' She went on to tell him about the notice she'd seen.

He let his exasperation show now. 'Why didn't you tell me this yesterday?'

She felt her face flush. She hated to be caught out. 'It just . . . The whole thing. Lucy. I couldn't think of anything else.'

He nodded, clearly unsatisfied, and went back to the notice. He seemed as puzzled by it as she had been, and asked her about people in the park, people she saw regularly, any problems with flashers, any other odd or worrying people, *anything*. She found herself saying No . . . no . . . no, never . . . no.

Then she told him about the wheel yard, about the gate being open, about her visit to the wheel. His face didn't change, but she felt as though she could read the thoughts behind those expressionless eyes. She stepped hard on her desire to apologize, to explain, and tried to go through her story calmly and clearly. He took her over and over it. She closed her eyes, trying to make the picture clear. 'It was my reflection,' she said. 'I waved at it, and it waved back.' The sinister, farcical picture of Emma, dead, waving back at her disturbed her equilibrium further, and her voice tailed away in her explanations.

It seemed it was almost over. She began to relax now that he wasn't pushing her for information she didn't have, wasn't asking her questions she couldn't answer, wasn't making her feel like a culpable fool for keeping information back. It was important to explain that she hadn't seen either Lucy or Em, but she needed to tell him about the man – the youth? – she had seen near Shepherd Wheel. 'I only saw one person in that part of the park.' She sent her mind back to the odd, jumpy feeling the figure had given her. 'I thought it was someone I knew at first, but . . .'

'Who was that?' McCarthy's tone was bland, but she knew at once she'd made a mistake.

'Oh, it wasn't,' she said quickly. Too quickly. 'I just thought it was. At first.' She could feel her chest start to tighten and the air she was breathing becoming thin and insubstantial. She concentrated. Breathe slowly, evenly. Keep calm. *I hold you responsible for this!* Her father's litany. McCarthy just went on looking at her. More prevarication would only make it worse. After all, it hadn't been Ashley. Her voice came out in uneven jerks, and she had to stop speaking and gulp for air. 'Just for a moment. I thought . . . it was Ashley Reid . . . from the Alpha Project . . . only it wasn't . . .' It couldn't have been more unconvincing if she'd deliberately lied.

*   *   *

55

McCarthy was working through the computer files. He was angry, and he wanted to talk to whoever had interviewed Suzanne Milner the evening before. He should have done it himself. But they had the information now. At around a quarter past ten, the wheel yard had been open, and someone, a young man answering a particular description, had been around there, actually coming from the direction of the yard.

He was puzzled as well as angry. He was good at reading people in interview situations, but Suzanne Milner had been strange. Yesterday she'd been fiercely protective of her friend, later she had been almost flattened by shock. Today she had presented the façade of a carefully groomed academic and had managed to get right up his nose. She'd come in, a picture of cool elegance, very different from the old-jeans-and-sweater image she'd projected yesterday. At first he'd interpreted her attitude as hostility. She'd sat there straight-backed, tilting her head and studying her fingernails before she answered each question, shooting quick glances at him and looking away as soon as he met her eyes. She seemed to be treating the whole thing as a game, giving him minimal, uncooperative answers to the questions he needed answering.

But it was a façade, he'd realized, as the interview had moved on. What he had mistaken for hostility was, in fact, tension, but it seemed more a tension associated with her surroundings than with him. It was almost as if she was having trouble concentrating on the interview at all.

He looked at his notes. Her confusion about the park – he could accept that. She'd been in shock, focused on finding the dead woman in the water. Her sheer embarrassment at having to admit that she'd been near Shepherd Wheel at the crucial time, and hadn't mentioned it, had been convincing.

But had she tried to slide that sighting past him? If so, why mention it at all? It was odd. He'd *known* there was something else, and he'd been right. Ashley Reid from the Alpha programme. Why were alarm bells ringing in his mind? He knew that name. OK, let's see what Ashley who wasn't there might have been doing. Let's see what he'd been doing the last time he'd been arrested and charged. He typed the commands into the machine, and waited.

The photograph on the screen showed a young man with heavy dark hair and dark eyes. He looked out at McCarthy with a faint smile, his eyes wary. He was nineteen – a bit older than most of those sent on the programme. McCarthy ran the record back. Reid had served a short youth custody sentence three years ago – got into a fight and glassed his opponent. Most of his other offences were typical of a disruptive juvenile: shoplifting, twoc, minor vandalism. But Reid had moved on to breaking and entering. He had more than one conviction. He should have been sent down. Why the Alpha Project? McCarthy read on. Reid was classified as having 'learning difficulties'. McCarthy was surprised. The face that looked at him from the photograph didn't give that impression. He'd been identified as particularly suitable for the experimental programme that was running at the Alpha Project. Not so much bad as easily led, his probation officer had said, the fall guy for more intelligent companions. That had been the argument that had kept him out of prison.

McCarthy raised a sceptical eyebrow. Then he noticed that Reid had an outstanding charge against him, one that was due to go to court. University campus security had found him late one night in the shadows behind the chemistry building, the route across the car park that made a useful, but lonely, shortcut. He was facing a charge of going equipped for burglary. He'd been carrying a torch, a lock-knife and some heavy-duty adhesive tape. In McCarthy's eyes, in that location, that wasn't going equipped for burglary, it was going equipped for rape.

The world of chemicals is ordered, predictable and, for those who understand it, safe. It was evening, and Simon let his eyes follow the straight lines of the tiles running along the shiny floor, across, making right angles and patterns of squares. Small squares, and larger squares each containing four small squares, and larger squares still each containing four of the smaller squares each containing four of the small squares and on and on forever. Order.

He mixed the three solutions, acetimide in water, calcium hypochlorate in water, sodium hydroxide *careful now* in water. Watch the heat! He put the solutions in the freezer.

There were heavy benches in rows. Strips of light on the ceiling, bright, bright, bouncing off the surface of the glass, the bottles, the tubes, the shapes, the curves. The light mixing and shattering into chaos.

The important thing was to keep the temperature low. Experiment had shown him that a stainless steel bowl suspended in a mixture of ice and salt worked fine, as long as he was careful and patient. Molecules sit in their patterns, break down on the right stimulus, recombine in patterns that it is easy to predict. Absorbing and beautiful.

The light reflecting, refracting, lines against the glassware, shattering again and again and again.

He put the first solution in the bowl, stirring to get the temperature down. Then, slowly, carefully, he added the second, working under the fume hood. *Care!* Once, once only the order, the ratios, the time, *something* was wrong, and the disinfectant smell of chlorine began to seep into the room.

Now he could sit and wait. Two hours. Tonight he'd brought his drawing pad with him. He opened it to a new page. The sheer whiteness, the blankness of it pleased him, and he sat looking at it for a long time. Footsteps on the shiny floor. A face, smiling. Just a face. Faces need to be drawn, carefully delineated in sharp pencil lines to give them meaning. 'Hello, Simon. I haven't seen you at . . .' Malcolm. Tutor. Tune it out. Not important. The beauty of the white began to evade him, and he picked up his pencil. '. . . so close to your finals.' Nod. That's not enough. Say, 'Yes.' It was important to get it right in the centre. The pencil began to create a picture, fine lines, fine detail, unclear at first to anyone who can't see the patterns that have always been so clear to Simon.

'. . . catching up. This lab's empty tonight, but Barry's next door if you need anything. They'll be locking up at nine.' Their eyes meeting. Simon, looking away, nodding. Say, 'OK. All right.' Footsteps. Door. Gone. Simon looked at the clock, and returned to his drawing.

Two hours. He added the contents of the third flask now, cool not cold. The solution turned a clear white, like milk, like paper.

Hours to wait now. Leave, down the shiny corridors and the lights in the ceiling, and the chaos as the people walk here, there, and all the patterns disturbed. Say, 'Goodnight.' The security man, old, 'Night.' Looking down, not noticing, used to Simon's comings and goings. Out of sight and back to the room with the shiny floor. Wait.

Lights out. The security man, back soon. Wait, watch, sleep. Sleep. Dream . . .

The torchlight wavering on the path ahead. Fading, as though the batteries were giving up. The rain spattering against them, and a puddle gleaming in the thin light. And on the path ahead . . . Staggering under the weight as she slumped against him. The stuff had been good, strong. *Quiet, be very quiet.* The path by the dam, now. The night, black beyond the circle of faint light on the ground. The torchlight catching the rain, shining and glittering. Shining and glittering like the mud in the dam, the thick, black mud and the sucking sounds drawing your feet in and releasing them. And the place where the mud was disturbed, the place where you could dig.

Oh, no. Please not that. And the gleam colder than the gleam of firelight, making the metal burn with ice.

Not that! And the soft, muffling sound of the mud in the darkness.

Simon's eyes snapped open. That dream again, and now there was another one, rushing along a shadowed path, looking for something that wasn't there, feeling it hard on his heels, the chaos, the chaos, the chaos.

He looked at the clock, its black hands on its white face calming him, steadying his breathing. *Just a dream, Si. Don't worry about it.* Several hours had passed. It was midnight. The night watchman never came up here so late. Simon began heating the water bath.

5

Dennis Allan's home – once Emma's home – was a maisonette on the estate overlooking Gleadless Valley. Tina Barraclough got lost on her first attempt to find the address, working her way through the confusing maze of two- and three-storey blocks that studded the valley side. From the distance, the estate gave a sense of openness, of green parkland dotted here and there with buildings whose fronts were multicoloured with fluttering curtains, washing hanging on the balconies, painted doors. From closer up, the decay was more apparent. There was rubbish on the grass, bare, muddy patches. The paintwork on the buildings was peeling. Nearby, the blocks were boarded up. Further down the hill, they were encased in scaffolding, surrounded by the mud and rubble of a building site, tarpaulins and polythene sheeting flapping in the summer breeze.

The Allans' block was one that was awaiting refurbishment. Police cars were parked in front of the row of garages that formed a basement to the building. Barraclough pulled up beside them. The doors of the garages were uneven and chipped, decorated with tags and slogans and names: CASSIE B AND CLAIRE D WOZ ERE! BAZ FOR CLAIRE D! SLAGS LIVE HERE. The garages had once been painted in primary colours, red and blue and yellow. Traces of the paint could still be seen.

Barraclough went up the concrete stairway to the first deck, to number twelve, the Allans' maisonette. Though the rubbish chute seemed to be jammed, stuck open and overflowing, the stairway itself was swept clean, the front doors painted and most of the windows trim with nets and potted plants. One or two doors were open as people watched the police team arrive, but the doors closed again as quickly when neighbours were approached. Barraclough opened the door to number twelve and went in.

Having got permission to search the house, Brooke had given instructions for the place to be turned over. 'I want anything – anything at all that tells you what's been going on there. Anything that says Emma went back after he says she left, anything that tells us about her. I want the lot.'

The maisonettes were laid out to a pattern. Barraclough had a friend who lived in a council maisonette on another estate, and she could have found her way round this one with her eyes closed. A kitchen to the left of the front door, a corridor leading into an L-shaped living-room with French windows opening onto a small balcony. Upstairs, a windowless bathroom, a separate toilet, also windowless and smelling faintly of urine. A bedroom and a tiny second bedroom – Emma's. According to her father, the room hadn't been touched since she left. 'I wanted her to think she could come back. I wanted her back,' he said.

Emma had been seventeen. Barraclough was twenty-four. She wondered if those seven years would be a big enough gap to make a barrier. She could remember being seventeen. She couldn't remember seventeen feeling any different from the way twenty-four felt, except that life seemed both easier and more difficult at twenty-four. Barraclough cast her mind back. Seventeen had been rows with her mother about her exams. Had it been arguments about late nights and boys, or was that from when she was younger? Barraclough felt as though she'd been making her own decisions for a long time, but maybe her mind was deceiving her. Seventeen. Emma had lived here with her mother who apparently thought nothing about inflicting her own miseries on her family. Her father – was he the ineffectual ditherer he seemed, or did that pathetic exterior hide a more sinister, more manipulative psyche? Emma must have been unhappy. She'd run away twice. Why had she come back – and why had she finally left?

Barraclough looked round the small room, trying to get a

feel for Emma, get a picture of the living girl, rather than the dead woman on the slab in the mortuary. There was a single bed under the window, and a melamine wardrobe against the wall, the kind that had hanging space and shelves and drawers. It was clean and tidy, and the bed was made up. The room was the room of a younger girl, the room of someone who was growing up, moving on. Emma had not bothered to change or update it. The bedding and curtains were brightly coloured with a cartoon motif – Bart Simpson. *Eat my shorts.* Emma's choice? Her mother's? Either way, the bedding and curtains were faded. They weren't new. A torn Spice Girls poster was above the bed, something that Emma would probably be embarrassed to own if she had retained much awareness of the room. A photograph of Royal Trux, one that looked as though it had been cut from a magazine, was pinned to the opposite wall.

Barraclough opened the wardrobe door. A stained fleece dressing gown hung on a hook – it looked too small for Emma to have worn it recently – and a party dress, black, lycra, very short, halter-neck top. A real jaw-dropper. A RECLAIM THE STREETS flyer was stuck to the inside of the wardrobe door. A pair of old trainers lay on the bottom.

She pulled open the drawers. There was nothing there apart from a half-empty packet of Rizlas, the card of the packet torn, and the remains of a cigarette. Barraclough picked up some of the tobacco and sniffed it. The undersides and backs of the drawers yielded nothing. She looked round the room again. There was a rucksack on the back of the door. She opened it and looked inside. It was empty apart from a couple of flyers – free parties by the look of things, Smokescreen and DIY Sound System. Underground, deep house. She checked the side pockets of the bag – for a moment, she thought she'd found a diary and her heart jumped, but it was a wallet, the kind you get from banks and building societies for holding cards. She flicked through it. It contained a cash card, a bus pass and a chain store credit card. Odd, for an unemployed teenager. Had Emma been in debt? She flicked through the cards to see if there was anything else in the wallet, and a couple of photographs dropped out. She picked them up. The first one showed a young woman at a party or a disco – the background was dark, with people indistinct in the background. The light – possibly a flash – had caught the woman, and she was laughing and holding her hand up in protest. For a moment, Barraclough thought it must be Emma, but the hair was darker. On the front of the photograph someone – the woman in the picture? – had written TO EM. She turned the photograph over. On the back, in a different hand, it said SOPHE. HULL, '97. Sophie Dutton?

The second photograph was a snapshot of a group of people, blurry and out of focus. It looked as though they were setting up some musical equipment. In the foreground, clearer than the other figures, was a woman, about the same age as the woman in the first picture, Sophe, but the picture was older. There was something about the style of clothes, the make-up, that said seventies, and not seventies revival, either. The clothes looked clumsy, without the stylishness of more recent fabrics and designs. Barraclough looked more closely. The woman could be a younger version of a photo she'd noticed downstairs, a very young Sandra Allan. She looked at the other people in the picture, but it was impossible to make out any detail. She turned the picture over. There was a date scribbled in faded ink. It looked like November 197— The last digit was unclear, and there was another word she couldn't quite read: —ELVET. Above that, in what looked like more recent ink, someone had written, SO WHAT ABOUT THIS? She looked at the photo again. There was something about the woman – girl, really. The way she was standing, awkward, unbalanced. Barraclough frowned. It reminded her of . . . Of course! The woman in the photograph, the woman who was probably Sandra Allan, was pregnant. She looked at the smudged date again. Sandra Allan had had a child before she had Emma. What had happened to it?

Dennis Allan's face flushed as he looked at the photograph that McCarthy passed to him. 'Do you recognize any of these people?' McCarthy asked him.

He shook his head, then said, 'Sandra, of course. I don't know . . .' He peered at the picture. 'I don't recognize any of them,' he said. 'It's hard to tell.' McCarthy nodded. The photograph was indistinct. 'I don't know where this came from,' he said. He'd known Sandra towards the end of the seventies, he said. He'd been in a band, and Sandra had been the singer for a while. 'I left in '77,' he said.

McCarthy asked him about Sandra's pregnancy. Allan's face flushed again. 'We lost touch when the band broke up,' he said. He caught McCarthy's look and said with real indignation, 'It wasn't mine. I wasn't her boyfriend.' The band, Velvet, had broken up in '78, when another member had left. 'I met Sandra again in '81,' he said. 'We got married in 1982, just before Emma was born.' His face looked forlorn.

Barraclough liked nosy neighbours. She particularly liked house-bound nosy neighbours. Best of all, she liked house-bound nosy neighbours who were quite up-front about their hobby. It was always a frustration and a delay to find your way tactfully around 'I mind my own business' and 'I keep myself to myself.' Rita Cooke was seventy-three. She had the shuffling gait and twisted hands of arthritis, but her mind was whip sharp, as, apparently, were her eyes. And she'd lived next door to the Allan family for ten years. 'I don't know which was worse,' she said happily, pouring Barraclough a cup of tea. 'That Sandra, always got a long face on her, always sighing and moaning. She'd come round here and it was, "Oh, Dennis's done this and Dennis's done that and poor me." What she needed was a few real problems, take her mind off herself.'

'What did her husband do? What did she complain about?' Barraclough took another biscuit.

'Oh, something and nothing. He worked nights, you see, and she didn't like being on her own, or he wouldn't back her up with the girl – "He lets her talk to me how she likes" – or he didn't understand about how ill she was. You know. Mind you' – Rita Cooke wanted to be fair – 'he was just as bad. In his way. "Yes, love, yes, love, oh, what shall I do?

64

Oh, I can't cope." It's no wonder that child went to the bad.'
She waited for Barraclough to pick up the bait.

'How do you mean, Mrs Cooke?' Barraclough asked
obligingly.

'Oh well, I only know what I saw. She was out all the time.
All night, sometimes. And she had some very odd-looking
friends, not that they came here much. Not unless there
wasn't anyone here.'

Barraclough nodded. 'Would you recognize any of them?'
she said.

Mrs Cooke gave her a sharp look. 'I might be getting on,
but I've still got my sight,' she said. Barraclough hastily
nodded again. 'There was one lad – didn't like the look of
him at all. He used to hang around a lot and wait for her.
I'd have sent him off, but you've got to be careful these days.'
Barraclough got a description of the youth. Tall, pale, dark
hair and eyes. 'Quite good-looking,' Mrs Cooke conceded.

Barraclough asked her about Sandra Allan's death. For the
first time, the old woman seemed a bit reluctant to speak. 'I
don't know,' she said. 'She had a big row with the lass –
shouting and screaming. I couldn't hear what they were saying, but it went on for a while. Then the lass is off out, door
slamming, and he starts. I've never heard him shout at her
before. She went out for about half an hour . . .' Barraclough
checked the time. They knew about that. She'd gone to the
chemist to collect a prescription, the prescription for the pills
that she later overdosed on. 'Then she didn't go out again.
I saw him going out to work, four o'clock that was. I thought
she was going to come round here like usual when she was
upset, but she never did. It was quiet after that. I heard him
come back at six the next morning. Then I got woken up
again by the ambulance.' The old lady frowned, looking
uncertain, frail. 'I never thought she'd do it,' she said, looking
at Barraclough with troubled eyes.

Suzanne gave up on work. She felt as though something
trusted and familiar had let her down. She looked out of her
kitchen window and saw Jane in her small yard, working in
the early evening sun on the tubs she used to grow herbs.

Lucy was crouched over some game involving building blocks and the animals from her wooden farm. Mother and daughter.

She remembered her own mother, that close, intense relationship that had been the centre of Suzanne's child universe. She could remember coming in from school every day, her mother lying on the settee, the disorder of the morning still to clear up, the food to prepare before her father came back from work.

As a child, she had just accepted her mother's illness. As an adult, she could see that it had deprived her of the things that a normal childhood should have: a mother who looked after you, friends, uninterrupted schooling. But as a child, she had liked it. It had made her feel important and wanted. She remembered her mother the year before Adam was born, always on the settee, always in bed. But she could remember a party, her friends round a bonfire, sausages on sticks and her mother laughing as she watched them bob for apples. When had that been? *You've worn your mother out, Suzanne! How can you be so thoughtless!* Her father. She shook her head. Memories of childhood were not what she wanted just now.

She knocked on the window and, when Jane looked up, she mouthed, Tea? Jane smiled and nodded and, five minutes later, Suzanne was carrying mugs of tea out into the garden, and some apple juice for Lucy. The day was fine, the sky a deep blue, with just a few clouds racing in the breeze that kept the air warm rather than baking hot. Suzanne took off the sweatshirt she'd been wearing over her T-shirt, and sat on the low wall that divided the two gardens, watching Jane work. 'It's just tea,' she said, indicating the mug.

'That's OK.' Jane pulled up a long-rooted dandelion and looked at it. 'You know, they used to cultivate these things. I tried making dandelion coffee once. It was disgusting.'

Suzanne looked across at Lucy who seemed to be involved in her game, oblivious to the conversation between the two adults. 'Have you heard anything more?' Jane looked at her. 'From the police, about Emma.' Surely Jane didn't need reminding.

'Yes, I know.' Jane went on looking at Suzanne, then she

said, 'You still look very tense. I don't know – I haven't heard anything directly.'

'How do you mean, directly?'

Jane knelt back on her heels and sipped the milkless tea Suzanne had given her. 'I'm sure this stuff is better for you than people say,' she said, indicating her mug. 'Of course, you just don't know what's in it.'

Suzanne wasn't sure if Jane was being deliberately evasive, or if she was just thinking out loud while she sorted out an answer to Suzanne's question. She couldn't ask again, because Lucy came over and looked at the glass of apple juice. 'Is that mine?' Suzanne nodded, and Lucy picked it up carefully, holding it with both hands.

'Sorry,' Suzanne apologized. 'It's a bit full.' Lucy nodded, concentrating as she lifted the glass to her mouth. 'What are you doing?' Suzanne indicated Lucy's game over at the other side of the yard.

'Playing.' Lucy drank some more juice and looked at the level in her glass. 'I'm going to take some for the people,' she said.

'People?' Suzanne looked across to where wooden toys were assembled on some twigs and leaves. The peacock feather was stuck in the ground like a flag above them.

'They're on a boat,' Lucy explained. 'Escaping from the monsters. Tamby's guarding them.' She carried her glass carefully back to where she'd been playing.

Jane pulled a face. 'Still monsters,' she said. 'They spent a long time with Emma's father,' she went on, 'but I don't know why. Joel told me.'

Suzanne had to do a quick mental pivot to realize that Jane was now answering her earlier question. 'Emma's father? How does Joel know?'

Jane shrugged. 'Joel made it his business to know. I don't ask. Joel wanted to know if there was anything they weren't telling us – that we should know. He was worried.'

'Well, so he should be.' Suzanne wasn't giving any ground on Joel. 'She is his child. His only child.' This concern, uncharacteristic of Joel in her experience, made her feel slightly warmer towards him.

'Oh, she isn't. His only one, I mean.' Jane sat back on her heels, detaching a snail from one of the plants. She looked at it. 'I don't want that.' She threw it over the wall into the garden of the student house. 'He had a child from his marriage.'

Suzanne was genuinely shocked. She hadn't known. 'He never said anything. I'm sure he never told Dave.'

'No. There's no contact.' Jane had finished working on the tubs now, and was looking at them with calm pleasure.

'What, never?'

Jane fixed her blue eyes on Suzanne. 'Never.' She gauged Suzanne's reaction for a moment, then said, 'I know how it looks. And I don't have many illusions about Joel. I know what he's like. But there's Lucy, you see.' She rested back on her heels, her hands clasped round her cup. 'Joel was just a bit of fun – I knew he wasn't someone to take seriously. I didn't actually plan for Lucy to happen.' Suzanne nodded. Jane rarely talked about this. She was a very self-contained and private person. 'Lucy needs to know that her father loves her,' Jane said, glancing back at where Lucy was still absorbed in her game. 'And if that means I have to make allowances for him, well, what does it matter? If I pressure Joel into doing more, he'll just vanish. And what good will that be for Lucy? She'll find out what he's like as she gets older, but, just now, she needs to know he loves her.'

'Does he?' Suzanne had never, until recently, seen much sign of this in Joel.

Jane sighed and shook her head. 'I don't know. As much as he's capable, may be. Though this thing has really given him a jolt. He was straight up as soon as I told him – he was pissed off that I didn't call him straight away – and he's sticking around. Oh, he's off today because he's working, but he's coming back tonight.'

Suzanne felt depressed at the thought of Joel being around. She remembered her encounter with him that morning. 'He seemed upset that the police had interviewed Lucy,' she said doubtfully. She found Joel in his new incarnation as concerned father a bit hard to believe.

Jane nodded. 'He said I shouldn't have allowed it. He

thought it had upset her. I think she needed to talk about it, and she needs to know that someone is doing something. It was good for her to see the police – she knows that there's someone to chase the monsters away. And we all needed to find out what happened – to Lucy, as well as Emma. I think Joel knows that really. He just hates to admit he's wrong.'

'Do you know any more about what happened to Lucy?' Suzanne looked across the garden to where Lucy was rearranging her toys, her face serious.

Jane shook her head. 'Lucy still says she went to the playground on her own, then she hid in the woods because she didn't want to go to the hospital, I think. But it all got mixed up with Tamby. Each time she tells it, it gets more and more like one of her stories. I agree with Joel about any more interviews. I've told the police I'm not asking her again. I want her to forget.'

Suzanne needed to talk. Jane listened quietly as Suzanne told her about the interview with DI McCarthy, and her worry that she'd unwittingly implicated Ashley. 'I tried to explain,' she said, 'but he didn't believe me.'

Jane looked at her with exasperation. 'You worry too much. Leave it up to them. It's not your problem any more. You did the right thing. You told them what you saw. They'll deal with it.' She thought for a moment. 'McCarthy. Was he the fair-haired one? Cold and distant? There's something very sexy about men like that. He should have been wearing a uniform.'

'Who? Who should have?' Suzanne was thrown.

'Your DI McCarthy. And you had him to yourself for a whole hour?' Jane sighed. 'All Lucy and I got was some female with a stuffed rabbit.' She looked at Suzanne. 'It's not your problem,' she emphasized.

Suzanne looked at Lucy who was engaged in carefully burying one of her toys in the narrow border at the bottom of the yard, her hands and face muddy, her hair tousled, her face intent.

Dennis Allan sat at the small coffee table in the front room. It was dark; the heavy curtains were drawn. He didn't want people looking in, staring, whispering. He'd heard what they had been saying. *Him. . . his wife. . . now his daughter. . . the police. . . murder. . . murderer. . . Murderer.* He held his hands round the mug of coffee, sipping it occasionally, not noticing that it was cold. How had it happened? He looked at the photographs on the glass cabinet, safe in their frames, safe like he wasn't any more, like his family wasn't any more. Sandy in her wedding dress, white, he'd wanted that, though his mum had had a bit to say. Well, under the circumstances, Emma already on the way . . . Emma, in one of those oval frames the school photos came in, ten, smiling. Emma and Sandy on holiday, squinting in the sun, smiling. Emma in cut-off jeans, her blonde hair dyed a funny yellow, that awful stud through her nose, not smiling any more. Emma last Christmas by the tree, caught unawares, playing with the cat. Smiling now.

How had it happened? He'd tried so hard. *I did try, Sandy.* Nothing. *I love you, Emma.* Nothing. The answer came, unwelcome and unasked for. *Like mother, like daughter.* His own mother's sour disapproval that had blighted the early years of his marriage. He felt his eyes fill with tears. He was weak. People thought he was weak. He'd seen the veiled contempt in the eyes of the detective. Did they think he didn't notice? They thought they were so clever. Well, let them work it out.

Eight o'clock that evening, Suzanne decided she was going to the pub. There was a comedy night, she could talk to some friends, have a drink and just get away from it for a while. She put on the black trousers she'd bought several weeks ago and hadn't worn yet and a silk top that Jane had given her. She twisted her hair back and caught it in a clip, put on some lipstick.

She was just checking the contents of her purse when there was a knock at the door. Suzanne opened it. She was surprised to see Richard Kean, the psychologist and her mentor from the Alpha Centre, his head almost touching the top of the doorframe, his bulk filling the small entrance hall as he came in. Richard had never been in her house before.

70

She invited him into the front room, wondering what it was he wanted. He looked at her, taking in her make-up, the new clothes. Suzanne always dressed conventionally, even severely, for work. Until recently, she'd dressed conventionally, severely, for everything. 'Sorry, I've interrupted you. You're going out.'

'No, that's fine. I'm only going to the local. Do you want a coffee?' Suzanne wondered if he might join her down at the pub.

'I'd rather have a cold drink.' He looked hot.

'Beer? Or a soft drink?'

'Coke? I'm driving.' Suzanne went through to the kitchen to get the drinks. He wasn't likely to want a trip to the pub if he was driving. When she came back into the room he was standing by the wall looking at her photographs. 'Is this your son?' He was in front of the picture of Adam, the one taken just after his eleventh birthday. 'He's about the same age as my Jeff.'

'No.' Suzanne swallowed a sudden bitter taste. 'No, that's my brother, Adam.'

'Oh, right, he looks a bit like you. Is this recent?'

'No.'

'What does he do, then? Is he an academic too?'

Suzanne found it hard to say. 'No. Adam – he died, when he was fourteen. Six years ago.'

'I'm sorry. I'm really sorry.' He looked embarrassed. He didn't ask any questions. He didn't want to know. 'Look, Sue, this is really a business visit. It couldn't wait until Monday. I had a call from Keith Liskeard.' Suzanne recognized the name of the Alpha director. 'He says he's had the CID round asking questions.'

Suzanne's stomach lurched. She should have warned them. 'About Ashley?' she said.

Richard looked serious. 'You do know about it.'

'Well, yes . . .'

He went on before she could tell him what had happened. 'Look, Sue, I realize you were in a difficult situation – if you saw Ashley you had to tell them, no one's saying you shouldn't have done. But you should have let us know. I

71

would have hoped you'd have come to us *before* you went to the police. It's part of the commitment you make—'

'Wait a minute!' Suzanne was caught completely off balance. 'What exactly do you think happened? What do you think I said?'

'I can understand when there's been a crime like that, if you saw Ashley near the scene you'd naturally—'

'I didn't.' Suzanne felt a cold push of anger.

'What do you mean?' He looked confused.

'I didn't see Ashley and I didn't tell them I'd seen Ashley. I didn't volunteer to talk to them, I had to . . .'

'Yes, that's what I'm saying . . .' He tried to pick up the initiative again but she overrode him.

'It's all a stupid misunderstanding. I specifically told them, specifically told DI *fucking* McCarthy that I didn't see Ashley.'

He looked at her in silence for a minute. He obviously didn't believe her. 'There are some issues with Ashley at the moment. This couldn't come at a worse time for him.'

'What do you mean?'

He looked uncomfortable. 'I'm sorry, I can't say.'

Their endless confidentiality! Maybe if she'd been given the information that Richard was referring to . . . 'Why don't you ask Ashley? He'll tell you where he was.'

Richard looked uneasy. 'It's almost certainly because of these other issues . . . He hasn't been to the centre since Thursday evening. We need to find him, get him to tell his story to the police before this gets out of hand.'

Suzanne found that her anger was being taken over by a sense of insecurity – had she done something wrong, something stupid? 'I think you'd better go,' she said.

'Yes. I'm . . . OK, right.' He turned in the doorway. 'Keith is very unhappy about it,' he warned.

She went to the pub by herself in the end, but left early. She talked to a few people: some of Dave's friends who'd been her friends as well when she and Dave were married; one or two people she knew from the university. It could have been a pleasant evening, but she found that she didn't really want to talk to anyone. The comedy evening was a let-down

72

as well, though the rest of the audience seemed to enjoy it well enough. To her, the comedian's laddish jokes were pointless and unfunny. She left early. He heckled her as she was leaving. 'There's another one off for her pension!' It seemed that being over twenty-five was funny in itself now.

She walked back past the park gates and paused, looking down the path towards the woods. It was dark. She could see a small group of people hanging around in the shelter near the entrance. Teenagers, she assumed, though it was too dark to tell. Further in, the shadows were black under the trees. She could see a light flickering in the darkness, but otherwise it was quiet and still. The group by the shelter watched her as she stood under the street light. She could walk through the gate, follow the path to the third bridge, go out the gate there and be on Dave's doorstep, be where Michael was. She couldn't think of anything that would induce her to walk into that black silence.

6

Steve McCarthy had been home for an hour. He'd got home after eight-thirty and gone straight to his computer to log on to the network. His evenings would be like this now, until this case was over. There was always more information pouring in, more details often burying important details, and he intended staying on top of it all.

McCarthy was ambitious. He'd joined the police after leaving school, choosing to go straight in rather than going on to do a degree. He still wasn't sure if that had been the wisest decision. He'd done well, promotions had come in good time, sometimes sooner than his best expectations, and he knew he was seen as a team player with a good future ahead of him. He was thirty-two, and the next hike up the promotions ladder was the important one.

He was working on their current database now, getting it to look for patterns in relation to other offences in the Sheffield area over recent months. He typed another command into the computer, getting it to sort the information in relation to drug offences. While he was waiting, he dug his fork into the takeaway he'd picked up from the Chinese on the way back. Cold. He looked down at the polystyrene tray. His chicken chow mein had somehow transformed itself into a grey, glutinous mass. He pushed it away impatiently. He could get something out of the freezer later, stick it in the microwave. He picked up his mug of coffee with little optimism. Cold as well. He couldn't work without coffee. He went through to the kitchen and pushed the switch on the coffee machine.

The flat was modern, two-bedroomed. McCarthy had

74

bought it because it was fitted out, convenient and he could move straight in. He'd heard someone say once, or he'd read somewhere, that a house should be a machine for living. McCarthy understood that. He wanted the place he lived in to service him. He wanted to go in and find it warm when the weather was cold, cool when it was hot. He wanted to be able to cook at the push of a button, wash at the flick of a switch. He wanted to have any disorder that living created reordered before he returned.

'Christ, McCarthy,' Lynne, his last girlfriend, had said, 'why don't you just lock yourself away in a cupboard at the end of the day?' Another time she'd said, 'What you need, McCarthy, is a wife. An automatic, rechargeable, super-turbo, fuel-injection wife.' He'd laughed and started massaging her back, running his hands over her neck and shoulders in the way he knew she liked, because he hadn't wanted to have another of their vicious, cutting rows, and she'd pulled him into the chair and they'd had a quick wham bam thank you, ma'am – or thank you, sir, and then they'd gone into the bedroom and spent longer, spent most of the evening, exploring each other and drinking wine. But he and Lynne only had that: they had sex and they had the job. They couldn't spend all their time screwing and working – though to McCarthy it had sometimes seemed as though that was exactly what they did – and the relationship had ended when Lynne got the job that he had aimed at, got *his* promotion in fact, and the whole flimsy edifice had fallen apart in the volcanic aftermath. He still felt angry and bitter about that, and he determinedly shut it out of his mind.

He took the coffee back into his work room and looked at the screen. There was very little there that he didn't already know. He noted the fact that Ashley Reid had a drugs caution – hardly surprising he'd missed it, McCarthy thought, in the long list attached to that young thug's name. And, now, this could be interesting: Paul Lynman, one of the tenants at 14, Carleton Road, the student house, had a conviction for possession. McCarthy pulled up the details. OK, it looked like a my-round deal – he'd been caught with almost enough speed to pull down a dealing charge – but not quite. He'd insisted, wisely, that it was for his own use, but he'd probably been buying for a friend as well as for himself. Worth chasing up, though. There was nothing conclusive, no real links. McCarthy rubbed the skin between his eyebrows in an effort to concentrate. He'd heard something about a problem at the Alpha Centre, something about Es and speed. And had there been some kind of action round the university? He needed to talk to someone from drugs.

He looked at his watch. Ten-thirty. He wondered what to do with the rest of the evening. Listen to music? Watch the telly? He felt a sense of things closing around him, as though his life was shrinking to the walls of this flat, the route to and from the office, the office itself. Maybe Lynne had been right. Maybe he should start looking for that cupboard.

Sunday morning, Suzanne got up early, was showered, dressed and at her desk by eight o'clock. She planned to put in a solid day's work, to forget everything that had happened since Friday. For an hour, she tried to read and make notes from a research paper that she'd had on her desk for a week. Her mind refused to focus. When she reached the end of the ten dense, closely printed pages, she realized she might as well not have read it at all. She tossed it irritably into her paper tray, not bothering to put it into its correct basket. She rubbed her forehead, and looked at the waiting tasks arrayed around her desk. She thought about Jane's method for focusing – there was some kind of yoga trick. Something to do with emptying the mind. She closed her eyes and tried to concentrate on the nothingness that was behind her eyelids.

Focus. . . What had Richard meant when he said that Keith Liskeard was very unhappy? Keith had always been less than enthusiastic about Suzanne's research. She remembered him nodding in agreement when one of the social workers – Neil, she thought – had said that the Alpha lads weren't rats in mazes for researchers to play games with. Suzanne had swallowed the antagonistic response that had leapt to her tongue, and again patiently gone through the reassurances that at this stage all she wanted to do was observe, she would do nothing without the approval of the staff, would keep them

76

informed at all times. It had been time-consuming and frustrating, and she had been angry at the way they put labels on her and stereotyped her in the way they were accusing her of doing to the young men who were sentenced to the Alpha programme. She was tired of the phrase *middle class*, tired of *academic* as a term of abuse ... She realized that Keith would not be sorry of a chance to get rid of her.

This wasn't working. She opened her eyes and looked at the array of papers on her desk. OK, reading was out. She needed something concrete to do. She decided to put some data into the computer to set up the first stage of her analysis. It needed doing, but it was a mechanical task that she'd been putting off. She didn't need to concentrate for this, and it would keep her occupied.

But once again work seemed no escape. Suzanne keyed data into her computer, the mindlessness of the task leaving her vulnerable to thoughts that wandered beyond her control. She thought about Michael's small figure climbing the steps up to Dave's front door. She thought about Lucy's contained self-possession; she thought about Joel leaning easily against the worktop, smiling. She thought about the sudden interest in DI McCarthy's eyes. She thought about Richard's look of disappointment. He was the only person at the Alpha Centre who'd given her any support. *How can you be so unreliable!* Her father's exasperation and reproach echoed in her mind.

The computer beeped at her. *Shit!* She'd hit the control key by mistake. Thank goodness the programme she was using was fairly idiot proof. She leant back in her chair and stretched. Maybe a walk would do her good. It was all tangled up in her mind. Michael, Dave, her problems at the Alpha Centre, her research ... Emma. She tried to picture Emma in her mind, but all she could see was the white face under the water, the face that wavered and became Lucy's, then wavered again and became Adam's. She pressed her hands over her eyes. No good.

She went down to the kitchen, put the kettle on, sorted through the dishes in the sink until she found a cup that wasn't too bad, rinsed it and put a spoonful of coffee in. She remembered how Dave used to refuse to have anything to do with instant coffee. She ladled two spoons of sugar into the cup, and added the top of the milk. That reminded her of Michael. She'd bought the full-cream milk for his weekend.

Then she sank down on a stool, holding her cup, as the panic hit her. Familiar, so familiar, but never any easier. She was back in the hospital, feeling drunk with a kind of elation she had never known before. *It's a boy, Suze!* She could remember Dave's face close to hers. *Let me hold him.* Suzanne, reaching out, was tired, relieved, amazed. She remembered the tiny, perfect face, the small body wrapped in a hospital blanket. Her baby. She held him. His eyes opened and looked into hers for the first time, a clear and perfect blue like the first time she'd held Adam, her mother in the hospital bed, the nurse carefully handing her the blue-wrapped bundle. And a stab of fear almost doubled her up, leaving her trembling, with a knot in her stomach, a feeling of panic and impending disaster. She felt as though a terrible danger was teetering over the child, catastrophe and chaos lurching towards him – from her. She mustn't touch him. She was . . . somehow, she was going to hurt, to damage this child beyond repair. The baby stirred and uttered a protesting cry.

Remembering, Suzanne felt herself break out in a cold sweat.

Since leaving home, Emma Allan had stayed in the student house on Carleton Road. Sophie Dutton had lived there, and Emma had apparently shared Sophie's room, and then lived there by herself once Sophie had left. 'Strictly against our rules,' the university housing officer said. He had the list of the recent tenants. Paul Lynman, who'd been studying modern German, gave a home address, presumably his parents', in Derby. Gemma Hanson and Daniel Grier, also students of modern German, had gone to Germany as part of their post-graduate study. 'They left in May,' he said.

Barraclough had been given the task of making contact with Sophie Dutton, who was proving elusive. According to the university records office, she had left officially on May 14. Her tutor had put it down to exam panic, and tried to persuade her to stay. 'She would have passed, probably done quite well. But a pass was all she needed. First-year exams don't count towards your degree.' But Sophie had been adamant.

But whatever she'd told her friends, she hadn't gone home, nor had she told her parents of her decision. 'She's in Sheffield,' Sophie's father had said. 'She's been there all year. Sophie left her course? Rubbish.'

His irritation was apparently aimed at Barraclough who clearly couldn't detect her way out of a paper bag, but perhaps concealed the anxiety of a parent watching his child take those first steps in independence. 'We're the last people to know what she's doing.' His irritation switched to anxiety when he realized that his daughter was not in Sheffield, or at least not where they thought she was. He wasn't able to give Barraclough any information about Sophie's contacts that she didn't already have. 'Sophie hasn't been in touch much,' he said. 'Not after the first few weeks. Her mother's had a bit of a go at her about it, but Sophie just says, "Oh, don't fuss."' Barraclough managed to establish that Sophie had been home for Christmas, but had only stayed for a few days. She'd made a couple of phone calls since then, and sent them a jokey postcard from Meadowhall.

The house had only recently been vacated. 'It's earlier than we usually end the let, but with two of them off to Germany, and the fourth tenant having left, it seemed fair enough to let the last one go.' He was apologetic. The house had been cleared out. All their houses were used for summer rents and needed to be ready as soon as possible. 'This one's let from the beginning of July,' he said. Anything personal left in a house was dumped and sent to the local tip.

The cleaners who had done the houses on Carleton Road couldn't remember anything particular about number fourteen. 'Did that poor lass that got killed live there?' the supervisor of the team asked Barraclough. 'It's shocking.' She shook her head. Her words were conventional, but she seemed genuinely moved. 'No, I can't remember anything about number fourteen. There can't have been anything, it was only about a week ago we did it. I'll tell you what. They were all pigsties the houses on that road. They may be bright, these kids, but they've got some filthy habits.'

The house was next door to Jane Fielding's. Inside, it seemed too small to contain the four – sometimes five – adults who had lived there. Steep stairs ran up from a small entrance lobby. A door to the left led into a downstairs front room with a bay window. There was a bed, stripped, a carpet, a wardrobe and a small desk. The room was crowded with just that small amount of furniture.

To the right was a communal room and a kitchen. The kitchen was equipped with the basics: cupboards, worktops, cooker and fridge. The edging on the worktops was damaged, showing the MDF inside the marble-effect plastic.

Upstairs, there were two bedrooms and a bathroom. And on the next floor, in the attic, there was another small bedroom. Barraclough looked out of the dormer windows and wondered about fire. There was no fire escape. Did they have one of those fold-away ladders? It looked like a death trap to her.

Sophie Dutton, whose room Emma had shared, had had the attic room, but, like the others, it was stripped to essentials now: a bed, a wardrobe, a desk. It must have been cramped with two of them in there, Barraclough thought, squeezing past the inconveniently placed wardrobe. The room was clean, but there was dust in the corners and bits on the carpet, as though the cleaners had run out of energy as they moved up the stairs. Looking at the evidence of less than thorough cleaning, Corvin arranged to have the rooms checked for prints. But unless that check came up with something, the search of Carleton Road was a bust. They found no traces of Emma, and nothing to tell them where Sophie Dutton had gone.

Suzanne closed the door on her study and set to work to clean up the house. She worked meticulously from the top to the bottom, dusting, vacuuming, washing, until the distracting disorder was replaced by something closer to the order and system she had in her study. It took her nearly three hours, and by the end she felt tired, hot and grubby – but was filled with a sense of achievement.

A plan was beginning to form in her mind. Her research at the Alpha Centre was under threat. Richard hadn't actually said so, but . . . She could put all her energies into producing a really good analysis of the little bit of material she had, but that wouldn't be enough to impress the people who made the decisions. She needed to undo the damage she had – unintentionally – done. She wanted to do that anyway. She owed it to Ashley.

She thought about the first time that she'd met him. He'd just been a face in a crowd at first. She had a vague memory of a boy with dark hair and eyes and a sudden, warm smile – someone fleetingly, but disturbingly, familiar. With hindsight, she knew that he had been interested in her, curious. It was his attention to her that had drawn her attention. But it had been a week or so before they finally spoke to each other.

She had been in the coffee bar one day – a big, high-ceilinged room with an assortment of chairs, some tables, a drinks machine in one corner. Like the rest of the building, the coffee bar was shabby, showing the wear and tear of constant use but no personal ownership. Rules about vandalism were strict, and there was little graffiti at the Alpha Centre, but the damage of constant use, the damage of poverty and the damage resulting from damaged people with damaged lives had all made their mark.

The air always smelt of frying, steam and cigarettes. There was a serving hatch at one end of the room that was locked and shuttered at that time of day. A metal grill protected its brown painted wood. The main part of the room was taken over by a full-size snooker table, which was one of the few things at the centre that the lads evinced enthusiasm for. There was always a game going on, whether it was officially break time or not.

She was idly watching two of the Alpha's clients, Lee and Dean, experimenting with fancy shots. Richard had suggested that these two would be good candidates for the first stage of her research, and she was trying to get to know them. Dean she found hard to read, and though he had shown her no overt hostility, there was something about him that worried her. She always felt edgy when he was around. Lee, on the other hand, had seemed friendly in the middle of his hyperactivity and fast-talking wit. That day, he'd offered to teach her how to play snooker, and though she knew the basics, she'd accepted, seeing this as a way of breaking down some more of the barriers. She'd caught Ashley's eye as Lee was demonstrating how to hold the cue, and he had, almost imperceptibly, shaken his head as if in warning.

And the muffled comments and laughter as she'd leant over the table lining up her cue, the way Lee positioned himself behind her, the loose-lipped smile on Dean's face made her realize that she was being turned into a target of sexual innuendo and mime. She'd made the fundamental mistake of assuming that superficial friendliness meant they had no hostility towards her. She didn't know how to cope with that kind of behaviour from a group of youths – it was more unnerving and more demeaning than careless innuendo on the street. It was focused, personal, malicious. She'd walked away, knowing that this was acknowledging defeat, aware of muffled comments and laughter, and met Neil's eye from where he'd been standing in the door of the reception office watching unseen. His face carried the unspoken comment: *I told you so.*

She'd moved across to the far side of the coffee bar, lit a cigarette, trying to make herself less visible, feeling angry with herself for not handling the situation well, when Ashley had caught her eye again and given her a sympathetic smile. A few minutes later, he'd sat down beside her, where she was aimlessly turning the pages of her work folder.

'Don't mind them,' he'd said. He'd bought her a Coke from the machine, and she found that, and his support, oddly comforting. Then he'd looked at her folder. 'What are you doing?' he'd asked. His voice was quiet, his accent broad Sheffield. She'd told him a bit about the university, and asked him about his interests, his plans. He didn't really have any, he'd said. He hadn't bothered with school much. But he liked drawing. 'I'd like to do art at college,' he'd confided. A brief exchange, but encouraging.

Another time, he'd pulled a small sketch pad out of his pocket and shown her some of his work. To her untutored eye, it looked good: bold line drawings catching the movement and atmosphere of the city. She recognized the shops near Hunters Bar, and the park. They were delineated with a few strokes of the pencil, lively and vivid, filling the paper with a sense of movement. She was impressed and told him so. He'd given her a quick, private smile.

It was Adam he reminded her of, that must have been what gave her that flash of recognition when she saw him. He had the same warm smile. Adam's face used to light up like that when he saw her, and Adam had that same confiding way of talking. *I'll tell you a secret, Suzanne*, he'd say when he was – what? – seven, eight? And he'd whisper in her ear about some misdemeanour that she was to keep secret from their father. *I won't tell*, she would say. That was her role. She had to protect her father from worry, and Adam from their father's anger. *But you mustn't do it again.*

She was tidying the kitchen now, but she had lost the momentum and realized she was aimlessly moving things from one surface to another. She ran hot water into the sink, scooped up the dishes that were scattered across the worktops, and dumped them in the water. She'd wash them later. She thought about her study, the papers on her desk, her computer with the pages of data half typed up. Screw work. She was going out for a walk.

Late that afternoon, Barraclough was trawling through the records, trying to find Sandra Allan's baby, the child born sometime towards the end of the 1970s, or possibly 1980. Sandra's recent death saved a lot of work. Copies of her birth certificate were in the file. Barraclough checked. She'd been born in Castleford, West Yorkshire, in 1963, daughter of Thomas Ford, van driver, and Elizabeth Ford. Were the parents still living in the area? Where were they when Sandra's baby was born?

Barraclough checked the file on Sandra Allan's death. Next of kin was obviously Dennis Allan. She couldn't find any reference in the notes to Sandra's parents. She went back to the database and checked. Yes. A Thomas Ford, with a matching date of birth, had died five years ago in St James's Hospital, Leeds. She could get the address off the death certificate, if this was the right Thomas Ford. That would give her an address for Elizabeth Ford, Sandra's mother.

She looked at the time. There were a couple of people coming in from the house-to-house that she was supposed to interview. She'd have to get back to it tomorrow.

The man from the museums department, John Draper, wore baggy jeans and Jesus sandals. He carried a folder of papers, some books and an air of energetic enthusiasm. McCarthy, who had arranged to meet Mr Draper at Shepherd Wheel, felt depressed. He was doubtful about the value of this contact, and didn't relish the thought of listening to yet another academic demonstrate his boundless knowledge of an area of minuscule breadth, minuscule relevance to the present day and minuscule interest to anyone with a life to live. And all delivered in a tone of patronizing deprecation for the benefit of the stupid Plod who couldn't walk and chew gum at the same time.

In the event, McCarthy found himself getting interested as John Draper explained quickly and succinctly how the power of the river system had been harnessed, and how the chains of workshops and wheels had grown up along the five rivers that had carved out the valleys on which the city was built. 'No problems with recycling and waste,' Draper said. 'Not from your power source, anyway.'

'There must have been a price.' McCarthy knew that someone always paid for the free lunch.

'Oh, yes, there was an environmental cost,' Draper agreed. 'Wildlife patterns were disrupted. And the mills did pollute. Waterways were seen as natural sewers – chuck in all your waste and see it vanish. To become someone else's problem. Still, that's not what you're here for.'

McCarthy looked along the dam. All the activity had died down now, the search of the workshop moving on to the laboratory and the scientists. 'I'm not sure exactly what we are here for,' he admitted. 'It just seems as though someone

84

has been using this system, and what I need to know is: were they just exploiting what was here, or have they been manipulating it somehow?'

'Manipulating it?' Draper looked puzzled. 'Oh, I see what you mean. Liz Delaney said that the wheel was turning when the body was found?'

McCarthy nodded. 'I can't see why. There's no logic in that.' McCarthy didn't like the idea of illogical crimes. Any crime, particularly an unplanned one, may seem illogical to the outside observer, but McCarthy knew that all crimes had their own internal logic, and finding that logic, that pattern, was an important key to solving the problem. Sometimes, the very illogicality was the logic – the attempt to confuse by the random act, that could never be truly random. *You have left your mark, and I will find it.* 'Also, the wheel stopped again. The woman who found the body said the wheel stopped while she was in the yard.'

'Let's go and have a look,' said Draper cheerfully. They'd met on the bridge where the road divided Bingham Park from the woods, and were standing on the bridge looking down at the weir above Shepherd Wheel dam. They went into the park by the gap in the wall that led to the steps. Draper showed McCarthy the way the weir channelled the water along the goit and into the dam. 'The weir has deteriorated, of course,' he said. 'It's a crime the way this system has been allowed to decline.' He caught McCarthy's glance. 'It's important to keep some of our history intact, wouldn't you agree, Inspector? Learn from our yesterdays?'

'Depends what you learn.' McCarthy was only prepared to concede so far.

'Oh, no doubt. Always. True of anything.' McCarthy looked at the shaggy-headed scholar who was studying the top of the weir with minute interest, and couldn't decide if the man was taking the piss or not. He waited to see if the perusal was to any purpose, or if Draper was just making the most of an opportunity to commune with his beloved remains. 'This is . . .' Draper put his hand on a small bar that protruded above the edge of the path. 'I was wondering why the water was so low.' He looked at McCarthy. 'In the dam.

The water is very low. I was assuming it was the silting problem we've got along the whole system, but . . .' He indicated the bar. 'This is the shuttle that regulates the flow of water into the dam. It's been set to virtually stop the flow.'

'Someone's shut the water off?' McCarthy wanted this clarifying.

'Exactly. I'll have to tell them. Get the flow restored.'

McCarthy looked across the dam, where the sun was gleaming off the mud banks and turning the surface of the water into a dark mirror. Despite the disruption of the past week, he found the scene peaceful – but it was the peace of desertion, a place abandoned, where the water-birds swam undisturbed beside the overgrown allotments and the shuttered silence of Shepherd Wheel.

The two men walked along the side of the dam. Draper looked down at the mud, marked with the prints of the water-birds, emerald green with new moss, littered with twigs fallen from the trees, soft-drink cans, sweet papers. They went down the steps at the far end of the dam and round the front of Shepherd Wheel to reach the entrance to the wheel yard. McCarthy didn't break the silence. He had a feeling that the other man was mulling something over and he didn't want to disrupt his train of thought. As they reached the wheel-yard gate, Draper paused with his hand on the padlock. 'Of course, if you wanted to run water through without moving the wheel, you might think that lowering the level of water in the dam would do it. You'd be wrong, of course.' He looked up at McCarthy, still fiddling with the key in the lock. 'It solves your problem about the wheel stopping, though. With the water as low as this, there'd only be enough to turn the wheel for about twenty minutes. If that.'

It seemed so obvious, McCarthy couldn't believe he hadn't thought of it himself. 'Could that, what did you say, shuttle have been moved accidentally?' Or could Emma's death have been carefully planned, rather than the sudden outburst of killing violence that it seemed?

'It's never happened before that I know of,' Draper said doubtfully. 'It doesn't shift to a knock.'

Vandals? McCarthy wondered. No, vandals wouldn't be content with the simple resetting of the level of the dam. They would have torn it apart, destroyed it. For some reason, the river workings didn't seem to attract their attention. Draper fiddled with the key and unlocked the padlock. 'Half these bloody keys don't work,' he said. They were in the wheel yard now, and Draper wandered across to look down on the decaying wheel. 'You know,' he said, 'there's been a mill here since at least 1556.' He was silent for a moment. 'She was in there,' he said, 'your little girl?'

The phrase sounded strange to McCarthy. A little girl. A drug user. A sexually active woman. A little girl. 'Yes,' he said.

'And the wheel was turning. She'd been pushed in from the inside?' McCarthy nodded. 'Pushed into the water, and . . . The wheel is damaged – I'm surprised it turned.' McCarthy waited, not feeling the impatience he usually felt when experts waffled their way to the point. He felt as though Draper was putting his thoughts together out loud. 'There's a long tail goit here,' Draper said. 'The water channels back through a conduit – comes out about fifty metres from the wheel. Small and narrow. When the mill isn't working, there isn't enough current to move anything much through it. She'd probably have jammed in there anyway. Maybe he opened the pentrough to wash her into the conduit.'

He caught McCarthy's eye. 'Sorry. Look, the water comes through here' – he indicated the wooden tank above the wheel – 'from the dam, and turns the wheel. It falls into the channel below the wheel, then it runs out through that conduit' – he indicated a narrow archway in the stone, under the water – 'and back into the stream about fifty yards along. If you dumped a body down in that channel and ran some water through, it would wash the body into the conduit. Shut the water off again and there it stays. I wonder how long before anyone would have thought to look?'

Logic. It was clear and logical. Would they have looked? Would they even have looked in Shepherd Wheel, locked up and secure? Would they have looked at all for a missing, troubled seventeen-year-old with a history of drug abuse? But the wheel turned. The killer hadn't expected that. The wheel turned. 'Thank you, Mr Draper,' he said.

The blocks were abandoned now. The warren of deck access, walkways, stairs, lifts – which hadn't worked when the flats were inhabited, and certainly didn't work now – was in darkness, the windows and doors of each flat boarded up as they became empty, the stairways sealed off, the lift doors jammed shut. They stood in dark stillness, waiting for the demolition team that would, eventually, erase them.

As the bona fide inhabitants moved out, other inhabitants moved in. The boarding was ripped off the doors and windows, the pipework and the cables were pulled out, the old boilers ripped off the walls in a swift and brutal asset strip. The flats were left open to the rain and the wind, the wood rotted, damp pervaded the concrete, water dripped on the walkways and formed in puddles on the landings. But they provided shelter of a kind. In some of the flats, there were signs of habitation: graffiti on the walls, the remains of fires on bricks in the middle of rooms, blankets, cups, plates.

Lee picked his way along the front of the second block. A burnt-out car blocked the pavement and he turned into the flats along the lower walkway. The flats had been boarded up, but most flats showed signs of later entry: boarding pulled off the doors, off the windows, broken glass, trailing wires. The walkway stank of piss and, from the broken-in doorways, the smell of shit made him gag. He knew what was in those flats, the silver foil, the needles, the detritus of a habit he abhorred. Pills were OK, crack and brown were for wankers.

He moved quickly, ignoring a figure slumped by the stairwell. Lee could handle himself, but he preferred to avoid trouble if he could. Mostly. He squeezed past the broken security barriers, went up the landings almost to the top of the tower, then along the deck. He counted the flats until he came to the one he wanted.

Lee put his head to the door and listened. Silence. He looked round. Nothing. He knocked lightly on the door. '*Lee.*'

After a moment, the bolts on the door were pulled back. Lee slipped through, pulling the wad of money out of his pocket. A few minutes later, he was running quietly down the stairs, a small zip-lock wallet tucked safely inside his jacket.

7

Monday morning, the lab reports from the post-mortem on Emma Allan came through, along with the results of samples taken from the search of Shepherd Wheel. There were detailed accounts of timings, fibres, detritus, blood analysis, body fluid analysis, stomach contents, that confirmed what they were already pretty sure of. Emma Allan had died in Shepherd Wheel between about ten and noon on the day she vanished. This was useful, important to confirm, because they all knew the danger of reading the obvious, jumping to conclusions, and getting it badly wrong while precious time ticked away. Fibres from the grate proved to be blue cotton denim, of the kind used to make jeans. It came from a strong, heavy-duty weave, work jeans rather than fashion jeans, the report suggested.

Possibly because of Emma's immersion, scrapings from under her fingernails revealed no traces of her attacker. Or possibly she had put up little resistance, either because she knew and trusted her attacker, or because of the interesting cocktail of recreational drugs in her bloodstream, including heroin. Her earlier caution for possession was clearly just a tip of a much larger iceberg. This was no real surprise.

But there was one unexpected plum in the pie – one that even McCarthy hadn't expected. They had found three sets of recent prints during the search of Shepherd Wheel. One set was still unidentified. One set was Emma Allan's, as they'd expected. But someone else had been in that workshop, and had touched things after Emma had touched them. His prints overlay Emma's, smudged them. He was on the computer. He was well known to the local force. Ashley Reid.

At the briefing, there was the buzz that indicates an investigation is starting to move. Brooke turned the briefing over to McCarthy to cover the Reid connection. McCarthy ran through the details: the possible sighting, the prints and Reid's recent arrest. 'It isn't enough. We don't know when Allan left those prints,' McCarthy pointed out. 'If she was in there on one day, she could have been in there on another. Probably was. The Fielding child said that Emma used to go off when they went to the park.' He remembered Lucy's voice, matter of fact, unemphatic. *And Emma went to chase the monsters and I went to the playground.* 'We've been trying to bring Reid in as a witness since Saturday. No one knows where he is.'

McCarthy passed round the drugs information he'd pulled up at the weekend, and went over his interview with Suzanne Milner again. 'What's a bit odd here is that Milner mentioned Reid specifically to say she hadn't seen him. Barraclough?'

'Why did she mention him? How did his name come up?'

McCarthy didn't know. It puzzled him as well. 'Either she saw him and didn't want to say – but she walked into it and had to make the best of it, or it's like she said: she saw someone she thought looked like him. She was very defensive about it. I don't know how well she knows him.'

He ran through the details of Reid's most recent arrest, noting the expressions of exasperation and anger when they heard the fact that Reid had got bail. 'Why would they do that?' Barraclough could still be surprised by court decisions.

'I didn't check back on all the details. He was already on the Alpha programme, under supervision.' Barraclough looked disgusted. McCarthy caught her eye and nodded his agreement. 'We've got to find him. We'll need samples – the prints won't be enough on their own. We want him pinned down on this. There's nothing that points to the father, but we haven't got the results back on his samples yet. And it would help if that sighting could be confirmed.'

McCarthy was tired and the day had barely started. The dead face of the woman in the water kept returning to him.

The buzz from the early news, the match-up with finger-prints in Shepherd Wheel, was replaced with a sense of urgency. They knew the signs. Ashley Reid was dangerous, and he was still out there.

Suzanne spent the morning in the library. She'd spent much of the previous night trying to think of ways to undo the damage, and drawn a blank. She felt angry at the way her actions had been interpreted, but she knew that, in a situation like this, crying 'unfair' was pointless. Anyway, as soon as she'd mentioned Ashley's name, as soon as she'd seen that gleam of interest in DI McCarthy's eyes, she should have contacted Richard and told him. She was at fault.

The only thing to do was to press on with her work, and so she was at the computer catalogue by eight-thirty, doing one of her regular checks through journals looking for recent research into language disorders. The terminals were awkwardly placed, the seats too high, and she had to lean forward to see the screen. Her hair fell in her eyes and she fished around in her bag until she found a clip. She twisted her hair back off her face and jammed the clip in place. Better.

After half an hour's searching she found the reference she'd been looking for. Someone in California was researching into evidence of brain damage in persistent offenders. She wasn't sure if it would be relevant, but language disorders could arise from certain types of brain damage. It was possible that she and this researcher were coming at the same problem from different angles. As she skimmed the paper, she recognized things that were relevant to her research: ... *clear evidence from imaging of the frontal lobe. . . aphasia. . . sociopathic patterns of behaviour* . . . She jotted the reference on an index card and took the journal to one of the reading desks.

She worked in the quiet of the stacks; the endless rows of shelves and the pools of light in the darkness restored her equilibrium. As she read, she felt the excitement of seeing solid backing for her intuitions. Here was someone who was identifying organic brain damage in persistent offenders. Damage in areas of the brain that affected language. Physical evidence to support her more indirect observations. Recent events had shaken her faith in her abilities. For the first time since her interview with DI McCarthy, she began to think that it might be all right after all.

Soon after eleven, she began to flag. She realized she'd been working for nearly three hours without a break, so she left her books and notes on the desk and headed across the campus towards the students' union. The sun was shining and the sky was clear. She closed her eyes and turned her face up to the sky, enjoying the warmth and the patterns of light and shade against her eyelids.

When she opened her eyes, she was a bit disconcerted to find herself face to face with DI McCarthy himself, coming down the steps from the road past the red-brick admin. building that gave the university its ivy-covered centre. They had almost collided. He looked faintly surprised, possibly at the sight of her standing there like a sun-worshipper. She grimaced, then hastily smoothed her features out. She felt at a disadvantage. She would rather have her rematch with McCarthy in the severe garb of professionalism, but she was dressed for working in the stacks in old jeans and a T-shirt. There were ink stains on her fingers from a leaking ballpoint, and, for all she knew, on her face as well. The clip was coming out of her hair. She thought she caught a gleam of amusement in his eye, but when she looked again, he was his austere, impassive self. 'Ms Milner,' he said. He sounded pleasant enough, but he didn't smile.

Suzanne nodded in acknowledgement. She didn't know what to call him. She thought maybe you said 'constable' or 'sergeant' but she wasn't sure if you said 'inspector.' Or would it be 'Inspector McCarthy'? She settled for a wary, 'Hello,' catching at her hair as the clip fell out and clattered onto the pavement. 'It's Suzanne, by the way.'

'Steve,' he said. He picked up the hair clip and gave it to her.

'Thanks.' She pulled her hair off her face again and pushed the clip back in.

She expected him to move on, but he stayed where he was, looking at her and then at the open campus ahead of him. 'I don't usually come into the university,' he said. 'Is there anywhere to get a cup of coffee round here?'

'There's a coffee bar in the students' union,' she said. 'You can get espresso and americano and things there.'

He shrugged. 'Hot and full of caffeine would do for now.' He looked at her again as though he'd just thought of something. 'Have you got some time? There's something I wanted to ask you. I'll get you a coffee.'

Suzanne was suspicious. *Something I wanted to ask you.* 'Is it something to do with—' She almost said 'Ashley', but caught herself in time. 'With Emma?'

'There are one or two gaps you could fill in.' He looked at her, waiting to see what she would say. She thought about Jane, what Jane had said the other day. Jane would probably have made a pass at the bleak DI McCarthy. She wondered how he would react to that. In her experience, very few men put up much resistance to Jane, but she thought she might put her money on McCarthy.

She realized she hadn't said anything, and he was looking at her questioningly. 'All right,' she said, cautiously.

He did smile then, at her wariness, and said, 'Don't worry. They fed me before they let me out this morning.' That surprised her into laughing. OK, possibly he did have his human side. They walked across to the students' union in silence.

The coffee bar was quiet. McCarthy bought her a double espresso, pausing to chat to the woman who was serving the coffee, getting involved in a quick exchange of banter, just for a moment seeming very different from the man who'd been brusque and unsympathetic with Jane, and cold and impatient with her. Maybe he just compartmentalized a lot.

He offered her a cigarette and then lit one for himself. Before he could say anything, she said, 'What are you doing up here?'

He looked at her for a moment before answering. 'Trying to track down Sophie Dutton.'

Suzanne was surprised. 'Sophie's gone home. Didn't you know?'

He didn't answer that, just kept on looking at her as he knocked the ash off his cigarette. 'I wanted to talk to you about the Alpha Project.' He stopped as though he had just thought of something, and looked at her with genuine curiosity. 'Why there?' he said.

Suzanne ran the question through her mind, looking for pitfalls. It seemed safe enough. 'Why not?' she countered.

He seemed to take that as serious comment. 'Most of those lads should be locked up,' he said. 'I wouldn't choose to spend any time with them. If I didn't have to.'

Suzanne set her jaw. 'There are reasons,' she said, 'for the way they are.'

'Oh, there are always reasons,' he agreed. 'It doesn't make them any less dangerous.'

She looked at her hands. She wondered if he really believed what he was saying, or if he was trying to get her wound up and talking incautiously. 'I don't think they're dangerous,' she said. 'It's mostly car theft, stuff like that.'

'Car theft is dangerous enough, if you get hit by a joyrider.' That was a debating point. Any driver was dangerous if you thought about it like that. She waited to see what else he would say. 'What you need to remember is that most of them are seriously disturbed. Don't judge them by your own rules.'

She had the feeling that he was warning her about something. She thought about the lads she'd got to know. OK, Dean was aggressive and difficult. He had a history of disturbed behaviour and substance abuse. The centre workers always treated him with caution. Richard had once admitted to her that he thought Dean's case was a hopeless one. And Lee masked something sinister behind his quick wit. Ashley was different, though: quieter, less aggressive. She wanted to get him off the topic. 'And that's just the social workers?' she tried.

He started to say something, then laughed as he caught her eye, and she smiled back in a moment of rapport. Jane was right. He was attractive. She relaxed a bit. She wondered why he was just talking, not asking her questions about Emma. Maybe he was trying to put her at ease.

'You still haven't told me,' he said. 'Why the Alpha Centre?'

95

'It was the best place for my research.' She explained her theory about people whose communication skills were damaged. She was used to being on the receiving end of scepticism, but he seemed genuinely interested and asked her some surprisingly well-informed questions. Then she wondered why she was surprised. Criminal behaviour was as much his area of expertise as it was Richard's. She told him about the Californian research she had found that morning, and the way it supported the work she was doing. He listened, and told her about some of the people he'd had to deal with. She found herself warming to him, finding him easier to talk to than she'd expected. He seemed prepared to accept her as an expert in her own field. She told him about the reactions she'd had from the Alpha workers: Neil's dour disapproval, Richard's earnest solemnity.

He smiled at that. 'They can be a bit protective,' he said. She could hear something underlying his diplomatic words, and looked at him quickly. He met her eyes, and she read an unspoken opinion that was close to her own. She felt that unexpected sense of rapport again. She was starting to enjoy herself. He went back to her research programme. 'So how often are you up there?'

'I just do the one afternoon and the one evening.' That was all she'd been allowed.

'A week?' He reached across for the ashtray as he spoke.

'Yes . . .' She pushed it over to him.

'How many hours a week?' He stubbed the cigarette out half smoked, unlike her own student habit of smoking them down to the filter.

'It depends. Three hours, four maybe.' She couldn't see where he was going.

'And you work with all the lads together?'

'Mostly. Sometimes—' But she stopped herself. She wasn't going to tell him about the tapes, not until she'd cleared it with Richard. 'Why do you want to know?'

'I wondered how well you knew Ashley Reid,' he said. 'Have you had any contact with him away from the centre?'

So that was it. He was trying to show that she was protecting Ashley because they had a kind of – something, she didn't know what. Trying to show that she wasn't impartial, that she would lie, in fact. The barrier was there again. He wasn't an attractive man gently chatting her up over a cup of coffee, he was a professional interrogator. 'I've only ever seen Ashley at the centre. I met him for the first time about eleven weeks ago, and I've seen him on and off at the centre since then. Some weeks, I haven't seen him at all.' That wasn't strictly true. She had spent more time with Ashley than any of the others, and though there had been one week when Ashley had left early, he was always there.

'OK.' He seemed happy to accept that. 'We're having some problems tracking him down. I thought you might have some ideas.' She shook her head, waiting. He was thinking over what she had said. 'As I remember, you said when I interviewed you that you *caught a glimpse* of the person, of his face.'

'Yes.' She was beginning to get that knot in her stomach again.

'But you can't be sure, can you, that it was or that it wasn't Reid? You just saw someone answering his description.' His voice implied that this was logical, reasonable. 'Listen, Suzanne, we think he was at the scene. You could help us with the time. By your own admission, you hardly know Reid – not to tell at a glance.' He looked at her again. 'You saw this person walking away from you towards the woods. He looked back over his shoulder. You thought it was Reid, and then you thought it wasn't – but really, you can't be sure either way.' *Just tell us where Adam is. We want to help the lad, Suzanne.* 'Look,' he said, 'you just need to tell me what happened, what you saw. You're not responsible for Reid.'

I hold you responsible for this, Suzanne. She froze. Adam's face in the picture; Emma under the water. A young man with dark hair walking away, looking back, quickly, furtively. Could she trust what she remembered? She looked at the man sitting opposite her. He was waiting for her to answer, looking faintly puzzled. Had she said something? She shook her head. 'It's like I told you,' she said. 'I saw someone who reminded me of Ashley Reid. I didn't think it was him at the

97

time, and I still don't think it was.' He didn't say anything. 'I'm sorry. That's what I saw.' She was going to start babbling, explaining, justifying in a minute. She didn't meet his eye as she stubbed out her cigarette and picked up her bag. 'I'm sorry, I've got to go.'

McCarthy watched her disappear through the door, feeling a sense of frustration. Everything about her said that she was lying to him, and he couldn't see any reason for it. Just possibly she'd been sheltering Reid in some misplaced benevolence when he'd talked to her before, but she'd had time to think since then. She wasn't stupid. He'd told her they had information that could put Reid on the spot. All he'd asked for was confirmation.

He stayed where he was and finished his coffee. The coffee bar was painted cream and blue, the carpet echoed those colours, and the whole effect was light and airy. The rows of tables by the windows said canteen, but the area where he had been sitting with Suzanne had low tables, bars with high stools, greenery, all arranged to create comfortable, private seating. There were a few people scattered around the tables, a low buzz of talk, but nothing to disrupt the general air of sunny quiet. He thought about the canteen at police headquarters. Adequate, but there was no carpet, no greenery, just an acoustic that amplified and echoed the noise of conversation and the grating sound of chairs on lino. It all seemed designed to increase the sense of tension and pressure under which they worked these days. He wondered what students did to deserve this air of calm and peace that always impressed him on the few occasions he came on to the campus. *Get that chip off your shoulder, McCarthy.*

He ran his conversation with Suzanne through his mind. He hadn't meant to upset her – she wasn't coming across the supercilious academic this time. She'd been friendly; a bit wary at first, but then she'd become genuinely engaged as they'd talked about her work, seeming suddenly confident and in control. He'd found what she was saying interesting. She'd sketched a vivid picture of the Alpha team closing ranks in horror, including a slanderous impersonation which had made him laugh, and then, as he'd rather reluctantly moved on to business, suddenly it had all collapsed, and she had looked frightened and lost.

He'd been pleased when he'd seen her standing by the wall, her face turned up to the sun, smiling, very different from the way she'd looked before. She'd spotted him, and her smile had changed to a frown, hastily modified when she realized he had seen her. If he was honest, he'd admit that he was watching her because he enjoyed looking at her. She reminded him a lot of Lynne, except there was a fucked-upness about her that there never had been about Lynne. A vulnerable Lynne, a Lynne without that intimidating competence. He'd enjoyed the process of breaking down the barriers of her resistance until she'd confided in him, but then, without meaning to, he'd put the boot in.

And he still didn't have his confirmation that someone answering Reid's description had been seen in the park around the important time – he was going to have to talk to Suzanne again. He checked his watch and finished his coffee. He had a trip to Derby on his schedule.

It was playtime. Lucy shook her head when Lauren asked her if she wanted to join in their game. 'Go on, Lucy, you've got to play. It's my game.' Lucy shook her head again, and wove her way through a group of boys who were shouting and pushing near the seats. She heard Kirsten's voice behind her.

'Her babysitter got killed. The police came to her mum.' There was a buzz of chatter. Lucy clenched her fists. She would show Kirsten. But she had something more important to do. She went to the wall that looked out over the road and scrambled up a bit, holding onto the railings. She could see the shops on the other side, people rushing up and down. There was the shop where Mum got all her *flowers and herbs*. Daddy was always talking about Mum's flowers and herbs. There was the shop with all the cheese. Lucy didn't like going in there. It smelt funny. She gripped the railings harder and scrabbled her toes into the irregularities in the stone. There were cars parked all the way along the road. Pollution. That's what Mum always said. All the people looked ordinary. There was Mrs Varney, who babysat for Lucy sometimes. There was the lady with the funny shoes. And Kath from the fruit shop with her baby in the pram. Lucy waved, and Kath waved back. The strange feeling that had been inside her all morning began to go away. It looked as though it was all right, as though maybe she didn't need to worry. She craned her neck to see further along the road.

And he was there, just outside the bookshop. He seemed to be looking at the books, but Lucy knew he was only pretending. Grandmother's Footsteps. She was looking now, and everything was still, nobody was moving. The monsters were still there, and they were closer. She didn't know what to do.

The monsters were still waiting.

'You're going to get me the sack, guys.' The young man looked at the two detectives waiting for him in the manager's office. 'Look, can't this wait until I finish? I need the money . . .' His voice trailed off. He looked uneasy, like someone with something on his conscience. He'd been working on Friday, at his keyboard all day in the Derby office, working to supplement the loan that hadn't even covered his rent for an academic year. McCarthy liked the uneasiness, liked the fact that Paul Lynman, undergraduate and ex-resident of 14, Carleton Road, flatmate of Emma Allan and Sophie Dutton, was frightened of losing his job. The quicker he answered their questions to their satisfaction, the quicker they would leave him alone.

'We'll make this as quick as possible,' he said. Lynman nodded. 'I want to ask you some questions about Emma Allan and Sophie Dutton. You shared a house with Sophie from last September. And we understand that Emma Allan was an unofficial lodger there for a few weeks.'

Lynman looked taken aback. He hadn't expected this. McCarthy wondered what he had expected, to have looked so worried, so uneasy when they announced themselves. 'Emma?' His look of unease began to grow. 'She's Sophie's friend. I don't really . . . And I haven't seen Sophie for weeks.

She's left . . .' He looked at McCarthy. 'I wasn't there in September. I moved in in October. I was living with my girlfriend, but there wasn't room. I didn't know them . . .'

McCarthy thought. 'Why did you move in so late?' The house was for four people. The university was short of accommodation, so how had there been a room available in October? A room in a premium area, as well.

Lynman looked at him, weighing up the question. 'The place was full, but then someone moved out, so they needed someone else. I knew two of the people there, they were on my course, Gemma and Dan.' The students who were in Germany. 'So . . .' He shrugged.

OK. McCarthy shelved that. 'Mr Lynman, did you see the news yesterday?' Lynman's bafflement was convincing. It looked as though he didn't know about Emma. So why the panic McCarthy thought he had seen?

'No, I don't bother with . . . What news?'

'Emma Allan is dead, Mr Lynman.' He watched as the young man's face registered the knowledge.

'I didn't . . . I told her . . . What happened?'

McCarthy didn't want to soften it. 'She was murdered.' Lynman's face showed first disbelief, then shock as he realized that McCarthy meant what he was saying, wasn't playing some elaborate trick. He went white and grabbed at the wall for support. Corvin steadied his arm and pulled out a chair, raising his eyebrows speculatively at McCarthy.

Lynman put his hand over his mouth. 'Oh shit. Oh shit.' He put his head in his hands. 'I'm going to be sick,' he said.

McCarthy nodded to Corvin who went to the water cooler outside the office door. 'Just take deep breaths,' McCarthy advised as Corvin offered the paper cup. Lynman looked at both of them, took the cup and sipped at the water. He was crouched down in his chair, looking hunted. McCarthy looked through the glass walls of the office, and saw the manager at the other side of the room, standing over someone's desk, peering across. The light was bright, flat, fluorescent. There was no way of knowing that it was a clear sunny day outside.

McCarthy reversed a chair and sat down opposite the

young man. 'Paul,' he said. Time to establish relative status. 'You *told her*. What did you tell her?' Lynman's eyes wavered away from McCarthy's. He didn't answer. 'You didn't know Emma was dead . . .' Lynman shook his head in quick affirmation. 'But you weren't too surprised. Now, we can do this the quick way, or we can do this the slow way, but you're going to tell me everything you know about Emma. I need to know about Sophie as well – we can't find her. She isn't where she's supposed to be. You can talk to me here, or you can come back to Sheffield and help us with our inquiries there.' The familiar phrase made Lynman's head jerk up as he looked at McCarthy. McCarthy waited. He was aware of Corvin settling himself into an authoritative stance behind him. Thug mode. Good.

Lynman ran his tongue across his lips. 'Christ. I can't . . . *Em*. It's . . .' He looked at McCarthy in indignant protest. 'It's doing my head in.' McCarthy waited. 'I don't know anything about it,' Lynman said in sudden alarm.

'But you know something about the drugs, don't you, Paul?' McCarthy smiled blandly at him.

'Oh, Christ.' He looked scared. 'I did . . . Look, it was Emma. She's OK, Emma, she's fine. Was fine. She just – she was short of cash, man, we all are.'

'What did she do, Paul?' McCarthy's voice was bland, avuncular.

'It wasn't anything . . .' He looked at the two men in panic. Whatever had been worrying him when they first arrived seemed to have coalesced with his current panic. His eyes travelled between McCarthy and Corvin.

Corvin shifted slightly. 'This is a waste of time. Let's take him back to Sheffield,' he suggested.

'No!' Lynman didn't want that. 'Look, I just don't want to get anyone into trouble.' McCarthy translated that into Lynman's not wanting to get himself into trouble. He began to talk. Emma had got herself a lucrative sideline. She'd got access to good pills. 'Real E,' Lynman enthused, forgetting himself for a moment. 'The stuff you get now is mostly shit.' And good speed, paste. 'It was cheap, too.' He brooded for a moment. 'She wasn't dealing,' he said. 'She was just selling to students, you know?' McCarthy couldn't see the distinction, personally, but he nodded, waiting. Lynman went on to describe an efficient and profitable operation. Emma sold to other students and to her friends. She sold to her friends at prices that were lower than street prices, sold to others for a bit more. 'But everyone knew it was good stuff. You went to Em for good stuff. She wasn't a dealer, see.'

McCarthy thought about it. 'And Sophie . . . ?'

'Well, Sophie used pills sometimes. We all did.' He rubbed his hand nervously over his face. 'Sophe thought Em was getting in a bit heavy just lately.' McCarthy caught Corvin's eye. If Emma was running a lucrative pills operation, why was she so eager to earn peanuts childminding for Jane Fielding? He needed to think about that. 'And then something happened,' Lynman said. 'Emma had a row with her mum and walked out, and next thing I know, Emma's in the house and Sophie's packing up her course and going home. She said she didn't want her parents to know she'd dropped out, not until she'd got a job. She said Emma could join her, once she got settled in. That was why we let Em stay at Carleton Road, see. We needed someone to help with the rent, and Sophe wanted to be able to get in touch.'

'And where's Sophie now?' McCarthy knew they needed to talk to Sophie Dutton urgently.

Lynman shook his head. 'She went home.' He shrugged, looking at the two men.

McCarthy looked at Corvin. 'You'll have to come back to Sheffield with us,' he said to Lynman. 'We need a full statement from you, and we need to know all of Emma's contacts, who she sold to, who she bought from.' Lynman started to protest, caught McCarthy's eye, and slumped in defeat.

Suzanne dumped her bag as she came through the door and crossed the yard to Jane's. Apart from her brief time with Steve McCarthy, and that didn't count, she hadn't talked to another person all day. She was tired of books. She wanted conversation.

Lucy's voice responded to her knock, so she went in, just as Joel came through from the middle room to answer the door. She thought he'd gone back to Leeds. Lucy was sitting at the table drawing, and looked up at her. 'Hello, Suzanne,' she said after a moment. 'I'm doing drawing,' she added politely.

'Hello, Lucy.' Suzanne wasn't sure if she wanted to stay. She didn't want to talk to Joel. He was watching her and when she looked at him, he gave her that slow smile.

'Hi, Suzie. Take a seat.' He settled himself on the settee and ran his eyes over her. His smile broadened at some private joke.

'Is Jane around?' She decided she wouldn't wait if Jane was out. Her last encounter with Joel was still in her mind.

'She's working.' Joel yawned and stretched, as if the thought made him feel tired. He was like a cat, Suzanne thought, with that same quality of relaxed watchfulness, that ability to look as though he belonged wherever he settled. 'She needs to get some stuff in the post tonight. She'll be finished soon. I'm babysitting.'

Lucy looked at the two adults. 'I'm not a baby,' she said.

Joel looked across at her. 'No,' he agreed. 'You're a brat.'

Lucy's face expressed disapproval as she thought about this, then relaxed into a brief, self-contained smile.

Joel winked at Suzanne who quickly turned her attention to Lucy. 'What are you drawing, Lucy?' It looked as though it was the monsters again, but Lucy covered the paper with her arm.

'It's a secret,' she said, looking at Suzanne coldly.

Joel laughed. Lucy compressed her lips and went on colouring behind her shielding arm. Suzanne felt she didn't really have a choice, and sat on the edge of the low armchair, rather than beside Joel on the settee. She saw him register this as he gave her another amused smile. Lucy clattered her hand through her box of pencils and huddled over her drawing.

'So what's been happening in *your* life?' he said, taking in her jeans that were dusty from the stacks, the ink stains on her T-shirt where she'd absent-mindedly wiped her hand. He leant back in the chair, not saying anything, just looking at her. She found it hard to sit naturally, suddenly conscious of her face, her hands, her body.

104

She racked her brains for something to say, a way of getting back the initiative. She wished she'd left as soon as she'd seen Joel, but if she went now, she would look stupid. 'How come you're still here?' she managed after a moment. It came out bluntly, and she realized that it sounded like a criticism. He would certainly construe it as such. Joel hated to be criticized. Just for a moment, his eyes narrowed, then his face settled back into its usual ironic smile. He was as good at hiding his emotions as DI McCarthy, except that McCarthy didn't go to the trouble of looking pleasant. *What you see is what you get.*

'Just giving my daughter some support. Keeping the police off her back, if her mother can't do her job properly.' He crossed his ankle over his knee.

She felt a spurt of anger. 'It's all done, though, isn't it?' she said. 'They said they didn't need to talk to Lucy again.' She kept her voice low, aware of the child at the table.

'So Jane says. I'm just keeping an eye on things.' He looked across at Suzanne. 'Just being around,' he said, with slow emphasis. 'For Lucy.'

Like you're not for Michael. 'You should know all about being around for your children,' she snapped.

Something flickered in his eyes. 'Always best to be consistent with them, isn't it, Suzie? No telling how they might turn out otherwise.' He was watching her steadily now. 'They get out of control, into trouble, and next thing . . . Well, who knows?'

Listen to me, Suzanne! She dug her nails into the palms of her hands. She wasn't going to react, wasn't going to fight back, not in front of Lucy. It had been a mistake even to start. 'Isn't that right?' he said. Lucy looked up.

'I wouldn't know,' Suzanne said. 'Look, Jane's busy. I'll come back later.'

She stood up, and he got up as well, carefully polite, to see her to the door. As he passed the table, and Lucy curled her arm protectively over her picture, he snatched it from her and held it up. The corner of the paper had torn where Lucy had clutched at it. 'Look, Suzie,' he said. 'Our Lucy's drawn some people.' Two figures, in skirts, one with fair hair, the other not coloured yet.

Lucy's face screwed up, then she jumped down from her chair. 'You spoilt it now,' she shouted. 'It's all spoilt.'

Suzanne's hands were clenched into fists and she wanted to hit him. He was looking at her over Lucy's drawing. His eyes were bright. *You wouldn't play the game but I made you!* She heard feet on the stairs and Jane came into the room looking triumphant. 'Done,' she said, waving a large envelope in the air. 'All finished, packaged, ready for delivery. I must get to the post office.' She took in the scene, Joel and Suzanne staring at each other, Lucy fighting back tears. Lucy never cried. 'What's wrong?' she said. She knelt down in front of Lucy. 'What's wrong, love?'

Joel was suddenly there, all contrition, with his arms round them both. 'Suzie wanted to see Lucy's drawing. It was a secret. I didn't realize. And now she's all upset.' He tickled Lucy under the chin and smiled at her. 'I'm sorry, Lucy-lu. I didn't mean it.'

Lucy looked at him, and then at her mother and Suzanne. She took the drawing back that her father was holding out to her. She looked puzzled, sullen. Jane stroked her hair, flashing a reproachful look at the two adults. 'Maybe you could draw another one,' she suggested.

'It's spoilt,' Lucy said with finality. Then she looked at her mother with some calculation. 'Can I have ice cream for tea?' she said.

Joel burst out laughing. 'Her father's daughter. Of course you can,' he said, ruffling her hair.

Jane frowned slightly, assessing Lucy. 'I need to get to the post office,' she said. 'This has to be there tomorrow. I'll only be fifteen minutes.' She was talking to Joel who was pulling on his jacket as she spoke.

Suzanne said quickly, 'I'll stay here,' she said. 'I was waiting for you anyway.' She looked at Joel, trying not to put any challenge in her eyes. 'You get off if you've got to go.' She wasn't leaving him with Lucy.

He paused, his eyes narrowed, then he said, 'OK.' His smile was cool and satisfied as he followed Jane out of the door. Suzanne let her breath out. She turned to Lucy, who had gone into the kitchen.

'Have you finished drawing?' she said.

Lucy nodded. 'Now I want a drink. I can get it myself,' she added, severely, as Suzanne stood up. Suzanne stood in the kitchen door, watching as Lucy pulled a small red stool across to the worktop and stood on it to reach the tap. She climbed down with the glass of water held carefully in both hands. 'You made Daddy cross,' she said, her voice hovering between accusation and question.

'I didn't mean to,' Suzanne said.

Lucy looked at her assessingly. 'It's my sisters,' she said after a moment. She sounded quite proud. 'But it's a secret.'

'Your sisters?' Suzanne realized that Lucy was talking about her picture. She wondered, as she often wondered about Michael, if only children were always lonely.

'I've got sisters,' Lucy went on looking dreamy, 'and brothers and sisters and I'm going to have lots and lots of sisters, and Michael can have lots of sisters,' she added generously, 'but I'm going to have more.' Her voice moved into a sing song. 'And Tamby's going to have . . .' Her voice faded to a murmur as she went across to the shelves and pulled down her roller boots. 'I'm going to skate,' she said.

Polly Andrews was Paul Lynman's girlfriend. Though she had never been an official resident of 14, Carleton Road, she had spent a lot of time there, and knew Emma Allan and Sophie Dutton. 'It was more comfortable than my flat,' she confided to Barraclough and Corvin. 'I wish I'd managed to get the room when that creepy guy moved out.' She twisted herself round at the interview desk, and looked behind her. 'Bit of a dump,' was her verdict. She wore a pair of shabby jeans, a skimpy black top that left her shoulders bare and stopped short of the pierced navel. She had a tattoo on her right shoulder, a knife and something that looked like devil's horns. 'OK if I smoke?' She stretched her legs out, the heavy boots looking incongruous against her small-boned fragility. Her face was pale, but with the creamy pallor of health. There were freckles across her nose. She was twenty-one, a university student. She looked about twelve. Barraclough thought she did a good job of projecting the sexy schoolgirl image. Corvin certainly looked uncharacteristically benign. Polly lit a cigarette, and then leant forward on the desk looking directly at them, waiting. Corvin was letting Barraclough lead on the interview, and she started with the easy questions: Emma's friends, contacts, routines. Polly was co-operative, chatty, but she had nothing to add that they didn't already know. Emma was well known at 14, Carleton Road as Sophie's friend, and when she found herself homeless, the other tenants had raised no objections to her sharing Sophie's room. 'Well, they couldn't really,' she said. 'Not Paul, anyway, because I was always there.'

'It must have been very crowded,' Barraclough observed. She'd seen the rooms at Carleton Road. 'Sophie had the attic room, didn't she?'

'Yes. Emma dossed on one of those exercise mats with a sleeping bag. She rolled them up and shoved them in the roof space during the day,' Polly said cheerfully, smiling at Corvin, who smiled back. 'They pack us in like sardines.'

She could shed no light on Sophie Dutton's whereabouts. Her eyes opened in surprise when Barraclough asked her. 'She's with her parents. Didn't you know that? She was going home until she could find a job. Maybe she got something and didn't want to tell her parents, you know, that lap dancing, strippagrams . . .' She looked at Corvin and smiled again. 'You can make a fortune,' she confided. She shrugged to indicate that she couldn't understand why Sophie wouldn't have told her.

'What kind of work was Sophie looking for?' Barraclough asked. If she was prepared to do lap dancing . . .

Polly couldn't help there. 'Oh, anything. She wants to be a writer, so it's all, you know, material.'

Barraclough went back to Emma. 'What about boyfriends? Did Emma have any boyfriends?' If Emma had been going to a rendezvous, they hadn't been able to find the name of any possible candidates, though Paul Lynman's evidence opened up some new possibilities.

For the first time, Polly looked – Barraclough tried to put a name to the expression on her face: evasive? Puzzled? 'She didn't really talk to me about things,' Polly said after a

108

moment. 'She was Sophie's friend.' Barraclough took a leaf out of McCarthy's book, and waited Polly's silence out. 'She was seeing someone. She talked about someone called Ash . . .' Barraclough was aware of Corvin's sudden interest. *Ash. The Ash Man. Ashley Reid.* 'But he never came to Carleton Road.' She shook her head at the name Reid. 'It might have been,' she said. 'I don't know. Em never told me.'

'What about "Ash Man", "the Ash Man"?' Barraclough tried.

For a moment, she thought she saw recognition in Polly's eyes, but the girl shook her head. 'No,' she said. She paused, looking uncertain. 'I saw her after she'd left Carleton Road,' she said. 'It was . . . I think it was about ten days ago, a Wednesday or a Thursday.' Eight or nine days before Emma's death. 'She'd been shopping, she had all these bags from those shops on Devonshire Street, you know?' Barraclough knew the shops well – designer wear, avant-garde, way beyond her pocket. 'She said she'd met someone.' She bit her lip, thinking. 'Emma asked me not to tell anyone.'

'It's a bit different now, though, isn't it, Polly?' Barraclough wasn't too convinced by the display of reluctance, but she still got the feeling that Polly was puzzled by something. 'She'd met someone. A new boyfriend, do you mean?'

'He was older,' Polly said. 'Emma said he'd got some work for her. I don't know if he was her boyfriend or not.' Barraclough assumed that 'boyfriend' was synonymous with 'sexual partner'. 'She had all this money . . .'

Barraclough asked her about the drugs. After distancing herself from the whole thing, she told more or less the same story that Paul Lynman had told McCarthy and Corvin, except she made the operation sound a lot less organized. 'Emma knew someone who could get good stuff,' she said. 'So she'd get some for everyone.' It was no big deal, she insisted. Barraclough asked her about heroin, and she appeared genuinely shocked. 'No. Never. Nothing like that. Emma was on . . . ?' Her eyes slid away from them, but she didn't add anything else.

* * *

109

Suzanne didn't go back home. She needed to think, and the park was the place she came to get her mind in focus. Now it looked open, spacious, the sky high and blue with distant wisps of cloud, the grass green and the trees heavy in full leaf. She walked through the main gate at Hunters Bar and followed the path past the small playground and the field where teams played football on Sundays, the school had its sports day, the travelling fair pitched every summer. She went on past the café, crossed the stone bridge to the first dam, and watched the ducks for a few minutes. She didn't think about anything in particular. She followed the path on to the next dam, where the iridescent blue of a kingfisher caught her eye, and she watched it as it flashed between the two islands where the water-birds nested, then vanished down the river.

She needed to sort things out. It was all getting out of control. She needed to identify the problems, so that she could deal with them one by one. She tested them in her mind. *Joel*. Should she tell Jane about her encounter with him? It would sound like nothing to someone who hadn't seen it. Wait and see. Joel's new-found concern for Lucy would soon evaporate, and then he would be back to occasional visits. *The Alpha Project*. Leave it and see what happened? It was probably better not to wait. She could phone Keith Liskeard tomorrow and arrange to see him. Then she could explain exactly what had happened. She'd better talk to Maggie, her supervisor, as well. She should have done that today.

Ashley. Without meaning to, she'd focused police attention on Ashley, and he'd responded the way Adam had done. He'd run away. When Richard had told her that Ashley was missing, she'd thought of Adam. The Alpha grapevine was very efficient. As soon as the police started looking for him, he would have known, she was sure of that. And he would know where the information had come from. Ashley had trusted her.

She tried to shut it out, but she kept hearing Steve McCarthy's voice: *I hold you responsible for this*. No, he'd said, *You're not responsible. . .* In her mind, his face became like her father's, his eyes looking at her with cold judgement. *There is right, and there is wrong, Suzanne. I expect you to know the difference.*

It's not that simple, she pleaded, but his face was gone. She was looking over the bars of a cot, looking at the tiny face against the white of the shawl, the fists clenched, the face screwed up, the mouth seeking. 'He's going to cry,' she said. 'Can I hold him?'

'That's right, Suzanne, you hold him, see, like this . . .' And the weight of him in her arms, the baby smell and the dark blue eyes that looked at her. 'Your little brother, Suzanne. You're going to be a big help to your mother, I know you are.' Her mother. A white face on the pillow, a thin, tired whisper. *Take care of him, Suzanne.* She was entranced by his face, his hands, his smallness.

She knew where she was going. She went out through the gate and crossed the road into the next park. To her left was a grassy slope that was a sea of daffodils in the spring. The path was wide and straight in front of her, inviting her into the cool shadows of the woods. She looked at the noticeboard. The piece of paper was gone. TAKE CARE. . . Her feet felt heavy, and she was tempted to turn around and go home, but she knew she mustn't. The trees were shading her eyes from the sun now, but it gleamed through the branches in sudden flashes, dazzling her as she walked.

She came to the bridge, the one that led to Shepherd Wheel. She looked across at the building. It was locked up and silent. It looked the same as it always did, and it looked as though it had closed itself up on dark secrets. She mustn't let her imagination run away with her. It was just a workshop. She was glad that the wheel yard would be locked. If it had been open, she would have had to go round, look down again into that dark, still water.

There were tapes across the doors, black and yellow police tapes, which looked like ribbons tied on a statue – inappropriate and incongruous. She crossed the bridge. There was no barrier there, and the police can't have been too worried about their crime scene any more, because there was no one there to keep people away. She walked along the path and

111

up the slope to Shepherd Wheel dam, the dam that existed to power the wheel. The water was still low, but the flow between the mud banks looked stronger, as though the dam was filling up again. The ducks quacked mournfully at her as she passed.

She stopped at the end of the dam, where it met the stream. There were steps up to another bridge here, to the road. Suzanne looked at the water. It tumbled down a weir that returned it to the main stream. She looked back at the dam. The shadows rippled across the surface of the water. Shepherd Wheel was still and silent under the trees. Suzanne had made a decision.

She knew what she had to do. She had to find Ashley.

Barraclough felt as though she had been relegated to the paperwork when the interesting, the important things were happening elsewhere. She looked at the notes in front of her. Where had Emma been in those last weeks of her life? She had left her father's house and gone to Carleton Road. She had left Carleton Road at the end of May, but there was nothing to tell them where she had gone. She had given Jane Fielding the address of her father's flat, but she hadn't been living there. And yet she'd been around, active, and apparently earning money. Polly had seen her. Polly's story had given them a link they hadn't had before – Emma had a boyfriend called Ash. Polly wasn't able to confirm it, but given everything else they had, the prime candidate was Ashley Reid. Ashley Reid . . . Barraclough frowned. Emma had clearly been a troubled and difficult young woman, but everything that Barraclough had seen told her that Emma was also bright and intelligent. According to the information they had from the Alpha Centre, Ashley Reid was of below average intelligence. What would the attraction have been? And then, according to Polly, Emma had found someone else. Jealousy. One of the clearest motives in the book. Barraclough knew her Shakespeare.

They'd requested Reid's file from social services. She had been landed with the job of going through it. His life – his nineteen years – had been difficult. Barraclough saw enough

112

of the effects of crime not to be sentimental about offenders, but as she read through Reid's file, she felt the anger she often felt at the lives some people were born to.

Ashley had not come into the care of social services until early 1989, when he was nine. His parents were Carolyn Reid, formerly Walker, and Phillip Reid. His parents were British, but he had been born in America, where his parents had emigrated in 1978. His mother had brought him to England and left him and his elder brother, Simon, with their uncle, her brother Bryan, in 1984. It seemed to have been an unofficial arrangement. Barraclough frowned. Surely there should have been some kind of official involvement. She said as much to Corvin, who was reading through Polly Andrews's statement.

'Not if they were told the kid was with his mum and it was all happy families,' he said. 'Not unless there was reason to worry. They've got enough on without looking for work.'

'I wonder if the uncle and aunt are still around.' Barraclough looked at the names. Bryan and Kath Walker. 'I wonder what they could tell us.' She went back to the file. The social services had been unable to trace either parent. Ashley's mother had apparently gone back to America. There was no reference to his father in any of these notes. Bryan and Kath Walker had taken both boys in, but Simon had gone into care early on. He was autistic, and too much for his aunt and uncle to handle. They had brought Ashley up with their own child, who was five years older. Michelle. Would Ashley have kept contact with his cousin? She made a note to check.

After five years, the Walkers put Ashley into care. They described him as being 'out of control'. There was some kind of friction between the children. There had been attempts to track Carolyn Reid down. The Walkers had reported her last known address in Utah, but, as far as Barraclough could tell, there had been no trace of the woman. She'd abandoned her children and vanished. The notes reported problems with Ashley's development. They described him as being in reasonable physical condition but withdrawn. He had behavioural difficulties and a low reading age. As far as

Barraclough could tell, no one had made a specific diagnosis to account for his problems. He'd been moved around the care system, but had never been adopted or even put into long-term foster care. As he got older, the problems that had plagued his adolescent years began. Truanting, vandalism, theft, violence. *A child is for life, not just for Christmas* . . .

She needed to find out where Ashley's family was now.

Simon coming through the park, in the dark through the woods. The pathways made patterns in front of his eyes. The lines and cracks of the tree bark told stories of how the tree had grown and developed and thrived. He stopped and watched the way the street lights played on the patterns as the breeze blew the leaves about, making shadows and light, shadows and light. Here, the path was steep, taking him up a narrow track that led to the wall. Here, it led through the passage and then the gate.

Then the road, quiet, the street lamps lit but shadowed by tall hedges and shrubs. Walls of brick, rectangles, doorways. Spaces of light and planes of shadow, planes with the shadows washing like water across and back.

A face at the window, a pale blur with dark smudges for eyes, fine hair tangled round her face. Like a drawing, then *recognition*, a blank square and her face in the middle, quiet and still looking out into the darkness. Then – gone. *Lucy.*

Lucy climbed into bed and lay back against the pillows. He was still there. He was in his place, watching. She could tell when she looked out of the window. He was hiding in the darkness, but she could see his feet just where the light shone under the tree. A car went down the road, and Lucy watched the light run across the ceiling. They were coming. They were getting closer. She couldn't watch all the time. The policewoman wanted to know, but Lucy wasn't telling. Emma didn't understand. Lucy knew. And Lucy wasn't telling. Not anyone.

114

8

It rained that night. Early on Tuesday morning, a walker in the park took an unaccustomed turning across the river to the Shepherd Wheel dam. This early in the morning, the ducks were unfed, and swam hopefully towards the path, circling in the water below him. He listened to the calls of the birds, and waited for a few minutes. A friend had told him about herons in the park, and he wondered if, at this quiet time of day, he might see one. He looked up at the sky. Clear and blue. It was going to be a fine day. He strolled slowly along, noting the way the mud that had built up was slowly disappearing under the water again. He looked at its soft, glistening surface and the water that ran from the weir, carrying trails of mud as though it was washing the banks away. The feet of the wading birds had left prints and he looked at them, wondering which birds had been there.

There were things sticking out of the mud: twigs, mostly, from small branches that had fallen into the water. There were one or two empty cans, some bits of paper. His eye was caught by a twig that looked almost like a hand submerged in the mud, a hand reaching up for help. He remembered the legend of Excalibur, the arm clothed in samite – whatever samite was – reaching out of the water holding the mystical sword. He smiled to himself, walking along the path nearer to the twig, waiting for the illusion to vanish with closeness, the 'hand' to turn into what it was, a bunch of sticks. His mind was half occupied with problems at work – nothing serious, he was just turning things over in his head – when he was pulled back to focus on the mud again.

It was a hand. He squinted and rubbed his eyes, trying to

get the thing on the surface of the dam to change into the twig he *knew* it really was. It was a hand.

It must be a doll, a shop-window dummy that someone had dumped, a . . . His mind ran out of ideas. It was grey, the skin wrinkled, the nails looking . . . He was suddenly aware of his stomach, his throat. He felt cold. He looked up. The trees were sharp against the sky, every leaf clearly defined. There was a hand sticking out of the mud. He turned back to go down the steps, and his legs wouldn't hold him. He was sitting on the top step and the sun was shining and his hands were shaking and he didn't think he was ever going to get warm again.

They thought they'd got a real nutter at first, a well-dressed man, educated voice, babbling about mystic arms and samite or something. When he managed to get his story out more coherently, a car was dispatched to investigate, and eventually McCarthy found himself back by the dam, looking down as the men dug into the wet mud, opening up the shallow grave. McCarthy moved back from the edge. He didn't allow his face to show anything, but the stench was overwhelming. He looked up at the summer trees that hung over the dam, and breathed in the air that smelt of water and cut grass. Then he moved back and looked down at the body, the features and form blurred by the processes of putrefaction, but still disturbingly human, disturbingly real. The body had been there for two or three weeks, the pathologist thought. 'I can give you a better estimate once I've had a closer look.'

The Lady of the Lake. McCarthy, who had been a fan of the King Arthur legends in his teens, had picked up the reference made by the distraught walker. But this woman – the pathologist was prepared to commit herself that far, to something they could all tell anyway – this woman hadn't been holding up a mystical sword to a king. Her hand looked as though it had been scrabbling desperately through the mud, reaching for the surface. McCarthy hoped that was just an illusion. Two women, one in the dam, one under the wheel, both dead in the same waterway. What had John Draper said? *Of course, if you wanted to run water through without moving the wheel, you might think that lowering the level of water in the dam would do it.* But if you wanted to dry out the mud in the dam, just a little, then lowering the level of the water would certainly do it. McCarthy watched as they lifted the body carefully from the mud and laid it on a body bag. For her, it was all academic now.

Suzanne put the phone down. Keith Liskeard, the Alpha director, had written to Maggie Lewis, her supervisor. The research project was suspended. Indefinitely. A copy of the letter had been sent to Suzanne. She looked at the morning's post that she hadn't yet opened. The letter was there. She read it as she talked to Maggie, holding the phone awkwardly against her shoulder. The letter cited *problems with the group*, but also *lack of experience in working in this context*. That was an irony that roused Suzanne's anger. 'I want to see you,' Maggie had said, her tone peremptory.

Suzanne had prevaricated, and had managed to postpone the meeting until the following week. She knew what Maggie wanted – a talk, one of those 'little talks' that somehow ended up being documented, and became part of the paper that dogged you through your working life. She wanted to have something to offer Maggie in her own support. She knew why Maggie was reacting so badly. The research funds were limited. Suzanne had talked her into supporting the programme at the Alpha Centre, on the grounds that it would attract a lot more money once they had some concrete findings. And now, what could they do with the money they'd committed to Suzanne? It was too late to start another research programme, to try again somewhere else.

Suzanne had had to admit to Maggie that she'd been aware of the problem since Saturday night. 'I was coming in tomorrow to tell you,' she'd said, knowing that it sounded thin. She had said, without much hope, 'Richard, Richard Kean seemed to think the problem could be sorted out.'

'That's not what Keith Liskeard said when I phoned him.' Maggie was really angry, and Suzanne couldn't blame her. 'He said that they now realized that the Alpha wasn't a

117

suitable venue for primary research.' They'd to-and-froed a bit and, by the end of the conversation, Maggie had softened somewhat, was prepared to concede that Suzanne was perhaps sinned against as well as sinning, but the word – unspoken – *unprofessional* hung in the air between them. Maggie scheduled a meeting for the following week, with the threat of a meeting with the Head of Department to follow. Suzanne knew that unless she could vindicate herself completely, her prospects as a research academic were seriously damaged.

She felt tired. She looked at the photo on her desk: Michael giving his toothy camera smile, the smile that had appeared as he got old enough to be camera-conscious. His first school photograph. She looked beyond it to the wall. Adam smiled back at her.

Her mother should never have had her second child. Adam was a late arrival in her parents' lives. Her father must have been over fifty when Adam was born. And her mother . . . *Of course, Adam ruined your mother's health*, her father would say, as the little boy sat quietly at the table, carefully pulling the crusts off his sandwiches. Multiple sclerosis – Suzanne was able to give a name to the illness that had made her mother an invalid for most of Suzanne's life, and had killed her when she, Suzanne, was thirteen. And it was true, the strain of a late pregnancy had caused the already advanced illness to run riot through her mother's body. *Take care of him, Suzanne . . .*

The doctors had advised an abortion when the pregnancy was diagnosed, but Eleanor Milner wouldn't hear of it. *Worst mistake we ever made*, Suzanne's father said when he brought Adam back from the police station after yet another incident of vandalism, another incident of stealing. *I thought I brought you up to know right from wrong!* That had been aimed at Suzanne, who apparently no longer knew or, at least, was not able to instil in Adam this difference. She had tried, but her best had proved useless, or worse than useless.

That last time. She remembered the familiar face of the policewoman who worked with the juveniles. Another break-in, a warehouse this time. Adam and his friends, after sweets, boxes of sweets. She shook herself impatiently. The thought of it could still make her eyes sting. This time, it had been worse. The watchman had seen them and given chase. One of the lads had hit out, and the man had been hurt. Adam had run, hidden himself away, terrified of the consequences.

She remembered the policewoman's voice, calm and implacable. *Just tell us where Adam is. We want to help the lad, Suzanne.* But there was only one kind of help the police could give. She could still hear Adam's despairing cry as the magistrate handed down the sentence, the time that was, in weeks, so short, but to Adam, lonely and frightened, must have seemed like an eternity he couldn't face. *Listen to me, Suzanne . . .* She'd told them, told them that Adam wouldn't be able to cope with what was happening to him. They'd been brisk, offering her impersonal reassurance.

And she'd let him down. She'd gone in search of lawyers, of social workers, of the people who'd been so clear that all Adam needed was help and support. And left Adam, left him to be taken away on his own and terrified. She could remember the report, not even front page, buried on page three of the newspaper: THIRD SUICIDE IN YOUNG OFFENDERS' CENTRE. She remembered her father's face when the police officers had arrived that morning, and she had had to tell him. *I hold you responsible for this!*

She looked at Michael's picture. *I hold you responsible . . . responsible . . . responsible . . .* She had tried to keep Michael safe the only way she could. *Listen to me, Suzanne . . .*

She sat up, remembering something. The Alpha tapes! Ashley's tape! She ran up the stairs to her attic study, and looked at the row of cassette tapes on the shelf behind her desk. She frowned as she saw how disordered they were getting. Then she remembered. She'd left the tapes in her desk at the department. She sorted through the pile of notes in her in-tray until she found the transcript. There it was! She went back downstairs and began to read.

Q. So what do you like to do then? In your spare time?
A. So . . . ?

Q. *What do you do?*
A. I thought we were together.
Q. *What? Sorry, Ashley, I didn't get that.*
A. So, I'm sorry.
Q. *Ashley, do you want to do this? Only . . .*
A. I'm telling you!

He'd said it, *I'm telling you!* Like a plea, like the way Adam had said *Listen to me!* And she hadn't listened, she'd just transcribed the tape and felt good because Ashley couldn't communicate what he wanted to say. And now he was in trouble. This time she would listen. This time she would do something.

There was a knock at the door and she jumped. The door was locked; it took her a moment to find the key. It was Jane, a tatty cardigan pulled over the top of her paint-spattered work jeans, a look of agitation on her face.

'In the park,' Jane said, 'It's in the park again . . .'

Suzanne stared at her in bewilderment. Jane took a breath and tried again. 'The police, they're all over the park again. Suzanne, they've found something else, someone else.' Jane had been walking to the shops and had seen the cars outside the park. Curiosity had sent her closer. 'I thought it might be something to do with Emma,' she said, but there were police at both gates and they wouldn't let her in. 'They wouldn't tell me, either.' She'd gone to the newsagents in the end, her intended destination, and the woman there had told her. 'She said they'd found a body in the Shepherd Wheel dam.'

Suzanne had a picture in her mind, a picture of a tall, dark-haired figure, his pale face looking back at her as he turned towards the allotments. She could no longer remember the face she had seen. 'Ashley . . .' she said.

'What?'

'Was it a man, a young man?'

'I don't know. She didn't know.' Jane twisted her hair round her fingers.

Suzanne's mind worked frantically. What had McCarthy said? *We think he was at the scene.* Except he hadn't been . . .

Or had he? McCarthy had said Ashley was missing. And now a body had turned up in the park. *Ashley, I'm sorry!*

The temperature of mud is constant and cool. Bodies buried in mud are often well preserved, the processes of decay slowed down. The woman's features were still discernible, blurred and waxy, but someone who had known her in life could well, now, know her in death. Barraclough knew her. Barraclough had only seen her photograph, but the transformation of the vivacious young woman snapped in the disco lights of a nightclub into the still, putrefying cadaver on the mortuary slab made her eyes sting as the pity of it overcame her. TO EM. She felt her nose clog up, and sniffed to clear it. Crying in the autopsy suite was hardly the act of a professional. She wiped her nose on the back of her hand and glanced across at McCarthy, who was assessing the body with dispassionate interest.

She wondered if any of the work he did affected him. She had seen him like this before, looking at the victims of road accidents, reading reports of child abuse, looking, as now, at the victims of brutality, talking to the relatives, people who had lost loved ones to that same brutality, with a level, emotionless gaze. She had thought, at one time, that he was just better than most at concealing his feelings. She was familiar with the importance of machismo among the male officers – women, too; but the emotion came out – in sick jokes, in drinking, in anger towards perpetrators. She had never seen anything much disturb McCarthy's equilibrium.

The pathologist was brisk and matter of fact. 'I can't tell you if it's the same killer or not. Yet,' she added. 'The lab results might give us something. I can't say that it isn't either.'

This slow deliberation irritated McCarthy, who wanted to push the woman into some kind of speculation. 'So what can you tell us?' he said.

'She was young – under twenty-five. She was, as far as I can determine, in good health.'

Come on! McCarthy thought irritably. 'So how did she die?'

The pathologist picked up her clipboard. 'It'll all be in my report.'

McCarthy wondered why he always thought of her as *the pathologist*, rather than – what was her name? – Anne, or even the more formal Dr Hays. He never saw her outside of her professional environment. She seemed to have no life other than that of the dead. Maybe that was it. 'We need a summary before the briefing,' he said.

She looked at him over her glasses. He wondered if she had perfected that gesture as a way of asserting her authority. He waited. 'Briefly, Inspector,' she said, 'there is very little to report. Cause of death is undetermined at present. She appears to have drowned in the mud. How that happened is a matter for speculation. There is some evidence of a struggle but not much. Like your previous victim, she did not put up much of a fight for an apparently healthy young woman. The lab reports may give us more information.' For a minute, McCarthy thought that that was all she was going to give them, but she frowned, her eyes focusing into the distance, and went on, 'We're looking at a murder victim, and I think she's another victim of the same killer. That's unofficial.' She looked at the two officers, and for the first time she seemed to McCarthy to be taking a personal rather than a professional stance. 'You wouldn't drown in that mud if you just fell in. Well, you'd be unlucky. If you were unconscious, if you landed face first, if the mud was particularly soft . . . it might cut off your air supply. There are bruises on her arms as if someone held her down.' She caught McCarthy's eye. 'Like the first one,' she agreed.

McCarthy tried to picture a struggle by the dam, someone caught in the mud, another figure, shadowy, but becoming clearer, someone with murderous intent. The victim's terror, the assailant's . . . what? What emotions did a killer feel at such a moment? He pulled his mind back to the practicalities of the situation. It would have been messy, noisy, likely to attract attention. 'How quick would it be?'

'Not quick enough, I shouldn't think,' the pathologist said briskly.

*　　　*　　　*

122

The Duttons lived in a small village outside Hull. The M18 was quiet, and McCarthy was happy to let Barraclough drive while he ran aspects of the case through his mind. How likely was it that both women were victims of the same killer? They were close friends, they were physically alike, they had died – or at least their bodies had been found – in more or less the same place. That was pretty conclusive. How did it look with Ashley Reid as the main suspect? A scenario with a single murder had given McCarthy no problems. His own interpretation had been an abortive sexual encounter and a sudden, vicious attack. But the evidence of planning, the evidence of a drugs connection, had made him revise his thoughts. Reid was, apparently, not very intelligent. Another murder, and one that had been successfully concealed, didn't fit, and he was adjusting his mental picture to find ways to accommodate it.

'What do you think?' he asked Barraclough, out of the blue.

The sudden interruption of the long silence startled her for a moment. 'About this latest, you mean?'

'I wasn't talking about the last budget.'

'It's not—' He registered the brief flash of protest on her face at his tone and reflected that he probably hadn't been very fair. He didn't intend doing anything about it. He waited. 'Well,' she said, cautiously, 'it looks as though it must be the same person – or people.' She checked her mirror and pulled out to pass a heavy lorry. 'It must have involved some planning, which suggests that the first one – I mean the first one we found, Emma, was probably planned as well.'

'Not necessarily,' but McCarthy nodded to show that he followed her logic.

'We think that Emma's killer knew her. So did he know Sophie as well? Or was Sophie the only intended victim and did Emma just get in the way somehow?' She was quiet for a moment, thinking. 'Sophie's been in the mud for three or four weeks, they said. She was still at the university in May. Do we have a last sighting?'

McCarthy shook his head. 'They're looking for that now.'

'OK.' Barraclough ran the details through her mind again.

'The obvious thing is the drugs connection. If Emma was dealing on the campus, trod on someone's toes . . .'

'It's possible. But don't forget there are a lot of small-time dealers around the university. If she got in someone's way, she might have got beaten up, but why take the risk of killing her?'

'Do you think Sophie left because someone was threatening her?' Barraclough looked at him for a moment and then back at the road.

McCarthy shrugged. 'Something happened. But don't forget the trouble in the Allan family.'

Barraclough said, 'Emma left home in March. After a row with her mum. A few weeks later, Sophie is killed. You think there's a connection?'

McCarthy nodded. 'It might all tie in with the drugs thing again. They have a row because they find out that Emma's got herself involved in trouble? They have a row because they aren't getting their cut? Or it's something else altogether.'

They needed to put more pressure on Dennis Allan, find out what he was hiding. McCarthy went back to his thoughts as Barraclough negotiated her way through the centre of Hull. Too many connections.

The Duttons lived in an old farmhouse about half an hour's drive from the centre of Hull. The village, Penby, was typical of the area: small, dispersed, set in the middle of flat spreading fields separated by dykes. The houses were red-brick with pantile roofs; the outbuildings were utilitarian. The roads were narrow and in poor repair. 'Third one along,' said Barraclough as they came to a T-junction. She turned the car and pulled up on the grass verge. The ground was muddy. There was a short drive up to the house that ran past the kitchen door and along to a garage. The door stood open, but there was no one in sight.

'Are they expecting us?' Barraclough thought it was probably a stupid question as she asked it, and McCarthy's lack of acknowledgement confirmed this. He knocked on the door, waited and then knocked again.

'Sorry. I was feeding the hens.' A woman came round from the back of the house. She gave them a smile that tried to conceal her anxiety. She was wearing trousers and rubber boots. Her short hair was jet black. Barraclough found herself wondering where Sophie had got her colouring from – if this was Sophie's mother. Barraclough could see no resemblance. 'Mrs Dutton?'

She nodded and offered McCarthy her hand. 'Maureen,' she said.

'I'm Detective Inspector McCarthy from South Yorkshire Police . . .' Barraclough listened as he went through the formalities of introduction, watching the woman's face. 'Mrs Dutton, is your husband here?' McCarthy moved nearer to the purpose of their visit, and Barraclough found she didn't want to be there, didn't want to see the woman's friendly, worried face collapse into grief and dismay. For her, Barraclough thought, her daughter was still alive. For McCarthy, and for Barraclough herself, Sophie Dutton was almost certainly dead.

The woman's eyes began to hunt around the room, as if she was looking for something normal and everyday to fix on. 'He'll have seen you arrive. He's been expecting you,' she said. 'Would you like a cup of tea? Or coffee, or something?' She crossed the kitchen and filled the kettle as she spoke, looking at them inquiringly.

'Shall we wait till your husband gets here?' McCarthy said, and the uncharacteristic gentleness in his voice surprised Barraclough.

Maureen Dutton looked round, cleared her throat, said, 'We could go through to the other room. It's a bit more comfortable.' She took them through to a sitting-room at the front of the house. It had the same rather shabby used look about it that the kitchen did. A pair of boots stood on the low table. Books and magazines were piled up in corners. A settee in one corner, opposite the television, presented a homely enclave with some knitting stuffed under a cushion, an open book on the arm, a pair of slippers on the floor.

Maureen Dutton's eyes looked through the window behind them and her face cleared. 'Here's Tony now,' she

125

said. Barraclough looked at the big, solid man coming across the field towards the gate. Thick black hair, grey beard, dressed in working clothes, like his wife. They waited in silence as he pulled off his boots and came through from the kitchen. He shook hands with McCarthy, and, after a slight pause, with Barraclough. 'You don't have to be embarrassed,' he said, looking at them. 'You've come to tell us our Sophie's in trouble. We know she's been mixing with a bad crowd. She's been a bit . . . headstrong, lately.' They had prepared themselves, braced themselves for the worst. Sophie was in trouble, and they were going to deal with it. They were going to stand by her and help her get through it. Barraclough could tell by the expression on the man's face, and the way the woman straightened her back. *We don't want to hear this, but we're ready.*

'In what way, Mr Dutton?' McCarthy said.

'It's Tony. Well, she was . . .' He looked at his wife.

'She wanted to find her mother,' Maureen Dutton said, baldly. 'We always knew she might want to do that. We'd never have stood in her way.'

'Sophie was adopted?' McCarthy's voice was that of someone clarifying a point, but Barraclough could detect the slight edge in his voice.

'Yes. We took her when she was four. There was never any question of her not knowing.' Maureen Dutton looked at her husband, and the two of them moved closer together. 'Then, when she started looking, there was a letter. Her mother had written a letter to be given to her if she ever tried to find her birth family. That's why she took the place at Sheffield, I think. That's where her family came from.'

'And did she find her mother?'

'No. I don't know . . . She hardly writes or phones.' Maureen Dutton bit her lip.

'Did you have a . . .' McCarthy tried to select a diplomatic word. 'Was there any disagreement about it?'

'No.' She looked sad. 'Not from us. But I think Sophie felt guilty, felt that she was letting us down – we'd perhaps try to persuade her against it.'

'I did.' Tony Dutton looked grim. 'Whoever her mother is

126

– well, she wasn't that interested in Sophie when she was little. Put Sophie into care. You don't do that to your kid.' McCarthy was aware of Barraclough's nod of approval. 'I'm worried she'll get hurt, that's all.'

'Tony's right.' Maureen Dutton shook her head. 'But you can't budge Sophie once she's made her mind up. I'd just like to know what's happened. I don't push it, because she's very touchy about it. She'll talk when she's ready.'

Tony Dutton shifted his feet uncomfortably. 'Look, there's no point in beating about the bush,' he said after a moment. 'You'd better tell us what it is she's got herself involved with.'

Before McCarthy could answer, Maureen picked up a small photograph from the mantelpiece. 'Sophie,' she said. McCarthy looked at it and showed it to Barraclough. The girl from the photograph found in Emma's bag looked back at them. In this picture, she looked younger, less sophisticated. It was taken outside the house they were now in, and she was smiling in the kitchen doorway, muddy boots on her feet and a small white dog in her arms. Barraclough had a sudden flash of the blurred, waxy face on the autopsy table. She braced herself.

McCarthy looked at the Duttons who were waiting, their tension becoming more apparent, for him to tell them why he was there. 'Mr Dutton, Mrs Dutton. I'm not here because Sophie is in trouble with the law. I'm afraid it's more serious than that. We're investigating a second death.' Barraclough saw the woman's face clench, her lips move silently. 'The body of a young girl was found this morning, in Sheffield, and we think' – Barraclough saw the man's hand grip his wife's arm – 'that it's your daughter, Sophie.'

9

The life on a smallholding doesn't stop in the face of tragedy. Neither of the Duttons would let the other go alone to identify the body of their daughter, and it was the small hours of Wednesday morning before Brooke's team had the confirmation they were expecting. The lady in the lake was Sophie Dutton. Her father, trying to numb his grief with rage, had insisted on talking to Brooke, had threatened to lay complaints against the whole team, had hit out blindly against an attack that came from inside him. McCarthy recognized guilt. This was the useless, agonizing guilt of the parent who had not been able to protect his child.

Sophie's background, after her adoption, had been unexceptionable. Her mother had, according to Tony Dutton, effectively abandoned her, signing her over to local authority care and vanishing. In consequence, they knew very little about her family background. 'We think her mother may have had another child,' he said. 'She talked about "the other baby", used to ask about "the other baby". Me and Maureen, we'd have given anything . . .' He stopped talking for a moment and looked at his wife. 'But those that don't care for them can just have them like shelling peas.' He was reaching for his anger again.

Maureen Dutton sat in calm silence, and Barraclough thought that she looked like a porcelain figure, like a doll, like someone whose reality had been hollowed out of her from the inside, leaving no visible damage, no wounds, leaving . . . nothing.

*   *   *

Kath Walker, Ashley Reid's aunt, greeted Barraclough and Corvin with a grudging, 'You'd better come in,' and sat unsmiling as they explained what they wanted. There was no point, she told them, in their asking about her husband. 'Bryan and I separated ten years ago,' she said, in answer to Corvin's query. 'We're divorced now. I haven't seen him since two Christmases ago. He drinks,' she added. 'Our Michelle keeps in touch. He sees her sometimes. When he's short of cash.' Barraclough looked at the woman's severe face, her carefully groomed hair, the way she sat upright and rigid, and wondered what it would have been like to be delivered to this woman at the age of four, young, bewildered, vulnerable. 'There was nothing but trouble from the word go,' she said, when Corvin asked her about Ashley and his brother, Simon. 'Not surprising, really. Bryan's sister, Carolyn, she was into all that hippie stuff. Drugs. Music. "Free love", they called it.'

'But you and your husband took the kids in,' Corvin said, as if acknowledging the generosity of the gesture.

Kath Walker looked at him stonily. 'We were family. Those kids needed somewhere. "Just for a few months," Carolyn said. "Give me a chance to settle in my job, get us somewhere to live. Just a few months." Next thing we know, she's gone back to America. Bryan and me, we couldn't have another, so we thought . . . But those two . . .'

'What was the problem, Mrs Walker?' Barraclough thought she had seen a gentler side to the woman under those words.

'Bad blood.' Kath Walker's mouth snapped shut.

'Bad blood?' The woman obviously hadn't liked her sister-in-law, but what about the father, what about Phillip Reid?

'It was in his family,' she said. 'In Bryan's family. They all went wrong. Simon, the older lad, he was wrong in the head. We couldn't have that, not with our Michelle. He'd just look at you, like you weren't there, and he'd stare at things in this creepy way he had. He was always doing the same thing, over and over and over. And then if you got him mad . . .' She looked at the two officers. 'They put him away.'

'When was that, Mrs Walker?' McCarthy had said he wanted Simon Reid locating.

She squinted her eyes, calculating. 'She, Carolyn, brought them to us in 1984. That was when it was, 1984. Once we knew she wasn't coming back. We couldn't manage Simon.'

'So what happened to Simon. Is he still in care?' Barraclough had not been able to locate Simon in the records.

'He was only there for a few weeks, then Bryan's mother took him on. He went to live with her.' She waited, then added, 'I don't know any more than that. I had my hands full with the other lad. And Bryan.' Simon's grandmother was Catherine Walker, she told them, but she had been in a home for several years. Kath Walker had no knowledge of who had taken Simon in after this. Barraclough sighed, thinking of the paperwork ahead.

'So what happened to Ashley in the end?' Barraclough tried not to make the question confrontational. Their information said that Simon Reid was autistic. Could she have coped with an autistic nephew, along with a second, younger child, a child of her own, an alcoholic husband and a pub to run? She didn't think she could have done it. Who was she to judge this woman?

'He was trouble, too. We were watching him, in case he went the same way as Simon. Bryan wasn't having that. Bryan always wanted a lad, but Ashley, he wasn't a proper lad, not like we wanted. He wanted his brother and he wanted his mum. "You'll have to want," I told him in the end. She left him. She didn't want him and the sooner he got that sorted, the better.' She met Barraclough's expression head on. 'It's not always best to be soft with kids. Sometimes they need to know the worst. Ashley needed to know his mum wasn't coming back.'

Barraclough nodded. Maybe the woman was right, but there were ways and there were ways. 'So what happened with Ashley in the end?'

'Well, you know about that.' Kath Walker didn't drop her gaze. 'We had to let him go. He was wrong in the head, like his brother. Bad blood.'

'How do you mean, Mrs Walker?' Corvin's voice sounded cheerful in Barraclough's ears.

'It's that family,' the woman said. 'It came out with Bryan in drink. And his mother, she's not been able to look after herself for years. Senile.' She said it like an obscenity.

'What about Carolyn? What about their mother? What happened to her?' The social services hadn't managed to track her down, but their resources were limited, Barraclough knew. Had she been in touch with her brother or her sister-in-law? Had she at least tried to find out what had happened to her children?

Kath Walker's face was set and cold. 'We had a couple of letters, after she went back,' she said.

Corvin tried again. 'And nothing after that?' Kath Walker shook her head. 'You don't have a current address for her?'

Again, the head shake. 'I gave the last address we had to the social.'

'What about her husband?' Corvin asked. 'Phillip Reid.'

Kath Walker sniffed and raised her eyebrows. 'Husband,' she said.

'But they were married,' Corvin said.

'Oh, yes, but only because they had to, for him to get into the country. She had work, but he didn't. Passports and things. He was off as soon as she was expecting again. Bryan had to send her money. I ask you!'

'Do you know where he is now?'

The woman shook her head. 'No, and I don't want to. Nor did Carolyn. I said, "What about their father?" when she asked us to take the lads. "He doesn't care," she said. "I've got to do this myself."' She looked at Corvin and Barraclough. 'And before you ask, the answer's no, I haven't heard from him since.'

Polly Andrews had said that Emma stowed her belongings, or some of them, in the roof space when she was sharing a room with Sophie Dutton. The original search of Sophie's room had not included the roof space – the search team had found no access to it. Now they were back, to see if Emma's missing things were still up there, ignored or forgotten by the cleaners.

The attic room looked dustier, less bare and empty than Corvin remembered it. The smears from the fingerprint powder were still on the windows and the carpet and mattress looked dirty. The housing officer looked round and clicked his tongue. 'The standard of cleaning gets worse each year,' he said. 'OK, access to the roof space.' He indicated the wardrobe against the dormer wall, and two of the search team braced themselves against it, staggering a bit as it moved more easily than they expected. 'It's only cheap, pre-fab stuff,' the housing officer said apologetically. 'Right.' He pointed to a small, vertical trap that was flush with the wall and hard to see. 'We sealed off the roof space in the other room, but this trap-door provides access where it's needed. Private landlords use these as fire exits – you used to be able to get right along the row through the roofs – but that's illegal now.'

Corvin nodded, and one of the team unlocked the trap and it fell onto the floor. A puff of dusty air blew out. He shone his torch into the darkness, illuminating the sloping roof, the beams with insulation fibre running between them, and saw, stuffed round the corner for ease of collection, a suitcase and a rolled-up sleeping bag. He reached in and pulled them out. A torn piece of paper fell onto the floor. Corvin looked the case over. There were no identifying marks on the outside, no address or name label. The case was blue, a weekend case, plastic, scuffed, but not too heavy, suggesting it was full of clothes or something light.

He opened the suitcase. As he'd suspected, it contained clothes: a pair of jeans, a couple of sweatshirts clearly in need of a wash, and some towels, also dirty. A pair of worn trainers were stuffed into the bottom of the case. These weren't Emma's clothes, or Sophie's. These belonged to a man and, judging by the size of the trainers, a big man, or a tall man at any rate. At the bottom of the case there was a zip-lock bag. The bag was stuffed full, and Corvin could see through the transparent surface that there were bundles of pills wrapped in plastic bags inside, and a notebook with a red cover. Well, well. Emma's stockroom. An analysis of her supply might lead to their supplier.

Carefully, he pulled out the notebook and flicked through the pages. He was hoping for a list of customers, or something else that would give them more of a lead into Emma's drugs life, but most of the pages had been torn out. Those that were left were blank. He looked inside the cover. Under the pencilled-in price was the name S. DUTTON, and the address, 14, CARLETON ROAD, then, in larger figures, the year, 1999. He remembered Polly Andrews saying, 'Sophie wants to be a writer.' This could have been her diary. But she, or someone else, had made sure that no one was going to read it. He picked up the piece of paper from the floor. It was a small piece, lined, ripped across. Closely written words in blue ink: *. . . and the park was beautiful. We talked, really talked, for the first time. We talked about the river and the trees and the birds . . .* The writing ran off the edge of the torn page *. . . just like me. I didn't know, I really didn't know . . .* Corvin shrugged. It meant nothing to him. 'Get forensics to go over this lot,' he said. 'And get copies of this' – he indicated the paper – 'straight away.'

One of the team called him over. The man had found marks on the carpet that they'd missed last time, marks of a piece of furniture that had stood there for some time, leaving its impression indelibly etched on the cheap carpet. This was obviously the place where the wardrobe had once stood. Corvin had wondered why, if Emma and Sophie used the roof space regularly for storage, the wardrobe had been pulled across it. He looked at the carpet where the wardrobe now stood. The carpet didn't have the same, single set of deep marks. Instead, there was a larger flattened area, as though the cupboard had been regularly moved and put back not quite in the same place.

It was gone half past three by the time McCarthy's car pulled up outside the Fielding house. Jane Fielding had known Sophie for nearly a year and Emma for several months. There were things McCarthy needed to know that maybe she could tell him. He wasn't unhappy with the timing. He wanted a chance to talk to Lucy. He wasn't sure what he was going to say – he didn't have a lot to do with children. He thought about his occasional – very occasional – visits to his sister's, when he became this stranger called Uncle Steve, and found himself the object of the curiosity of his nephew and niece who, disturbingly, carried traces of his sister and his mother in their faces. He played football, he bought presents and they seemed to like him. He remembered how strange it felt when four-year-old Jenny had thrown her arms round his neck and told him she loved him. 'Cupboard love,' Sheila had observed, drily. She had no illusions about her brother.

Brooke, as senior investigating officer, had decided that Lucy would not make a credible witness in court; McCarthy was in full agreement with that. Thirty seconds' innocent prattle about monsters and the defence would have a field day, but an informal, unofficial chat might just give them some pointers. She was, apparently, a bright child. Her story of monsters, of 'the Ash Man', of 'Tamby' interested him and frustrated him. He wanted someone to translate those stories into terms he could understand. He wanted to find out if all of this existed only in Lucy's imagination, or if she was trying to tell them something they needed to know, only they couldn't hear her.

'Have you noticed,' he said to Barraclough, 'that there seem to be children involved round the edges of this case?' He wanted Barraclough's perspective.

She thought. 'There's Lucy, of course, and then that earlier child Sandra Allan had. And Sophie Dutton was adopted.'

'Have you completed that search? For the first child?'

Barraclough shook her head. 'I'm getting back onto it tomorrow,' she said. They had both done the arithmetic. Sophie Dutton had been born in 1980. Sandra Allan had been pregnant sometime in the late 1970s. Sophie Dutton could have been that missing child, and if so, it would explain the bond that had apparently developed between her and Emma. And had Sandra's death been the push that finally drove her away?

As they pulled into Carleton Road, McCarthy saw that Lucy Fielding was sitting on the steps outside number twelve. She was tugging at the lace on her roller boot. He shelved the matter of Sophie Dutton. He wanted to talk to Lucy.

Lucy looked up as he opened the car door, and he saw a blank watchfulness come over her face.

Suzanne listened to the rattle of Lucy's skates on the paved yard, on the asphalt of the passage and on the flagstones at the front. Jane was shut away in the room she used for a studio, working, and Suzanne was keeping an eye on Lucy as she played in the yard and on the street. Using the sound as a guide to Lucy's whereabouts, she wandered through to the front room, worrying at a ragged nail with her teeth and thinking again about what Jane had told her, about someone else, about another body in the park. She had listened to the local news the evening before but there was nothing. The paper, that morning, had carried a brief, uninformative story. She could see Ashley's face in her mind, the way his eyes came alive as he saw her, so like the way Adam's used to light up as she came through the door from school or, later, from work. *Suzanne, Suzanne, look what I've done! Look at me, Suzanne! Listen to me, Suzanne!*

She realized she had let her attention drift, and she could no longer hear the rattle of Lucy's skates on the paving stones. She looked out of the window and saw that the police van that had been outside the student house all morning was gone, but two squad cars were parked higher up the road. She'd been aware of disturbance for most of the day. The houses were all linked, and noise travelled easily from one to the other.

Lucy was outside on the pavement, she saw with relief. But she was talking to someone. Suzanne squinted through the branches of the cotoneaster that grew raggedly in her front garden. McCarthy! What was he doing here? He was leaning against his car, and he and Lucy seemed to be involved in some kind of discussion. Was he supposed to talk to her without Jane? Suzanne tried to see what was happening. Tina Barraclough was in the car, her chin on her arm in the open window as she listened to what Lucy was saying. As Suzanne watched, she saw McCarthy lift his foot up and point to his shoe. Lucy responded by lifting her roller-bladed foot and apparently demonstrating some quality of her skates that McCarthy had been asking about.

They were talking about skating. It seemed so incongruous, somehow. Since their encounter in the coffee bar, McCarthy had grown in her mind into a figure like her father, someone who filled her with an undefined unease. But as she watched him amiably chatting with Lucy about skating, he looked friendly and approachable. He knelt down and tightened the lace on one of Lucy's boots, talking to her as he did so. Lucy nodded, looking solemn.

Suzanne thought about calling Jane, then she decided it would be quicker if she went out herself and saw to what was happening. She took a deep breath and went through the side door into the passage, and then out into the bright sun of the road. McCarthy and Lucy both looked at her, and she was disconcerted to see the same sudden blanking of their faces. She was used to Lucy, who always responded to the new behind a closed and uncommitted mask, while she decided how to react. In McCarthy, she found it unnerving.

He stood up as she came onto the pavement. 'Suzanne,' he said, by way of a greeting. His tone was neutral.

'Did you want something?' She kept her voice cool, aware of the contrast between her middle-class accents and the northern ones around her.

'I was showing him my skates,' Lucy said, apparently deciding that Suzanne's intervention was benign. 'His skates had the wheels in the wrong place so he kept falling over.'

'Spent most of the time landing on my arse,' McCarthy agreed with a companionable grin at Lucy. Lucy giggled.

'You can have a go with mine,' she offered. Suzanne was surprised. Lucy was usually very self-contained and unwilling to make overtures of friendship to people she didn't know.

'Not with my big feet,' McCarthy said. 'Anyway, I've got further to fall now.' Lucy nodded, seeing the sense in this. McCarthy suddenly turned his attention to Suzanne. His face was impassive again. 'I'm here to see Miss Fielding,' he said. 'She doesn't seem to be in. Are you looking after . . .' He nodded at Lucy who was showing off on her skates, doing turns and twirls.

'I'm . . . yes. Jane's in, but she's working. She won't hear the door. You'll need to—'

He interrupted her. 'It's not very bright having her out here with no one looking out for her after what happened on Friday.'

Suzanne flushed. She had remembered, as he joked with Lucy, how much she'd liked him that morning they'd talked in the coffee bar, but now her misgivings came flooding back. 'I was watching her from the window,' she said, aware that she sounded defensive, but also feeling that his implied criticism was unfair.

He was about to say something but, before he could respond, Lucy came skimming up and brought herself to a stop, staggering slightly as she'd been moving faster than she usually did, to impress McCarthy with her skill. 'It's easy,' she said.

'You're a good skater, Lucy,' said Barraclough from the car window, joining in the conversation for the first time. Lucy gave her a closed look and declined to comment.

McCarthy crouched down again in front of Lucy and said, 'Remember what I said, Lucy, OK?'

Lucy nodded, her face serious. McCarthy touched a finger to the end of her nose, and she smiled at him. Suzanne was struck again by the rapport that seemed to have sprung up between them. She watched, thinking of Joel, and thinking how much better it would be for Lucy to have had a father who would fight her corner – McCarthy's criticism had made her angry, but it was motivated by a genuine concern, and a valid one. And how much better it would have been to have had a father who could have engaged her in that gentle humour, been interested in what she was doing. For a moment, she wanted to confide in him, tell him about her worries for Ashley, about her problems with the Alpha Centre. Then her father's patrician features formed in her mind, and his voice, *Can't you do anything right?* in those tones of weary exasperation. And she saw Ashley's pale face (*Listen to me!*) under the water, in the dam, cold, silent, dead.

McCarthy was aware of Suzanne Milner as he reinforced his warning to Lucy. *Be careful. Don't play alone.* He shouldn't have taken it out on her – he'd assumed that Lucy was playing, apparently unsupervised, a few hundred yards from the park where she'd vanished just a few days ago, but Suzanne's swift response to his arrival demonstrated that she had been doing as she said, watching out. Lucy skated off up the passageway. He nodded to Barraclough who went after her, and he stood up slowly, watching Suzanne. She looked as if she wanted to say something. She ran her hand through her hair, pushing it off her face. She looked at McCarthy uncertainly.

'What's wrong, Suzanne?' Her T-shirt was tight-fitting, and she obviously wasn't wearing anything underneath it. He was aware of a faint perfume that hung around her. He kept his face impassive, his eyes on hers.

'Nothing,' she said, after a brief pause. There obviously was something, though. He could see her trying to work out the words. He waited. For a moment, he thought she was going to turn away and go back in, when she touched his arm. 'Steve . . .'

'What is it?' She was biting her lip, looking undecided.

'Jane said that you'd found someone else in the park.' He said nothing; waited. 'Another . . . Someone else.' She didn't want to spell it out.

'Yes.' Suddenly, McCarthy was alert. What was her interest in this, apart from ordinary curiosity? This didn't look like curiosity. He remembered that he'd planned to look her up, to see if there was anything on record that would explain her contradictory attitude. He'd do that when he got back to the station. He leant his arm against the car and looked at her. 'She didn't know who it was, or anything. If it was a . . . man or a woman. I just wondered . . .'

McCarthy knew the information would be in the late edition of the local paper today. It would be in the nationals tomorrow and on the news. There was no reason not to answer her questions, but he wanted to know why it was so important to her. Her hands were clasping and unclasping – a nervous tic that he'd noticed before. She looked down, following his eyes, then wrapped her arms round her waist. 'I just wondered, was it . . .' She was having trouble controlling her voice. It caught, and she looked away, biting her lip.

138

She took a deep breath. 'Was it Ashley Reid?' Now she was looking straight at him with the intent stare of someone who has asked a question and knows the answer is something she doesn't want to hear. She knew, McCarthy thought, that he was going to say yes.

He almost gave her the answer she expected, just to see what she would do, what she would tell him in the moment of shock, but instead, he shook his head slowly. 'No. It wasn't Ashley Reid.'

She relaxed as the tension went out of her. 'I thought . . . I'm sorry.' She brushed her hand across her eyes. 'I thought it was him.'

And why the fuck, McCarthy wondered, would she think that?

McCarthy left Barraclough to deal with Jane Fielding once they had broken the news about Sophie. He listened to the sounds of tea being made, Barraclough's calm voice engaging her in conversation, casual and informal. McCarthy had formed the opinion that Jane Fielding's vague dreaminess was actually a useful shield for a shrewd mind. He hoped that Barraclough might be able to get behind that shield while shock and distress kept the woman distracted.

He went to find Lucy who had stayed in the back room as they talked to her mother. Jane Fielding didn't miss that. 'Don't tell her,' she warned. McCarthy shook his head.

Lucy was sitting at the table, and watched him expressionlessly as he came into the room. She wrapped a protective arm round something on the table in front of her. 'I'm doing drawing,' she offered by way of an overture, and McCarthy took this as an invitation to sit at the table with her.

'Can I see?' he asked.

She thought about it. 'This one isn't finished,' she said. 'You can see the others.' She slipped down from her chair and took his hand. 'Over here,' she said, pulling him across the room where drawings were pinned haphazardly to the wall. To McCarthy's eyes, they were a random jumble of childish scribbles, brightly coloured, depicting a world where flowers and animals were as tall as people, houses were boxes

139

that sprouted chimneys at awkward angles on their roofs, the sky was a blue line and the sun shone unremittingly. He looked at some of the captions for guidance. He had a feeling that Lucy would judge him by his response to her drawings. *My dog in the park. Flossy my cat in the park. Me and my sisters in the park.* 'You haven't got a dog,' he said.

She looked at him assessingly. 'I have *really*,' she said.

'Oh.' McCarthy needed a guide. This child fantasized, Alicia Hamilton had said so, but he had no way of telling the fantasy from the reality. 'Where is he?'

Lucy looked at him. 'My dog's a girl,' she said.

'My dog was a girl, too,' he said, feeling his way.

'What was her name?' Lucy looked interested.

'Sally,' McCarthy said.

Lucy nodded. 'That's a good name. My dog's called Sally too. She lives in the park.'

McCarthy felt as though he was stepping on cobwebs. 'What about your cat? And your sisters? Where do they live?'

'In the park.' She was a bit impatient with his slowness. 'We all live in the park. All of these are in the park,' and she encompassed the wall of drawings with an expansive gesture.

McCarthy looked again. *My dog in the park. Flossy my cat in the park. Me and my sisters in the park.* There was another one with writing on. He looked closely. *The Ash Man's brother in the park.* These were all pictures of people smiling, the blue sky above, the ubiquitous sun shining. These were happy pictures. There was one painting that was pinned in a corner away from the others. This one had no writing, there was no sun and no blue sky. The figure loomed at the front of the drawing, the face wasn't smiling. He looked down at Lucy. She was watching him carefully. He thought he knew who this might be, but he wasn't sure how she'd react if he got it wrong. He waited and, after a moment, she said, 'That's in the park too. That's the Ash Man.'

Q. *So where do you go in the evenings? When you go out?*
A. So . . . ?
Q. *In the evenings, Ashley. Where do you go?*
A. The Alpha.

140

Q. Yes, I know. But what do you do when you don't go to the Alpha?

A. To the Alpha . . .

Q. But when you don't go?

A. (Pause.)

Q. Ashley? I know you go to the Alpha some evenings. What do you do on the other evenings?

A. On the other evenings . . . er . . . (pause) . . . the flat.

Q. Where's that?

A. The garage. With . . . Lee's name on . . . and . . . em . . . so . . . sometimes, not now.

Q. What did you do last night?

A. Went to the place so . . . (Pause.)

Q. Which place, Ashley?

A. I'm telling you. It was in the park and so . . . she said she was going.

Q. Yes.

A. And I couldn't . . . (Pause.)

Q. But which place is this, Ashley? Is it the flat?

A. No . . . (Pause.) By the flats . . . em . . . Simon brings the stuff so . . . she didn't like that. (Pause.) It was loose, you see, and so didn't want . . .

Suzanne rubbed her eyes. She'd read the transcript of Ashley's tape right through, but she hadn't found much to help her. It was so hard to follow, because he didn't seem to understand her questions, muddled his responses, didn't seem to know what he was talking about himself half the time. She wished that she could re-interview him. At the time, she hadn't been bothered about the lack of clarity – she'd been pleased. It had been what she was looking for. Now, she didn't understand. Who was he talking about? Was he talking about his brother? Richard said that Ashley's brother was in care, was autistic. Ashley had never had a family. Maybe he fantasized like Lucy.

Where was this 'place'? Where was Ashley?

She knew he went to the Alpha Centre. Except, according to Richard, Ashley had done a runner. So he wasn't at the centre any more. Thanks to the confidentiality system at the

Alpha, she didn't even know where he lived, in which part of Sheffield she should start looking. Except . . . *Use the brain God gave you, Suzanne.* He obviously wasn't at home, or wherever he lived, because no one could find him. He couldn't be at his usual haunts, not the ones that everyone knew about.

So where would he go, that McCarthy couldn't find him, and Richard couldn't find him? And what made her think she could do any better? He would go to his friends, of course. Friends that no one would know about? She didn't know his friends. Who could he trust? Simon? She went back to the tape.

> A. On the other evenings . . . er . . . (pause) . . . the flat.
> Q. *Where's that?*
> A. The garage. With . . . Lee's name on . . . and . . . em . . . so . . . sometimes, not now.
> Q. *What did you do last night?*
> A. Went to the place so . . . (Pause.)

Or Lee. Lee from the Alpha Centre? The garage with Lee's name on? She thought. Lee and Ashley were sometimes together, she remembered. She'd seen them playing snooker, seen them smoking together outside, been struck by the contrast between Ashley's silence, his pale face and heavy dark hair, and Lee's noisy red-headed vigour. But she'd never thought of them as friends. Lee was quick and cruel. He tormented the slow-witted Dean, was quick to take advantage of others, as she knew to her cost. She remembered Ashley's warning. He'd seen the trap before she had. Richard had said that Ashley was a loner. Her observations seemed to confirm that. He'd also said that Ashley had learning difficulties. She'd taken that on board – Richard must know. But Lee wouldn't have any time for someone who wasn't bright, she was pretty sure of that.

She thought back over her encounters with Ashley. Apart from the interview, the tape, he'd shown signs of being withdrawn, but he hadn't struck her as being unintelligent. She wondered what she would have thought if Richard hadn't said anything. A picture came into her mind. She remembered sitting in the coffee bar one evening, after the programme was finished for the day, watching Lee challenging Richard at snooker. There had been an interested and partisan crowd round the table. She had stayed back, observing. She'd looked across the room and caught Ashley's eye. He'd been watching her and, just for a moment, she saw a speculative, almost calculating light in his eyes. Then he'd given her his gentle smile, and turned back to the game. She hadn't thought much about it at the time, but, remembering it now, she was convinced. Ashley wasn't subnormal, or special needs, or whatever label had been pinned on him. Ashley was perfectly intelligent. So why did he hide it? She felt frustrated. She hadn't got enough information, and had no access to any more.

But she did! Richard. She was pretty sure he felt bad about what had happened. He'd tried to give her some warning, and he'd been very uncomfortable when he'd told her what was happening. She could use that. She needed a reason to contact him. He was interested in local history. They'd talked about the village where he lived, Beighton, one of the old communities that had been engulfed by the urban sprawl of Sheffield. He wanted to know something about the history of his house. 'I keep meaning to look it up in the archives,' he'd said, 'when I've got time.'

'I'm down in the stacks at the uni all the time,' she'd said. 'I'll look up one of the old maps for you.' One of those promises you make and never get round to. But he wasn't to know that. If she tracked him down at the university, gave him the map, pretended that she'd found it before the trouble, he'd feel even more guilty. He'd feel he had to talk, and then she could ask him about Ashley – legitimate questions about the diagnosis of learning difficulties, and then some casual ones about Lee. Lee could find Ashley for her. She was suddenly convinced. She looked at her watch. It was almost five. She could go up to the library now, look up the map and get it copied. She needed to pick up her tapes from the department as well. Ashley's tape, at any rate. The transcript wasn't enough – it wasn't finished, and anyway, she wanted to listen to it again. If she took it out of its case, no one would notice it was missing.

She was just dumping her keys and her purse in her bag when there was a knock at the door, and Jane came in, looking pale and upset. Suzanne realized that in her relief about Ashley, she'd forgotten everything else. 'What's wrong?' she said. 'What is it?'

Jane gripped her hand. 'Suzanne, the body in the park.' Suzanne's breathing tightened. Surely McCarthy wouldn't have lied to her? 'It's – I don't know how I'm going to tell Lucy. It's Sophie. They found Sophie dead in the park.'

Suzanne felt numb. Something that had seemed only incidentally, accidentally, connected to her life, suddenly became central, focused.

'Sophie? Your Sophie? Are they sure?'

Jane nodded. 'Her parents identified her this morning.' But Jane hadn't come round for comfort, or just to tell Suzanne the news. 'They want me to look at some pictures, of people that Sophie might have known. I saw the people she went round with. I want to help. I want to do it as soon as possible. I want them to catch him.' Jane's usual air of vague detachment had gone. She was focused the way she focused on her work, on her daughter. 'I want to go with them now. Suzanne, could you look after Lucy for me?'

Suzanne still felt frozen with shock. She heard the words as if they were coming from a distance. 'Yes. Of course. I was going to walk up to the library. She wouldn't mind spending half an hour in the stacks, would she?'

'That would be perfect. I don't want her near the news or anything. I want to tell her myself.' Jane's lips were compressed the way Lucy's were when she was concentrating, when she was expressing disapproval.

'Don't worry.' Suzanne ushered Jane out of the door, and watched as she got into the car with McCarthy. She noticed that Tina Barraclough wasn't with them, and found herself wondering if Jane would enjoy McCarthy's undivided attention as much as she had said she would. She looked back up the road towards the student house. The police cars were still there, and now a university housing department van.

Sophie. Sophie wasn't a dead woman in the park, a murder victim. She was the happy-go-lucky student who looked after Lucy, who'd been more like a big sister to Lucy than a carer.

She realized that she hadn't been surprised when the complex, troubled Emma had come so seriously to grief. But Sophie was happy and full of life. It was ridiculous that Sophie was dead. That was the word that kept coming into her mind. Ridiculous. No one had the right to take that life away from her. *It's all we get,* Suzanne pleaded to the figure, dark and faceless, who seemed to lurk in the back of her mind. *It's all we get.*

People moving like random particles across the forecourt, weaving in and out of the straight lines of the cars, parked in rows. Unpredictable movement, no order, no pattern. People bumping into him looking at him, expectant. Say, 'Sorry.' *Can't tell, can't tell.*

Simon could understand the laboratory where the bottles and jars were ordered and labelled and what they contained was predictable in what it would do and the way it would behave. He could understand the library, once he was in among the shelves and the books all in rows, all with a place where they belonged.

But sometimes, whispering and laughing and people-sound interfering with the patterns in his head. A face. 'Hi, Simon!' Fellow student. Say, 'Hello.' 'Fancy a coffee?' Coffee, people, conversation, no pattern, no order, nothing to understand. Say, 'Can't just now. Thanks.' Lost them! Looking, looking. Just a moment ago, over by the shelves, over by the door. *Where? Where?*

There.

Lucy sat at the computer terminal and wriggled herself into a more comfortable position. Suzanne was just round the corner, looking at books, books that were huge and had to be lifted off the shelves with two hands. They were dusty and had made Lucy sneeze. 'You'd better keep out of the way of this dust,' Suzanne had said, and she had shown Lucy how to search on the computers. 'You just stay here,' she said.

But the computers were boring. She looked round her. The shelves were all around her, towering up to the ceiling. Everywhere you looked, there were shelves, *secret shelves*, Lucy thought. You could get lost in the secret shelves. Suzanne told her, 'Don't go far. If you do get lost, follow the yellow line' – she showed Lucy a yellow line on the floor – 'until you get to the door, then wait for me. I'll come and find you.'

It was like the story about the monster in the maze. The *minotaur*. Lucy had a picture of a man fighting the minotaur. She slipped off her stool and crouched down at the bottom of the shelf, looking underneath it. You could just see through to the other side, and there were more shelves and more shelves. She squirmed along on her stomach, trying to see. There were Suzanne's feet. She was standing on tiptoe. She must be reaching up to a high shelf. She didn't know Lucy was watching. Lucy wriggled further along.

It was very quiet in the library, in the *stacks*. 'There's no one else down here usually, not now the exams are over,' Suzanne had said. 'So no one will mind if you go on the computer.' Suzanne had taken her into the library up some steps. There were lots of people there. Then they'd gone through a small door and down some stairs, and there were all the secret shelves, miles of secret shelves, but Suzanne had said, 'Come on,' and they'd gone to another door and down more steps. The door had swung shut behind them with a *boom*. There was another door at the bottom of the steps. 'Come on,' Suzanne had said. That door had closed like a whisper. And it was so quiet, Lucy's ears felt squashed, and the air felt old and dry.

More shelves, more secret shelves. Lucy had run round them, laughing, wanting to make a noise, and then she didn't know where she was. Everywhere she looked, there were just shelves. In front of her, rows and rows, and in the distance it got dark. Behind her, just the same. She looked to where the door was, but there were just shelves again. Then Suzanne was there, and told her about the yellow line. Lucy thought that maybe she wanted to go home. 'Does Michael like the secret shelves?' she asked.

Suzanne had smiled. 'That's a good name. Yes. He likes playing with the computer. I'll show you.' She showed Lucy that each of the shelves had lights. 'You can turn them on if you need them, but turn them off afterwards.' Lucy didn't want to go home then, not if Michael liked the shelves. And now she did like them, now she understood about the yellow line. It was like the minotaur again. She could kill the monster and then follow the yellow line to escape. She looked down the rows of shelves into the darkness. Not the monsters. The monsters were in the park.

She got braver, and walked down a whole row of shelves. For a minute, she was lost again, and then there was the yellow line, and she found her way back. She didn't want to go too far, though, not into the bit that was dark. She could play Grandmother's Footsteps; she could pretend that the seekers were tiptoeing round the shelves, and she had to see them, to look at them to make them stop. If she didn't see them, they could tiptoe right up to her and grab her from behind.

She heard a faint *boom*, and then it was quiet again. She tiptoed round the shelf. Looked. *Got you!* Then she ducked behind and hid. They followed her round the shelves, and she ducked round again and caught them moving. *Got you, too!* It was harder to see now, because she was further away from Suzanne's light. She didn't turn her own light on, because then the seekers would know where to find her. There was another light now, somewhere through the shelves, across the dark bit. She could hide and scramble her way across to the other light, then she could watch and catch them when they tried to follow.

The other light went out. Then came on again a bit nearer. Grandmother's Footsteps. Sometimes, in the playground, you could hear them moving, and you could turn round and say, 'Got you!' And they had to go back to the beginning, but sometimes you couldn't hear them at all, and then you had to guess, and when you turned round they were all as still as anything, but they were all a bit nearer, a bit closer,

147

but you couldn't see them move. They couldn't move if you watched them.

She could hear one of them now, soft feet, *pad, pad, pad,* getting closer. She peered round the shelf. No one. Not there. She moved across a row and into the next line of shelves, moving quietly now, listening. *Pad, pad, pad,* getting nearer, going slowly. They moved slowly when they weren't close, they moved slowly so that they could stop or hide if you turned round. When they got near, they moved quickly, *padpadpad,* to get you before you could move.

She crouched down and peered under the shelves. Nothing. *Pad, pad, pad.* Soft and slow. She ducked round the next shelf in her game and whispered, 'Got you,' but the game didn't work any more. Her whisper seemed to stir the dry air, rustle among the shelves. The footsteps stopped, started again. *Pad, pad.* Stopped. Came closer. *Pad, pad, pad.* Lucy slid round the next shelf, quiet now. She could hear breathing in the dark. She looked under the shelf. She could see feet now, in those soft trainers that made no noise. The trainers were dirty, covered with dried mud. The feet turned, stepped, hesitated. Lucy held her breath. She wanted to cough, she could feel her chest getting tight. It was all right, it was just a game. She stayed still in the dim light. *Tamby?* she said in her mind. *Like a mouse,* he said.

She turned her head, looking along the ground. No yellow line. Slowly, she turned back. No yellow line. She wanted to run among the shelves as fast as she could, run away from the muddy trainers that would come after her *padpadpad,* closer and closer. Then the feet turned again and began to move along the shelves, towards the end of the row, towards the aisle leading to the next row where Lucy lay hiding. Her chest tightened again, and she gave a wheezing cough. She couldn't help it.

Suzanne tied the ribbon on the last map book. Sod's law, of course. The thing you want is always in the last book. It was her own fault for not taking time to use the catalogues. She'd been trying to be quick for Lucy's sake. Lucy! She was being very quiet. 'Lucy,' she said, and went to the aisle where the computer terminals were. Nothing. No one there. She felt irritated. The scope for one of Lucy's hiding games was immense down here, she suddenly realized, and if Lucy was annoyed enough with her to subject her to a full-scale hide, then she was in for an uncomfortable hour.

But she didn't know that Lucy was hiding. Suppose she had gone upstairs and got lost? She decided to check the door, see if Lucy was waiting there as they had agreed. Maybe Lucy had wandered off and used the yellow line to find the way out. She checked her watch. It had only been about twenty minutes since she last saw her.

Lucy wasn't by the door. Suzanne felt uneasy. She ran her options through her mind. If Lucy was angry, was hiding, then calling would be a bad move, because it would tell Lucy that Suzanne was looking for her, was maybe worried, and that the game was worth playing. If, on the other hand, Lucy had wandered out of the stacks, then she needed finding at once. 'Lucy,' she called. 'Shall we go and get some sweets?' Lucy wasn't allowed sweets. Jane would kill her, but Suzanne reckoned it was a price worth paying to flush Lucy out. Silence. 'Lucy?' she tried again. Nothing.

She'd better go and get the librarian, get the campus security on the job. She felt nervous, but at the same time convinced that Lucy hadn't gone far. For all her hiding games and her monsters, Lucy was a sensible child. 'Lucy!' The still, dry air mocked her with silence. There was a sense of falling dust. She needed to go and get help, but something made her reluctant to leave this level, to leave the stacks where she was sure that Lucy was, somewhere. Then she heard a sound across the stack, coming from the far shelves. A cough, just one, but it sounded tight, asthmatic. *Oh, God! Lucy!*

'Lucy!' she called. 'I'm coming.' She grabbed her bag that had Lucy's inhaler in it and, as she ran, dodging among the shelves, trying to pinpoint the place the sound had come from, she heard someone else moving through the stack, soft sounds moving fast. She ran up the far aisle, looking down each row. It had been from here, she was sure. She heard the muffled *boom* of the door, and again, and then she was looking down at Lucy who was crouched on the floor, reaching for breath. Suzanne whipped out the inhaler and held it to the child's mouth. She heard the hiss of the release, and then Lucy was breathing more easily, then more easily still. She sat up against the shelf, and looked at Suzanne warily. Suzanne waited.

'It was a monster,' Lucy said.

'What was? Lucy, it was asthma. Why did you go so far?' Her fright was making her feel angry. Lucy looked at her, her face closing into stubborn blankness. Suzanne tried to get her mind back on track. 'I was just worried, Lucy, when I couldn't find you.'

Lucy thought about this, and relented. 'It was Grandmother's Footsteps,' she said. 'And the monster made me have asthma. But it was all right, because of Tamby. The monster's gone now.'

As they made their way across the campus towards the students' union, Suzanne's eye was caught by someone moving quickly away from the library entrance. A tall, dark-haired figure. She stared. It surely couldn't be . . . The figure turned for just a moment, and Ashley's eyes caught hers across the car park. Then he was gone. She made to follow, then looked down at Lucy who was still pale, still short of breath. For a moment, the frustration almost overwhelmed her, then she managed a smile. 'Come on, Lucy,' she said. 'Let's get you a drink.' And turned away.

10

Thursday morning, McCarthy's phone rang as he was reading through Paul Lynman's statement again. Polly Andrews had confirmed Lynman's story in its essential details, apparently without any prompting. And a supply of pills – almost pure MDMA if the preliminary reports from the lab were correct – had been found concealed in the roof space in Carleton Road. However, Lynman had left 14, Carleton Road to move in with Polly Andrews, a fact that neither of them had thought to mention. And the forensic evidence from the suitcase and the zip-lock bag containing the pills had been interesting. Emma Allan's prints were there, which was to be expected if Lynman's story was true. But two other people had left prints on those bags. Neither set belonged to anyone who was identifiable through police records, but one set matched the nameless set found in Shepherd Wheel. They needed to get Lynman and Andrews in again and put them through the wringer.

The phone was an unwelcome distraction. He picked it up. 'McCarthy.'

It was Anne Hays, the pathologist. 'I wanted to talk to your boss, but he's in a meeting,' she said. 'I thought this had better not wait. I've been doing some more tests on the blood from the Allan case. The samples from the father.' McCarthy made an affirmative noise. Those samples hadn't led anywhere in the end. They had found no traces of Dennis Allan in Shepherd Wheel. 'Partly, I was following a hunch . . .'

McCarthy wondered if it was a characteristic of pathologists that they never got to the point. 'And?'

'This is just based on blood group, you understand. The DNA will take longer – that's with the lab now.'

'Yes.' McCarthy understood that.

'Well, Emma's blood group is O. Dennis Allan is AB. I went back into the records to look at the mother's blood group. We did the PM here. She was A.'

'Which means?' McCarthy thought he knew what this meant, but he wanted it in the black and white this woman never seemed willing to provide.

'It means, Inspector,' she said briskly, 'that Dennis Allan was not Emma's father.'

Half an hour later, Brooke, called from his meeting by McCarthy, was in his office with Anne Hays and McCarthy himself. He polished his glasses as he listened to the pathologist outline her findings again. 'I think it must have been at the back of my mind,' she said. 'It was only a couple of months ago we did the PM on Sandra Allan. It was just a hunch.'

'Steve?'

McCarthy had been running this new information through his mind, matching it up with what they already had. 'There was a major row between Emma and her mother, then between Dennis Allan and his wife. Something happened that day to make her take an overdose – a serious one. Suppose he just found out. Suppose Emma found out that her dad wasn't her dad . . .' He looked at Brooke and shook his head. 'I don't know how. But if she did, she has a major row with Sandra and leaves home. It was as serious as that – she left home and didn't go to her mother's funeral.'

'She didn't forgive her father, either,' Brooke said.

'She was seventeen.' Anne Hays had a seventeen-year-old daughter of her own. 'It's a very judgemental age, very black and white. To err is human, to forgive is not our policy.'

Brooke gave a rueful grimace. His own daughter was fifteen. 'Then there's the Sophie Dutton complication. Was she Sandra Allan's child?'

'DC Barraclough's looking into that,' McCarthy said.

Brooke nodded. 'Let me know as soon as she finds something. Anyway, Emma and her parents have a massive row.

She didn't go back. Then there was the row between Allan and his wife. Either he knew and was angry she'd let the daughter find out, or he didn't know – until then.' McCarthy thought about Allan's demeanour during the interview. He had been hostile, evasive. McCarthy was certain the man had been lying about something. 'He was ashamed of what he found out?' Brooke suggested. 'He felt a fool – having another man's child landed on him?' It was possible. It didn't account for the fact that, to both McCarthy and Brooke, he had looked guilty, not ashamed. 'Is there anything to link him to the killing? To Shepherd Wheel?'

McCarthy shook his head. 'There was a lot of useful stuff came out of Shepherd Wheel – fingerprints, hair, fibres – but none of it links with Allan.'

'So what are we saying?' Brooke asked. 'We're saying he might have killed his daughter because she wasn't his? Wouldn't it have been the wife he went for?' Sandra Allan's death had apparently been accidental. It had resulted from an overdose, an overdose she had taken after her husband went to work, taking pills she had collected from the local pharmacy after he had left. But there had been no suicide note.

If Dennis Allan had killed the girl he had thought was his daughter, what was the connection with the death of Sophie Dutton? Sandra Allan had had a child before Emma was born. Was Sophie Dutton Emma's half-sister? And if she was, how did this connection link with her death? What about the drug connection? And what about Ashley Reid?

The information gave Brooke enough to bring Dennis Allan in for questioning and to have another look at the flat, this time in search of information about the Allans' marriage. Barraclough sat at her desk, working with the team going through bags of papers retrieved from the flat. She had a photograph album in front of her, and was making notes of names and dates, friends and contacts from the early days of Allan's career. 'Look at this,' she said to Kerry McCauley, the other DC in Corvin's group. She was looking at a photo of Dennis Allan from 1972. 'You could see what she saw in him.' A young man with auburn curls framing an attractive, slightly androgynous face leant against the wing of a sporty-looking car. There was another picture of the same man with what was clearly a rock group, very early seventies, a lot of feathers and psychedelia. Corvin came over to have a look. 'He was in the music business,' Barraclough said. 'It looks as if he was doing quite well – sports cars, flash clothes.'

'It's only a souped-up Cortina,' Corvin said. 'He wasn't doing that well. Everyone was in a rock group in those days.'

Most of the photos were of Allan with musicians. As she turned the pages, the same faces began appearing: Dennis Allan with a man and woman. The man had long hair, a moustache and beard; the woman, too, was very much of the times, her auburn hair parted in the middle and hanging like curtains round her face. Some of these pictures had names and dates written underneath them: VELVET, 1975; LINNET, DON G., '76. There was one picture of the trio on a stage, the men with guitars, the woman singing. Velvet. She remembered the photograph they'd found in Emma's room: —ELVET, 197— The photograph that Dennis Allan had claimed not to recognize. Velvet. It must be the name of a band. Don G.? Linnet? Nicknames? Other bands?

There were other pictures: Allan with a rather severe-looking woman, neat and elegant. There was a facial resemblance – was this Allan's mother? Several pictures of Allan with young women, in mini-skirts, flared jeans, all with long straight hair, heavily made-up eyes and pale lips. As far as Barraclough could tell, the same woman didn't appear twice. No sign of Sandra.

She turned the pages over. 'Velvet' appeared intermittently. There was no indication that they'd been particularly successful. They seemed to have done gigs in various parts of the country: Leeds, Summer '75, King's Head, Barnsley, '75, Castleford, March, '76. The line-up seemed to vary sometimes. In '76, a different figure appeared in the pictures, someone who, though he was dressed in the – she supposed you would call it slightly hippie – style that the others affected, looked much more like a business man, an entrepreneur. Had Velvet found a manager? This man was Pete, Peter. By the end of 1977, the woman with the auburn hair no longer appeared in the pictures. Barraclough looked closely. Here, for the first time, a slim, very pretty girl, a lot of wavy fair hair, standing with her arms round the two men. Sandra. She looked at the writing under the picture. All it said was Huddersfield, 1977.

This time, Dennis Allan wanted a solicitor. He proved more robust under questioning than McCarthy expected. He was quiet, polite and adamant. He insisted he knew nothing about his daughter's death. 'I loved Emma, Inspector,' he said, twisting a broken rubber band through his fingers. He flinched when McCarthy asked him about Emma's parentage. His face flushed and his eyelids reddened. 'I didn't know,' he said. 'I . . . That was what we had the row about. Emma knew. I don't know how, but she knew, and she just threw it at Sandy that day. I came back in the middle of it. She just told me, just like that.' He looked at McCarthy in appeal. 'I didn't want it to come out,' he said. 'Not now they're dead, not now Emma's dead and Sandy's dead.'

McCarthy pressed him, wanting to know the when and the how of Emma's awareness, but Allan shook his head. 'Sandy said that no one knew.' But someone had known, and that person had apparently told Emma. On his solicitor's advice, Allan said no more. 'My client has explained the omission in his earlier statement,' the solicitor said. 'I think anyone would find that explanation reasonable, Inspector McCarthy.' Similarly, he refused to answer questions about Sandra, other than to claim ignorance again of any earlier child. McCarthy wasn't satisfied, but he decided to leave it for the moment.

Allan couldn't tell them much about the people in the photographs. He insisted he couldn't remember their names. 'You were in a band with them for, what, three years, Mr Allan, and you're asking me to believe you can't remember their names?' McCarthy waited.

'I can't remember,' Allan insisted. 'It was twenty-five years ago. I started a band, I'd been playing guitar for quite a few gigs. Then I started Velvet with some of the musicians who were around. We didn't get a lot of work. It wasn't always the same people.' He looked at the photo with names written underneath it. 'That was Linnet,' he said, indicating the woman. He caught McCarthy's look. 'I think she was Lyn, she sang, so Linnet. Why not? It was the seventies. Everyone was using different names.' In the first flash of humour McCarthy had seen, he added, 'We had one singer who called herself Gandalf.' He shook his head when McCarthy asked him about the man. 'I don't remember,' he said. 'He was just Don G.'

He laughed rather bitterly when McCarthy asked him about the smartly dressed man who appeared in the photographs from 1976, Pete. 'That was our manager, our so-called manager,' he said. 'Peter Greenhead.' He apparently had no problems with that name. 'It was a rip-off from start to finish.' Greenhead had worked with the band for less than a year. At the end of that time, he owned the rights to the few songs they had written, and ended their contract, taking their singer with him. Shortly after that, Allan had left. He didn't know what had happened to the others.

McCarthy thought, his face expressionless. Velvet looked like a dead end, except for that photo in Emma's room. SO WHAT DO YOU THINK OF THIS? But that was probably to do with Sandra. McCarthy decided to leave it for now. The man was too calm, too collected. He needed a bit of time to brood, a bit of pressure, a bit of stress.

McCarthy had forgotten about his intention to look up the records – if any – on Suzanne Milner until late that morning, after Dennis Allan had left, promising to be available if he was needed. 'I'm not going anywhere,' he said. When McCarthy did remember, he wondered if it was worth spending the time. It was shaping up to be a long day with a lot of hassle. He wondered if there was any chance of him getting away on time. It was a beautiful sunny afternoon. Home wasn't a particularly attractive prospect – it felt like an extension of the office at the moment. He felt drawn to the idea

156

of an evening drive out into the Derbyshire countryside, a walk across the tops somewhere peaceful.

Milner wasn't a common name. It wouldn't take long. He logged on to the system. OK, if he was looking for something, how far back should he go? He realized he didn't know how old she was. He looked at his notes and did a quick calculation. Thirty. Obviously a respectable citizen now. She claimed to have lived in Sheffield all her life. Right. He decided to go back ten years, and keyed his query into the computer. He remembered the complications of married names and maiden names, and checked back in his notes. Right, she used her maiden name, Milner. Her married name was Harrison. He set his search up under both names, but he had a feeling that he was looking for a youth thing here. It would help to explain what, to McCarthy, looked like an obsessive interest in young offenders.

There was nothing in the records for Suzanne Elizabeth Milner. But Milner was a fairly unusual surname. There were very few Milners, with that particular spelling. It was worth spending a few minutes over. He pulled up more details for what there was, and found himself looking at information relating to one Adam Michael Milner. Michael – the name of Suzanne's son. Coincidence? McCarthy pulled up the whole record. About ten years ago, Adam Milner had been a one-man crime wave, starting with shoplifting, vandalism – his first recorded offences at age ten – then graduating to car theft, breaking and entering.

McCarthy's eyes skimmed the page. *There it was!* Next of kin – Suzanne Elizabeth Milner, sister. His curiosity aroused, he sent down for the file, and caught up with some paperwork while he was waiting. When it arrived, a remarkably heavy file for someone who would be – McCarthy did a quick calculation – only twenty now, he picked it up and began to fill in the gaps. Adam Milner had caused some major headaches, but reading between the lines, McCarthy got the impression of a child who was more of a fall guy than anything else. He mixed with a crowd that was pretty notorious. McCarthy recognized some of the names. Milner was the youngest and always the lad who got caught, always the lad who took the rap. A report would go in about a group of youths stoning cars, the patrol car would get there, and there would just be Adam Milner. Someone would report kids stealing from a local shop. Adam Milner would get left behind in the stampede. McCarthy flicked through the pages, calculating.

So he was right. She had had some bruising experiences with the police, and when she was quite young. He looked at the dates and frowned. She seemed to have had sole responsibility for the lad, and she must have been only, what, nineteen, twenty, when he first came to police attention. He could understand why she might blame the police at the time – shoot the messenger – but why the hostility he thought he saw now? Or was it just him she didn't like?

What had happened to Adam Milner? On past form, he was probably banged up somewhere. He didn't feel like trawling through the whole file. He looked for the names of the officers who had dealt with him. It was possible . . . Yes! One he knew. Alicia Hamilton, in fact. He checked his watch. What were the chances of catching Hamilton? He picked up the phone.

He was in luck. She was on her way out for lunch, and, with the awareness of the tight schedules that they all worked to these days, was perhaps not happy, but prepared to spend a few minutes filling in some details for him. 'Is there some kind of link with the lady in the lake?' she said, when he explained what he wanted.

'Unlikely,' McCarthy said, and went on to explain the connection with Suzanne Milner that he'd just pulled up.

'I knew that name rang a bell. Of course, Suzanne Milner. Adam's sister.' She paused, as though she was gathering the facts in her mind, then went on, 'OK, the Milners. Dad and two kids – the mother had MS, died a couple of years after the boy was born. The father seems to have pretty much abdicated his responsibility for the lad as far as I could tell. The social worker – I can't remember who it was, but I'll find out if you like—'

'I'll get back to you if I need that. I just need the basics at the moment.'

'OK. Well, the social worker said that the father left his daughter – that would be Suzanne, right – to bring up the boy. It wasn't a good situation, but they didn't think there was much to do about it. Reading between the lines, I got the impression they didn't rate the father, but you know how these things go.' McCarthy didn't, as such, but he assumed the comment was rhetorical. 'Anyway, the lad starts getting into trouble – well, you've seen all of that, and young Suzanne is there trying to pick up the pieces . . .' McCarthy listened as she ran through the story. The lad had clearly been immature, disturbed, very dependent on his sister.

'He'd play tough,' Hamilton said, 'but he wasn't. I think we were getting somewhere with him, but then – it was one of those stupid things – he and his mates did a break-in at a warehouse. Sweets, would you believe? And the watchman got hit, had a fall, fractured his skull. No,' she said in response to McCarthy's swift inquiry, 'it wasn't Adam Milner who hit him. And the man recovered fine. But it meant they were up on a serious charge. Milner ran away from home, went into hiding. But of course his sister knew where he was. I talked her into telling us. It was the only thing she could do. Well, he got a custodial sentence. He went to pieces in the court, calling for his sister, fighting, the whole works. She was married by then, expecting her first baby. Anyway, he was sent to . . .' McCarthy recognized the institution, a ramshackle sprawl that had started out as a good and effective establishment with an enlightened programme for dealing with the vulnerable youths who came into its care, but that, like so many, had collapsed into a containment facility as the pressure of numbers built up and up.

'You know how it happens,' Hamilton continued. 'He left home that morning, was sentenced in the afternoon, the escorts didn't do anything about getting him any food, gets to the place at about eight that evening, through reception and locked up in the living unit with the others – they didn't know him and he didn't know them. You can imagine it, kind of. He's frightened, hungry, miles from home – and bullying is endemic in those places, don't let anyone tell you different.'

After six days of incarceration, just before his fifteenth birthday, Adam Milner had knotted his torn sheet into a rope and hanged himself by slow strangulation in the shower. There had been an internal inquiry, the results of which were confidential. Someone had had his knuckles rapped for a minor infringement, and new procedures were recommended. 'That's it,' Hamilton said. 'The life and short times of Adam Milner.' Her tone was brisk. 'How is Suzanne? I tried to follow up there, but she didn't want to know me. You could understand it. The father died of a heart attack shortly afterwards. Attracted quite a lot of sympathy. Not from me, I might add. I mean, why start being there for your children when you've made such a good job of not being there in the past. I heard Suzanne had a boy. I hope that worked out OK for her.'

McCarthy made a non-committal sound. From what he had seen, it hadn't worked out OK at all. His mind set into the impassive mode he used to carry him through crime scenes, through interviews, through post-mortems. *I touch nothing, and nothing touches me.* He thanked Hamilton and put the phone down, promising to return a favour some time. He looked at the photograph of Adam Milner. One of those fresh-faced youths who hadn't even started shaving. Curly hair. A look of Suzanne around the eyes and mouth. Rather an appealing smile. He pressed his fingers against his closed eyes. *Quis custodiet ipsos custodes?* Or something like that.

OK, that explained a lot.

Lucy sat on her own in the playground and unpacked her school bag. She took out her lunch box and her drink bottle. She looked at the sandwiches her mum had made for her. The bread looked fresh and crumbly, and there were bright green bits of parsley mixed up with the egg. They were her favourite sandwiches, and she'd asked for them specially, but she wasn't hungry now.

She wasn't talking to Kirsten. She wasn't talking to anyone. Kirsten had shouted after her, shouted something horrible about Sophie. 'My mum says that Lucy Fielding's babysitter . . .' Kirsten wouldn't say anything about Sophie again, not anywhere where Lucy could hear her. Lucy had waited quietly until Kirsten got brave, until Kirsten came and pushed her face right into Lucy's, until Kirsten thought that she had won. Then Lucy had punched her clenched fist right into Kirsten's tummy, as hard as she could, and Kirsten had gone *whoof* and fallen over. Miss Boyden had been cross, but she'd been cross with Kirsten as well as Lucy, so that was all right.

But she still had the funny ache in her middle. Mum said that Sophie was dead – just like Emma was dead. Lucy had thought that Mum was wrong. Mum often got things wrong. She did her drawing and she didn't really *listen*. But Lucy knew, now, that Mum was right.

The monster had been in the library, in the secret shelves. She thought she knew the places where the monsters went. Sophie had told her. But Sophie couldn't tell her now. And Emma couldn't tell her. And now the monster had come out of the park. She would have to be careful. Tamby would have to be careful. *Be careful*, she whispered.

Very, very careful, he reassured her.

Suzanne checked in her diary. She felt a bit nervous, felt the clench of apprehension in her stomach at the thought of what she was planning to do. She had the map for Richard, she could make him feel in her debt, but she wasn't convinced that it would be enough to make him talk to her and tell her what she wanted to know. There was a better way. She knew which days he worked at the university, the days when he wouldn't be at the Alpha Centre. And today was one of those days. She went to her bookshelves to find the copy of *Offending Behaviour*, the bible of the youth probation workers, that he had lent her a couple of weeks before. She couldn't find it at first, and then realized it was with the books she hadn't got round to putting back on the shelves, the books that were stacked rather intrusively on her desk. She slipped the book into her bag, remembering as she did so that she now had Ashley's tape in there. She spent ten minutes tidying away the papers and tapes that had somehow got disordered across her desk again. OK, her visit to the Alpha was to see Richard and to return his book – also, if she'd got it wrong and he happened to be there, to give him the map of old Beighton. And move on to plan B. Plan A required ten minutes on her own in Richard's office.

The road was so parked up she had trouble easing the car out of its space, and she was tense and jangled before she actually set off. By the time she got to the Alpha Centre, her throat felt tight and her back was damp with sweat. The building that housed the centre was in a leafy suburb; it was big, stone, standing back from the road. The road was a wide, tree-lined sweep, almost Edwardian in its elegance, but the first impression of middle-class affluence was dispelled by the signs of deterioration and neglect. There was litter on the pavement. The gardens were overgrown and uncared for. The windows of the houses were dark and empty, or hung with torn and dirty curtains. The front doors had several bells. There was no sign outside the Alpha. The centre wanted anonymity. There were still enough private houses for the residents to object to a centre for young offenders being opened in their area, particularly young offenders with histories of violence and drug abuse.

She parked the car and walked towards the building, which had started to feel familiar, like home. She saw that graffiti still disfigured the front door: Lee's tag, LB, in strident blues and reds, rather ornate, rather elaborately done. It was overlaid by cruder tags, white paint swirls and blotches, barely distinguishable one from the other. She felt an unsettling mix of emotions as she stood there: anger, guilt, anxiety. She mustn't let herself get distracted by what had happened. She was here to find out about Ashley, to find a way to Ashley. That was the important thing. She rang the bell and, after a minute, Hannah, one of the centre workers, opened the door. She looked surprised when she saw Suzanne, and a bit wary. Suzanne smiled, feeling as though she'd forgotten how, as though the muscles of her face could no longer perform the action naturally. 'Hello, Suzanne?' Hannah said.

So she wasn't going to let Suzanne in without good cause. 'I've come to see Richard.' It was humiliating as well. She was like an employee who'd been sacked in disgrace, making a friendly call on her old workplace.

'Is he expecting you?' Suzanne's heart sank. It sounded as though Richard was there after all.

'No,' Suzanne said. 'I just had some stuff to leave for him.'

'You can give it to me. I'll see he gets it.'

Hannah sounded quite friendly and Suzanne suppressed her anger. 'I need to see him. Is he here?' She needed to know. And if he wasn't, she needed to get through that door and into his office.

'No. This is his university day.' Despite her friendly tone, Hannah stayed uncompromisingly in the doorway. *As though I'll try to break in.*

'That's a nuisance. He's got a book of mine I need to collect as well. Maybe I could just . . .'

'I'll tell him,' Hannah said. 'If you let me know which one it is.'

Fuck this. She wasn't going to stand on the doorstep arguing with Hannah. 'Who else is here? I need to see someone,' she said, and pushed past Hannah, who stood back reluctantly to let her in. Neil appeared in the doorway of the downstairs office. 'Hi, Neil,' she said, trying to sound everyday, friendly. 'I need the book back, the one I lent to Richard. And I've brought him some stuff.'

'He isn't here.' Neil wasn't trying to be pleasant.

'Yes, Hannah said, but I need the book today. I've brought this as well.' She waved the folder she was carrying, then tucked it securely under her arm again. 'I think Richard's got the book on his shelves.' That was a good move, because the shelves in Richard's room were packed with books. It would take a major search to find out that it wasn't there.

Neil seemed to be weighing his choices. She wanted to say, What are you so worried about? You've won. Except he hadn't. Not yet. 'OK,' Neil said, 'I'll take you up there.' Suzanne had hoped to be on her own, but she smiled pleasantly at him.

'Thanks. Sorry to take up your time, but I've got a tutorial . . .' That was a mistake. Teaching was over. There were no tutorials. He didn't notice, but led the way up the stairs and through the convoluted passageways of the Alpha building. Suzanne noticed he was taking her a roundabout route that would avoid the coffee bar and snooker room. Obviously he didn't want her talking to the lads. She felt angry again, and this helped her to focus on what she planned to do. She didn't need to feel guilty when she was being treated like this.

Neil unlocked the door to Richard's office and waited as she put the file on his desk. She picked up some scrap paper and scribbled a note. She was aware of Neil studying the room. No papers on the desk, filing cabinets locked up, nothing out that she shouldn't see. She started looking along the shelves, frowning. 'He's got so many books . . .' she said.

Neil was starting to show signs of impatience. She went on looking, keeping her head back to show she was still only on the top shelf, moving along slowly. 'I'll get Hannah,' Neil said. 'I'm supposed to be in with a group now.'

'OK.' Suzanne let her voice sound abstracted, but her heart was starting to thump. Neil turned, began to go, turned back, then said, 'Hannah will be up in a minute.'

'OK,' Suzanne said again, and then he was gone. She listened as his footsteps hurried along the corridor. She needed to be quick. Richard kept the keys to his filing cabinet in the pull-out tray in his desk. She looked. There were five of the little silver keys that opened filing cabinets. He obviously kept old keys. There was only one cabinet. She picked up the keys, dropped one in her nervousness, picked it up, tried it in the lock. Not that one. She tried the next one. Her hands were trembling and it was difficult to get the key into the lock. *Calm down!* Not that one. The next one. And the one after that. None of them worked. She looked back at the desk. There, at the back of the tray, on a small key ring, another set of keys, a pair this time. She dropped the useless keys back into the drawer, and tried these new keys. She listened. Silence. No sound of anyone coming along the corridor.

The keys turned and the drawer slid open. What did she want? The top drawer had files with things like *Correspondence, Meetings, Pay*. She pushed that drawer shut and moved on to the next one. Here! Case files. *Andrews, Arnold, Begum, Booth*. . . She flicked through. *Reid*. She wanted to pull the file out of the drawer and take it home, hope that it wouldn't be missed, but she knew she couldn't do that. She flicked through; *Charges, Convictions, Reports, Personal details*. She didn't have time to read it. She looked at the sheet with the personal details on. Date of birth, address – she began jotting notes on a piece of paper. Ashley's address was a hostel – he wouldn't be there. Before? Green Park, a tower block near the city centre. But Green Park was due for demolition. She listened. It was still quiet out there. What had happened to Hannah? Address, *quick*. She sent a quick vote of thanks to whoever might be listening that she had learned shorthand at college. His school. She scanned the sheets quickly, trying to get the gist of Ashley's life, the things she didn't know. But this wouldn't be enough. He wouldn't be anywhere that was in this file, or McCarthy would have found him.

She waited for a minute, her hand on the drawer. It was still quiet out there. She pushed Ashley's file back into its place. Lee. If she was right, Ashley and Lee were friends. He might be keeping some contact with Lee. He talked about meeting up at the flat, by *the garage with Lee's name on*. . . Would that be near where Lee lived? Lee's file. What was Lee's surname? *Think*. Bradley! It was Bradley. She heard a door opening along the corridor. Hannah! She ran her fingers along the files – *Bradley* – and frantically flicked through the paper in Lee's file. There it was; *Personal details*. She checked the address, pushed the drawer shut, turned the key and whipped it out of the lock as Hannah came through the door.

The pull-out tray was still open. She moved across to stand in front of Richard's desk. 'Still looking,' she said over her shoulder. Her voice sounded odd to her. She slipped the key back onto the tray, and let her body push it shut as she moved closer to the desk. 'I'm beginning to think it isn't here.' She looked at Hannah. 'It just occurred to me, Richard is at the university, did you say?'

Hannah nodded. 'Yes.'

'Well, he knows I need it, the book, so maybe he's dropped

165

it off in the department. Perhaps I'd better go and check there. Anyway, I've left this stuff for him.' She patted the folder on the desk. She wondered what Richard would say when Hannah or Neil told him about the book she'd been looking for. She'd never lent a book to Richard. She hoped they wouldn't realize what she'd been doing.

Hannah cleared her throat and said, rather awkwardly, 'Neil said to tell you to make sure you'd got all your stuff.'

She saw Suzanne off the premises. As Suzanne was heading for her car, half triumphant at having succeeded, half ashamed at her subterfuge, she saw Richard's Range Rover pull in to the car park. *Shit!* Or maybe it was a good thing. She waited, watching as he uncurled his large frame from the car. He saw her, and looked embarrassed, hesitant. 'Oh. Hi, Sue.'

'Hi. I just dropped some stuff off for you. It's on your desk.' She took a deep breath. Attack first. 'I may as well tell you – I pretended I needed to look for a book I'd lent you. Hannah and Neil didn't want to let me through the door, and I got pissed off. I wasn't going to be treated like a criminal.'

Richard looked harassed. 'Well, strictly speaking, your authorization . . .' He scuffed his foot along the ground. 'Neil goes by the book too much,' he said.

'Has there been any news about Ashley?' She looked at him closely. He shook his head. 'Well.' She held out her hand. 'I'll be off. I might see you in a few weeks. Goodbye.' She turned away and walked to her car. She was pleased to see he looked uncomfortable. He'd feel a damn sight worse when he found the map of old Beighton she'd left on his desk.

11

Polly still looked about twelve years old. She looked like a twelve-year-old who had been blatantly, decisively caught, but had decided to brazen it out. She looked at McCarthy defiantly. She glared at Corvin and slumped down in her chair. McCarthy was not being gentle. One set of the unidentified prints on the zip-lock bags were Polly's. A search of the flat she shared with Lynman had produced a matching bag with a much depleted store of pills. He leant back in his chair and looked at her. Polly glowered at him. 'At the moment,' he said, 'you two are the only names I've got. Of anyone who's still around to charge, that is.'

He saw the blood rush into her face. That had got her mad. 'You don't care, do you? You don't give a shit!' She looked genuinely distressed. She probably was. Emma and Sophie had been her friends.

'I don't like drug pushers,' he agreed, keeping his voice level.

Her face twitched. She was under a lot of pressure. Two friends suddenly and violently dead, what must have looked like a harmless deal – everyone knew that Es were no more dangerous than dope – suddenly threatening her from both sides. She must have been terrified. 'I'm not . . .' she said, and looked at both men again.

'A pusher?' said McCarthy pleasantly. 'That's what it looks like to me.'

'Who? I told you! It was Emma. And Sophie.' She wouldn't meet his eye.

'It's Sophie as well now, is it?' McCarthy kept his face benign, but he was starting to get pissed off. She was wasting their time, and she was going to be in a hell of a lot of trouble. 'I don't believe you, Polly. My information says it was nothing to do with Sophie Dutton. I've only got your word for it that it was anything to do with Emma Allan. Do you know the penalty for dealing class A substances?' Her face went whiter, and she looked round the room, blinking rapidly. She was starting to panic, McCarthy thought.

'If I tell you . . .' She looked at the two men and leant forward across the table confidingly. She still looked very young. One of the thin straps of her camisole top – a lacy scrap that contrasted oddly with her baggy trousers – slipped down her arm. McCarthy could read her mind. She was used to people being nice to her. She was used to older men being gentle, fatherly. For all her streetwise appearance, she didn't know enough to come in out of the rain. He watched her slowly gathering her wits, trying to charm them and get the situation under control. Time to give her another spin.

On cue, Corvin leant across the table towards her. Polly's eyes filled with tears and she smiled tremulously as he came closer to her. For a few seconds he looked her straight in the eye. 'You're not getting it, are you?' he said. Then he shouted, thrusting his face into hers. 'Shit! Or get off the pot! Right?' Thug mode.

Polly jumped. Her eyes appealed to McCarthy who raised an inquiring eyebrow at her. Her lip quivered. She wasn't used to this, not at all. He'd checked into Polly's background. Father in banking, a manager of a local branch. Mother a primary school teacher. Polly was an only child. Someone from Polly's background wouldn't think twice about taking an E, smoking a bit of dope, but dealing? Getting involved on the fringes of dealing? He was pretty sure he knew the answer, and he intended getting it out of her.

She was in tears now. A bit of TLC and she'd talk. McCarthy felt as though he'd spent the last hour pulling the wings off a butterfly. He pushed a box of tissues across the desk at her. She didn't look at him as she pulled a handful out and wiped her face. He waited for a moment, then said, 'Come on, Polly, be sensible. I want to get the people who did this to Sophie and Emma. I want the name of Emma's

168

supplier. I can't ignore drugs on this patch . . .' – *I'm not making any deals* – 'I know you're not the prime mover here, but you haven't given me anything to work on. Tell me what you know, and let's take it from there.'

She looked at him with tear-filled eyes. She sniffed, blew her nose, sniffed again. 'It was Paul's idea,' she said.

Extract from interview with Polly Andrews:

Paul had this idea, you see. We knew Emma was getting stuff, you know, Es, and Paul thought . . . No! He wouldn't have touched the smack. I don't know where Emma . . . I don't know where she got any of it. Anyway, we knew where Emma kept the stuff. Yes, I think Sophie knew. I don't think she was too happy, you know? Well, after Sophie left, and Dan and Gemma went to Germany, well, Paul thought before he left the house . . . you see, Emma didn't really live there and she was mostly somewhere else by then. I don't know where. She just came back to Carleton Road occasionally. Paul thought that he'd just get any stuff that was in the roof. Only he had this job and he thought Emma might come back, so I went. No. We weren't going to sell it, it was just for us. It was because there was a lot and I only took half. Paul said I was daft, but . . .

When you came, he thought it was the drugs, he thought maybe what happened to Em was something to do with the drugs. We knew about Em and the smack, so he thought . . . he's very quick . . . he'd tell you about the drugs and about Em. If she was dead it wouldn't . . .

Ash Man? You mean Ash Lady . . . Yes . . . But it started as a joke, see. There was this programme on Channel 4 last year about people selling opium in London in the 1920s. You could then. No one stopped you. I think . . . But women who sold opium, they called them Insi-Por. It means 'Ash Lady'. You see? Em sold Es, she was seeing someone called Ash – Ash's lady, Ash Lady. It kind of stuck. Ash Man? No, no one was the Ash Man.

It was all Paul's idea . . .

Suzanne hadn't seen Jane on her own since her trip to the police station on Wednesday. She couldn't ask questions when Lucy was there. She wanted to know what had happened. There was something else she needed, something else that was beginning to fill her with that sense of urgency. She wanted to plan her weekend with Michael, arrange time with Jane and Lucy, take them out somewhere maybe, suggest a shared meal, arrange some time for the children to be together. She knew, and knew it with a guilty clutching in her stomach, that she was planning to have as little time on her own with Michael as possible, as little time to worry that the words she might use, the decisions she might make, the things she might do would work their black alchemy and leave her, sometime in the future, sometime not so many years ahead, watching him pulled away from her, calling her, pleading: *Listen to me . . . listen to me . . . listen to me. I'm telling you . . .*

She was just planning to go across to Jane's when she heard the back door open and Jane's familiar voice calling, 'Suzanne! Hello?' She went through to the kitchen where Jane was putting the kettle on. 'I brought you some apple and ginger,' she said by way of greeting, waving some teabags at Suzanne.

'How did you get on? Yesterday? Is there any news?' Jane looked tired. There were lines under her eyes that hadn't been there before. She, Suzanne, hadn't really known Sophie – she was an acquaintance, but Sophie had been Jane's friend, and Lucy's friend as well. 'How's Lucy?'

Jane pulled a face. 'Oh, it's just . . . I want to get her away from it all. Lucy's not said much. I'm worried. She's gone awfully quiet. Except about the monsters. Joel's no help – he just keeps telling me to keep Lucy away from the police.'

Suzanne reflected that Joel had never been any help with Lucy. Despite her misgivings about him, she found herself agreeing with him about the police. 'Maybe he's just worried about the effect that all the questioning will have on her. It might make her brood about it more, you know.'

'Maybe,' Jane agreed. 'But actually, they didn't ask to talk to Lucy again. I think they were a bit thrown by all the monsters last time. They asked me what I thought, if she'd said anything to me since, you know, but she hasn't. They

170

got me to look through some photographs, to see if I could recognize some of the people I'd seen Sophie with.'

'Did you?' Suzanne wondered whose photograph Jane had seen.

'One or two, mostly people who used to call at the house.' Jane poured water into the cups. A spicy smell filled the room.

Suzanne thought that she wouldn't have been able to recognize anyone who called at the student house, or anyone she may have seen Sophie with. But Jane, for all her vagueness, had an artist's trained eye, and was a keen observer. 'Was one of the photos . . .' She was aware of Jane's quick glance. 'It's someone I know from the Alpha Project,' she explained.

'Oh, the one you got into trouble over.' Jane nodded, remembering.

'Yes. Was he one of them? Tall, fair skin, dark hair?'

Jane nodded. 'Pale and romantic, sort of Death of Chatterton? Yes, they showed me that one, and yes, I've seen him. In the park, with Emma. Not at the house.'

Suzanne's heart sank. 'You told them.'

'Oh, yes. That cheered your friend Steve up. He took me apart about that, but you see someone in the park, well, you see someone in the park.' She shrugged. In the middle of her anxiety, Suzanne was diverted by the thought of McCarthy trying his various tactics to pin Jane down to exact answers. She knew from her own experience it would be like wrestling with smoke.

'Do you think he had something to do with it? Ashley? The boy in the photograph?'

Jane shrugged. 'Someone with a face like that could probably get away with anything,' she said. 'He reminded me of Joel.' She sipped her tea. 'This stuff always gives me a lift. Drink yours. It'll do you good. Listen, what I came to tell you . . .' She looked down for a minute, not meeting Suzanne's eyes. 'I heard from my publisher yesterday. They want a meeting now they've got the drawings. I'm seeing them tomorrow, but I'm going up to London today and staying till Sunday. Lucy needs a change of scene. Joel's got some kind of deal in progress there, and he seems to want to spend more time with Lucy, so I thought we'd make a weekend of it.' She held her cup in front of her face and looked at Suzanne over it. Suzanne realized that Jane knew exactly what this news meant to her, and that Jane felt anxious.

'Oh.' She heard her voice sounding flat. She tried to make it more cheerful. 'Michael will be disappointed.' She felt a heavy weight descend on her. The weekend that had loomed over her with weighty responsibility, anxieties that she couldn't quite name, now faced her like a sheer cliff she didn't know how she was going to climb.

After Jane had gone, promising to drop in and say goodbye, Suzanne went through her preparations for the weekend methodically. There was no reason to panic. She would meet Michael from school, and take him to the park . . . No, not the park. She would take him swimming and they could go and have something to eat at the students' union – he liked that. He could have pizza and salad, his favourite. Then they could go home, and she could let him play games on her computer. And before she knew it, it would be late, and he could go to bed, and that would be one evening sorted out. *Don't you even want to be with him?* a voice in her head remonstrated. She looked at the photo of Michael on the table. It was just a picture of a small boy. She let her eyes drift to the photo of Adam on the wall. *Responsible.* . . She felt the panic and fought against it.

She built her preparations as a wall. She made up the bed in Michael's room with his racing car quilt that had been his special Christmas request, got out his pyjamas and his favourite towel. She checked the fridge and made a note of things to buy: the ham, the strawberry yoghurt, the cheese triangles that had gone to waste from his aborted weekend just six days ago. Was it really so recent? She checked her watch. Two o'clock. She needed to do something to help her relax, to try and get rid of the cold lump that had settled in her stomach. A few days ago, she would have gone to her study, done some work, but that was part of the anxiety now.

She remembered Ashley's tape in her bag, slipped out of

its box on the shelves in the data archive in the department. She could listen to it again, see if she could find any further clues to places she might look to try and find him. She let her mind take a few steps in that direction. There was a sense of action, of purpose. What did she know already? Ashley talked about *the garage* – OK, that wasn't very specific, but she knew from listening to the talk in the coffee bar, and the talk in the staffroom, that Dean at least had been hanging round the flats at the bottom of Ecclesall Road. She got the impression that there was some kind of contact – drugs, she'd assumed – that took him there. Her illicit trawl through the papers on Richard's desk had given her a recent address for Lee: the same flats.

There was a garage, an all-night garage, down there, which was close to the point where the social scene from the town centre tangled with the pubs and restaurants of Ecclesall Road, especially on Friday and Saturday nights, when the pubs spilt out onto the pavements, and the whole of the main road became a promenading party around the pubs, the eating houses and, less openly, the blocks of flats: concrete and green grass leading through to the remains of the urban park – now more or less built up – and the old red light district, and then on to the university. The modern blocks gave way to tree-lined streets with dark and pot-holed roads, the elegant rows of terraces and the old stone mansions turned over to multiple occupancy or business use. Working girls still walked these streets, waited on the street corners where the maze of by-ways allowed cars to travel slowly past, the interiors dark against intruding eyes. Two minutes' drive from here, Peter Sutcliffe, the Yorkshire Ripper, had finally been apprehended. This was where affluence and poverty met, where expensive wine bars crowded against multi-screen pubs, where taxis and police cars, prostitutes and dealers competed for trade, where students exercised their right to irresponsibility, the employed threw off the shackles of the week and enjoyed the profits of their work, and the market that throve in a range of commodities operated in a range of venues, some well populated and lively, some dark, empty and alone.

The phone rang, breaking Suzanne's chain of thought. She realized she had become distracted by the problem of Ashley to the point that her anxieties about the weekend had faded into the background. She picked up the phone. 'Hello.'

It was Dave. 'Suze. I'm glad I caught you. Look . . .' His voice sounded conciliatory.

'It's OK,' she said. 'I haven't forgotten. I'll collect Michael from school tomorrow.'

'No, look, it's . . .' She wondered what he wanted. It wasn't like Dave to beat about the bush. She waited. 'This weekend. I'm sorry to mess you around, but can we change it?' He waited into her silence, then said, apologetically, 'It's probably . . . Look, you probably can't . . . I wouldn't ask if it wasn't important.'

Dave wanted to change the weekend. Almost at the last minute, he wanted to change it. Dave, who blamed and attacked her when the panic got so bad she couldn't cope with Michael, Dave who shouted about consistency, Dave who said things like *He's not a bloody pet, Suze!* 'Change it how?' She kept her voice neutral, trying not to let her confusion show.

'I was going away, but there's been a hitch. I've got a visitor for the weekend now, and she's bringing her kid with her. I thought it would be a good time for Mike and Becca to meet.'

The girlfriend. And the girlfriend had a child, and was, no doubt, an excellent and conscientious mother. 'Becca?' The name didn't sound familiar. It was Carol, surely. *Carol does eggs with faces on.* Suzanne was playing for time, but the sense of relief, the sense of an awful weight lifting, and lifting in a way that she didn't have to feel guilty about, was beginning to overwhelm her.

'Carol's daughter. She's Mike's age.' Dave sounded cagey, defensive.

So it was Carol, and Becca was the daughter. The relief was edged with a sharp pain, which gave a bleakness to her voice when she answered. 'It sounds serious,' she said. 'I mean, it sounds as if it's going somewhere.'

Dave would almost never discuss his life with her, but

even he had to see that she had a right to know about this, this introduction of someone into Michael's life who might, in the end, have more rights over her son than she had herself. It hurt. 'Well, it's early days,' he said now, cautious, prevaricating.

'But not that early.' She wanted to know, she had a right to know what was happening in Michael's life. Or did she have any rights with Michael? Did she deserve any?

'No.' Dave's tone was measured. 'Michael and Carol have met a few times. He likes her a lot. Hasn't he told you?' There was a challenge here. *He doesn't talk to you about what matters.*

But he does! she wanted to say. *Carol does eggs with faces on.* They could have a row about this. She could refuse Dave's request. He wouldn't insist. He wouldn't put himself in the wrong like that. But . . . She took a deep breath. 'OK,' she said. 'But explain to Michael that this wasn't my idea, that I wanted to see him. Tell him . . .' *Tell him I love him even if I am useless to him.*

'Thanks, Suze. Really, thanks.' And he did sound truly grateful. His voice was warm the way it never was these days when they talked. 'And I'll make sure that Mike knows what happened. And he can come to you next weekend – we'll be back on schedule like that.' Trust Dave to think of the practicalities, even now. Suzanne's once-a-fortnight weekends were her access rights, and Dave liked to have those weekends occurring at regular, expected intervals. 'Drop in for a coffee one afternoon. That way, you'll get to see Mike sooner. Any afternoon,' he added expansively.

She put the phone down a couple of minutes later. She'd sold her weekend with her son for a few grains of approval from her ex-husband and relief from the crippling anxiety that the prospect of Michael's visits engendered. She'd see him during the week in the safe environment of Dave's house, where she could sit with him, read him stories, listen to his chat, and she would have him at the weekend when Jane and Lucy would be there, and it would all be all right. And it wasn't her fault. It wasn't!

*   *   *

175

Steve McCarthy pulled the box from the top of the freezer and looked at the label. Chicken in something or other. He shoved it in the microwave and pushed the timer buttons. There was some bread in the cupboard, just about OK without toasting. It'd do.

He'd got in about nine, dumped the files he'd brought back with him onto his desk, opened a can of beer and headed straight for the shower. There was no point in pretending he was going to do anything other than work this evening. He was starting to feel an oppressive sense of urgency, as though someone or something was trying to catch his attention, as though someone had been calling his name, but he couldn't work out where the voice had come from. He was tired, and he found it hard to focus his mind.

Children. The thought came from nowhere. It had started with Lucy, Lucy Fielding. McCarthy thought about the small, fair-haired child with her tales of monsters and fantasy friends, her pride in her skating prowess, her strange drawings, her closed-face watchfulness.

Then there was a missing baby, Sandra Allan's child born before her marriage to Dennis Allan, half-sibling to Emma. And Michael Harrison, Suzanne's son? Surely just an observer on the sidelines?

The timer on the microwave pinged, and McCarthy took the now slightly distorted packet out, burned his fingers opening it, and dumped the contents onto a plate. A piece of chicken steamed briskly in an anonymous white sauce. He looked at it without enthusiasm as he buttered a piece of bread. He remembered Lynne teasing him about his eating habits. *You'd be happier if you could just plug yourself into a wall socket, McCarthy.* Teasing, yes, but with the undercurrent of viciousness that had been the hallmark of their relationship. They had been good at finding – and attacking – each other's weak points.

And it was true. For McCarthy, particularly when he was working, food was just fuel that kept him going: instant meals, dial-a-pizza. But for Lynne, everything had to be enjoyed, had to be as good as it possibly could be. She liked to cook. Sometimes she'd brought stuff round to his flat and turned the kitchen into a rich-smelling den of herbs and spices, turning strange, unpromising-looking items into casseroles and soups, serving them up with wonderful bread that he didn't know you could buy and salads that were crisp or moist or pungent. It always seemed like a distraction to McCarthy, almost a betrayal, the drift into sensual pleasure in the context of a demanding case. Lynne had never seemed to see any contradictions. And she was as ambitious as he was, he knew that – he'd paid that price. He thought again about the plum promotion that he had worked for, wanted, been the obvious candidate for – the job that would have taken him up to London, given him the experience and expertise that he needed for the next, important climb up the ladder – after that, the sky was the limit. And Lynne had gone for it, and Lynne had got it. *You were a close second, Steve.* He remembered the consoling voice of his then superintendent. Second was no good to McCarthy.

It wasn't only the promotion – though he and Lynne could not have survived that – but the fact that she didn't need him, clearly didn't need him, that their relationship, whatever it was, had never been a factor she thought worth considering. OK, it had been his pride that was hurt, he could concede that. But he hated the idea that all through their time together – a short nine months – she had been the one who had been in control. She had decided when their relationship started, she had decided when it finished, and when they were together, it now seemed to him, it had been her tune they followed, not his.

He realized he'd eaten the chicken without really tasting anything. He pulled his mind away from Lynne. He didn't want to be distracted by his anger. Now he was thinking about Suzanne Milner. Another problem. There was something she hadn't told him. He'd handled her badly, misread her at the beginning, and now she didn't – wouldn't – trust him. Maybe, given her background, she wouldn't trust anyone who worked for the police. Her concern for Ashley Reid worried him, and he wasn't sure exactly why he was worried. Did she realize that her brother, with his string of vandalisms and minor thefts, was a very different candidate from Reid?

177

His vague concern sharpened as he thought about the set-up at the Alpha Project. Secrecy and need-to-know. She probably knew very little about what the people she was working with had done, or what they were capable of doing. She talked as though she thought they were children, or near children.

It worried him, this naïveté. He remembered how she'd looked when he talked to her on Carleton Road, and hoped she at least had the sense to cover herself up a bit when she mixed with the Alpha youths. He wondered if she even thought about it. He'd found her disarray the other day – a just-shagged-in-the-back-of-a-Mini kind of disorder – far more disturbing than any calculated provocation. It worried him that she had been – apparently – unaware of it.

12

Tina Barraclough and Peter Corvin took the picturesque route from Sheffield to Manchester, crossing the Pennines over the A57, the Snake Pass. The road ran straight past fields and moorland, past the Ladybower and Derwent reservoirs and then began its twisting climb. The hills of the dark peak rose on either side, the inhospitable wastes of Kinder Scout and Bleaklow. Barraclough had once had a boyfriend who went hill-walking in the peaks, and for a while she had shared his enthusiasm for donning heavy boots and gaiters, catching the small train or the bus out into the Derbyshire hills, and climbing up onto the tops, to the inhospitable moors and the heavy peat, where fewer people ventured. They'd gone up onto Kinder Scout often, and she could remember the bleak land that lay there, so unlike the gentle beauty of the heather moors. They'd crossed the peat uplands and navigated their way to Kinder Downfall. The fog had come down unexpectedly once, and she'd realized then why people still died on these hills.

Now its dark height looked forbidding rather than inviting as they climbed the narrow road that took them to the top. Corvin cursed and braked as a car suddenly appeared in front of them, ambling up the steep climb, the driver, hat pulled firmly down, chatting to his front-seat companion, gesticulating at the landscape as he drove. The road was narrow and twisting. 'We should have gone by the Woodhead,' Corvin growled, his face dark and angry. 'Fucking Sunday drivers.' There was a bend in the road about a hundred yards ahead. Corvin changed down to second and flicked on the lights as he floored the accelerator. Barraclough closed her eyes as they shot towards the bend, the acceleration pushing her back into her seat. Then they were past.

'That was a bit close,' she said, trying to keep her tone mild.

'No. I know this road,' he said cheerfully. He sounded pleased that he'd managed to rattle her.

They were at the summit soon, and then they dropped down to Glossop and began the journey through the urban sprawl towards Manchester.

Manchester centre was very different from Sheffield. It had suffered less during the war, and its Victorian stone buildings were more or less intact. It always gave Barraclough a sense of imposing heaviness, dark and serious. Peter Greenhead had offices near Piccadilly on one of the side streets opposite the Plaza. The offices were on the first floor above the shops, an unlikely venue, Barraclough thought, for someone who was apparently a successful operator on the clubs scene.

They climbed the narrow staircase to the first floor, and went in through dark wooden doors marked GREENHEAD HARPER. A receptionist, who looked to Barraclough more ornamental than efficient, was working at a VDU. She greeted the officers, her blonde prettiness bringing out Corvin's rarely displayed charm. She checked their identification, the time of their appointment and the fact that it was in Peter Greenhead's diary with a speed that belied Barraclough's initial impression, and kept the initiative firmly with her. As officers investigating a serious crime, they could have insisted on seeing Greenhead, appointment or no, but there was no need to point that out, nor did she give them the opportunity. She pressed a button on her phone and said, 'Mr Greenhead. Detective Sergeant Corvin and Detective Constable Barraclough are here.' She'd remembered their names from one glance at their documentation. Greenhead's Manchester operation was clearly more slick than it appeared. 'You can go through,' she told them, favouring them with an attractive, impersonal smile.

Peter Greenhead was exactly how Barraclough imagined a slightly seedy, middle-aged business man would be. His hair – what was left of it – was long, reaching his shoulders, and was brushed across the balding patch on top of his head. He wore a gold watch, possibly a Rolex, though she couldn't get a close look at it. His suit jacket was slung over the back of his chair, and a slight paunch hung over the top of his belt. After her experience with the receptionist, she reminded herself not to judge him by appearances.

He was genial, apparently happy to talk to them. Presumably he had no bad conscience about his dealings with Dennis Allan's band, Velvet, or a confidence that whatever had happened was either sanitized by time or by the law. 'Hello, good morning, did you have a good run over?' He ushered them into seats in the austere but comfortable office. 'Coffee?' He went over to the intercom. 'Paula. Coffee please.'

He sat at his desk looking at them, and Corvin seized the initiative that he rather seemed to have lost. 'Mr Greenhead. We won't take up too much of your time. As I told you, we're interested in Dennis Allan who was a client of yours in the seventies, I understand.'

Greenhead steepled his fingers and thought. Corvin waited. After a moment, Greenhead spoke. 'Is Dennis in some kind of trouble, Officer?' He made no pretence about having forgotten the name.

'Routine inquiries.' Corvin gave the bland reassurance, and Greenhead nodded.

'Well, my association with Dennis was minor. He was the founder member of a group – Velvet, as you know – and I became their manager for a short time. They were really not very good.'

'So why did you take them on?' Corvin was clearly having problems, as Barraclough was, in seeing Greenhead as a man who would bother with a group of no-hopers.

Greenhead thought again before he spoke. He seemed cautious with his words. A man who sails close to the wind? Barraclough wondered. 'When I say they were not very good, I don't mean that they had no talent. The guitarist was rather good, and the singer was excellent. They'd written some songs as well. They just didn't work as a band. It was Dennis who was the problem. He just didn't have a nose for performance . . . or the talent, I'm afraid.'

Barraclough couldn't resist the question. 'But you did quite well out of the songs?'

He looked at her and smiled. 'Yes. That was the deal. Instead of my ten per cent, they gave me rights to three of their songs.' He shook his head. 'Dennis was the one who signed for the rest of the group.'

Corvin pulled out his file. 'Did you know his wife, Sandra Ford she would have been then?' He waited for a moment, then showed Greenhead a photograph of Sandra, one of the portraits from Dennis Allan's flat. 'And we're trying to track down the people in this picture.' Linnet, Don G. 'Do you recognize any of them?'

Greenhead was looking genuinely thoughtful now, as if he couldn't quite decide what to say. Corvin stepped in. 'Sandra Ford, Sandra Allan, that is, died earlier this year.' He paused, and Barraclough could see he was weighing up whether to tell Greenhead that the death wasn't considered suspicious, or whether the man would co-operate more if he thought that the crime they were investigating was Sandra Allan's death. He waited.

'I see,' Greenhead said slowly. 'Well, I'm talking about over twenty years ago, you understand.' He looked at the officers to make sure that they did. 'I don't like to speak ill . . . Velvet did some tours, bottom of the bill for bigger groups, you know. Sandy came along as an unofficial extra. I didn't know about that, not until after. She was a bit . . . wild. The roadies called her the tour-bus bike.'

'And she got pregnant,' Barraclough said.

Greenhead shrugged. 'So I understood from Dennis. He tried to get some money off me for her – he said I owed the group. Most of this was after my involvement.' He looked at the two officers. 'Oh, I don't think it would have been his child. He was a bit quixotic about her.'

He looked at the other photographs. 'That's the guitarist. I can't remember his name. They called him Don G. That's the singer,' he said, pointing to the woman Dennis Allan had called Linnet. 'I tried to persuade her to go solo, but she wasn't interested. It was just a bit of fun for her.' He looked genuinely regretful. 'She had real star quality. In my opinion.

She left the group to have a baby shortly after I ended the contract.' He smiled. 'There was a lot of it around. She was a nurse.'

'What was her name?' Corvin said. 'Apart from Linnet?' Greenhead frowned. 'Bloody silly name,' he said. Corvin nodded. 'Let me think. It was . . . Linnet, Linn . . . Linn . . . Carolyn. That was her name, Carolyn.'

Barraclough felt the jump of recognition. Greenhead looked at her and raised his eyebrows. She felt irritated with herself for being so easy to read. Maybe she should take some lessons from McCarthy. 'Just remind me, Mr Greenhead,' she said. 'When did that contract end?'

He smiled blandly at her. 'I didn't say, Officer. But I can tell you. It was in 1977, autumn 1977.'

As soon as she and Corvin were out of the office, she said, 'Did you hear that?'

Corvin nodded. 'Carolyn. Ashley Reid's mother was called Carolyn.'

'And his brother was born in 1978 – so that fits as well, her leaving the band to have a baby.' She thought for a moment. 'I should have realized. The DI asked me to find out what happened to Simon Reid. I couldn't find anything. But he isn't Simon Reid – she wasn't married then. Do you remember, her sister-in-law, that Walker woman, said they got married to go to America. So her son might have been registered as Simon Walker. Maybe they never got round to changing it before they left.'

Corvin whistled between his teeth as they walked back to the car. 'Did you notice something else?'

'What?' Barraclough was still trying to work out how they could check if 'Linnet' was Carolyn Reid, the name she had seen in Ashley Reid's file.

'He knew Sandra Ford.'

'Well, he said so.' Barraclough was puzzled.

'No, he knew her as soon as I mentioned the name. Didn't you notice? And he wasn't surprised when I told him she was dead.' He whistled happily as they walked back to the car. 'You drive,' he said. 'I need to talk to base.'

*   *   *

183

Suzanne made her mind turn to practical things. It was Friday. It was her weekend with Michael. Only she wasn't seeing him this weekend after all. The strawberry yoghurts, the special ham and the cheese triangles – she hadn't had to buy them. The bed with his racing-car quilt – she took the cover off and put the quilt away. It wouldn't be needed.

She looked at her watch. It was after nine. She was getting into bad habits. She showered and pulled on a pair of old jeans and a T-shirt. She went up to her study, but the general disarray in the usually neatly ordered area depressed her. Even her desk was disorganized, with papers and tapes scattered over it. She thought she'd tidied it. There was no point in doing any work anyway. Not just now. She went downstairs to the kitchen and remembered that she hadn't made it as far as the dishes, either. The kitchen was still relatively clean, but the sink was full of a daunting mass of cups, plates, cutlery, floating in a soup of cold water. It smelt. She plunged her hand into the sink and pulled out the plug. The greasy water drained away. She ran water over the dishes until the room smelt fresher, then filled the sink again with hot water and detergent. She'd let them soak for a bit.

She took down a packet of cereal, realized that she didn't have a clean bowl, and in the end she ate a handful of the cereal dry. It was the sort of thing that drove Jane mad. 'You should respect what you eat,' she'd told Suzanne once. 'It's what you are.' Well, that was OK. Dry cornflakes just about summed it up really. She ate another handful and switched on the kettle.

She needed something to do, and none of the things she needed to do seemed possible. She ought to work, ought not to assume that the whole thing was over – but the idea of working seemed overwhelmingly difficult. She could wash the dishes, that would be something, but even that seemed impossible. Irritated by her own indecisiveness, she wandered through towards the front room. The dark of the little entrance lobby and the stairs matched her depression. The stairs and landing got no natural light if the doors were shut. She'd been meaning to decorate, at least to get rid of the uninspired and dingy cream paint that she'd slapped on over the old wallpaper when she'd moved in.

She turned the light on and looked at the walls. The old paper was peeling off. The whole area looked dull and shabby. OK, that was something to do. She needed something hard and tiring. She'd strip off all the wallpaper and spend the weekend painting the walls.

In theory, it was McCarthy's day off. In practice, he knew he'd be lucky to get any kind of break until the case was over, or until the investigation ran into the ground. He'd arranged to meet Richard Kean up at the university – Kean hadn't seemed particularly enthused at the idea of McCarthy coming to the Alpha Centre – and they had spent a futile half-hour going over all the information they had in relation to Ashley Reid. 'Ashley isn't typical of the kind of lad we see at the Alpha. The kind that gets into trouble, sure, but not persistently serious trouble. Ashley did get into some serious stuff. It was his mental state that kept him out of prison last time. And then this latest thing.'

To McCarthy, this was so much waffle. He wanted to know about Reid's contacts, the places he went, the things he did. 'That's for the courts,' he said. 'I just want Reid. Who did he hang out with, who can tell us where to find him?'

Kean shook his head. McCarthy knew that Kean didn't like him, but he also knew that the other man would co-operate. The office that they were in was a bit away from the main campus, in a modern block that was built back from the road and screened by trees. The office itself was nothing out of the ordinary – a cubicle, almost, with a desk, a terminal, a filing cabinet. But the window looked out over the tops of the trees as the hill dropped down into the valley below them. McCarthy looked at the sky – a deep blue with wisps of cloud – and then at the green tumbling away down the hillside. He was reminded of the tranquillity of the place where he'd had coffee with Suzanne, that time she'd described Richard Kean and the other Alpha workers to him in less than flattering terms. The thought made him want to smile and he suppressed it.

'Our first records of him are from when he came into care when he was nine. His parents divorced when he was three.' Kean shuffled through his papers. 'What's interesting is he was born in America. His mother was a nurse, worked in San Francisco for a couple of years. She seems to have brought him and his brother back here after the divorce, when Ashley was four, and left them with her brother. No sign of the father. It was all unofficial.' But within five years, both children had been in care. 'It was voluntary care – the family said they couldn't cope,' Kean explained.

McCarthy knew most of this from the notes Tina Barraclough had put together. He'd been hoping that Ashley had talked to one of the workers at the Alpha and told someone a bit more about his background. 'Did he stay in touch with his brother? Were they kept together?'

Kean shook his head. 'I don't know much, but the brother went into care before Ashley. He's autistic. He needed special care, so he wouldn't have gone into an ordinary children's home.'

'And Reid never talked about it?'

'Not to me. And I was his case worker.' Kean frowned, thinking. 'He never mentioned his brother. If you want to know about that, you'll need to talk to the family.'

McCarthy made a note. He knew that Corvin and Barraclough had spoken to the aunt. He wanted someone to talk to the rest of the family. There was an uncle and a daughter, and there was this brother. He was certain that Reid didn't have the resources to lie low without someone helping him. His aunt and uncle looked like long shots. They'd put the child into care and had, apparently, had no contact with him since then. But the cousin and the brother needed more checking.

Kean was talking. 'Ashley's been pretty isolated at the Alpha. He gets on OK with the others, but he's got a talent for not being noticed.' Kean frowned as if he'd only just realized that. 'I don't think he has any friends there. He played snooker with Lee Bradley sometimes, but I doubt there's any more to it than that. Lee's very bright. He'd have no time for Ashley.'

186

'He's, what, educationally subnormal, Reid?' McCarthy ignored Kean's frown. He couldn't remember the proper labels, what term you currently used for 'thick'.

'He was identified as special needs by his last school,' Kean said after a moment. 'I've only been working with him for about ten weeks. I'm not so sure, now. He's functionally illiterate, but that could be because he wasn't much given to attending school. But he's . . . You don't notice Ashley, not if he doesn't want you to, that's his talent. When he first started at the Alpha, I thought he was one of those lads who was easily led – you'd ask him to do something and he'd do it. No questions, no argument. But that made it difficult to get to know him – you'd think you had a nice, co-operative character on your hands, and then, well, I've worked with him for nearly three months now, and I couldn't tell you much more about him than I could at the beginning. You can't keep yourself hidden like that if you're . . .' He hunted for the word.

Thick, McCarthy supplied, mentally. 'What do the other centre workers think?'

'They're beginning to think the same as me,' Kean said. 'Somehow, he's managed to keep everyone at bay, give nothing away; in fact, not co-operate at all. But no one noticed until he went missing. That's the point I'm trying to make. You don't notice Ashley if he doesn't want you to. I think we've made some bad mistakes with that lad.'

McCarthy considered this. If Reid was brighter than they thought – if he was bright enough to run rings round the Alpha staff – then he was bright enough to be their intelligent killer. The scheme with the water-wheel had been too elaborate, but if it had worked, they probably wouldn't have found Emma yet – might not even be looking for her, as they hadn't been looking for Sophie. That was bright.

Richard Kean spoke again. 'The only person who seemed to make any real contact was Sue Milner. Ashley talked to her.'

Suzanne. That odd defensiveness when he'd talked to her about Ashley. 'How do you mean?'

'Well, when she was with us, he'd quite often make a point of talking to her, sitting with her in the coffee bar. The other lads used to tease him, say that he fancied her, things like that.'

McCarthy heard his voice sounding colder than he'd meant. 'And did he?'

Kean thought about it. 'Probably,' he conceded.

McCarthy didn't like the idea of Reid on the loose, interested in Suzanne Milner. He was reminded of his earlier misgivings. 'And the other lads, do any of them talk to her?'

Kean looked suddenly evasive. McCarthy came alert. 'I don't know . . .' Kean was looking more uncomfortable. 'It's not really an issue,' he said. 'Sue doesn't work at the Alpha any more.'

McCarthy raised an eyebrow. He could see that Kean was wrestling with a decision. He waited, and slowly the story of Suzanne's somewhat unceremonious dismissal from the centre came out. McCarthy kept his face impassive, but his mind was turning this information over. He couldn't see what it had to do with the investigation, though he felt some kind of vicarious responsibility. No wonder she'd been hostile towards him. But he needed to keep his mind on the job. The rest really wasn't his business. One thing that did interest him, though. Suzanne obviously knew Ashley Reid better than she'd let on – well enough to know if she'd seen him in the park or not. He needed to talk to her again, but this time, he wanted her co-operation.

McCarthy put his hands in his pockets and leaned against the banister watching Suzanne as she scraped paper off the wall, pulling large strips off with angry strength, peeling the walls down to the bare plaster. She must have been working at the same frenetic rate for a while, because she had stripped the stairwell and most of the landing. She'd called him through when he'd knocked at her door, and looked at him without comment when he stood at the bottom of the stairs. She continued with her work, waiting for him to tell her why he was there. 'Want any help with that?' he offered after a moment.

She gave him a guarded look, assessing the sincerity of his offer, then said, 'You can make a cup of tea if you want,' and returned to scraping at a stubborn bit of paper. McCarthy went into the kitchen and switched the kettle on. He looked round for cups, and ended up washing two from the sink that was overflowing with unwashed dishes. He was about to make the tea when he went back to the sink, refilled it with hot water and set to washing the whole lot.

Then he took the two cups back to the landing. She took a drink and put her cup on the floor, assessing the wall with her eyes. 'Thanks,' she said as an afterthought.

He sat down on the stairs, after brushing the worst of the mess off with his hand. 'I didn't make that for you to leave it to go cold. Or for you to drop plaster into it.' He retrieved the cup. 'Sit down. Have a break.'

She went on pulling at strips of paper, then dropped the scraper on the floor and came and sat next to him on the stairs. 'So what did you want to see me about?' she said after a minute.

'Nothing. I wanted to see if you were all right.'

She gave him a look of open scepticism. 'You mean you've got some more questions.' She went on drinking her tea.

'OK,' he said. 'I've got one.' She turned his own technique on him and waited him out. 'Are you still certain that it wasn't Ashley Reid you saw in the park that day?'

She opened her mouth to answer, then stopped. She ran her hand through her hair, pushing it back from her face. She seemed genuinely uncertain. 'I can't remember what I saw any more. If I try to picture it, I don't see it the way it was. I remember that I was certain at the time.' She looked at him. 'I told you.'

He nodded in acceptance. He hadn't expected anything else, but he was pretty sure, now, that she was telling him what she thought she had seen, as best she could. 'I heard what happened about your job.' The landing was dark, the doors to the rooms closed, keeping out the natural light. But even in the dim light of the bare bulb, he could see she looked washed out. Her hair was untidy and kept falling in her face. There were pale circles under her eyes, and she kept biting her lip nervously. He glanced down at her hands. He remembered carefully manicured nails the first time he interviewed her – now they were bitten down and unpainted. She reached for her cigarettes, and he got out his own packet and offered it to her. She took one, and leant forward for him to light it. No bra again.

She put her hand against his to steady the lighter, and he let his awareness of her touch show in his face. She held his eyes for a moment. 'I should be giving this up,' she said after inhaling deeply.

'Why does everyone say that when they have a cigarette? If you want to give up, give up. If you don't, just enjoy it.' Lynne's anti-smoking rhetoric had turned him into a militant pro-smoker.

'I suppose so . . .' She didn't sound too convinced. They sat in silence for a while, then she pinched out her cigarette and slipped the half-smoked end into her packet. The broke smoker's economy. 'I suppose I ought to get back to this.' She looked at the mess without enthusiasm.

'Why the rush? It's a beautiful day out there. This is rainy-day work.' He found it ironic that he was the one preaching the *carpe diem* philosophy.

She bit her lip. 'I've got a free weekend. I thought I'd pass the time . . .' She looked at him. 'Michael, my little boy, he was supposed to be coming this weekend, but there's been a change of plans, so . . .' She rested her chin on her hand, suddenly looking defeated.

McCarthy surprised himself. 'Come on, I'll take you out for the afternoon. It's my day off.' Which he hadn't planned to take, in the middle of the investigation. 'We can go out into Derbyshire for a couple of hours, go for a drive or something.'

She looked surprised. 'I'm too scruffy to go anywhere.'

He looked at her and grinned in agreement. 'You are a bit. I can stand it. Or take some time – no rush.'

She thought about it for a moment, then said slowly, 'OK . . .'

He put his hands up. 'No tapes, no hidden agenda.' That made her smile. She tried to hide it, then caught his eye and laughed. He went outside into the sun and leant against the car waiting for her.

Twenty minutes later, she emerged, her hair still damp

from the shower. She'd put on a skirt and a loose cotton top. She looked cool in the bright sunlight. He opened the car door to let her in.

He headed out along Ecclesall Road South. He thought they could go via Ringinglow, maybe walk up a short way where the ground was easy. She was quiet for a while, not quite sure of him, not relaxed in his company. Then she said, 'Why are you doing this?'

He kept his eyes ahead, though the traffic was light, swinging the car round onto Ringinglow Road. 'Any reason why I shouldn't?'

'Why does a policeman always answer a question with a question?' she shot back. That made him laugh, and he felt her relax in the seat beside him. He was glad she didn't press it, because he didn't know why he was doing this, when the work was piled up on his desk and his team was working flat out.

He drove past Burbage Rocks which, even on a weekday, had its share of parked cars, and went on past Higger Tor and Carl Wark. He pulled off the road where it began to wind down the side of the valley, fields and trees tumbling away on one side, grey rocks on the other. There was a gate where a path ran through some trees and up onto the moorland. The sign on the gate said PRIVATE LAND, but McCarthy knew from past experience that you could walk there undisturbed.

The path wound up a short way, then they were walking in the heather and the bilberries. The ground was uneven, and she stumbled once or twice. Once he held her arm to steady her but otherwise they walked in single file, following the narrow sheep track towards the top of the hill. Once they had reached the top, they sat in the heather looking out across the valley. A breeze had started up that ruffled their hair and cooled them down after the climb.

McCarthy's mind was a blank. He lay back beside her and looked up at the sky. She stayed sitting up, looking across the valley to the rocks on the other side, resting her chin on her knees. 'You can't devote the whole of your life to it,' he said after a moment.

'To what?' she said. 'Scraping wallpaper?'

The slightly bitter humour encouraged him to go on. 'Feeling guilty,' he said.

'What do I feel guilty about?' She sounded genuinely curious.

'You tell me,' he said.

She looked down at him where he was lying in the heather. 'Why do you think I feel guilty?' she persisted.

He looked up at the clouds and thought about it. 'I don't think you feel guilty. I *know* you feel guilty. What I don't know is why.'

She put her chin on her knees again and went back to her contemplation of the valley. He watched her. Her shoulders looked tense, and her position no longer looked relaxed, indifferent, but protective, as though she was shielding herself from an anticipated blow. 'Where shall I start?' she said, surprising him. He'd thought she wasn't going to answer. 'Shall I start with being an unnatural mother?'

'No. Start with your brother. Start with Adam.'

She whipped round in shock as though he had hit her. 'What are you trying . . . ?' He knew she was looking at him, and he made himself stay relaxed, staring up at the sky, watching the clouds. It probably hadn't been the best time to use interview tactics. 'How did you know about that? Who told you?' She was kneeling up now, facing him. Her voice was agitated, but he couldn't tell if she was angry or not.

'No one told me. I found out.'

She was quiet for so long he thought she'd decided not to say any more, but eventually she said in a rather muffled voice, 'How long have you known about Adam?' She lay forward in the heather, supporting herself on her elbows. She had a heather flower in her hands and was slowly picking it to pieces.

'Only a day. I looked it up.'

She was frowning in concentration, studying the flower in an effort, he thought, to keep her mind off things she didn't want to think about. 'Why?'

He rolled onto his side, facing her, propping his head on his hand. 'I wondered why it was a battlefield every time I talked to you.' He took hold of her wrist lightly, running his fingers a little way up and down her arm. 'What happened to your brother was criminal negligence – but not yours, Suzanne. You did everything you could. Who else did anything?'

'Adam, he . . .' The tone of calm rationality she'd adopted cracked a bit. She coughed. 'Adam, he . . . I . . . didn't . . . I could have . . .'

'Could have what?' He wanted to pin her down to what, exactly, she thought she could have done differently.

'Could have done something,' she said. *Something.* I just left it. In the end, I just left it and he . . . did it. I should have . . . I don't know. I just know I didn't do anything.' She rubbed her hand across her forehead in a gesture of tired despair.

'A lot of people made mistakes where your brother was concerned. Some people made worse than mistakes.'

'It isn't that easy,' she said. He squinted up at the sun. The sky was cloudless. He couldn't think of anything else to say. She was probably right. She wasn't stupid – she must have worked out a long time ago that the people charged with the care of her brother hadn't done their job properly. But he had been her brother, her responsibility, and he had died. The fact that she should never have had that responsibility didn't seem to be an issue with her.

Her head was bent so that he couldn't see her face, just her hair falling forward. It had dried in the sun and he could see threads of chestnut and gold running through it. And . . .

'Grey,' he said. 'A grey hair. You worry too much.' He didn't want to talk any more. He could feel himself drifting into deep waters.

She looked at him and shook her head. 'I can't help it,' she said.

No more talking. He put his arm round her, pulling her down towards him as he lay back in the heather again. He could smell that faint perfume as he kissed her, and feel her breasts pressing against him. He slipped his hand under her top and ran it up and down her back, gently, slowly. He felt her stiffen and wondered if he'd misread her again, but then he felt her relax against him. He didn't want to rush her – they had all afternoon. For a while, they just lay there in the sun and he let his hands run over her skin, feeling it smooth and warm against the slight roughness of his hands.

He kissed her again and pushed her top up, rolling over, holding her close, so that she was lying beside and below him. He was still kissing her as he put his hand on her breast, as her mouth opened under his. Her nipple felt hard against his fingers. He helped her pull the T-shirt over her head. 'It's going to be bloody uncomfortable in all this heather,' he murmured.

She was unbuckling his belt, undoing his trousers, pushing them down to free him. Her skirt had ridden up round her waist. He kissed her stomach, running his tongue round her navel. He pulled her pants down round her knees, and felt her legs move as she worked them down the rest of the way and kicked them off. He slipped his hand between her legs and she made a sound somewhere between a gasp and a moan. He wanted to bury his face in that musky wetness, but now he couldn't wait, and the scratches from the heather in their half-undressed state seemed just another sensation as he pushed into her and there was just their breathing, and the heat of the sun, and the way she was moving and her gasp of, 'Steve' . . . as he felt her hips jerk and then he was holding her tightly and he was saying, 'Suzanne, oh Christ' . . . And then they were lying on a bed of twigs and leaves, and his clothes were tangled uncomfortably round him, and he could smell her perfume mixing with the smell of heather and the smell of sex, and he felt happier than he had since . . . when? Since he couldn't remember.

Barraclough was winding up her search for Sandra's baby. She knew what she was going to find. Sandra had been pregnant at the end of the seventies, after Velvet broke up. Sophie Dutton had been born in 1980. She had been adopted, and had come to Sheffield in search of her mother. She had never communicated the results of her search to her adoptive family, but Emma Allan had become her close friend.

Sophie had probably found Sandra Ford quite quickly –

she may already have had the name, some means of contact from the letter her mother had left for her. And had the neurotic, worn-down woman living her complaining life in a shabby maisonette with her ineffectual husband proved to be the kind of disappointment that Barraclough imagined she would be? Sophie probably had dreams about her real mother, dreams that may have carried her through the troughs of adolescence, provided a more vital background than a smallholding on the east coast could provide, no matter how loving her adoptive parents had been. And instead she had found Sandra Ford. But she had also found Emma, her half-sister. Emma, troubled and constrained, the child of a difficult marriage, the child of deceit. Sophie and Emma had been inseparable, everyone had said it. And how had Dennis Allan reacted to this?

Might it have seemed better to him if Sophie were to go, to leave, to be removed from their lives for ever? And then, had the thunderbolt of Emma's birth hit him, and had Emma become something else he must remove from his life, destroy? And his wife, of course, conveniently dead as well. It made a clear and elegant pattern. It was like dropping the last pieces into a jigsaw puzzle, feeling them slip in without resistance.

And it was here in the records. Sandra Ford, now living in Sheffield, had had a child in – but that couldn't be right. March 1978. Two years before Sophie Dutton was born. Barraclough had been so *sure*. But it was clear and unequivocal. Sandra Ford had given birth to a girl. She had called her daughter Phillipa. What had happened to her?

Barraclough thought about the unhappiness that had haunted Sandra's adult life, then went back to the registers. And there it was, dated for the same day as the birth, a death certificate, showing that Sandra Ford's child had lived for only a few hours.

Then she realized something else, something she should have seen at once. In 1978, the year of her daughter's birth and death, Sandra Ford had been just fifteen years old.

13

Suzanne came floating up from empty space. Her dreams these past few nights had been filled with images of tension, places where she hunted in vain in gathering darkness, buildings with endless corridors tracked in a growing panic until she jerked awake to realize, once more, she was dreaming – *listen to me, Suzanne, listen, listen, listen . . .* But now she was waking up from a sleep of welcome blankness, into a bed that felt crumpled, the sheet bunched underneath her, a smell of cool air, soap, sex. Someone was moving around. That was what had woken her. She opened her eyes into a white dimness, where Steve McCarthy was quietly taking something out of a drawer over by the window which was covered by a translucent blind. He looked as though he'd just come out of the shower. His hair was wet and tousled, and he was carrying a towel. He must have heard her move, because he looked round, saw she was awake and smiled. 'I didn't mean to wake you yet,' he said. 'You looked as though you needed the sleep.' He looked tired.

She sat up, rubbing her eyes, and checked her watch. Six o'clock. 'What are you . . . ?'

'I've got some stuff I need to do before I go in. Should have done it last night, but I got distracted.' He sat down on the side of the bed, pulled up the sheet and wrapped it round her. 'Cover yourself up, or I'm not going to get it done.'

She laughed, feeling that buoyancy that had lifted her spirits before. Steve McCarthy. Five years of self-imposed celibacy spectacularly broken in one afternoon and one night. She wound her arms round his neck and kissed him. For a moment, he responded, then he pulled himself away.

196

'Come on. Or I'll have to lock you up for obstruction.' He held her wrists lightly in one hand. 'Shit. I'm in no state to get my clothes on now.'

She laughed again and let him stand up. 'I'll get up in a minute.' But she lay back down again and let her mind drift. She could feel the sting of the scratches on her arms and back that she hadn't noticed at the time. Everything had changed so suddenly. After their quick, almost frantic coupling in the heather, they'd walked back down the path, stopping once to kiss and to look at each other with bewilderment. He'd said, 'My place?' and she'd nodded, not wanting to leave him and not wanting to go back to the emptiness she had left behind just a couple of hours before.

He lived in a flat in a modern block. She got a vague impression of impersonal comfort. She didn't really notice much. He took her straight into the bedroom and they pulled each other's clothes off as they fell onto the bed. A detached part of her mind was amazed. How was it that a cold, unemotional man like Steve McCarthy could be a warm and passionate lover? They spent the rest of the afternoon and the evening there. As the sun got lower in the sky, it shone through the bedroom window, sending the shadows slanting long and dark across the room. He lay on his side, looking at her, letting his fingers trail lightly across her skin. 'You're lovely,' he said. He went and got a bottle of wine from the kitchen, and later he phoned for a pizza. 'I don't do food,' he said.

'What's wrong with dial-a-pizza?' she said. 'As long as it hasn't got pineapple on,' and he laughed and looked relieved. He seemed to take it for granted that she was staying, and she couldn't think of any reason why not. Her last memory was the clock display showing 00:03 as she drifted off to sleep with Steve's arms wrapped round her.

She woke up and realized she must have fallen asleep again. He was dressed now, sitting on the side of the bed, leaning forward, looking at her. When he saw she was awake, he said, 'I have to go soon. I'll be in the shit with Brooke for vanishing yesterday, so I need to get in. I've got a lot to do.'

197

She rubbed her eyes. 'I thought it was your day off yesterday.'

'It was. It doesn't make any difference.' He didn't look too serious. He was watching her with a half-smile, very different from the detached, impassive McCarthy that she had been familiar with. 'I'll take you home – you've got time to grab a shower, things like that.' He pushed her hair back from her face, and traced the outline of her mouth with his fingers. 'I could think of things I'd rather do today,' he said.

The sight of him concentrating on her made a shiver run through her, as though he was running his fingers lightly across her skin. His face seemed to soften and her breathing became uneven. Her face felt warm. They looked at each other in silence for a moment, then he leant forward to kiss her, pulling the sheet away.

The phone rang making them both jump. 'Shit!' He buried his face in her neck, and she held him tight, willing him not to answer it. But he picked up the receiver and gave her a resigned smile. 'McCarthy.' He put his hand over the mouthpiece. 'Work. OK, Suzanne, help yourself to anything you need. I'll make coffee when I've dealt with this.' She heard him talking as she got up. 'Yes, OK. What? When? You're sure? OK, about . . . give me half an hour.' She turned on the shower and the noise of the water drowned him out.

He was in the kitchen making coffee when she went through towelling her wet hair. 'You need to go,' she said. The call must have been important – he had changed, was the McCarthy she remembered from the interview room. He looked abstracted, distant.

'Yes. It's OK, have a coffee, we've got time.' He offered her a cigarette and pushed a cup over to her, flicking through the pages of a folder he had open in front of him.

'Is anything wrong?' She wasn't sure how to react. She found herself thinking of him as a different person, as McCarthy. The man she had just spent the night with was Steve – Steve whom she felt comfortable with, relaxed with.

He smiled at her, Steve again, but still distracted. 'No. Just something on the case, something we didn't expect.' He indicated cereals, bread, milk. 'Help yourself.' He was back with the file. Suzanne could recognize the absorption. This was how she was when something in her research began to ring bells, when a previously hidden pattern began to emerge. And she thought about her work, and about the chaos in the house, the half-stripped walls. She thought about the empty weekend in front of her. Suddenly it seemed unbearably lonely. She sipped the coffee, feeling the tension that had vanished yesterday afternoon building up inside her again.

She looked at Steve, absorbed in his work, and wondered if she should tell him about – about what? It was all supposition. She had nothing to tell him except her own belief that Ashley was not responsible for Emma's death. He could only act like a policeman. She needed something concrete to bring him. Ashley talked to her. He didn't talk to anyone else – or no one at the Alpha, anyway. He might talk to her, and she would *listen*, like he'd asked her to ... Then she would have something to bring to Steve.

He looked at his watch, and then looked across at her. 'Ready?' She nodded. 'You haven't eaten anything.'

'I'll have something when I get back.' The tension had taken her appetite away.

He took her hand and circled his fingers round her forearm. 'You're too thin.' She liked it that he was concerned. She tried to remember the last time someone had said something like that to her. She needed to trust him.

'Steve ...' He looked a query at her as he locked the door. 'It's ...' She could see the lines of fatigue etched in his face. She thought about the gruelling schedule he seemed to work to, and wondered how long it was since he'd had a full night's sleep. She had nothing useful to tell him, and he didn't need her worries. 'It doesn't matter.' He didn't pursue it, and she wasn't sure if she was relieved or sorry. He dropped her off at Carleton Road with a promise to phone her the following day, Sunday.

She let herself into the house, and the depression and the dread were waiting for her as soon as she crossed the threshold.

* * *

199

It was the news about Corvin's and Barraclough's visit to Manchester that had galvanized McCarthy. According to Peter Greenhead, Dennis Allan had known very well about his wife's first child. And something else, more unexpected, had turned up. Carolyn, Velvet's singer. Was she Ashley Reid's mother?

Brooke grunted at him when he arrived in the incident room for the briefing. 'What do you think this is, Benidorm?' So he knew McCarthy had been out of circulation for part of the previous day. He decided the best policy would be no comment.

Brooke was clear about what he wanted. 'We need to know if there's a connection here. If Emma Allan's parents – whoever her father was – and Reid's parents knew each other, then it's relevant. And what kind of hornet's nest did Sophie Dutton stir up when she started looking for her mother? OK, she wasn't Sandra's child—'

'Unless Sandra got pregnant again,' Corvin said. 'Greenhead said she put it about.'

'Right. Check it.' McCarthy saw Barraclough wince. She'd been landed with the archive-checking for this case. Brooke looked at her. 'Any progress with this brother of Reid's? This Simon? Reid could be hiding out with him, wherever he is.'

Barraclough said quickly, 'I've got an address for the grandmother. The Beeches. It's an old people's home at Grenoside.' The outskirts of Sheffield.

Brooke nodded. 'OK. Steve, fill us in on Dennis Allan.'

McCarthy thought quickly and said, 'There's something about Sandra Allan's death. That's what made Allan jumpy when I interviewed him. I think we should go back to that, talk to the neighbours again. I need something to put pressure on.'

Brooke wound up. The drugs connection seemed to be no more than a student deal. 'Don't ignore it,' he said. 'Emma Allan was supplying, she was a heroin user, and she'd taken something the day she died. They've had drugs problems at the Alpha Centre, and Ashley Reid is a clear link there. But as far as we know, Sophie Dutton wasn't involved at all.'

'What about Lynman and Andrews?' Corvin wanted to know.

'We're charging them,' Brooke said, his face set. 'With dealing, and with wasting police time. That might frighten the name of Emma's supplier out of Andrews.'

Brooke looked at the pictures on the wall. Sophie and Emma looked back at him, their similarity noticeable to someone who was looking for it. 'Are we being spun around by a lot of detail?' he said. 'Are we just looking for someone with a taste for girls who look like that?' He shook his head. 'Right. Steve, get your people on the Allan thing. I want to know why he's been lying to us. And I want to know if this Linnet woman is Carolyn Reid. If she is, I want to know where she is. I want to know if there's a connection between Dennis Allan and Ashley Reid.'

Half an hour later, McCarthy, going through the urgent stuff on his desk, caught up with the details of Corvin's visit to Manchester. 'You think Greenhead knows something?' he said, following on from the report back in the briefing.

'There was something he knew about Sandra Ford, but whether it's got anything to do with this . . . We're going back over twenty years.' Corvin thought. 'I don't think he'd cover up for a murder, not unless he stood to go down for it.'

'What about having another go at him?'

Corvin shook his head. 'If we go after him again, he'll surround himself with lawyers nine deep. I've had dealings with him before.'

McCarthy thought about it. 'So we either need something concrete we can push him with, or a reason to get him to co-operate?'

'It'd be easier,' Corvin said.

As the door closed behind her and she looked up at the stripped wall and the litter of torn wallpaper on the stairs, Suzanne's feelings seemed to flatten and darken. A heavy fatigue was draining the energy out of her, as if, once she was on her own, she had no reason to keep upright, keep going.

She knew this feeling well, and she knew what she had to do to fight it. She dredged up some small reserves and began to sweep the strips of wallpaper down the stairs. This time it worked, and she felt her energy returning. Once she had cleared the stairs and landing and taken up the dust sheets that she'd put down to protect the carpet, she felt better. But it was dark on the landing and the stairs, and the darkness threatened to bring back the depression she had so far managed to defeat. She bundled all the paper into a bin bag and put it by the door. She'd take it out later. What to do next? She allowed the thought of her research to drift into her mind. She sampled it, and decided it wouldn't hurt to look. One thing she could do would be to finish typing up her handwritten transcripts, get all the interviews onto the computer.

She tested the thought again, and found she could cope with it. She went up the stairs to the attic and closed her study door behind her. She frowned as she looked round at the papers strewn on her desk. Maybe next week she could timetable a couple of hours for tidying up her study. The thought quite appealed to her. She switched on her computer and pulled the transcripts out of her desk drawer.

The mechanical act of copy typing allowed her mind to drift. She steered it away from the places where the blackness was lurking and allowed it to focus on more gentle things. Sunny days. Landscapes laid out in front of her, slightly misty with the new green. Shadows on the rocks. The heather moors and the bilberries.

Steve . . . She tried that thought with the caution of someone stepping onto uncertain ground, feeling for the place where the solid land gave way to the grassy overhang. He was going to phone her tomorrow, and then . . . ? Time would tell. What was he doing now? That was the wrong question to ask. He was looking for Ashley.

Her hand drifted to her notebook and the addresses she had found. Ashley had lived on the Green Park estate, where the tower blocks were being demolished. And so had Lee, before his family were moved. Lee had his family. Ashley had no one. The story she had seen in his file, just in her brief reading, had told her that. Care. Lack-of-care. One children's home after another, institutional, bleak and cold. She thought about something Richard had said, one of the few things he'd told her about Ashley. *Some of the lads – they have horrific backgrounds, things you can't imagine. But it isn't always that which does the damage. Take Ashley. Ashley's never had anyone who loved him, not for himself. That's the root of Ashley's problem, I think. No one wanted him. He's never had anyone who really cared about him. That's hard to cope with.* It was probably easier to hide behind a façade of clouded perception, and keep your real self hidden deep. But Ashley had shown her a bit of his real self, enough to make her care. Lee would know something, she was sure, now. He wouldn't tell her anything, but he might pass a message on. He might tell Ashley she wanted to talk to him.

She looked at Adam's photograph, and Ashley's pale face seemed to come between her and the picture she knew so well. His dark, serious eyes looked out instead of Adam's, his heavy dark hair imposed itself on Adam's short curls. His smile – cautious and guarded – replaced Adam's cheerful grin. She had let Adam down – her father had been right. In the end, it had been her responsibility. She couldn't let Ashley down.

The district nurse was a brisk woman with a no-nonsense voice and the air of someone who had more to fit into a twenty-four-hour day than could be reasonably accommodated. She introduced herself as Janet Middleton, and talked to Barraclough while she was packing up her car. 'I'll have to get on with this,' she said. 'You don't mind.' It wasn't a question.

'You visit Rita Cooke on the Gleadless Estate, is that right, Mrs Middleton?'

Janet Middleton checked the contents of her bag. 'Yes. Well, she was on my list for a few months.'

'You were there on the twenty-ninth of March, is that right?' Barraclough realized she was repeating herself. There was something about the woman that reminded her of a particularly fierce headteacher she'd had at junior school.

'Yes, I saw her Mondays.'

The efficiency that could put a day to a date reinforced the feeling, and her polite, professional smile began to feel slightly ingratiating. 'That was the day that her neighbour died, do you remember that?'

Janet Middleton nodded, her face serious. 'Yes. I met her a few times. She kept Mrs Cooke company, and she'd lend a hand with her shopping and things. A nice woman, but not a very happy one.' She grimaced. 'That's probably twenty-twenty hindsight. Mrs Cooke was upset.'

'Did you talk to us at the time?' Barraclough asked.

'No. There was no need. I mean it was all over by the time I arrived. Just a few interested neighbours hanging around, and poor old Rita in a right old tizz. She'd made a mess of putting her clock forward. She was an hour ahead of herself. She gave me earache for being so early.'

Barraclough thought. She'd forgotten that the twenty-eighth was the day the clocks went forward. But they wouldn't have missed that, the officers investigating the death. Rita Cooke's time was one of the things that supported Dennis Allan's story. 'Did you tell her?'

Janet Middleton laughed and shook her head. 'The last thing you do is tell someone of Rita's age that they've forgotten something. You particularly don't tell Rita. I just changed the clocks and didn't say anything. No harm done.'

Except, Barraclough thought, that Dennis Allan had actually come home an hour earlier than they'd thought. Would it have made a difference? He must have left work early. Why?

Janet Middleton was watching her sharply. 'I'm right, aren't I? No harm done.'

Barraclough knew better than to try and fool this woman, but equally, she didn't want any gossip floating round until they were sure. 'It sorts out a bit of a discrepancy in the timing,' she said. 'It wasn't a serious problem.'

Dennis Allan lit a cigarette and stared at the table in front of him. He didn't seem so much to be stonewalling as trying to think his way through what had become a problem he could no longer cope with. McCarthy had been working at establishing a rapport with the man, letting him see that they understood the nature of the shock that had precipitated – perhaps – the events of the case. And they seemed to be edging nearer something, something that was making McCarthy tense with impatience, waiting as they moved closer, moved away, moved closer again. Now he was going in harder.

Brooke thought Allan was their intelligent killer. McCarthy wasn't so sure. Allan was certainly hiding something, but his distress and tension became more marked when they moved towards his wife's death, rather than the death of his daughter, or of Sophie Dutton. He still claimed that his feelings towards Emma weren't changed by his wife's revelations. 'She was still my daughter. That doesn't change. It wasn't Em's fault. It was Sandy . . .'

McCarthy let the silence build up. 'Let's talk about your wife, about Sandra.' He saw the man's eyes flinch. His defences had gone up. *Come at him slowly.*

He spent a minute looking at the notes in the file relating to Sandra Allan. He didn't need to – he knew them almost word for word, but he wanted to wind the tension up a bit. He began by taking Allan back over his first meeting with Sandra and the early days of their relationship. He was aware of Allan's solicitor shifting in his seat, and kept his eyes firmly on Allan's, establishing a rapport based on his strength and the other man's weakness.

'Your ex-manager, Peter Greenhead,' he said, still watching Allan. The man's face flushed. 'He's done well.'

'I know.' Allan sounded petulant, grudging.

'Greenhead remembers your wife.' Allan looked at him, cautious now. 'He said,' McCarthy flicked through the papers in his hand. 'He said she was a bit of a groupie. He used the words "tour-bus bike".'

Allan looked at McCarthy with honest amazement before the impact of the words hit and he flushed a deep red. 'That's . . . It . . . Why would Pete say something like that?'

'Because it was true?' McCarthy suggested. 'Are you telling me it's not true?'

'No. I mean yes. It's not true. I'm telling you it's not true.' Now Allan began to talk, tripping over the words, more animated than McCarthy had seen him, more energetic in defence of his dead wife's reputation than he was in his own defence.

She had been in love with Velvet's guitarist, Don G. It had been a bit of a joke at first. 'She was just a kid,' Allan said. He didn't think the man had taken her seriously. She'd bunk off school if she knew they were rehearsing, make coffee, buy cigarettes, wash and iron stage gear. 'Sometimes she'd talk her way into the van, you know, if we were doing a gig nearby.' One time, she'd travelled a bit further afield with them. 'There didn't seem any real harm in it,' Allan said.

McCarthy couldn't see anything here that necessarily contradicted what Greenhead had told them. He pointed this out to Allan, who slumped down in his chair. 'This hasn't got anything to do with any of this,' he protested. 'Sandy's dead. Why rake it all up?'

His solicitor cleared his throat and asked for a short break. 'I need to discuss this with my client.' McCarthy nodded. He was happy for Allan to stew for a while.

When the interview resumed, he found, to his surprise, that Allan was willing to talk. 'My client is prepared to tell you this to establish that it has nothing to do with the crime you are investigating,' the solicitor said.

McCarthy was happy with that. He looked at Allan. 'OK, Dennis,' he said. 'You were telling me about Sandra.'

'I knew Don G. was into some wild stuff,' Allan said. 'I didn't think he'd bother with Sandy. She was only fourteen.' McCarthy wondered why they had allowed a fourteen-year-old to hang around the rehearsals, the tours. He didn't say anything, he just nodded again. 'Then after, she came to me for help,' Allan said. 'She'd got into some bad stuff. He'd got her into some bad stuff.' He shook his head at McCarthy's query. 'Just bad stuff, you can imagine. It's like that, performing, people get a bit . . .' He twisted his hands together, cracking the knuckles. He looked at McCarthy, at his solicitor, then looked down at the table. 'It was threesomes, foursomes, that kind of thing, all with pills, that's how they got her . . .' McCarthy kept his face expressionless, but Allan must have seen something, because he said, 'I didn't know! I didn't have a clue!' Then Sandra had come to him when she'd found out she was pregnant. 'She wanted someone to help her. She didn't know who the father was. But it was too late to do anything, you know . . .' He shook his head. 'She was just a kid.'

'What about Don G.?' McCarthy said.

Allan's face twisted. 'He did a runner,' he said. 'Because she was under age, I suppose. She was only fourteen and he left her to cope on her own.'

'What about her parents?'

'They just wanted to keep it quiet. She came to Sheffield to have the baby. She had family here.'

They'd lost touch. Allan had left the band, got a job. 'I met her again four years later,' he said. 'I'd always liked her, always thought she was, you know . . .' His face was sad. Sandra Ford had developed a drug habit, the addiction to tranquillizers that had plagued her for the rest of her life. 'Maybe she'd developed a taste for other things,' he said. 'I couldn't make her happy. I loved her,' he said. 'I thought I could help her.'

She and Allan had married a few months after that, when Sandra was pregnant with Emma. 'I thought he was gone for good,' Allan said. 'But I must have been wrong.'

McCarthy said, 'This Don G. was Emma's father?'

Allan nodded. 'She never got over him.' Allan shrugged. 'Don G.. Linnet called him that. Don Giovanni, see, because of all the women. She used to make fun of him – she was the only woman who didn't take him seriously. Not then. But his real name was Phil. Phil Reid.' McCarthy looked down at his notes again, not trusting himself to keep his face blank. *Reid. Phillip Reid.* He could see the pages of Barraclough's notes as if they were in front of him. *Father: Phillip Carl Reid.* Linnet and Don G.. Carolyn and Phil. Ashley Reid's parents.

The sins of the fathers.

The rest of Dennis Allan's story came out slowly but inexorably. McCarthy began the task of pulling out of the man the story they now realized that he wanted to tell: the story of Sandra Allan's death. McCarthy read through the statement Allan had made at the time. 'Dennis, you said on' – he checked the date – '. . . on the twenty-ninth of March that you got home from work at six a.m.'

Allan looked at his hands, and nodded. 'Yes.'

'And found Sandra dead. That's what you told us.' Silence. 'Is that right, Dennis?'

'Yes.' He whispered the word.

McCarthy looked at him. The guilt was etched on his face. 'Is it? Dennis?' He was aware of the solicitor shifting in his seat, thinking about intervening, but McCarthy had the whip hand now and silenced him with a look.

Dennis Allan's voice was quiet. 'It was Mrs Cooke saying I'd not got back until six. If it hadn't been for that, I would have said something before, something . . .' His voice faded, and he stared in front of him, his eyes unfocused. When he spoke again, his voice was a monotone. 'I'd left the house to go to work, and I was so angry, so angry with her. I'd done everything, I'd done so much. She kept telling me I couldn't cut it, I wasn't like Pete, I wasn't like Phil. Oh, yes, she used to talk about him. Then it was, "Don't leave me, I can't cope, I'll kill myself."' He looked at McCarthy. 'I could have made it back, you know. But Sandy, she wouldn't leave Sheffield. They said it was agoraphobia, but now I wonder . . . She must have met up with Don G. again in Sheffield. Did she hope he'd come back?' He rubbed his hands together as though they were cold.

'I did try to start another band, but then there was the accident. She'd been at me again, we'd got no money, Emma was small, she wouldn't stop crying, I don't know. I just went out and got drunk. Then I got in the car . . . I wouldn't have done it if she'd just . . .' McCarthy remembered Allan's drink-drive conviction, the dead child, the prison sentence.

Allan was silent. McCarthy judged the moment, and offered him a cigarette. Allan took it, and after a couple of drags he said, 'I left work early. I couldn't let it go. I had to sort it out with her. She was on the bed. Her breathing was all funny and she'd been sick and . . . There was this smell, and I couldn't . . . It wasn't like when she'd done it before. She'd left a note. I didn't know what to do. I read the note. I was going to phone . . .' He caught McCarthy's eye. 'I was. But I read the note, and then I just sat there, I didn't know what to do.' He looked at McCarthy with tears streaming down his face. Despite himself, McCarthy felt sorry for the man. 'And then I went back and I sat by the bed. And I held her hand and I told her . . . because I did, you see, I really did, that's why I stayed all those years, I loved her. But she wasn't breathing any more, not that I could tell. And I stayed a bit longer because there wasn't any hurry now, and then I phoned for the ambulance.' His hand was shaking as he drew on the cigarette.

'What happened to the note?' McCarthy kept his voice neutral, pushing Allan along the path he'd already chosen.

'I threw it away. I burnt it before I phoned. I washed the ashes down the sink. I couldn't let anyone see it. I couldn't!' He put his face in his hands.

McCarthy wondered what revelations the note had contained to disturb him so much. Wondered what revelation could be worse than the one Sandra had already given him. 'You'll have to tell me now,' he said. 'You know that, don't you?'

Allan's head drooped down towards the desk. He nodded once, briefly, almost imperceptibly. 'Yes.' His voice was hesitant, unsure.

'What did she say in the note? What did Sandra say?' McCarthy leant forward, getting closer to the man, trying to promote the feel of an exchange of confidentialities, of privacy, of secrets.

Allan kept his eyes on the table, his voice low, a monotone. 'It said about Emma, that now I'd found out, and it would all be over.'

McCarthy waited. He could understand why Allan had destroyed the note at the time, but now, this was no secret. What else was it that Allan didn't want to tell him? 'Dennis?' he prompted.

Allan's voice was a whisper. 'It said about Em. It said that Em had this boyfriend. It said that . . . That was why she'd done it . . . Sandy . . . She said it was her fault for not telling the truth. She said Em had a right to know.' He pressed his hands against his face. McCarthy waited. 'She said that . . . Em's boyfriend . . . The man she was seeing . . . It was Don G. It was Phil Reid. And Em didn't know.'

McCarthy closed his eyes and listened to the man weeping into the silence.

The flats were still and empty. The sun shone against the wall of the tower, warming the grey of the concrete, reflecting against the metal railings of the balconies. The windows were boarded up – they had been as each flat was vacated, but the boarding on the doors was soon smashed in and each flat denuded of its valuables, sometimes stripped almost to the brick, the wiring, the piping, the electrical fittings – all had their value and all had their market. The chipboard on the windows was warping where the winter rain had got in, twisting and pulling away from the frames. The graffiti artists had worked their way up the side of the building, and the boards were decorated with tags, names, dates, in paint that had dripped down the side of the building, white, black. The graffiti was crude higher up: the challenge was to place your tag in the most dangerous, most inaccessible place. Lower down, the artists had more time and some took a little more care. Here, 3D words sprang out of the walls and colours flaked off the brickwork and the metal of the garage doors.

A cat with the lean, intent look of a stray moved across the courtyard along the garage fronts. Some of the garage doors had been wrenched off, some were closed or half closed, offering some kind of shelter to people who needed somewhere out of the night, away from the eyes of other people. To the left of the block, one door, still bolted shut, carried an ornate LB, overlapping in red and blue, surrounded by a red circle.

The council had recently moved in again to secure the flats against intruders. The access to the stairways had been barred and chained, the flats on the lower decks boarded up. The workers had refused to enter the flats that had been broken into, with the smell of human waste, and the discarded needles and blackened tinfoil. They'd boarded the doors and windows and left. And now the other residents were coming back. There were voices around the back of the block, young, male, the sound of tyres squealing, the sound of a car engine being revved.

The cat retreated into the dark of one of the garages.

14

Brooke listened to McCarthy's account of the interview. 'He says that this "Don G.", this Phillip Reid, is having sex with his own daughter, and he doesn't see that as a motive for murder?' Brooke was incredulous.

McCarthy ran through the information they had. 'According to Allan, Emma didn't know about the relationship. She knew Allan wasn't her father, but she didn't know who was. And according to Polly Andrews, this "older man" Emma was seeing was a drugs contact, not a boyfriend.'

'OK, even if she's just selling pills to her father, it's a hell of a coincidence.' Brooke stared blankly in front of him for a moment. 'Set it out for me, Steve. Who knew and who didn't.'

McCarthy went through the story Dennis Allan had told him, slowly, bit by bit, laying out in front of the interviewing officers and his solicitor the story that Sandra had told her husband shortly before her death. Phillip Reid, Don G., had come back. He'd been living in America, had married, but his marriage had broken up, and he was back. Reid had been happy to start up what Sandra thought of as a relationship, but what to him was probably no more than a one-nighter. When she found she was pregnant again, she went looking for Reid, but he'd moved on.

'She knew his ex-wife's family, apparently,' McCarthy said. 'The Walkers. Or knew of them. She went to them to see if they could find him, but they couldn't.' She'd been seeing Dennis Allan, who had apparently kept in touch over the years. 'Maybe she thought the child was his,' McCarthy said. 'Or might be. He certainly had no doubts, not until Emma's bombshell.'

The Beeches was a large stone building. To Barraclough, it looked as though it had once had extensive grounds, but a new housing estate surrounded it, the houses looking like dolls' house ensembles with ornate exteriors and tiny patches of grass next to car ports and garages. Corvin cast a critical eye over the stone frontage as Barraclough pulled up. 'Cost a fortune to look after,' he said. 'Wants pulling down.' Barraclough could see rows of chairs in one of the ground-floor windows, and a head craning awkwardly round to look at them. There were steps up to the front door. Someone had constructed a concrete ramp to one side of the steps: ugly, but, Barraclough supposed, adequate.

They went through the front door. The floor was a scuffed, dull red, and the walls looked in need of paint. There was a smell of disinfectant overlying the faint smell of urine that Barraclough always associated with homes for the elderly. Barraclough looked round for somewhere to announce their arrival. Eventually she spotted a bell on the wall with RECEP-TION in small letters above it. She pressed it, and they waited again.

'Oh, fuck this,' Corvin said. 'I'm going to find someone.'

But just then a woman in a white overall came down the stairs and smiled doubtfully at them. 'Yes, it was me you spoke to,' she said when Corvin introduced himself. 'I'm the manager, Mrs Court. You want to see Catherine. She's expecting you.'

'Is she . . . ?' Barraclough wasn't too sure how to word her question.

'With it?' the woman said. 'She has good days and bad days.' She pushed open the double doors in front of them. 'Through here.'

They followed her along a corridor to another set of double doors. There was a background noise of crockery being shifted about, and someone shouted and banged against something. They were in a large sitting room, with chairs round the walls and in a row across the middle of the room.

Most of the chairs were occupied, the sitters staring ahead at the walls, at the floor, at nothing. The chairs were low, with deep seats. There wasn't really anything to look at, apart from the television. The smell of urine was stronger in here.

Mrs Court went over to one of the sitters and shouted in her ear. 'Catherine? Catherine? These people have come to visit you.'

A small woman with white hair and pale, fragile skin looked at them. She stood up slowly, helped by Mrs Court's arm. 'Have you come from Carolyn?' she said, looking anxiously at Barraclough.

Barraclough didn't know what to say. 'No,' she said, after a moment's silence. 'No, we haven't come from Carolyn.'

'They want to talk to you,' Mrs Court said, with the same exaggerated enunciation. 'They've come to take you for a walk.'

The woman looked at her and then at Barraclough and Corvin, frowning with bewilderment. 'I don't want to go for a walk,' she said.

Barraclough could feel Corvin shifting restlessly beside her. She tried to catch the woman's eye and smiled at her. 'We want to talk to you about your grandson, about Simon,' she said.

Catherine Walker was suddenly attentive. 'Do I know you?' she said, peering at Barraclough. She put her hand on Barraclough's arm and patted it gently. 'Do I know you?' she said again.

'No, Mrs Walker. I'm a detective. I'm Detective Constable Barraclough, and this is Detective Sergeant Corvin. We'd like to talk to you about Simon.'

'Simon.' The woman's eyes hunted round the room. She looked back at Barraclough. 'Have you come from Carolyn?' she said.

'This is getting us nowhere,' Corvin muttered.

'It's a lovely day,' Barraclough said, still looking at the old woman. 'Would you like to go out in the garden?' Not that there was much of a garden that she could see, but the gravelled area in front of the house was sunny, and there were some shrubs and flowers in the borders. Catherine

214

Walker took her arm and they moved slowly towards the door.

As they went out into the corridor, Barraclough felt the woman grip her arm more closely. 'Can I walk with you?' she whispered to Barraclough. 'I don't like it here. I don't know . . . My daughter's coming to take me home soon.'

'Is she?' Barraclough guided her towards the door.

'I haven't seen her for a while.' Barraclough looked down at the fingers gripping her arm, then into Catherine Walker's face and saw the fear and distress.

'I'm sure it's all right,' she said. 'Maybe your grandson will come.' They were down the steps now and in the sunlight.

The noise of traffic made the whispered words hard to hear. 'Simon's problem,' Catherine Walker said. 'He had his problem, you see.' Her face was blank, her eyes staring into the distance.

Barraclough nodded. 'Yes,' she said. She didn't want to distract this fragile train of memory.

'But he did very well.' Catherine Walker's smile was proud.

'Yes,' Barraclough encouraged again.

'I told him, "You can do it," I said. I think he was proud too.' There was a brighter light in her eyes now, as if her mind was freeing itself of the clouds. Barraclough felt more of an awareness of a person beside her. 'Our Simon, going to university. It's more than Carolyn ever managed.'

Barraclough expected the story to fragment in the woman's mind any minute. She had been holding her breath as she listened. 'I can't remember,' she said. 'Which university was it? Was it Sheffield?'

Catherine Walker looked at her. 'Of course it was,' she said. A slow bewilderment was growing on her face. 'Do I know you?' she said. 'Have you come from Carolyn?' Barraclough could see, from the corner of her eye, Corvin's thumbs up, and his jerk of the hand to tell her it was time to get moving.

They made their slow way back inside. Mrs Court was nowhere around when they returned to the sitting room. A harassed-looking woman in a pink overall steered Catherine Walker back to a chair and sat her down firmly. 'Come on,

Catherine, love, you sit down here. That's right. Come on.'
Catherine looked across at Barraclough. 'Have you come
from Carolyn?' she said. 'Is she coming to get me?'

Barraclough couldn't think of anything to say. She shook
her head. 'I haven't come from Carolyn. Thank you, Mrs
Walker. You've been very helpful.' And before the woman
could respond, she turned and followed Corvin who was
already heading back to the car.

Suzanne had waited for about an hour. She'd parked close
to the flats where Lee's family had moved after they left
Green Park, pulling into the forecourt of a garage. According
to the records, Lee still lived with his family. She was banking
on him going out on Saturday night, going into town. He'd
have to come this way. The garage was busy. She watched
the cars pulling in and driving away. She watched people
going into the all-night shop. It looked like the closest place
to the flats where you could get cigarettes, sweets, newspapers. She looked at the bright bands of primary colours,
red and yellow, the light from the canopy spilling down on
the pumps, the bright light from the shop window illuminating the forecourt as the evening darkened. A group of youths
were messing around on the pavement, using the forecourt
to shoot their skateboards through complicated manoeuvres
and leaps. Two girls, skimpily dressed even for a summer
night, swayed past on impossible shoes.

Then she saw him, strolling towards the two girls, watching
them as they passed him. There was no mistaking that red
hair, that distinctive swagger. She opened the car door and
got out, feeling less and less sure about what she was doing,
now that the moment had come. He was moving faster now,
and she hurried after him, calling, 'Lee! Wait.'

He turned round sharply. He didn't look surprised. 'Lee,'
she said again. She didn't know how to start. Her heart was
beating rather fast and she realized, ashamed, that she was
frightened. He stood in front of her, alert, ready to respond
to whatever threat – or promise – she was offering. She
stopped, still some way from him.

'What?' he said after a moment. He was wary and guarded.

216

She tried to look confident and collected. 'Lee, please, I need to talk to you. I just—'

He stepped back. 'I'm not talking to you,' he said. 'You grassed Ash up.'

Of course he would think that. To talk to the police at all was a betrayal. She knew that. 'I didn't,' she said. 'I found a dead girl, Lee. I didn't . . . They didn't understand what I was saying. I need to tell Ashley. I need to find him. Do you know . . . ?' She cursed herself as she heard the words blurting out in a rush. 'Can you tell him . . .'

The street was quiet now. They were in the shadow, away from the shop, and the stream of passers-by had ended. The cars raced past, unseeing. He relaxed his alert stance and, for a moment, she thought he was going to listen. He came towards her, and the darkness felt empty and dangerous. She stepped back as he gripped her arm. 'What do you want with Ash?' He was whispering, but his words were angry. 'It's not Ash you want. Understand? If you go looking, you won't want what you'd find.' His grip on her arm was so tight it was painful.

She tried to remember his good humour at the Alpha Centre, his camaraderie and fun, but all she could think of was the cruelty of his jibes at Dean, the coldness of his opportunism, the way his bright eyes sought out weakness. She was afraid, and he knew it. She tried to steady her breathing, telling herself that he had no reason to hurt her, that he wasn't violent – except she didn't know that, did she? She didn't know anything about him, not really, only what he had allowed her to know. 'Please, Lee,' she said, keeping her voice as level as she could, talking at a normal volume. 'Please tell Ashley I need to see him. Tell him I need to talk to him.'

People were coming along the pavement again, and he slackened his grip on her arm, his eyes crinkling at the corners with the smile she was more used to seeing. Almost gallantly, he turned her back to her car, opened the door and steered her in. 'What do you want with Ash?' he said again. 'I don't know where he is.' His face hardened. 'Now fuck off.' He banged the car door shut, and when she sat

217

there staring at him, he slammed his hand down hard on the roof. Unnerved, she fumbled her keys into the ignition and pulled away, steering erratically with one hand while the other fumbled with her seatbelt. A taxi swerved to avoid her, the driver mouthing abuse through his window. She was shaking.

Night began to cover the park. The shadows of the trees lengthened across the grass. The deeper woods slowly filled with darkness. The roof of Shepherd Wheel caught the last glimmerings of the sun, then the wheel yard became a pool of shadow, and the surface of the dam glittered darkly in the moonlight. Back along the path, the basement flat of the end house showed no light behind its torn curtain.

The bin still lay on its side in the garden, the contents strewn still further by the scavengers that came every night: the mice, the foxes and the rats. The small patch of carefully dug earth was still visible among the weeds. But the seedlings had wilted in the dryness of summer, the weeds were starting to grow, reclaiming the land that had been taken away from them. Through the window, the pictures still glimmered in the faint light. But now the sequence had changed again, running along the wall. First, the child, next, the youth; then the child, then the youth; the child, the youth. The child. The child. The child.

Suzanne had run. After her encounter with Lee at the garage, she had headed for home and for her study. She didn't want to think about it, about any of it. Tomorrow, she would tell Steve what Lee had said, her ideas about Ashley: let him deal with it. It was his job; it was what he did. The tapes! She'd never told him about the tapes. She'd wanted to clear it with Richard first. Well, screw that. She'd give him the tapes as well. Maybe there was something there. Something she couldn't see.

She sat in front of her computer, picking up the cassettes that were out of order on her desk and pushing them back onto the shelves. If she was going to give Steve the tapes, she should give him the transcripts too, typed up and legible.

Mechanically, she slipped the pages of transcript into the paper holder and began typing. At first, her fingers missed the keys and fumbled with the commands. But gradually she was drawn into the routine and, as she worked, her encounter with Lee became less vivid in her mind. After a couple of hours she finished the last piece, methodically saved the file and shut down. By the time she switched off her computer, it was almost midnight. She went down the stairs to her bedroom and looked out onto the road, watching the shadows from the street lamps on the bushes, the faint shine on the flagstones from the earlier rain. The wind was getting up, and the shrubs in the gardens were moving restlessly, sending their own pattern across the pavement. The road was deserted. She was suddenly aware of the empty houses around her: Jane and Lucy away for the weekend; the student houses empty for the summer. She was in the middle of a bustling city, but she lived in an enclave of ghosts.

She looked at her watch. She was turning into a recluse, and for what? For a piece of research she couldn't complete, and a grant that ran out in seven months' time. Maybe she should just give up, go to the careers advice centre tomorrow and start looking for a proper job. Her breath had misted the window and she wiped the pane clean. Then she looked more closely. There was someone across the road, standing in the shadow of the laurel hedge. She could see feet in worn trainers. As she watched, a hand moved, holding a cigarette. There was a shower of sparks as the butt hit the pavement.

She felt uneasy. There was no reason why someone shouldn't be standing there, no reason for it to be anything to do with her, but it was a good place to stand if you wanted to watch her house – and Jane's. She frowned, realizing she was biting her nail again. She went downstairs, turning on the light in the outside passage as she went past the door, then decided to have a look out of the downstairs window. She might get a better look at whoever it was. The overgrown cotoneaster outside the bay obscured her view a bit, but as far as she could tell, there was nobody there. She went out of the side door and stood at the gate, looking up and down the road. It was dark and silent. There were lights on in one of the houses a bit higher up, but she realized again how many of them had been turned over to student accommodation now. They were marked by their dark windows and the TO LET boards in the front gardens.

The house by the privet had a light in the window. Maybe the person standing in the shadows had been a guest, or a family member, banished outside to smoke. She was pretty sure that the couple who lived there – what was their name? – had a son who'd be in his late teens, or early twenties.

She felt irritated with herself for getting distracted. She went back in and closed the curtains. If anyone was watching, they certainly weren't going to watch her. She went upstairs and had a shower. She didn't feel like going to bed, so she put on her dressing gown and went back downstairs. She put a cassette into her stereo – Cleo Laine and John Williams, music to commit suicide to, Dave had dubbed it – and let the melody take her. Cleo Laine's voice slid over the notes as she sang about feelings, feelings of love . . . Only it wasn't feelings of love she was trying to forget, but feelings of responsibility, regret, guilt. If only— *Stop it!* She made a conscious effort and turned her mind to her plans for the next day. How much sleep had she had last night? Last night . . .

Then she was abruptly alert again. Her head felt full of bubbles and for a moment she didn't know where she was. The twiggy branches of the cotoneaster were knocking and scratching against the window as the wind caught them. She could see the moving shadows through the curtains. Then she listened. Surely that had been . . . There it was again. A knock, quiet and deliberate, at the door.

She moved to the front door and listened. The knock came again, and she said, 'Who's there?' clearing her throat as her voice came out high and nervous. No answer. Then the knock again. She peered through the spyhole, trying to see through the shadows. Her heart was beating fast. Then she could see his face, and she felt weak with shock. She leant against the door for a second, regaining her composure, then she said, quietly, 'Hang on,' as she unlocked and unbolted the door.

He was through the door before she could say anything. He slammed it shut behind him and leant back against it, looking at her, breathing fast. Ashley was in front of her, his face white, his hair tangled, his clothes stained and torn. 'Ashley.' She didn't know what to say to him.

'Listen!' His voice was an urgent whisper. He grabbed her shoulders, pushing her back into the room. 'Don't . . .'

'Ashley.' He looked awful – ill, and far less in control of the situation than she felt. 'What are you doing? You can't—'

'Don't tell them. He's looking for me.'

'Ashley.' She needed to get through to him. 'You've got to let me help you. You can't keep running away.' She looked into his dark eyes and felt that elusive sense of familiarity again. Adam? *Listen to me, Suzanne!* She took a deep breath. 'OK?' she said. 'Ashley? OK?'

'Where are they?' he said.

'Who?' Suzanne was confused.

'Next door. Loose . . .'

'It's all right, there's no one there. They've gone to London for the weekend.'

He relaxed and seemed to take in his surroundings for the first time. 'That's all right then.' He leant against the wall and closed his eyes. She couldn't let him disappear again. What had brought him to her door?

'Ashley. Let me help you.' She watched him come alert, looking at her warily. 'You need some food, and you need some sleep. Stay here tonight. We'll talk in the morning. I promise I won't tell anyone anything. Not until after we've talked.' She wasn't sure if he had agreed or not, but he followed her through to the kitchen where she cut some bread and made sandwiches. She wasn't hungry, but she sat with him as it seemed important to be companionable. She was glad, very glad, that Michael wasn't with her. She would have had no choice then. He ate ravenously, and for a while his attention was entirely taken up by the food. She wondered how long it was since he'd eaten. She ran options through her mind, wondering what to do for the best. She realized he was watching her again, waiting to see what she would do next. She needed time to think. 'Why don't you have a bath?' she suggested. 'Or a shower.' She tried a smile. 'You need it.'

221

His mouth twitched in response, but his eyes slid round the room. He didn't trust her, she realized with a pang. Why should he? Did she trust him? 'It's OK,' she said, wondering why he should believe her. 'I promise you I won't tell anyone until we've talked tomorrow, and I won't do anything without telling you first.' He looked at her, assessing her meaning, then gave an abrupt nod. 'Your clothes are falling apart,' she said. Didn't she still have some stuff of Dave's in a bag at the bottom of the stair cupboard? They were about the same size. She found him jeans, a sweatshirt, socks. He took them, still looking undecided and wary, then she showed him the bathroom and the towels in the airing cupboard.

She went into her bedroom and pulled on a pair of trousers and a jumper. As they had sat together in the kitchen, she had become aware that her dressing gown was flimsy, and aware that he was aware of it. She made up the bed in Michael's room. She checked her watch. It was nearly one. She went back downstairs and waited.

The sky dark and clear. The wind starting to blow. Watching the stars, in the cold in the park, waiting. Walking through the woods in the darkness, past the glittering river, past the shuttered silence of Shepherd Wheel, past the dam where the mud gleamed in the moonlight. *Remember. Always remember.*

Order. Walls of brick, rectangles, doorways. Planes where the shadows washed like water over the surfaces. Across and back. The window, dark, no face watching.

Where? A shadow against the lit square pulling the curtain across. A dim light in the doorway. Where? Darkness again. Where? *Where?*

There.

Waiting now. Waiting for it to get quiet, for the lights to go out and the hush of night to fall on the house.

The lines of the bricks like maps to draw the eye, up, down, sideways in a crazy pattern. Disorder, but it isn't, not really. Look, look, the pattern, whole and clear and beautiful, the eye racing along the lines, finding it, losing it.

Wait.

*   *   *

222

Half an hour later, he came down. He slid round the door and hesitated, looking at her. He seemed to be listening for sounds outside. Now he looked more the way she remembered him from the Alpha Centre. He'd put on the jeans she'd given him. He had a towel across his shoulders and his feet were bare. His skin was very white; his hair hung in damp curls round his face. The hair on his chest was dark. She couldn't think of anything to say. He came further into the room. 'There's a bed made up,' she said, her voice sounding artificial in her ears. 'I'll show you.' She realized she was going to have to pass him to reach the stairs. He stayed where he was, just in the doorway. As she came close to him, he said, 'You came looking for me . . .' and he touched her face, gently. Surprised, she looked up at him, and he kissed her.

For a moment, she froze, and he pulled her close against him, his arms round her so tightly she could hardly breathe. He was pushing her back onto the settee. 'Ashley! Wait, don't . . .' She didn't know what to do. She needed to think, to win back the initiative. She hadn't read his signals until too late, she'd got it wrong, wrong, wrong!

He was kissing her again so that it was hard to free her mouth, hard to speak. He was pressing her back into the cushions, his hands reaching under her jumper, pulling it off her shoulders, down her arms. It was like trying to swim against the current. She didn't know, for a moment, if she was fighting him or acquiescing. He was kissing her mouth, her neck, her breasts. She pushed against him as hard as she could. 'Ashley! Stop! I don't want . . .'

He relaxed his hold of her and was still for a moment, his head between her breasts. She had to fight a crazy impulse to put her arms round him and hold him there. Then he lifted his head and looked at her, his expression confused. 'Why did you let me in? Why did . . . ?'

Of course. Sex was one of the currencies in Ashley's world. She'd gone looking for him, she'd admitted him into her house, invited him to stay. What else had she expected? 'I want to help you,' she said. 'But I can't do this.' His head slumped forward. He wrapped his arms round her waist and pressed his face against her. She felt his warmth and the weight of him lying half across her. He whispered something and she had to strain to hear him as he whispered it again. 'I'm sorry ... love ...' She remembered Richard's words: *Ashley's never had anyone who loved him or cared about him.* She wanted to say something to show him that she did care about him, but she knew he would misunderstand her again. She felt his head heavy against her, and touched his hair, lightly. 'We're both tired. You're tired. We can talk in the morning.'

He lifted his head and looked at her. 'You'll let me stay?' She nodded. There were tears on his lashes.

She needed to be alone, to have time to think. She freed herself and stood up, pulling her jumper back up round her shoulders. It was torn. She stood away from him, not wanting to give him any signals he might misinterpret. 'You know where the room is. The bed's made up.'

He stopped at the door and looked back at her. 'I'm sorry,' he said again. Then he reached out for her, almost like a child reaching for comfort. 'Stay with me,' he said. For a moment, she wanted to hold him against her, do whatever he wanted her to do. He was young, he was lost and she wanted to comfort him.

'I said, sleep. We'll talk in the morning.'

He closed his eyes, steadying himself against the door-frame, then he smiled that warm smile. 'OK,' he said. He looked so young it nearly broke her heart. He pulled the door shut behind him and she heard his feet on the stairs.

The key sliding into the door, turning silently. The house full of empty air, full of the silence of abandonment. Stairs, where feet could tread one, two, three, four – always an odd number, always an itch in the mind. Feet stepping centrally onto each tread. One, two, three, four, five, six, seven, eight, nine, ten, eleven ... and stop. Knowing where to stop in the darkness. Along the landing, one hand on the rail, one hand on the wall, smooth and rough. Not equal, not balanced. Another itch.

More stairs. Narrow and twisting. And the room with the

moonlight flooding across it. A bed, stripped to the mattress. A wardrobe against the wall, crooked. Sliding it away, and there against the smoothness of the wall, smooth against the fingers, the trap-door.

The trap-door opened into dusty night. Then a moonlit attic. Another trap-door. Then the dust-filled shadows. Then a room with books, a desk, shelves. A chair, looking black in the moonlight. A door, open to the steep and narrow stairs leading into darkness.

Suzanne stayed downstairs, putting together a makeshift bed on the settee. She wrapped a wool rug round her against the chill of the early summer's night, and curled up against the cushions. Even though she was exhausted, for a long time she couldn't sleep. Then when she did, her sleep was fitful, disturbed. The wind was gusting now, sudden bursts rattling the windows and making the shadows move on the curtains. She lay awake, listening so she would hear if he got up, if he moved about, if he tried to leave. She dozed off, and woke suddenly. Someone outside. The wind gusted again and the twigs of the cotoneaster scratched against the window. She turned over, wrapping the rug more closely round her. It was draughty. She'd have to do something about that before the winter: replace the draught-excluder round the front door, try and seal the window frames. She settled her head on the pillow and closed her eyes. She was floating through the shadows, floating down the road, looking at all the houses dark in the moonlight. Lucy's monster was coming up the hill. She couldn't see it, but she knew it was there. It was a silent, gliding monster, but she could just hear its footsteps if she listened carefully. *Rattle, rattle* against the door, the creak of a floorboard.

Ashley reached out his hand and she smiled and took it. They were walking along the road, and it was all right now, it was safe, everything was OK. She looked at him, but he was looking behind them, and she couldn't see his face properly. *Listen to me, Suzanne!*

She was awake again. Something had woken her. The wind was making the door shake now. She listened for a minute. Gusting, a draught, *rattle, rattle*. She turned over again and pulled the pillow across to muffle the noise. Again the wind gusted, rising almost to a shriek, the shadows danced madly against the curtain, and the twigs of the cotoneaster scraped against the glass. She squinted at the clock. Three-thirty.

She closed her eyes again, and sleep came in the form of a long, dizzying fall. She was falling so fast that it was getting difficult to breathe. The air was catching in her throat and making her cough. She was in a field – the air would be clear here – chasing Adam across the grass, but she was still coughing. The field was burning, and Adam was running towards the flames.

There was a crackling noise and a bang, and she opened her eyes, but her dream went on. She was coughing in a thick darkness, and there was a smell of . . . of something burning, rubber, plastic. She struggled up, pushing the blanket off her. There was smoke in the room and it was thick and black. There were crackling, popping noises from the hall. She ran to the door, turned the handle. It wouldn't open. She tried again, rattling the door in its frame. It was jammed. How . . . ? Then she realized that the fire was just outside.

The window. She could open the window. She undid the catch and pulled at the handles, feeling the window rattle, and a draught of cold air sucked and swirled into the room. The window stuck. The fire roared and smoke billowed. She gasped with effort and the smoke gripped and froze her throat. She couldn't breathe. She retched and choked. The crackling of the flames was louder, and she thought she could see their flicker through the thickening smoke. She couldn't breathe. She groped round for something hard, something solid. She pulled books off the shelves, grabbing one as it fell, and smashed it into the glass. It rebounded and fell behind the settee. She reached for another one, a heavier one, that slipped and almost fell as she fumbled at it. She lined it up this time, and drove the edge of the book at the window with the force of her body behind it. The glass shattered and she fell forward through a blast of cold air. A sharp pain ran through her arm.

She was on the ground, lying in the flower bed outside the front of the house, retching and choking, reaching for clean air to fill her lungs. The entry was filled with smoke. Ashley! Ashley was still in the house! He was round the back in Michael's room! She couldn't stand up, so she crawled, the frantic screams in her head coming out as faint whispers, and she fell down the step onto the pavement as the silent road watched her.

McCarthy looked at the charring on the door. There was a sickening smell of burning, and the hall, the stairs and the landing were a blackened mess. The floor was awash with dirty water. 'It's mostly smoke damage,' the fire officer was saying. 'The fire itself was pretty small. There was something on the stairs that made a lot of smoke – very toxic, that.'

'How did it happen?' McCarthy knew that this was no accident. He felt frustrated at being here. He wanted to go to the hospital, to find out for himself how Suzanne was.

'Arson,' the fire officer said. He rubbed his fingers against the wood of the door and held them out to McCarthy. The smell was unmistakable. It reminded McCarthy of winter days in his grandfather's greenhouse, in the humid warmth with the smell of out-of-season blossom. Paraffin. 'Someone poured an accelerant through the letter box. Then they jammed the box open – give a good draught, you see. No, there's nothing accidental about this.'

McCarthy hadn't thought so from the minute he'd arrived, alerted by a call from the patrol that had routinely attended the fire. Ashley Reid had been found at Suzanne Milner's house, and was at the Northern General Hospital. It was almost daylight now, past five, and the scene-of-crime team were starting to work. 'OK if I go in?' he said. The fire officer waved him past, and McCarthy went through the door.

It looked very different from the way he remembered it. The stairs which ran straight up in front of him were smoke blackened, the wall a mess of soot and charred paper. To his left and to his right the doors were both coated with the same thick, greasy residue. The one to the left was slightly open. McCarthy looked at the door he'd come through, the one that had been attacked by whoever had started the fire. There was a Yale lock, bolts and a security chain. Using the end of a pen, he tested the bolts. They moved freely.

He went through the door on the left. The smoke had done its bit in here, and the water from the fire hoses made the carpet spongy under his feet. He walked through the room to the kitchen beyond. Apart from the broken lock on the back door, it was virtually untouched. The fire fighters had come in this way. McCarthy looked round. There was a plate on the worktop. Two cups were in the sink. One of the SOCOs was testing the door for fingerprints.

He went through to the front room. The door was closed, as it had apparently been during the fire. There was smoke damage in here, not quite as bad as the entrance and the dining room, but, instead, blackened areas around the door, and stains on the ceiling. According to the officers attending, the door to this room had been blocked, a piece of wood jammed under the handle. Suzanne had got out through the window, smashing the glass. One pane was knocked completely out; some jagged pieces of glass were lying on the floor. McCarthy saw blood on one of the shards, saw drops on the brickwork and the ground outside. He felt that sense of frustrated anxiety again.

He looked round. A bed had been made up on the couch, a makeshift job with cushions and a rug. Then he went up the stairs, looked in the room at the head of the stairs. A bedroom, Suzanne's by the look of it. The bed was undisturbed. Though the landing walls had been thick with smoke, in here the damage was minimal. A dressing gown lay across the bed. McCarthy picked it up. There was a faint perfume on it that took him back, disconcertingly, to the afternoon in the heather, and to the night in his flat.

The other room was chaos. The bed – a single bed – was pulled away from the wall. The bedding was strewn over the floor. McCarthy wondered how much of this was from the rescue. He understood that Reid had been pulled unconscious from the smoke-filled room and rushed to the ambulance that was waiting outside. He needed to talk to someone who'd been there. He went along the corridor to the bathroom. Here, there was no evidence of damage at all, apart from the smell of the fire. A damp towel lay on the floor, and some clothes, jeans, a T-shirt, were discarded by the side of the bath. The clothes were filthy and torn. A further flight of stairs led up to the attic. McCarthy looked up the stairway. It wound round, making a steep and dangerous climb. The stairs were dark and windowless. He pressed the light switch. Nothing. Maybe the electricity was off.

He came down the stairs again and went back to the front room. His phone rang as he was still formulating his message. It was Brooke. McCarthy listened to what he had to say, confirmed, listened again, and hung up. He stood in the middle of Suzanne's front room, watching the early morning sun make shadow patterns on the carpet and glitter off the shards of glass scattered around the window and on the ground outside.

There was a photograph on the wall, a portrait of a smiling boy with curly hair and freckles. He recognized the face from his search through the records. Adam Milner, the brother Suzanne had loved, protected, given up her childhood for, and lost. He felt an ache inside him, the ache he'd long ago learnt to ignore . . . no, not ignore, dismiss. *Not my concern, not my problem.*

Ashley Reid was dead.

15

Barraclough couldn't tell if McCarthy had been exasperated or angry when the records department at Sheffield University produced the name Simon Walker. He was a third-year student in the Department of Chemistry. He had lived in one of the halls of residence for the first two years of his course, briefly at 14, Carleton Road, then moved to a flat on Oakbrook Road, beside Bingham Park, just a few hundred yards from Shepherd Wheel.

Barraclough could hear the music of the funfair as she got out of the car. It was back down the road in Endcliffe Park, but the breeze was carrying the music, the creak and rumble of the machines, and the shouts and screams and the amplified voices calling to people to come and buy. She hadn't outgrown funfairs. She felt an urge to be spending the evening in the candy-floss and hot-dog environment, spinning on the waltzer, winning a huge green teddy bear on some rigged shooting gallery. Instead she was here to work, here in search of Simon Walker at his last known address.

The house was on the main road overlooking Bingham Park. It was a stone house that backed onto the park, its bay window dark, with torn nets, the upper-storey window obscured by a blanket, another house fallen victim to the creeping blight of multiple occupancy. The paint was chipped and peeling, the wood of the window frames starting to crumble at the base. At the back, the land dropped down into the park, down towards the river. The small back garden was below the level of the road, a basement flat opening out onto it.

Simon Walker had rented the basement flat, but the flat

itself was empty when Corvin, armed with a warrant, arrived with the search team. 'I knew he'd be trouble,' the landlord grumbled as he unlocked the door.

'How do you mean?' Corvin asked as they went into the room. Barraclough could smell the damp. She'd lived in enough run-down bed-sits in the earlier days of her career for the smell to take her back to a life of takeaways and cheap red wine, transient passions in front of fumy gas fires – a time of her life she had thoroughly enjoyed and had no desire to revisit.

The landlord considered Corvin's question suspiciously. 'He's a bit of a weirdo,' he said after a moment.

Barraclough was looking round the room as he spoke. It was not what she had been expecting. Student flats were sordid and messy – everyone knew that. This one was meticulously tidy. More than that, Barraclough thought. The books on the shelves were lined up and carefully arranged according to size. There was a small kitchen separated from the rest of the room by a breakfast bar. The single wall cupboard was filled with tins of sweetcorn, standing in neat rows in piles of three. She looked at the table in the window. Two unopened letters were lined up square with the table edge. On one wall was a sheet of paper filled with complex diagrams forming lozenge-shaped patterns, with letters and numbers attached to the lines. On the other wall, opposite the window, were marks, straight lines, as though something had been carefully lined up there in several rows. Whatever it was had been removed, leaving pieces of tape behind.

She could hear the landlord talking to Corvin as she tried to decipher the images she was seeing. 'He had this really strange look,' the man was saying. 'Like he couldn't understand a word you said.' There were leaflets and a free paper on the mat in front of the door, and a carton of milk that had been left on the breakfast bar had gone sour, its smell adding a slight taint to the damp air.

'OK, let's get started,' said Corvin.

Midday Sunday, McCarthy negotiated the one-way system through the city centre in response to an urgent summons from the pathologist. Anne Hays's office was at the bottom of the long hill that ran down behind the university. It was an undistinguished building among modern industrial blocks, next to the dual carriageway where the tramway ran towards Hillsborough. It was a place where people came and sat in a waiting room to find out the usually unremarkable truths that lay behind the deaths of their loved ones, to collect the certificates that would allow them to bury their dead. McCarthy felt that same frustration he'd felt earlier, of having to be in one place when he wanted to be somewhere else. A disgruntled security guard, his Sunday disrupted by the events of the night before, was on the door. McCarthy gave him a nod of acknowledgement as he went to the lift and said, 'Dr Hays is expecting me.'

He pressed the button for the second floor, and when he stepped out of the lift, turned right along the narrow, blue-carpeted corridor. The lights were fluorescent, recessed. The walls looked flimsy, as though they would cave in at a touch. The doors, spaced at regular intervals, were made of simulated wood with windows at the top, which let a vestige of natural light into the corridor.

He found Anne Hays's office and knocked. He wondered if she would actually say, 'Come,' and when she did, he opened the door and went in. She was sitting at her desk, and raised her eyebrows coolly at him as if she held him personally responsible for this latest incumbent of her table. 'Good morning, Mr McCarthy.' She was as formal as ever. She must have made an early start, but she was meticulously neat, and as correct as she always was with him – no reflections on the vagaries of teenage girls or the iniquities of the NHS system for his benefit. He wondered why she had asked him to call in, rather than submitting her report through to the investigating team.

She stood up. 'I'm afraid I've got something for you,' she said. 'You'd better come and see this.' She led McCarthy to the lift and they went down to the morgue. 'We did the post-mortem this morning,' she said, leading him to one of the fridges where the bodies were stored. 'We still need all the lab stuff, but I can tell you this now. It wasn't immediately obvious.' She unzipped the cover and pulled it back to expose the face.

McCarthy waited, wondering when she'd get to the point. He looked down at Ashley Reid, his face congested and swollen, disfigured by bruising and – something else. McCarthy looked more closely, and then back at Anne Hays, wanting now to know what she had to tell him. He had thought she was a young woman. Now she looked older. The light was giving her face that papery fragility of old skin, transparent and delicate. He was afraid for a moment that, if she smiled, her face would crumble and dissipate in the draught from the ventilation fan. He shook his head to clear it. He was tired.

She waited for his reaction before she went on. '. . . They tried their best to resuscitate the boy – nineteen, it's a crime.' So far, McCarthy thought, they were in complete agreement. 'So he was a bit battered by the time I got him. But I'm afraid there's no doubt.' Again, McCarthy was struck by the look of academic inquiry on her face, judicious, slightly distanced. 'Congestion of the face, petechiae, bruising to the neck.' She showed him, gently manoeuvring the head that lay between them. 'It would all be concealed by the smoke damage, of course. And, of course, no smoke in the lungs . . . You can understand how it happened. They got him out of there and went straight into resuscitation. Your first aim in a case like this is to save life.'

It took a moment for McCarthy to realize what she was telling him. Ashley Reid had not died in the fire. He had been dead before the lethal smoke reached him.

The forensic team worked fast. They knew which prints they had to match, and went straight to them. It was no surprise that they had an immediate hit with Ashley Reid's prints, but the second match they found was less expected. They had no name to go with these, but someone else had left fingerprints in Suzanne Milner's house, on the passage door, on the stair rail, and on her desk in her attic study. These prints matched with the unknown set found in Shepherd Wheel after Emma Allan's death.

Brooke called the team together late Sunday afternoon. He was angry, and made little attempt to hide it. They had had three promising lines of inquiry, two of which looked like coming up with their killer – Brooke would have put money on Dennis Allan as the killer of the daughter who was not his daughter, and the woman he thought was his wife's other child. But Dennis Allan had been in custody when Ashley Reid was killed, was guilty of another crime altogether, and, with his solicitor urgently coaching him, was unlikely to be charged with anything, or anything much. How easily could guilt distort the memory of a man who had found his disturbed wife apparently dead from an overdose after the row they had had, which had precipitated her suicide?

And Ashley Reid? Reid's death might have, could have cleared the whole thing up for him, though Brooke had never been as hot on Reid as McCarthy had been. The lad's apparent low intelligence had seemed to count him out as anything more than an accomplice, a puppet manipulated by more intelligent strings. But McCarthy's latest report suggested that Reid was of average or above average intelligence, more than capable of planning and carrying out the two killings. But not, unfortunately, capable of planning and carrying out his own murder. The evidence was unequivocal. Reid had died of strangulation, manual strangulation. Though the scene had been disturbed by the rescue, it looked as though he had been attacked in the room where he had been sleeping. He'd been subdued by a blow to the head, and then had the life choked out of him. The fire had apparently been set in an effort to conceal this fact. Despite the initial appearances, the fire had been set and started from inside the house.

'Whoever it was came along prepared, then?' Griffith asked. A premeditated attack with Reid's killer stalking him to Suzanne Milner's house, equipped for murder and arson.

'No.' Brooke indicated part of the fire report. 'Whoever it was used an accelerant that was already at the scene. Milner had been decorating. There was a bottle of paraffin on the landing. She said so.' An opportunistic attack? An unintended death?

Whoever it was who had strangled Ashley Reid, it wasn't Suzanne Milner. She was lucky to be alive. Someone had locked her in the downstairs room and nearly killed her as well. Her story was clear and consistent, but there were gaps. Barraclough knew – they all knew – she wasn't telling all of the truth. She claimed that Reid had come to her house that evening. She admitted that she had gone looking for him, but said that Reid had arrived independently. The evidence from the house suggested otherwise. Though a great deal of it had been destroyed by the fire and the damage done in extinguishing it, and in the attempts to rescue Ashley Reid, there was still enough to cast serious doubts on Suzanne's version of events. She claimed that Reid had never been inside the house before that night, and had only been in the downstairs rooms, the bathroom and the small bedroom. But Reid's fingerprints were in other places, particularly in the attic room that Suzanne Milner apparently used as a study. McCarthy was outlining their findings now, talking about fresh prints, overlaid prints – evidence of much more than a single night would account for.

Barraclough pulled her attention back to the briefing. 'So was she harbouring him all this time?' Brooke said.

McCarthy seemed uncharacteristically indecisive. He shook his head. 'I don't know. She says she wasn't.'

'Why would she harbour someone like Reid?' That was Liam Martin. It was a good point, Barraclough thought. Corvin made a crude suggestion that brought the relief of laughter. McCarthy's face set in cold, unforgiving lines.

Barraclough thought that she had never seen him so angry. They had interviewed Suzanne as soon as she left the hospital – against medical advice – just over an hour ago. Barraclough had felt sorry for her. She looked shocked and ill – as well she might – and had seemed to find it hard to concentrate. She kept saying, 'I'm sorry, I'm sorry,' as if she couldn't understand the questions she was being asked. She seemed bewildered by the evidence and retreated into confused silence.

For the first time in the years she had known him, Barraclough saw McCarthy lose it. As Suzanne repeated for the third time that Ashley Reid had never been in her house apart from that one night, he'd slammed his fist down on the desk and shouted, 'Exactly how stupid do you think I am, Suzanne?'

She had shaken her head, looking shocked and exhausted. McCarthy had said something about a break and slammed out of the room, leaving Barraclough to sort out the formalities. He'd sent Corvin in to complete the interview.

Thinking about this now, Barraclough remembered the scene at the hospital earlier that afternoon, when she had gone with McCarthy to talk to Suzanne, before the evidence from the house had come through. The nurse had said with some sharpness, 'She's not being very reasonable, but we can't force her to stay. Try and talk some sense into her,' and they had found Suzanne pulling on a torn and smoke-stained jumper, trying to collect her possessions together. McCarthy had told Barraclough to wait outside the cubicle, but she'd been able to see and hear most of what went on. Suzanne had tried to push past him, fighting him as he stopped her, saying, 'I've got to talk to him! I didn't listen! He tried to tell me and I didn't listen!'

McCarthy had grabbed her by the shoulders and shaken her until she'd shut up and looked at him, seen in his face the news he had to tell her. Then he hadn't said anything, had just put his arms round her, and all he'd said was, 'Suzanne, it's all right, it's all right.'

But it wasn't, Barraclough thought now, watching him in the incident room. Something wasn't all right with McCarthy at all.

The numbing effects of shock wore off as Sunday evening faded into Sunday night. Suzanne didn't know what to do. Her house was still being examined by police, by scene-of-crime investigators. She couldn't have faced going there anyway. Jane was due back with Lucy later that night. She had a spare key to Jane's, and now she was sitting in Jane's back room on the edge of the reclining chair, in the middle of Lucy's toys and drawings, watching the evening sky over the roofs of the houses. Lucy's one-eared teddy bear was tucked in a corner of the chair, and Suzanne picked it up, turning it round and round in her hands as she watched the evening star slowly become visible in the fading light.

Her mind kept replaying images of the past twenty-four hours. She thought about Ashley pushing her back onto the chair, the sudden flaring up of passion, its sudden end. She thought about the way he'd smiled at her as he'd closed the door behind him. She thought about Steve at the hospital, when she'd read the news – or the confirmation – of Ashley's death in his face. She thought about his face at the police station later, his anger, the things he said, the way he wouldn't believe her.

She saw feet moving stealthily up a flight of stairs, stairs where the walls were stripped bare, heard soft footsteps moving across a carpeted floor. She could see a door in the darkness, the letter box opening, rags dropping through, the flames beginning to blister the paint, finding the bin-liner full of paper she'd left behind the door, the plastic dripping and melting, the flames roaring up. She could see Ashley's face, white on the pillow, framed by thick, dark hair, see his hand dangling off the side of the bed, still, cold, as the smoke crept and twisted its way across the room.

She felt cold, even though it had been a warm day, and the evening was still pleasant and mild. She twisted the knob on the gas fire for warmth, and heard the pop as the flame caught. Flames licking up the door, catching the paper, flames and smoke filling the stairway – *it wasn't fire that killed him!* She stood up and looked for something to distract her.

Lucy's drawings. She looked at the familiar pictures. *Me and my sisters in the park. The Ash Man's brother in the park.* There was one she hadn't seen before. Unlike Lucy's other pictures, it was all in black – no colour. She looked at the caption. *The Ash Man.* Had Lucy drawn this new one after Emma's death, after that day in the park? Was it some kind of therapy? *The Ash Man*: the person from her fantasy that had helped to fix the idea of Ashley's involvement in Steve's mind.

Her attempt at distraction had come round in a full circle. She felt the weight of it fall on her again. Then she heard a

237

key in the lock, heard Lucy's voice animated and excited, '. . . and all fire engines and . . .' and Jane's voice, calm and gentle, calling, 'Suzanne? Suzanne? I just heard, I saw Mrs Varney . . .' and then Jane was there, and she drew Suzanne into her soft embrace, and the shadows retreated, for a while.

Something had woken Lucy up. She sat up in bed. The monsters had been chasing her, in the park, in a place with dark tunnels, and Tamby was saying, sadly, *Be careful, little Luce. Be very, very careful.* But she was at home in bed. She was safe. The curtains moved in the draught. No peacock feather by her bed, watching out for her. Tamby. Maybe Tamby was keeping her safe. She listened, made him say *Like a mouse* in her head, but there was no one there.

They'd been to *London*, her and her mum, and her daddy had gone too. London was big and noisy and dusty, and they kept going down, down with crowds of people pushing her and shoving her and there were tunnels with trains that came screaming out, and she was quite frightened. *Be very careful!* she said to Tamby in her mind, but he wasn't there. She'd clung onto her daddy's hand and he'd said, 'For Christ's sake, Luce,' and pulled his hand free and she was lost. And the train came roaring out of the tunnel and she screamed and then Mum was there and it was all right, and her daddy came back through the crowd holding a newspaper.

When they were coming home, a robber had stolen Mum's bag, and her daddy had said, 'Oh, for fuck's sake,' and her mum had said, 'Hush,' because she could see that Lucy was listening, and then she'd said, 'It's only a bag.' Lucy was *pissed off* with her daddy.

Now they were home again and she was *glad*. It was quiet and green at home and her daddy wasn't cross all the time. He wasn't cross at home, and he brought her presents. Sometimes. Lucy turned over and tried to get comfortable. Her bed felt all *wrong*. Suzanne was staying with them. Something bad had happened when they were in London. Suzanne had had a fire. Her house had nearly burnt down. There had been fire engines and sirens and things. Lucy would have liked seeing that. 'Was Michael there?' she'd asked Suzanne, jealously. Michael would boast if he'd been in a fire engine. 'No,' Suzanne had said, and her voice was all flat and funny. 'Michael wasn't there.' And then she'd started crying and Mum had put her arms round Suzanne like she was a little girl.

She needed to go to the toilet. She used to say *pee* like Mum did, but Mrs Varney said it was vulgar. That was a good word. Lucy liked that word. *Vulgar.* She climbed out of bed. The house was quiet and dark. She tiptoed along the corridor to the bathroom. She peered over the banister down the stairs, but it was dark and still down there as well. Mum must be in bed. And Dad must be in bed? She didn't know if her daddy was there or not. Suzanne was sleeping in the front room. Lucy had helped make a bed on the settee. She went along the corridor, past the attic stairs.

The door up to the attic was open, and the stairs vanished up into darkness. Mum said that Lucy could have the room in the attic for her own one day, but Lucy didn't want it. It was dark up there and smelt of dust and old things. A draught blew the smell into her face, and went away again.

Her eyes were becoming accustomed to the dark now, and she could see, along the corridor, the shapes of the pictures on the wall, Mum's drawings, photographs, things from every day that looked strange and wrong in the night. Round the corner, on the way to the bathroom, it was darker, and she had to feel her way along with her hands on the wall. But she didn't put on the light. If you were creeping through the tunnels, escaping from the monsters, you never put on the light. She'd put the light on in the secret shelves, and the monster had nearly got her. She opened the bathroom door, and the moonlight made shadows on the floor.

She peed, the trickle sounding loud in the silence, and then the noise of the flush sounding suddenly even louder. Lucy waited, expecting the house to wake up with the noise, but everything was quiet again. She listened. Then – it was just a sound like the house stretching in its sleep, like a sound in the wood; just one of those noises, Mum would say, if Lucy got scared by noises in the night. She waited, still, glad she hadn't turned the lights on. There it was again, the faint noise, and a sound like a slow *pad, pad* above her, like feet in muddy trainers, above her head. Lucy looked up at the ceiling. In the attic, in the old dust. Grandmother's Footsteps. *Like a mouse, like a mouse*, she whispered to herself, listening as she crept along the corridor. *Like a mouse.*

Be careful, Tamby had told her. Mr McCarthy had told her, too. *Be careful*, he'd said. *If you see the monsters again, tell me.* But you never did see the monsters. You just heard them, heard them creeping up behind you like Grandmother's Footsteps and when you looked there was no one there. *They're coming. They're coming soon!*

And the monsters weren't in the park any more. They were in the house.

16

Suzanne went through the motions of everyday life. She got up the next morning, woken by the sun pouring in through the window of Jane's front room. She showered and dressed, and at Jane's insistence ate a bowl of something dry and tasteless. She went across to her own house shortly after nine to meet Tina Barraclough for a final check that nothing had been taken from the house that they didn't already know about. It was strange going back again for the first time after that night. It seemed much longer than a day and a night since Ashley had knocked on her door, come to her for help. She felt detached as she looked at the boarded-up window; the staircase, a black, smoky ruin; the carpets sodden under her feet. Barraclough looked at her as she came through the door and said, 'They'll come and put new glass in today if you phone. Have you been in touch with your insurance?' Suzanne shook her head. She needed to, she knew. She just couldn't be bothered yet.

'Shall we get on with it?' Barraclough didn't want to linger. They checked through the house. There was nothing missing.

'I haven't got any valuables,' Suzanne said, 'apart from the computer and the TV.'

Barraclough was particularly insistent that she check her study. 'Someone was up here,' she said. 'He must have had a reason.' Suzanne looked round. The books were still scattered on the chair, the tapes scattered across her desk, the papers spilling out of the in-tray. She looked at Barraclough. 'I don't think there's anything.'

'The filing cabinet?' Barraclough suggested.

Suzanne looked. The top drawer was open. She couldn't

remember if she'd opened it herself or not. She checked the files. As far as she could tell, everything was there. She couldn't remember the details. But why would anyone want to steal photocopies of papers from academic journals? She remembered her passport and her birth certificate – they were both there. She looked at Barraclough and shrugged. 'There's nothing,' she said.

Barraclough's next appointment was with Simon Walker's personal tutor. He was a younger man than Barraclough expected, in his early thirties, she guessed, with friendly eyes and curly brown hair. She recognized him from Fagan's, one of her regular Wednesday evening haunts – though not this past fortnight. She always thought of university dons as elderly, vague and out of touch with the world that everyone else inhabited. Matthew Kiernan, *Doctor* Kiernan, she amended, seemed very much in contact with Barraclough's reality. Matthew Kiernan showed every intention of using their previous contact as an excuse to chat her up, and she rather reluctantly pulled him back to business.

'Simon,' he said. 'It's a bit of a coincidence, you coming here. I was just about to write to Simon.'

'Why?' The detective was now to the fore. She could see him recognize this and switch to a more impersonal mode. Other things were for other times. Maybe.

'He was absent from lectures and labs for the last six weeks of teaching. That's not unusual – not too unusual – with final-year students. It's unusual for Simon.' That crucial month. The time that seemed to have elapsed between Sophie's death and Emma's.

'You mean he's missing?' She remembered Sophie, and felt a sense of foreboding.

'No. He's been around. He just hasn't been attending classes properly. He's been in, he's been doing the work – that's why I haven't chased him up before.'

Barraclough checked her notes. 'Dr Kiernan, I haven't been able to get all the background detail on Simon that I need, but I do know that he was diagnosed as autistic when he was a child.'

242

Matthew Kiernan nodded. 'Yes, so I understand.'

Barraclough waited, then when he didn't say any more, she said, 'So, how come he's here, doing a degree course? Autism is a severe disorder, and this is . . .' *This is a university!* she wanted to say.

'Not a place for the mentally impaired?' Kiernan finished for her. OK, he wasn't above the thick Plods syndrome that McCarthy was always going on about. Maybe he wasn't so attractive. Kiernan went on, 'I'm sorry. You said you didn't have the background. Simon has Asperger's Syndrome.'

'I haven't come across – I'm sorry, I didn't catch the name?' Barraclough remembered Polly's description of Simon as 'creepy'.

'Asperger's Syndrome.' He looked down, chewing his lip, then caught her eye with a slightly apologetic smile. 'Actually, neither had I. Until I met Simon. It's a form of autism – it affects the way the brain processes information. There's no intellectual impairment – if Simon can sort his way through the last stages of the course, he'll get a good degree. He's a brilliant – an inspired – chemist. He has problems with language, with communicating. He has trouble forming social relations – so his behaviour can be a bit odd. That's why he was allowed to stay in the hall of residence. That's only for first years, usually. I was a bit surprised he decided to go into shared accommodation for his final year. It didn't last. He isn't good in groups.'

Barraclough thought. 'You said he had problems socially. Was he ever – did any of the students feel threatened by Simon?'

'Oh, no.' Kiernan was quick to reject that. 'No. Nothing like that. They just found him a bit odd sometimes – he doesn't always react the way you'd expect.' He saw the question forming on Barraclough's face and said, 'I can't give you any examples, I can't explain.' He looked at Barraclough's incomprehension. 'Simon's very bright. He listens. But he doesn't talk, or hardly at all. He can't explain things. He expects you to understand. He's not good with people. He's more comfortable with things.' He ran his fingers through his hair. 'I think he's had something on his mind recently. I

243

asked him if everything was OK, but he just said something about, "It's knowing how far to go," and seemed to want me to comment. I said, "I suppose so," or something like that, and that was it.'

Barraclough showed him the sheet of paper they'd found pinned to the wall in Simon's flat, the one with the diagrams. 'Does this mean anything to you?'

He looked at it closely, and frowned slightly. 'It's . . .' he said, and stopped. He looked at her. 'Simon had it?' Barraclough nodded and waited. 'Of course, it isn't significant. It isn't hard to get hold of this. It's . . .' He pointed at the diagrams. 'These are the chemical precursors to MDMA.' He looked at the sheet. 'This bit, it's a process for using safrole to get MDP-2-P.' He caught Barraclough's look of incomprehension. 'Sorry. Making MDMA, Ecstasy, isn't a particularly difficult process, not for a trained chemist. The problem is getting the chemicals. They're restricted. This is a process for getting round that. Talk to your drugs people. They'll know what this is.' He asked the question Barraclough had been waiting for. 'Is Simon in trouble?'

And Barraclough had no answer she could give. 'I don't know,' she said. 'Could Simon do this, get this, MDP-what-you-said, working in the lab?'

Now Kiernan looked wary. 'Our security is pretty tight,' he said. Which didn't answer Barraclough's question. And if she'd understood him, Simon had worked irregular hours, used the labs outside of official times. She didn't want him to clam up, so she left the subject. This was something to hand over to drugs. 'It's probably nothing,' she said. 'I was just curious.'

Kiernan wasn't fooled. He looked concerned. 'His grand-mother's in a home,' he said. 'She's got Alzheimer's. There's no family otherwise.'

'I'll let you know,' Barraclough said.

'Please,' he said, looking worried. Then he smiled at her. 'Will I see you at Fagan's on Wednesday?'

'Possibly,' Barraclough smiled back. If he did, it would be because the case was over.

*   *   *

244

McCarthy decided to talk to Kath Walker himself this time. She may have been telling the truth when she said that she'd had no contact with Ashley or with Simon in the years since they had left the Walkers' care, but he wasn't convinced. She had certainly not mentioned Sandra Ford, and her visit in search of Phillip Reid.

She was younger than he expected from Corvin's description, attractive and smartly dressed. She made no comment when he introduced himself and told her what he wanted, other than saying, 'You'd better come in.' The house was cold, and the room she took him into was almost clinically clean and tidy. She received the news of her nephew's death with little emotion. 'He was born to trouble,' was all she said.

'Mrs Walker,' he said, 'when my colleagues talked to you, you told them you hadn't heard from the boys' father, Phillip Reid. Is that right?'

She looked at him. 'That's what I said, and that's right.'

'But you had heard *of* him, hadn't you? Before Carolyn brought the children back from America?'

'Yes.' She met his gaze squarely.

It was like pulling teeth. McCarthy kept his voice patient. 'Can you tell me about that, Mrs Walker? Anything at all that you heard about your brother-in-law?'

She was silent for a moment, thinking. 'It was a couple of years before Carolyn came back. Eighty-one? Eighty-two? We'd been getting letters – she was only working part time, well, with the three of them to look after, it was difficult. Bryan had to send her money. Not that we were exactly rolling in it. I was sorry for her, I won't deny it, but I said to Bryan, you've got to think about your own first. He was soft on her, she was his little sister, he was soft before the drink got a hold. Anyway, next thing we know, there's this lass on the doorstep. She's looking for Don, she means Phillip, she says. "You're a few miles out," Bryan tells her. "He's in America." Well, it's all tears, and she's in trouble, and he's forgotten to leave her his address but she could always contact him through us. "That's news to me," I tell her. Bryan was soft. "She's just a kid," he said. He hated Phillip

Reid, said he'd . . . let Carolyn down, that's what he said. He kept in touch with the lass, Sandra, she was called. She *was* just a kid, really, but, like I say, you look after your own, and we couldn't help her. We didn't even know that he was back. Anyway, she was all right, she got married to her boyfriend. It's a wise man knows his own child, that's what I say.'

McCarthy wasn't in the mood for homespun wisdom. 'Why didn't you tell us this before?' he said.

The woman held his gaze. 'They didn't ask me,' she said.

McCarthy went over the details of Simon Walker again, but she seemed to know no more than she had told Corvin. She expressed surprise that Simon had done well and was working for a degree. 'You said something about Simon to my sergeant,' McCarthy said, referring to Corvin's notes. 'You said, "if you got him mad" . . . What did you mean?'

'He'd got a wicked temper on him. He was a big lad, too. Strong. Nothing would stop him. Bryan's big, he's got a heavy hand on him, but that lad . . . He had a wicked temper.'

McCarthy thought. He didn't want to leave the woman any more 'you didn't ask' loopholes. 'Carolyn Reid,' he said. He saw the woman's mouth tighten. 'What happened to Carolyn?'

Kath Walker tucked the corners of her mouth in. 'I thought you were supposed to be the detectives,' she said. 'She's dead. She died after she went back to America.'

McCarthy held on to his patience. *If you'd wanted to know that, you should have asked. I'm not a mind-reader.* 'When was that, Mrs Walker?'

For the first time, she looked uncomfortable. 'In 1988,' she said, after a moment. 'Christmas 1988.'

McCarthy did the sums in his head. 'What happened to her? She was only thirty-three.'

The answer was too quick, too prepared. 'I don't know. I didn't ask. She was ill.'

'Ashley went into care shortly after she died?' McCarthy said.

Kath Walker stiffened. 'He might have done,' she said.

McCarthy felt something tug at his mind. He kept his face

blank. 'Where did she die?' he said. At first, Kath Walker insisted that she didn't know, but eventually conceded that she might. 'It may have been the hospital in San Francisco,' she said.

'San Francisco,' McCarthy made a note. 'Not Utah?' She ignored that. He ran the interview through his mind. There was something she'd said that had caught his attention. He didn't want to let it go. 'Mrs Walker, you said—'

'Is this going to take much longer?' Her voice was sharp.

McCarthy had had enough. 'This is a murder investigation, Mrs Walker. You have already withheld important information from officers investigating, and if I wanted to, I could arrest you and take you back to HQ.' He'd be on dodgy ground, but he was just about pissed off enough to risk it. 'I'd prefer not to deal with the paperwork. Now—'

'I can't answer questions no one's asked me,' she said, defiantly.

'Mrs Walker, stop treating me like a fool, and stop pretending you're one. Now, you said Carolyn was working part time, "with the three of them." But her husband had left by then. What did you mean?'

She seemed slightly more friendly now, since he had been rude to her. He should have played her that way from the beginning. 'The three of them. The three kids.' She stopped, caught McCarthy's eye and went on. 'Didn't you know? There was Simon, and there were the twins, Ashley and Sophie. Carolyn kept the girl with her. She had a job, see, over in Hull. Nursing. One day, it's "I'll have the children once I'm settled in," then next thing we know, she's gone.' For once, surprise left McCarthy at a loss. The woman saw it and moved in triumphantly. 'Some detective,' she said.

Now they knew where Sophie Dutton fitted into the picture. She was the third child of Phillip and Carolyn Reid. Simon, with his damaged mind, Ashley, damaged in some undefined way. Sophie, the adopted child of loving parents, had walked into a maelstrom and had died. Emma was dead, and Ashley was dead. Brooke would have given a ransom to see the letter Carolyn had left for her daughter. It had directed her

247

to Sheffield, possibly to her family, or to her brother or her twin. Kath Walker was adamant that no one had come looking for Ashley and Simon. To her cousin? They needed to talk to Michelle Walker, Kath and Bryan's daughter.

Barraclough spent half an hour on the phone, contacting the vital statistics office in Sacramento, California. McCarthy had tossed the notes of his interview with Kath Walker at her, and said, 'I want the death certificate.' She half expected bureaucracy, delay, a series of frustrating hoops to jump through. Instead her request was received with courtesy and efficiency and the relevant record was promised by fax, 'momentarily'. She rang off in a flurry of 'thank yous' and 'you're welcomes'. She thought about Carolyn Walker – Carolyn Reid. Barraclough had very clear ideas about a parent's, particularly a mother's, responsibilities. She had felt hostility towards the unknown mother of Sophie Dutton because the woman had abdicated her responsibility towards her daughter, and, as it turned out, towards her son. But now . . .

Carolyn must have been twenty-three when Simon was born, twenty-five when she had the twins. Her husband seemed to have abandoned her in a strange country with a young child and two on the way. Barraclough wondered how well she would have coped herself. But Carolyn had tried. For four years, she'd brought the children up. Then, for some reason, she couldn't manage any more. Had she been ill? Four years after leaving her children, Carolyn was dead, at thirty-three. She'd come back to the country where she had family, she'd got work. She'd planned to make a home for her children, once she had settled in to her new job. And then she had gone, leaving her boys with the brother who had tried to look after her, and who wanted sons, her daughter to the lottery of the adoption system. Barraclough frowned. Surely Carolyn could have done better than that. She *wanted* Carolyn to have done better than that.

She checked her watch, and went through to the fax. Corvin was there, looking at some papers. She checked the tray, and the promised record from Sacramento was there. 'I've got it,' she said. 'Carolyn Reid's death certificate.'

248

They looked at it. Carolyn Reid had died in December 1988, of pneumocystis carinii pneumonia. Barraclough felt a pang of disappointment. She'd expected some kind of secret. She'd been expecting another murder. But pneumonia . . . ? She looked at Corvin.

'Thought so,' he said. He looked pleased.

Barraclough looked at him blankly. 'What?'

Corvin tapped the paper. 'AIDS,' he said. 'That type of pneumonia, it's a classic way to go, if you've got AIDS. I did a course.' Barraclough was surprised. He went on, pleased to show his knowledge. 'It was big in San Francisco – started with the . . .' He looked at Barraclough and modified what he was going to say. 'Started in the gay community.' He looked at the certificate again. 'She was a nurse. Must have done her training over here before she went to the States. That's probably how she got to stay. They couldn't find nurses who'd work with AIDS cases.'

'Is that how she got it? Working?' Carolyn had known she was going to die.

Corvin shrugged. 'Who knows? It could have been. Or she got it off her husband. Or from someone else. It was party time over there. Mind you, a nurse should have known to be careful.'

'I wonder why she went back.' Barraclough would have wanted her family.

Corvin grinned. 'You're too young,' he said. 'You don't remember. The papers were jumping up and down. The gay plague, they called it. Hospitals wouldn't treat you; undertakers wouldn't bury you. If you'd got it, you'd have been lynched. And no one would have taken the kids.'

Kath Walker had known. After her sister-in-law had died, the Walkers had known. And they had got her son out of their house as fast as they could and they'd kept his mother's death a secret. Barraclough felt her eyes sting. Carolyn had done what she could. It hadn't been her fault it wasn't enough.

Lucy sat in the playground on the little wooden stump, next to the gardens. All the children in Lucy's class had planted seeds in the spring. Mum had given her some *herbs*. Lucy had put her seeds in one of the little wooden tubs. She didn't want her seeds to be near Kirsten's. Kirsten said, 'My seeds will have flowers on.' Lucy had said, 'So will mine. And you can eat mine, too.' Now there were plants with green leaves growing. That was basil, that was chives, that was dill. Basil and chives and dill. Basil and chives and dill. It made a song in her head. She pushed her hand into the soil and felt it soft and damp and crumbly against her fingers.

She was going to Kirsten's party after school. Kirsten's mum was taking all of Kirsten's class to the funfair. Lucy didn't want to go. But her mum said she should, and if she didn't Kirsten would think she had won. She would think that Lucy was frightened to go.

Lucy sighed. She was glad they were home, but it hadn't really felt like home. It was like someone had come in and changed it while they were away. Suzanne's house looked all strange when Lucy saw it in the morning. There was wood over the window, and the bush with white flowers was all squashed and broken.

She looked over the playground wall to the shops. There was the big cat that lived at the bookshop. It slept on the piles of books in the sun, and Lucy would stroke it sometimes, and it opened its pink mouth and licked its paws. There was Mrs Varney who saw Lucy and waved. Lucy waved back and made a small smile, but it didn't feel right.

Really, she was looking for Tamby. She'd looked for him when she and Mum had got back from London. She'd looked out of her window, but there was no one there. She'd whispered the secret things, but he hadn't replied. *Like a mouse*, she whispered now. A breeze made the leaves dance across the playground and scattered dust on her face and on her dress. Lucy looked across the big roundabout to the park gate. Then she looked over to the shops again, then up at the sky. Now, she didn't know where the monsters were.

Michelle Walker was a vivacious young woman who greeted them like old friends and giggled and flirted with Corvin as she made them both coffee. She was vague in response to

250

Corvin's questions about her father. He seemed to have no stable address. She hadn't seen him for several months. 'He'll turn up again,' she said. 'He always does. Dad's a boozer. He was the last person who should have been a landlord. Talk about Dracula in charge of the blood bank.' She laughed. 'But I don't know where he is at the moment.'

'Tell me about your dad,' Corvin said. Barraclough was surprised that he'd seen through her laughter.

Michelle made a rueful face. 'He's an alcoholic,' she said flatly. 'I can remember a time when he wasn't, when I was little, but for most of my life, he's had a problem with drink. Then Mum threw him out, and he went right downhill. He's . . .' Her face was sad. 'I give him money, food, clean him up a bit when he comes round, but I don't like to see him now. I don't like to see him like that.'

Corvin nodded. 'OK. We're interested in your cousins,' he said. She frowned. 'Your cousins, Ashley Reid and Simon Walker. I understand they lived with you and your parents when you were children.'

'I don't really remember Simon,' she said. 'He had something wrong with him. I didn't have much to do with him. He frightened me, to tell you the truth. Kids are frightened of things that aren't, you know, normal.' She bit her lip, still serious. 'I remember Ashley. I haven't thought about him for years.'

'Can you tell us anything about him?' Corvin said. 'Can you remember what happened, why he went into care?'

'You'd be better asking Mum,' she said. 'Or Dad, if you can get hold of him. He'll be in one of his usual haunts. I'll tell you what I can. I was only nine when Ashley came to live with us.' She smiled at them. 'I didn't like him. I was jealous, I suppose. You know how kids are. He wouldn't leave us alone, me and my friends. We used to . . .' she grimaced. 'Kids are hateful. We used to lock him in the shed. And then he'd wet himself or something, so he'd get into bother with Dad. You didn't want to get on the wrong side of Dad, not when he'd been drinking.'

'Had a temper, did he? Your dad?'

'He was great when I was small,' she said, answering

Corvin's smile with her own. 'But it was the drink, later on, it made him . . . I knew to keep out of the way when he'd had a few.'

'Why did they take the lads in?' It seemed to Corvin to have been a family with enough troubles of their own.

'It was only a temporary arrangement at first. Then it seemed to become permanent. Mum couldn't have any more kids. She couldn't carry them. Dad wanted a boy.' Michelle twined her finger in her hair and tugged at it. 'Maybe that's why I was jealous. He wanted a boy who was a proper man, you know? I remember Mum saying to Ashley, "Boys don't kiss." I used to get a kiss and a cuddle, but Mum wasn't very good at that kind of thing. She was very hot on that, lads not being . . . you know . . . They thought Ashley was soft, needed toughening up. He used to cry all the time when he first came. He thought his mum was coming back. And then he missed Simon, I suppose. I hated it.' She pulled a face again. 'Me and Donna, we got Ashley all dressed up when he was about five. We said we'd play with him and we dressed him up in my party dress and we put make-up on him and everything. Then we let Dad find him. He didn't half give him a leathering. He didn't half go at him. I thought it was all right at the time. I thought it was what everyone did. Dad used to take his belt to me as well. But was . . .' She shrugged her shoulders. 'Poor little sod,' she said.

'It was odd, though. I've never really known what happened. They were always on at Ashley about not doing well at school, not doing the work, but then something happened. It was Christmas, and there was all this muttering and Mum going round with a face like this' – she pulled her face into a mask of horrified disgust – 'and the next I knew, they were putting Ashley in care. I always thought that what finished it for Dad was Ashley being retarded. They said at the school that he had, what do you call it, learning difficulties. But I don't really know. Mum won't talk about it.' She looked at them. 'I *do* think about him,' she said. 'I wonder what happened to him. Is he all right?'

*   *   *

Suzanne was left with the chaos of the fire. After Tina Barra-clough had gone, she stayed in her study, wondering how the disorder from the destroyed house had found its way up here. She supposed the police search had been responsible for some of it. She looked at the litter of tapes on her desk. They needed sorting back onto the shelves. She frowned. She thought she remembered doing that, come to think of it, last time she worked up here, the night that Ashley . . . She could see his pale face and dark eyes, but now he didn't look like Adam at all. Who did Ashley remind her of? It didn't matter. Ashley was dead. She closed her eyes, and she could hear his voice. *I'm sorry . . . love . . .*

She should have known. Now, when she looked back, she could see it clearly – the warm look in his eyes when he watched her, the way he sought her out and brought her things. He didn't court her with flowers and words, he brought her drawings, Coke from the machine, gave her his time and protected her from the casual cruelty of the Alpha Centre as best he could.

And Steve? Steve thought she was lying to him – had been lying all along. Possibly the one betrayal he wouldn't be able to forgive. And she had been lying, but not in the way he thought. She'd come so close to telling him, and instead she had gone looking for Ashley, and drawn him into the trap that someone had devised.

She'd planned to give the tapes to Steve. She'd forgotten about that. That was one thing she could still do. She looked quickly through the pile on the desk. Ashley's tape wasn't there. That was right, she could remember putting it back on the shelf. She looked on the shelf, but it wasn't there either. Puzzled, she checked in the recorder, but that was empty.

With her unease changing to alarm, she went through the tapes on the shelves again, this time checking that each tape was in the right case. Nothing. She pulled out her desk drawers and tipped the contents onto the floor, raking through each pile, knowing the tape had to be there and she just wasn't seeing it. She piled the stuff back into the drawers again and shoved them into the desk. *Think!* She hadn't, she knew she hadn't taken it downstairs. She forced her mind back to that evening, and it was still as clear as if it had happened just a few hours ago. She had finished working, and she had put the tapes back on the shelves. She remembered that now. She had stood by the window looking out into the road. That was when she had seen Ashley – only she hadn't realized it was Ashley at the time – watching the house. She pressed her fingers against her eyes. She'd come downstairs, and no, she hadn't been carrying anything, she'd gone straight to the door to look out. The tapes were up here.

But the other tapes, the tapes she'd put away with Ashley's tapes, were all still there, strewn on the desk. She looked under the desk again, under the easy chair, crawled around on the floor trying to see if it had been kicked carelessly into the shadow in a corner. Nothing. She rubbed her forehead with the back of her hand. The police had been up here searching. Had they found the tape and taken it? She hadn't looked at the list of things they'd taken away. It took her a while to find it, stuffed into the in-tray under a pile of unopened letters, the post from the last few days. She checked the list. No tapes were mentioned.

She went back up to the study and sat down, her head in her hands. The tape had gone. Ashley's tape had gone. And she hadn't told anyone about it, thinking it didn't matter, wasn't relevant. She thought. There *wasn't* anything on the tape that was relevant. For a minute, she was tempted to say nothing, to keep quiet about it. But she couldn't do that. Relevant or not, she had to tell someone. She had to tell Steve. She dreaded talking to him, knowing she would hear that cold, impersonal tone in his voice, an impatience to get her off the phone, but she couldn't go behind his back to someone else.

She tried his mobile first, hoping to get him directly, but it was switched off. She had two false starts before she found the courage to dial his extension, and when she finally got through, someone else answered. She asked to speak to him, someone took her name and she was left in the limbo of *hold* for so long she thought she must have been cut off.

Then the phone clicked into life again, and his voice snapped 'McCarthy' into her ear.

'Steve.' She was thrown by the abruptness. 'It's me.' *Oh, Christ, woman, get a grip!* 'It's Suzanne.'

A few beats of silence. 'Suzanne.' He sounded taken aback. He hadn't known it was her.

'It's . . . look, I . . . I was just . . .' She took a deep breath.

'Look, Suzanne, I'm busy. Is this important?' He was impersonal, businesslike again.

If she hadn't heard that uncertainty in his voice when he first spoke to her, she might have hung up, but she gripped the phone and said, 'It's important. Something's gone missing from the house. I didn't realize at first. I think it went missing that night . . . when—'

'OK,' he interrupted. 'What's gone? When did you notice?'

She told him quickly, tried not to justify herself, just saying that the tapes were routine, standard interviews, that she had just now realized that Ashley's was no longer on the shelves, that the tapes should have been on the shelves, not scattered on her desk. She was talking into silence, and she heard herself start to stumble over the words, to begin to justify, and stopped. Waited. His voice was tense when he spoke again. 'You've had a tape of Ashley Reid for the past ten days and you didn't think to mention it?'

'Yes.' There didn't seem anything else to say. She preferred his anger to his impersonal stonewalling.

She heard him sigh. 'Don't touch anything else. I'll get someone round there. I need to talk to you.' Before she could say anything else, he had hung up.

McCarthy decided to go round to Suzanne's himself. He wasn't sure if he wanted to see her, but he wanted to know about these tapes, and he wanted to know what else she knew, what else she had been hiding. He drew up outside the house, which looked derelict and forlorn, boarded up as it now was.

He went round to the back, assuming that door would be open. Lucy was in the shared back yard, sitting on a tricycle that looked too small for her, propelling it across the paving with her feet. She stopped when she saw him and looked at him in silence. 'Hello, Lucy,' he said. She didn't answer, but after a moment's thought, she gave him a rather wan smile. McCarthy remembered the friendship they'd established over skating. 'Isn't that a bit too small for you?' he tried.

She shrugged and pushed it along for a short way, as if to prove him wrong. She scrutinized him again with an intensity that he found disturbing. 'Suzanne's house burnt down,' she said. Was she just trying to bring him up to date with things she thought he ought to know? Or was she trying to tell him something?

'I know.' He wondered what to say next to keep her talking.

'It was the monsters,' she said, twisting the handles on her bike. 'And Tamby . . .'

He took a risk. 'It wasn't monsters, Lucy, it was people. There aren't any monsters.' Her face set in a stubborn blank. She was angry. She had expected better from him and was exasperated at his stupidity. He knew that feeling of exasperated anger well. 'OK,' he agreed cautiously. 'You say it was the monsters. Tell me what happened, Lucy.'

She looked at him warily. 'The monsters aren't in the park any more,' she said, 'and Tamby . . .' Her lip quivered. 'Tamby made . . .' A tear ran down her face, then another and another. She didn't cry like his niece, Jenny, did, mouth open, howling outrage or despair. She cried silently, trying to knuckle the tears out of her eyes.

He squatted down in front of her, bringing his head to her level. 'Lucy? What's the matter? Is it about the monsters, about Tamby?' She nodded, still wiping away the tears that wouldn't stop. 'Tell me,' he said, gently.

'What's up with our Luce?' McCarthy looked up. A man he recognized as Joel Severini was strolling across the yard, an expression of polite inquiry on his face. 'Aren't you supposed to get permission before you put an infant through the third degree?' He took hold of Lucy's wrist. She looked up at her father and then back to McCarthy. Her face was closed again, still wet with tears.

McCarthy cursed. She'd been about to tell him something.

He stood up slowly, giving Lucy a reassuring smile. He was thinking back. Corvin had interviewed Severini after Emma's death. Severini had had a solid alibi. He'd been working, in company, for most of the day, in his club in Leeds. The night before, he'd had company, again in Leeds. 'There was an authentically shagged-out schoolgirl to back that one up,' Corvin had said. 'Over sixteen,' he'd added, in response to McCarthy's query. 'But not by much. Pity. There's something dodgy about him. He's an arrogant shit. I'm surprised someone hasn't smacked his teeth in before now.'

Now, McCarthy looked at Joel Severini and remembered Suzanne's damning assessment of the man, the first time he'd met her. Jane Fielding hadn't demurred, he remembered, but she'd been distracted with worry for Lucy. According to Suzanne, Severini was an absent, non-providing father, but he seemed to have been around for his daughter since the park episode. He was prepared to withhold judgement. He looked down at Lucy again. 'Do you want to tell me, Lucy?'

Severini's face darkened, and he pulled Lucy behind him. She jerked her hand away from him. 'Get in the house,' he snapped. He turned to McCarthy. 'Perhaps you'd better tell me what she's upset about.'

'That's what I'd like to find out,' McCarthy said. He was interested to note that Lucy had not obeyed her father, but had gone back to her bike and was watching the two men alertly.

McCarthy smiled reassuringly at her. He didn't want her to see him and her father in an angry exchange. He wanted her to trust him. He wondered how he could signal that he'd listened, that he knew she had something important to tell him. Severini flashed him an angry look. Something had really got under the man's skin. 'We may need to talk to her again,' McCarthy said.

Severini had managed to regain his control, and his smile was back in place. He glanced across at the closed door of Suzanne's house and his smile broadened. 'Here to see Suzie? Well, well. She usually likes them a bit younger. I won't hold you up then.' He was just moving away when he turned back. 'A word of warning, *Inspector*.' He made it sound like a term of abuse. 'She's a bit of a head case, our Suzie.' He looked down at Lucy. 'Come on, you've got a funfair to go to.'

Lucy pulled away from him. 'I don't want to,' she said. She looked stubborn, unforgiving. She backed away, then turned and walked towards the house. She looked back at McCarthy once more before she went in.

The funfair was all in colours. The stalls and rides were painted blue and red and yellow, and music played as you walked past first the waltzers, then the cyclone, then the big wheel, and each music was different, loud, happy. Voices shouted as you walked past, and people screamed as the rides swooped them up and down and round. Lucy watched the octopus whirling people above her head, the waltzers spinning them round and round, and they screamed and smiled and laughed.

Kirsten had a huge ball of candy floss on a stick, and she was letting her friends pull streamers off and eat them, and then she would open her mouth and bite into the pink mass. Lucy could feel that pink, sweet cloud in her mouth. Kirsten wouldn't let her have any. Lucy wasn't going to ask, but Kirsten said, anyway, 'Lucy Fielding and all her friends can't have any of my candy floss,' and suddenly Lucy didn't have any friends and Kirsten did. Even Michael had gone and had some candy floss, and now he was standing near Kirsten with his mouth all pink and sticky. Lucy didn't care. She wouldn't be Kirsten's friend for all the candy floss in the fair. Candy floss was *vulgar*.

'I don't like candy floss,' she said to Kirsten. 'It'll make your teeth fall out.' She hoped Kirsten's teeth would fall out. She hoped Michael's teeth would fall out. Kirsten's mum was calling again, 'Keep with me, children.' And Kirsten's daddy was there as well, and Josh's mum, and Lauren's mum. Lucy had thought her daddy was going to stay, but he'd taken her to the funfair and said to Kirsten's mum, 'Can't stay. Work.' And he'd given Kirsten's mum that special smile and Kirsten's mum had gone all pink and said, 'Oh, don't worry.'

Lucy didn't want her daddy *anyway*. She wanted to have a go on something. There were stalls where you could win a big teddy bear, and stalls where you could win big plastic toys. There were hot dogs and hamburgers, and the smell of them made Lucy's mouth water, though Mum said they were disgusting. Like Sophie with the maggots. *Disgusting*. Maybe the hamburgers were made of maggots.

'Who wants to go on the dodgems?' Kirsten's mum said.

Lucy looked at everybody shouting to go on the ride. The cars stopped and there was a scramble, and Lucy went for a car with Michael, but Kirsten was there, and Kirsten pushed her and she couldn't get in the car, and then all the cars were full, and it was just Lucy and Kirsten's mum watching. 'Never mind, Lucy,' Kirsten's mum said. But she looked pleased. And off the cars went, and Lucy looked at the fair, and she could see now that all the colours were dirty, and the man on the dodgems had dirty hands and hairy arms, and the music was too loud. And everywhere she looked, the colours were cracked and peeling off, and the smell of the hot dogs and the maggot-burgers made her feel sick. Kirsten's mum was calling, 'Oh, watch out, Lauren, he's going to—. Oh, he missed! Look out, Josh!' Lucy stepped back. Then she stepped back again. Kirsten's mum didn't notice.

There was a crowd of people watching the dodgems. She moved round them, in and out, and soon she couldn't see Kirsten's mum. Then she went round the next ride, and the next, and then she had the fairground all to herself. There were a lot of people, but there was no Kirsten, and no Michael eating Kirsten's candy floss, and no Kirsten's mum saying *Never mind*. The waltzers whipped past her, noise and screaming and bright colours, and at the other side of her the octopus swooped and dipped. Her daddy was going to take her on the octopus this year, he'd said. He'd *promised*. But suddenly she knew he wouldn't. She watched it going up higher and higher and then coming down like flying. A voice boomed out, 'Come and ride with us,' and the music blared again, but in the moment's silence, she heard it, 'Lucy! Lucy!'

She looked round, but there was no one there. The noise from the waltzers was too loud. She slipped round the back of the ride, and she was at the edge of the fairground, where she could see wires trailing on the ground, and machines made strange noises, and there weren't colours any more. There it was again. 'Lucy!' She looked. Over in the trees, across the stream. Over in the woods in the shadows, she could just see him, like a shape in the darkness, and he was waving to her. *Come here, come here.* Tamby. And the cold, achy feeling that had been inside her went away. Tamby! She could feel the smile stretching her face. She waved back and began to scramble over the wires and cables. Tamby was back and he would keep her safe; he would know what to do now the monsters were in the house.

She skipped over the last cable and began to run, towards the trees, towards the dark shadows where he was waiting for her, when she heard voices calling. This time they came from the funfair. 'Lucy! Lucy!' She looked over her shoulder. Kirsten's daddy was climbing over the wires, waving at her. She didn't want to be found. She was going to find Tamby, and then Tamby would take her home. She didn't want to be at Kirsten's treat any more. She turned back to the trees where Tamby was waiting, but he wasn't there any more. She stopped and looked. Trees and shadows, dark places where there might be monsters. But there was no sign of Tamby. *Tamby*, she whispered. But there was just the silence in the trees and the music of the funfair.

17

McCarthy sat at Suzanne's desk and scrolled the transcripts down the screen. 'I'll need to print these,' he said. 'Take them back with me.'

'There's nothing there, is there?' she said, her voice still strained from the smoke damage to her throat.

He was angry with her, and his encounter with Severini hadn't helped, but his first white-hot rage had cooled a little. Maybe he had expected too much. He remembered that she had tried to tell him something, just as they were leaving his flat, and he'd been too preoccupied to pay much attention. He looked at her, feeling that confused mix of exasperation and anger – and other things that he couldn't afford to acknowledge. 'There might be,' he said. 'I think there is.' The name *Simon* had leapt off the screen at him as soon as he'd seen it. The rest looked like gibberish, but he needed to go through it, and he needed the tapes to help him make sense of it. 'I wish you'd told me about these,' he said.

She looked away from him, and bit at her thumbnail. 'I didn't think . . .'

'You didn't,' he said sharply. 'That's exactly what you didn't do.' He hit the print button and watched as the paper began to slide through the machine. He was angry with her about so many things. She'd had some kind of contact with Ashley Reid and hadn't told him. If they'd been able to find Reid earlier, he would probably still be alive. She'd had tapes with what might prove to be important information, and she hadn't told him. She'd left his bed and gone straight off in pursuit of Reid. If he was going to be honest with himself, that made him angrier than anything, that they could have shared all of that, and she'd still gone off after Reid.

She seemed to be reading his mind. 'I'm sorry,' she said. 'I . . . *Listen!* Ashley's never been here. I didn't know where he was.' He ignored that and took the papers out of the printer, checking to make sure he'd got everything. She tried again. 'I didn't find him. He found me.'

He suppressed an urge to meet her halfway. It would be so easy to accept what she said, accept that she'd made some bad mistakes – but that they *were* mistakes. Then he could take her home with him and spend the night blotting out the last forty-eight hours. He kept his voice neutral. 'Let's stick to the facts for now,' he said. He saw her flinch at that, and part of him – part of him he didn't like very much, but couldn't seem to control – felt pleased. 'I'm going to need you to go over these transcripts with me. I need to make sense of them.'

For an hour, they focused on the sheets of paper. In the absence of the tape, he had to rely on her knowledge of it, and kept pushing her to remember. He wasn't happy with her belief that some of the tape just didn't make sense. 'It made sense to him. I want to know what that sense was,' he said. 'This bit. Exactly how did he say it? Come on, Suzanne. How did he say it?'

The garage. With . . . Lee's name on . . . and . . . em . . . so . . . sometimes, not now. She struggled as she tried to remember. He made notes, moved on to the next bits. *I'm telling you. It was in the park and so she said she was going. . . No. . . By the flats. . . em. . . Simon brings the stuff so she didn't like that. . . It was loose, you see, and so didn't want . . .*

He went over and over it and, after a while, what had looked like meaningless nonsense began to form itself into some kind of sense. He was beginning to see patterns, and something was tugging at his mind, the signal that told him he'd seen more than he was aware of, and needed time to let these things come to the surface. He looked at her. 'OK, I think that's as much as we can do here. I'll . . .' Belatedly, his conscience stabbed him. She looked ill. Her face was white. She hadn't recovered from the effects of the fire and he'd bawled her out and put her through a gruelling interrogation about the transcripts. He touched her hand. It was cold. 'You need to rest,' he said. 'You should be in bed.'

She pushed her hair back from her face. 'I don't know what else I can say.' He didn't want to get into that. He didn't even want to think about it. He'd just get angry and say something he'd – probably – regret later. 'I don't want to go back,' she said, 'not while Joel's there.' She stood up and looked round. 'I'll just stay here till Jane gets back.'

McCarthy thought she looked ready to fall over. He was tired of being a bastard. He still didn't know what he thought, he still felt angry, but he said, 'You need to look after yourself.' Then, against his better judgement, he added, 'I'll phone you. We need to talk. I'll phone in a couple of days.'

'OK,' she said. 'But I'm fine, honestly.' She watched him as he went down the stairs.

After Steve had gone, Suzanne went back to her desk. She printed out another set of transcripts, and began to go through them again. Her thoughts seemed to be slow, as though her mind had lost all its energy. She found herself staring at the papers and seeing black lines of print running meaninglessly down the page. The sound of the phone made her jump, her arm knocking the papers from her desktop onto the floor. Her heart was thumping in her throat as she picked it up. 'Hello.'

'Suzanne.' It was Dave.

'Oh. Dave.' She tried to keep the flatness out of her voice.

'I heard what happened,' he said. 'Are you all right?'

How could she answer that? She wasn't all right. But that wasn't what he meant. 'I'm OK,' she said. 'Sore throat, a few bruises, nothing major.' Steve hadn't asked. He hadn't said, *Are you all right?* He'd just been angry. Except his anger at the hospital had been the anger of anxiety. It had been later that they found those fingerprints, things she couldn't explain. And now he believed that she and Ashley . . . She didn't know what he believed. He wouldn't talk to her.

'Suzanne?'

Dave had said something and was expecting an answer.

She pushed her mind back. 'Sorry. The line's a bit . . .'

'Listen, is your place habitable? What are you doing?' Surely he wasn't going to offer her accommodation.

'I'm staying with Jane, just for a few days.'

'Oh. Right. Good.' He seemed to be filling in time, as though he wanted to say something and couldn't quite bring himself to. She waited. 'Listen, Suzanne, Mike heard about the fire. It was all over the playground apparently. He's upset. I was wondering, I don't like to ask when . . . but if you're at Jane's . . . and if you're sure you aren't too bad . . .'

It wasn't like Dave to hedge. 'You want me to have Michael to come and stay?' Dave had never – *never* – asked her to have Michael outside of her official access.

'He asked,' Dave said. 'He's worried that you're hurt. If . . .' He sounded quite embarrassed. Then his voice changed, became brisker. 'It's not reasonable when you've got all the rest to cope with. Drop in for a coffee, let Mike see you're OK, that'll do.' He sounded happier now he was taking control.

'No. Just a minute.' Suzanne felt something she couldn't quite identify. Michael thought something had happened to her. He was upset. He wanted her. 'He can come and stay. Of course he can. He can share with Lucy. They love that.' Dave demurred, but she overrode his sudden misgivings. Maybe Michael did need her, just a bit. It would be safe if they were staying at Jane's.

They ended the phone call in a few desultory pleasantries, and she put the phone down realizing that now she had something she needed to do.

When McCarthy got back to the incident room, he copied the transcripts and his notes for circulation at the briefing. He knew that there was no point in sitting and staring at them any longer. He needed to let his mind work on them, come back to them later. He directed his mind away from the picture he had of Suzanne's white face as she told him she was fine. That led to other pictures of her – pictures of her lying in the heather, pictures of her in his bed. Did it matter, did it really matter that she'd lied to him? She had hardly known him, not well enough to trust.

But he had work to do. Now wasn't the time for personal stuff. They'd found the links between the victims. The common link was their father, Phillip Reid. Phillip Reid who had run off to America, abandoning his pregnant girlfriend, Phillip Reid who had left his wife in another country with a young child and twins on the way, Phillip Reid who had come back and fathered Emma, then vanished again. But he had been near, had been around, had had some kind of contact with Emma, his daughter – a sexual relationship, Dennis Allan said. A business relationship, Polly Andrews had implied. Had he been in contact with any of the other children? Had Carolyn's letter to Sophie allowed her to track her father down? Had Sophie led him to Ashley and Simon? And Simon had turned out to have a talent he could use – Simon, isolated by his condition – Simon was valuable. Unless the investigation got too close to the drugs. Then Simon would no longer be an asset, he would be a danger. They had to find him!

Liam Martin was sorting through the papers they'd collected from Simon Walker's room. McCarthy went across to have a look. He picked up a folder and flicked through it. 'Looks like a load of junk, sir,' Martin volunteered. The folder McCarthy was looking at contained half-completed forms, each one stopping at a smudge or a crossing out, as though Walker had been unable to accept any error and had had to start again. But then he'd kept the incomplete forms. McCarthy flicked through them. Applications for a driving licence. Applications for a student travel card. Bank forms, job applications, research grants. Several pieces of notepaper with the address of the Hall of Residence and the words *Dear Sir*. Definitely a few bricks short.

A second folder contained personal documents and included a passport. McCarthy looked at the photograph. Simon Walker had his brother's dark hair and eyes. The passport had never been used. There was also a birth certificate, exam certificates, GCSE and A Level. Whatever else Simon Walker had had problems with, he had passed his exams to date with commendably high grades. Martin showed him the papers they'd already sorted. In among the mountains of irrelevant junk – he'd apparently kept every leaflet, every flier, every circular – were more links with Sophie, Emma and Ashley. He had cards with addresses on, lists of personal details. He had photographs, each one carefully marked: Sophie, Emma, Ashley. There was one of Sophie in the park, smiling in the sunlight. There was one of Ashley and Emma, taken in front of a wall of pictures, frustratingly indistinct. Emma was laughing, her head on Ashley's chest, her eyes glazed, her pupils black wells. Ashley had his arms round her, supporting her. His face was serious. McCarthy looked at the picture. He'd only seen Ashley Reid on police records, and, finally, in death. He thought about the ugliness of the swollen, congested face that Anne Hays had showed him, the ruin of this pale, dark-eyed beauty. No wonder Suzanne had been beguiled.

But nothing they had found told them about Walker's current whereabouts, or the whereabouts of Phillip Reid.

Lucy sat on the carpet and pulled the yellow knitted pyjamas onto her teddy bear. She hadn't played with her teddy bear for quite a long time. She was too big for a teddy bear *really*, but tonight she was going to take it to bed with her. Michael was watching television. She looked at the screen as he started laughing. It was *The Simpsons*. Sometimes that made Lucy laugh too, but tonight she didn't feel like laughing.

Tamby was safe. She'd seen him. But Tamby had gone away again, and even though she'd sat in the garden watching, even when Michael got cross because she wouldn't play, and then Mum had said, 'Come and play with Michael, Lucy,' she'd waited, but he hadn't come.

She could hear her daddy's voice. He was cross again. He was cross with Mum about Michael. '. . . *her* fucking brat,' he said. She wished her daddy would go back to his house, go back to his house in Leeds. Now Mum was talking in the voice she used when Lucy wouldn't take her medicine. 'It's just for a night . . .' Lucy shuffled herself across nearer the door. '. . . just *great*, just fucking *great*. Listen, Jane . . .' and she heard cups banging in the kitchen. Her daddy was making coffee. Mum never banged cups. Mum never got cross.

Then Lucy heard footsteps in the passage outside, and the door opening. Suzanne came into the room, carrying sheets and quilts. She had Michael's racing car quilt. Lucy thought it was *silly*. She didn't want a quilt like a car, she wanted a quilt that was a horse. Mum was going to make her one. Suzanne smiled at them, but her smile looked all wrong to Lucy. It looked more like someone crying only pretending they weren't. 'Shall we do your bed?' Suzanne said to Michael. She looked at Lucy. 'Do you want to help?'

Lucy thought about it. 'OK,' she said, standing up. Michael stood up too, his eyes staying on the TV screen as the three of them left the room.

McCarthy's phone rang, and he picked it up wearily. The tension of the past three days was beginning to get to him. He was having trouble focusing. The different strands of the investigation floated randomly in his mind, and as he reached for the patterns he knew must be there, they drifted away into a confusion of names, faces, events. Barraclough put her head round his door, saw him pick up the phone, and put a cup of coffee on his desk. He nodded his thanks as he said, 'McCarthy,' and took a swallow of the coffee. It was black and sweet and, in a moment, he felt the artificial alertness of the caffeine.

It was one of the technicians from the fingerprinting section. 'We've matched up those prints you sent us,' he said, his cheerfulness a sharp contrast to the tension and foreboding that was weighing McCarthy down. He listened as the technician told him what they'd found. The prints taken from Simon Walker's flat, the only prints they had found there, matched the previously unmatched ones they had found at Shepherd Wheel, and the ones they had found at Suzanne's house after the fire.

Simon Walker suffered from a disorder that made him anti-social and reclusive, but he was also intelligent and resourceful. Simon Walker had *a wicked temper*. Simon Walker could fit the profile of their intelligent killer.

'Forget the Asperger's Syndrome,' the psychologist had advised. 'It will make him withdrawn, it might even make

267

him behave in a way that people find threatening or intimidating – but systematic violence like this, that's something else. If it's him, it's coming from something else in him. There isn't enough. I need to know more about his background, about all of them. There's a lot of anger here.' Tell me something I don't know, McCarthy had thought. But background was just what they didn't have.

The psychologist had come up with one suggestion. 'Maybe his anger comes from a history of rejection. His mother gave him away, but later she kept his sister. He wants his family, but he can't cope with people. So he thinks they'll reject him again. Maybe the only way to stop them from leaving you is to kill them.' McCarthy was unconvinced, but, on the other hand, Sophie's death had occurred around the time she had decided to leave Sheffield. 'I'm only speculating,' the psychologist had said. 'I don't have the data.'

Simon Walker or Phillip Reid? If Phillip Reid had killed to hide his involvement in a drugs deal – but that didn't make sense, not unless there was a lot more to the drugs deals than they had realized. Would he kill to conceal his relationship with his children? Again, McCarthy couldn't see any reason for that. It made no sense. Had he killed to hide his involvement with his daughter? If that involvement had existed, then yes, he might. McCarthy could see that.

On the other hand, if Simon Walker was their intelligent killer, and if his target had been his family: his half-sister, and his sister and brother, what was the motive there? Some impulse from a damaged mind that saw threat and danger where none existed? Would his oddness and his behaviour make him a monster in Lucy's eyes? And where would he go now and what would he do? There was no one left, apart from his father and himself.

The window was covered, but the sun, as it sank lower, illuminated the curtains, making the faded pattern of flowers glow in the early evening light. The flat was sparsely furnished: a table, some candles, a lamp suspended from the ceiling. And on the floor, confetti, white confetti, torn and scattered from sheets of paper that had been ripped again and again. On some of the larger pieces, it was possible to see the drawings, or parts of the drawings. This one could have been a fair-haired teenager. This one could have been a dark-haired youth. And a larger piece, and another. One picture, torn across. A child.

Suzanne supervised Lucy and Michael into bed, looking at her watch. She'd thought that Joel was going back, not staying another night, but he was still downstairs, an enigmatic and threatening presence. She stayed upstairs, talking to the children, reading an extra story lying on Michael's bed with him cuddled up on one side of her, and Lucy, uncharacteristically, cuddled up on the other. She felt as though she could stay there all night in their soft, undemanding presence, watching them sleep, watching over them – the way she'd wanted, against all sense and reason, to watch over Ashley. Michael was almost asleep. She disentangled him gently and tucked his quilt over him.

Lucy looked at her doubtfully. 'Are you staying in our house?' she said. Lucy's face was serious. She wasn't a child given to smiles and laughter, but tonight she looked worried and unhappy in a way that Suzanne hadn't seen before.

'Are you all right, Lucy?' she said. Lucy didn't respond. 'You don't look very happy,' Suzanne explained.

Lucy climbed into her own bed and picked up the teddy bear in yellow pyjamas that she'd brought upstairs with her. 'I'm sad about Tamby,' she said. 'I gave him my peacock feather to keep him safe.' She looked at Suzanne again. 'I want to go to sleep now,' she said.

Suzanne turned off the overhead light, leaving the dim night light that Lucy had started asking for. Michael was already asleep, sprawled on his back, his hands on the pillow by his face. She whispered goodnight to Lucy, and went along to the bathroom. Joel was still downstairs. She could hear his voice, and she knew he found her presence as welcome as she found his. She could just about have faced an evening talking with Jane, letting herself be distracted by Jane's vagaries, drinking enough wine to numb the way she felt, concentrating on getting through the hours, letting another day pass, and then another and then another, and surely, after a time, it would start to get better. But she couldn't talk to Jane with Joel there, under his shrouded, ironic gaze, trying to find some response to the gentle, almost polite way he spoke to her when Jane was there, while all the time his eyes were saying something else, entertained by her awareness of it and her inability to challenge him.

She had her escape route here. She got out the small pill bottle they'd given her at the hospital. 'Just enough sleeping pills for the next couple of nights,' the nurse had said. She hadn't used one last night, and she hadn't told Jane about them. She checked her watch. Half past nine. She'd been with the children for over an hour. She was going to take one of the pills now. In fact, she was going to take two, go next door to her house and collect the transcripts from her study, then go to bed. If the pills didn't work, she would pass the time by doing everything she could to reconstruct the sound of Ashley's voice, every pause, every stress, every intonation, and give it to Steve tomorrow.

She told Jane where she was going, and went down the passage to her house, unlocking the door and flinching at the smell of smoke and ashes. She would have to do something, get someone to clean it up, get rid of all the evidence of that night. Tomorrow. She didn't want to think about it tonight. She ran up the stairs to the attic. The transcripts were there. She collected them together, then remembered she had some handwritten ones that might help her. Where were they? She pulled open the drawer of the filing cabinet and began flicking through the files. Her head was starting to swim now, with the effect of the pills and lack of sleep. Maybe she should just leave it. She obviously wasn't going to do any work tonight. But she could do something tomorrow morning. There was a file marked *Transcripts*, stuffed full of bits of paper. She pulled it out and sank down in the easy chair to sort through it. She felt so tired. The writing blurred and danced in front of her eyes. It was difficult keeping them open. She let them close, succumbing to the heaviness. Just for a minute, just to clear her head, just to get rid of that swimming dizziness that was pulling her down into blackness.

Lucy pretended to be asleep. She lay there with her eyes shut, listening to Mum talking downstairs. Suzanne was going out. She heard the door shut. Then she heard the door open and shut again. She could hear footsteps in the passage, then another door opened and shut, and she heard footsteps on stairs, but a bit more far away. Suzanne was next door.

She opened her eyes and looked at the black shape of the window. The curtains moved. It was just the *draught*. She could feel it on her face. Mr McCarthy had said about the monsters, and she'd wanted to tell him, but then her daddy had got cross. And then she'd seen Tamby in the park, and she thought it was all going to be all right again, but now she wasn't so sure. She listened. The house was quiet. It was just making those noises that houses make, sometimes a creak, sometimes a clunk, but safe noises, house noises.

She could feel her chest starting to get tight. She reached for her inhaler and put it in her mouth. She clicked the button and felt it cool in her throat. She waited. Her chest felt better, but the inhaler felt wrong. It was nearly empty. She called to her mum who came quickly, her feet going *tap*, *tap* on the stairs. 'What is it, love?' Mum was whispering, not to wake Michael.

Lucy shook the inhaler at her, and Mum put her hand to her mouth. 'The new one. I'd forgotten. It was in that bag we lost in London. Don't worry, Lucy. I'll go to the special chemist and get another one. I'll do it now. Daddy's here.'

'Daddy can go.' Lucy didn't want her daddy looking after her, not when the monsters were here, in the house, hiding somewhere.

'Daddy doesn't know what to get.' Mum was looking worried. 'Suzanne's here as well. She's just next door and she'll be back in a minute.' Lucy thought about it. She was *cross* with her daddy. But Suzanne would make it all right.

She listened as Mum's feet went back down the stairs, *tap*, *tap*, *tap*. She could hear Mum talking to her daddy. She could hear Daddy's voice, but she couldn't hear what he was saying. Then the door opened and shut, and she could hear Mum's feet on the road outside.

Suzanne was up in her attic now, *clunk, clunk, clunk,* walking around. She would come back soon, Mum *said.* Now she could hear something else. Something was making footsteps downstairs. She listened. It was her daddy. Her daddy was *listening out* for them. Daddy's feet went *pad, pad, pad,* up and down and up and down. Then she heard the door of the middle room open, and her daddy's feet were coming up the stairs the way he did, quick and quiet. She heard him going along to the bathroom. She heard him pee, not a little trickle like when Lucy did it, but a loud splashy noise. She heard the clank as he pulled the chain and the whoosh of the water. Then she heard water splashing in the basin, and the click of the bathroom door. Michael made a whimpering noise.

Pad, pad, pad, back along the corridor. The bedroom door opened, and Lucy forgot to pretend to be asleep. She looked over, and her daddy was there. 'I'm going down to the pub,' he said. 'Suzanne's next door. She'll be back in a minute.' Daddy always went to the pub when he was *listening out.*

'Michael's waking up,' she whispered.

'He'll be fine,' her daddy said. 'Suzanne'll see to it when she comes back. Shut up and go to sleep.' He turned out the night light and closed the door. Lucy stared at the darkness. She heard her daddy's feet on the stairs, *clatter, clatter* now, and then the door opened and closed. She listened. Suzanne was quiet next door. Maybe she'd got her stuff. Maybe she was on her way back. She waited. Her eyes felt sore and tired. It seemed to be a long time. Then she heard the door open and shut, and knew that Suzanne was back. She didn't need to listen out any more. Her eyes closed by themselves.

McCarthy got himself another cup of coffee. He looked across at Barraclough and at Martin. He didn't know if they were working overtime, or if they were on the new shift. He rubbed a hand across his eyes, trying to remember. They were still looking through the papers from Simon Walker's flat. Barraclough looked at him and shook her head. 'There's nothing to tell us . . .' she said. Nothing to tell them where Simon Walker might be, nothing to lead them to Phillip Reid.

He went over to have a look. He picked up one of the remaining folders. It was bulky, but that was because it contained large sheets of paper, folded up. He opened one, and, for a moment, he couldn't understand what he was looking at. Bright colours, lines of blue and green, a daub of yellow, patterns. Then he recognized it and a cold wash of dread ran through him. It was a child's drawing. The writing wobbled across the top, and across the bottom. The letters were black, apart from the first letter of each word, which was a bright, poster-paint red. Across the top it said *The Ash Man's brother*, and, across the bottom, *in the park*. Lucy's drawing. She'd shown him another picture like this, a picture of someone else who was part of her fantasy world. The word, in red letters, jumped off the paper at him. *TAMB*. Tamby, her friend. Tamby, the Ash Man's brother. Simon Walker was Ashley Reid's brother . . . His mind whirled through the things she had said. *Tamby's my friend. . . He's Tamby's friend. Only not really. . . the Ash Man is Emma's friend. . . And Tamby is, too.* Simon Walker.

Lucy trusted him, and he was still out there. And the monsters. He should have stayed, he should have talked to her, he should have insisted!

He looked across at Barraclough who was opening a buff envelope, pulling out what looked like another birth certificate. She glanced at it, looked at it again, her frown of puzzlement suddenly changing to enlightenment, and to alarm. Wordlessly, she passed the certificate over to McCarthy.

They hadn't gone back far enough. It was the birth certificate for Phillip Reid. McCarthy read it. Phillip Reid had been born in Sheffield in 1956. His father was Joel Matthew Reid. His mother was Lucia Reid, formerly Severini.

McCarthy was wide awake now. 'I want Joel Severini in here, *tonight*! Get Brooke,' he said to Corvin. Then the full significance of what he had seen hit him. He thought of Ashley's tape. Ashley had said, '*I'm telling you!*' And he had. He had told Suzanne. She hadn't understood. McCarthy had read the transcript. He hadn't understood either. He remembered what Ashley had said, what Suzanne told him that Ashley had said, the night he'd broken into her house. He checked her statement. *Where are they? . . . Next door. Loose.* The house had been empty. Jane and Lucy had gone away unexpectedly. Ashley was worried, Ashley was panicking because he didn't know where they were, so he'd come to the only person who might know, and help him – Suzanne.

It wasn't *Loose* that Ashley kept saying. It was *Luce.* Joel Severini's name for her. *What's up with our Luce?* A line came to him from the transcript. *Simon brings the stuff so she didn't like that. . . it was loose, you see, and so didn't want. . .* Simon brings the stuff. Sophie, she didn't like that. It was Lucy, you see, and Sophie didn't want. . . *So, Em, Luce.* Sophie, Emma and Lucy. He'd read it, he'd known there was something there, and he'd missed it. It wasn't finished.

18

Suddenly, Lucy was awake. Something was different. Something was wrong. She listened. Michael was making funny snuffling noises in his sleep. She listened again. *Creak, creak. . .* very faint, very quiet. Lucy knew what that sound was. She'd heard it before. She sat up. It was all right. Suzanne was downstairs. She listened again. *Pad, pad*, quiet as quiet, along the corridor outside their room. She looked at the door. It was shut tight. She looked at the handle, waiting for it to start turning, waiting for the monster to come through the door. Maybe he didn't know they were there. *Tamby!* Tamby had been in the park. *Like a mouse*, Tamby would say. And Mr McCarthy. He'd said, *Tell me*. But Mr McCarthy wasn't here. And Tamby wasn't here. Her eyes felt wet and stinging. She'd find Suzanne. Or her daddy. She'd find her daddy. She looked at Michael who was sleeping. She needed to look after Michael as well.

She climbed quietly out of bed and tiptoed across to the door. *Like a mouse, like a mouse.* She turned the handle carefully. It made a small *click* in the quiet. Lucy froze. Listened. All quiet. She pulled the door open a little way and slipped out onto the landing. It was dark, but she didn't turn the light on. The light would bring the monsters. Where was her daddy? It was too quiet. He wasn't playing his music downstairs. She crept across the landing to the bedroom door. She pushed it open. She could see the bed in the moonlight from the window. It was empty.

Lucy pulled the door shut. Her daddy had gone to the pub. Suzanne was downstairs. She listened again. She couldn't hear anything. The stairs were dark, and the rooms were dark, she could tell. She started to go down the stairs, but then she looked down into the shadows below her. And she knew, *knew* that the monster was waiting down there, and Suzanne wasn't there, she knew that as well. She and Michael were alone in the house with the monster and soon it would come upstairs and there was no one to help them at all. *For Christ's sake, Luce. . . Like a mouse. . . Be careful. . . Tell me*. Her chest began to feel tight.

She backed up the stairs and to her bedroom door. The monster might be coming up the stairs now. She could hear Michael waking up, feeling the monster in the house as well. He made a whimpering, just-woken-up noise. 'Be quiet!' she whispered as fiercely as she could, and she felt him go stiff and silent. She didn't know what to do! *Tamby!* She didn't know if she said it in her head or out loud, but then she heard it. 'Lucy! Lucy!' Not a call like in the park, but a whisper, a whisper that seemed to say, *Quick! Now!* She took Michael's hand and they stood at the bedroom door listening. He was shivering. The voice came again, 'Lucy!' And it came from the attic stairs.

The attic! The attic with its darkness and its dusty smell and the strange noises on the ceiling. Her chest was tight. She couldn't *think!* She wanted her mum. She wanted Suzanne. Mr McCarthy had told her, 'Be careful, don't be alone', but her daddy had left her alone. She wanted Mr McCarthy. She could go to Tamby, go up the dark attic stairs and Tamby would keep her safe. *Be careful, little Luce*, he'd said. The whispered call again, 'Lucy! Quick!' She peered through the darkness, and there on the attic stairs, like a sign, was her peacock feather. Tamby!

She pulled Michael's hand and he came with her out of the bedroom and she ran with him up the twisting staircase. The room was full of *junk*. Her daddy said, *Throw it out!* But her mum put it all in the attic and now it made strange shapes in the darkness, and Michael whimpered as he tripped and nearly fell. She had to look after Michael. She was the oldest. 'Tamby?' she whispered. Where was he? She could see a light across the room, a light coming from a hole in the wall, the *roof space* where the smell of dust came from.

There were spiders in the roof space, and dark and dirt.

'Lucy!' And he was there, on the other side of the light, on the other side of the roof space, a dark shape like the cut-outs they made at school. If she and Michael could get through, they would be safe. She pushed Michael through the little door in the wall, a *secret door*, and then they were crawling over flat boards and over a little wall, and there was another secret door in front of them. Lucy pushed Michael. She thought the monster would be coming up the stairs now, coming to the secret door, coming into the roof space behind them, and it would pull her into the darkness and she would never escape. *Tamby!*

Michael disappeared, blocking the light for a moment and leaving Lucy in the dark, then she was tumbling through the little door herself and there was light from a bedside lamp and she looked round. She was in Sophie's room in the *student house*. There was a secret door into the student house. She looked round to find Tamby because she had been so afraid that the monsters had got him, that he was *dead* for always like Emma and like Sophie. And she saw Michael lying on the floor, and she saw feet in muddy trainers and then she knew, as she looked into his face, as her chest got too tight for her to call out or scream, that the monsters had got her too.

Suzanne woke suddenly from blankness. Her head was swimming and she felt cold and shivery. She tried to focus her mind. She'd fallen asleep. The pills had knocked her out as she sat in the chair. Her mind felt confused and blurred. She was in her study. Something had woken her. She had a vague image in her mind of a voice calling somewhere in the distance: *Lucy, Lucy!* It must have been a dream. She heard voices in her dreams all the time. It had come from – where? She had heard it close by somewhere, calling. Dreams. Her head spun and she let herself slump back into the chair. Michael and Lucy were playing, that was it. They were in a field, a dark field, and they were playing a tip-toeing, hiding game, and someone was calling them in one of those muted calls, almost a whisper, *Lucy! Lucy!*

277

She could hear a creaking noise, a soft thump, and then she was awake again, fighting against the dizziness. She needed to wake up, get back to Jane's.

A car engine started up outside her window, revving loudly for a few seconds, and then there was a screech of gravel as it pulled away. She heard another screech as it turned at the end of the road. The noise woke her a bit more. She wondered if it had disturbed the children. Michael sometimes got upset if he woke up in a strange place. She checked her watch. It was gone ten-thirty. Jane was looking out for them. It was all right. Jane knew where she was. She would have called her if Michael had woken up.

She stood up, swaying slightly, and carefully negotiated the stairs. It was like being drunk, only not so pleasant – more stupefying than euphoric. It was dark on the upstairs landing. She picked her way down the next flight of stairs, feeling her hands contaminated from contact with the walls, wiping them on her jeans.

Jane's house was dark. She had expected to have to negotiate an encounter with Joel, but the downstairs lights were off and the rooms were empty. They must have gone to bed. She went through to the kitchen and got herself a glass of water. She was tempted just to pull her clothes off and fall into the bed Jane had made up in the front room, but she needed to check on the children. She didn't want to carry the smell of smoke into the bedroom with her. She could have a shower – it would only take a minute. She went quietly along to the bathroom. The silence of the house closed around her. It must be the pills making her feel detached and distant, but the house felt empty, deserted.

Her shower woke her up. She listened again as she dried herself and pulled on her dressing gown. The silence worried her now. She could hear the sound of cars on the main road, but inside the house there was nothing, and the house felt dead. She went back along the corridor, the low wattage bulbs on the landing casting a dim light, towards the room where Lucy and Michael were sleeping.

The night light was off. The beds were mounded silhouettes in the darkness, the bedding humped up where

278

each child was sleeping, the pillows ... She looked again, trying to see through the darkness. The pillows looked empty, hollowed as though the sleeper had left. She moved into the room, waiting to see the forms of the sleeping children gradually come clear in front of her. But as her eyes became more accustomed to the dark, she could see that the mounded bedding was pushed back from the mattress, the pillows hollowed where the head of each sleeping child had been. But they weren't there any more.

The children were gone.

The phone lines were busy. It was the first hot night of the summer and people were out enjoying it. It was almost closing time, the first drunk and disorderlies were in the cells, a pub fight had resulted in a stabbing, cars were disappearing from their parking places or sometimes just losing their vital organs. One indignant caller reported the loss of his wallet, his radio and his front offside wheel. A celebration down by the canal basin had resulted in a near drowning, and now there were vandals or something in one of the parks. 'It was a car,' the caller insisted, 'going through the gates of Bingham Park.' The operator took the details, wondering what kind of priority a bit of illicit driving in the park would have. Probably looking for somewhere quiet to park up for a shag, he reflected. 'And I managed to get the details,' the caller went on. 'Or most of them.' The operator took down part of a number and a description: metallic. Red. A Corsa or a Punto. He told the caller they'd deal with it, and passed the information through. Someone would have to go and look. But there were a lot of things with higher priority than a bit of fun in Bingham Park. The phones were ringing again. It was going to be a long night.

McCarthy was driving towards Carleton Road. His mind was focused on one thing: keeping Lucy safe. How much Joel Severini knew or didn't know, the extent of his involvement, all of these were things that needed addressing, but were pushed to the back of his mind by the pressing need to ensure Lucy's safety. His radio crackled his call sign, and he pulled over and responded. Five minutes later he was outside 12, Carleton Road, where the cars, blue lights flashing, were already pulling up.

Lucy could smell the floor underneath her, damp and sour. She struggled her legs against the stuff that was holding them, but she couldn't get them free. It was dark. She could feel Michael lying next to her, but he wasn't moving. She listened. It was still, but there was a dripping sound, and sounds in the distance like cars on the road. It was cold. She was shivering and she couldn't stop. She felt sick.

It had all been black. He'd covered up her eyes and her mouth and she couldn't *breathe*, and he'd carried her and he'd carried Michael and he'd put her down somewhere hard where it smelt of petrol. Then she knew they were in a car, and he was driving them off, and she'd started to cry, but quietly, because he mustn't know.

She rolled over. There was light coming through a window behind her, but not very much light. She couldn't see anything in the dark, and there was a smell of dust, like the attic, like the roof, and a smell like old burning, like Suzanne's house after the fire. There was a *draught* blowing against her face. And there was the *drip, drip, drip* like a tap.

Her eyes wanted to cry, but she pushed her hands into them, angry. She was the oldest. She wasn't going to cry. 'Michael,' she whispered. Michael would be frightened and she had to look after him. She was the oldest. He was making noises, breathing in snorts and grunts that would have been funny if they'd been at home, in bed, but it wasn't funny here. 'Michael,' she whispered again, and pushed him with her feet. She felt him move and flop back. The Ash Man had given them sweets. Michael knew better than to take sweets from strangers, but the Ash Man had said 'Eat them!' in such an awful voice that Michael had eaten them. They were bright red, and the red had run down Michael's chin and dripped onto his jersey along with the tears that he was crying, but quietly, because the Ash Man had got hold of Michael's face and said, 'Shut *up*!' in a whisper that was more frightening than a shout when Michael had cried.

Lucy knew what to do when he had given her the red sweets. It was what she did when Mum gave her those special pills for *vitamins*. She pushed her tongue into the high place inside her cheek. She had hidden the sweets and then she spat them out when he wasn't looking. But Michael hadn't known to do that.

She heard someone moving in the darkness. He was there! He hadn't gone. She had to lie still, she had to be quiet. He mustn't know she hadn't eaten the sweets. He was talking now, muttering to himself like Mum sometimes did when she was working on a painting, but he sounded angry. She tried to hear what he was saying. '. . . and get rid . . . keep together . . . won't listen, won't do it *right*.' He seemed to be arguing with himself, and that made Lucy frightened.

It was hard to hear properly, because sometimes Michael's breathing was very loud and then sometimes it was so quiet it was like it wasn't there. Lucy pushed her fists into her eyes again. *Tamby?* she said, in her mind. But Tamby wasn't there any more. *You keep out of the way, little Luce*, he'd said, and she'd tried, she'd really tried. She was trying now, trying to be brave, but the tears just kept coming and coming and she didn't know what to do any more. The monsters had got Sophie, and they'd got Emma, and they'd got Tamby, and now they'd got her and Michael.

Stuck in a trap. *Like a mouse.*

Hazel Austen was standing in the doorway of 12, Carleton Road as McCarthy arrived. 'We're checking the house, sir,' she reported quickly. She directed him upstairs. The house felt like a tomb. Suzanne was sitting on one of the beds, a bed with a child's quilt designed to look like a racing car. Her arms were wrapped round herself, and her story was an incoherent stream of words about fields and voices. She was hyperventilating, and the more she tried to control her panic, the more incoherent she became. McCarthy sat on the bed beside her. He ignored the quick exchange of glances between Barraclough and Corvin, and put his arm round her, pulling her against him, letting her feel the closeness, stopping the words against his chest. He said meaningless things like 'It's OK' and 'It'll be all right' until the rigidity of shock began to leave her. Then, carefully, he began to ask the questions.

'I was dreaming,' she said. 'I fell asleep next door, upstairs, in the attic. I was going to do some work on that transcript. I wanted . . .'

McCarthy tightened his arms round her. 'It's OK,' he said again.

'I woke up. I thought I heard someone calling. Just quietly. Calling Lucy's name. I wasn't properly awake. It might have been part of the dream. And then there was a car. In the road. That wasn't part of the dream. It went off very fast. And I came back and . . .' Her voice was starting to waver out of control.

McCarthy was speaking against her hair. He didn't care if Corvin and Barraclough could hear him or not. 'You're doing fine, Suzanne. I need to know a bit more, sweetheart. Just a bit more. Was the door locked when you came back?'

Her hands dug into him as she tried to control her breathing. 'I don't . . . No. No, it wasn't.'

'And there was no one here?' He kept his voice quiet and insistent. Set up a pattern. Question, answer, question, answer.

She shook her head. 'No.' As she responded to each question, the picture came clearer. He had some kind of time scale now. She must have been back for about half an hour before she found that the children had gone. He closed his eyes. A lot could happen in half an hour. If the car she had heard was involved, they could be a long way from here by now.

'Sir?' One of the search team was in the doorway. McCarthy looked at him. 'We've found something in the attic.' McCarthy gestured impatiently for the man to go on. 'It's the trap-door to the roof space. It's open. You can get into the other houses, both directions.' The student house, empty and accessible to someone with a key, someone who might want to move between the three houses, Sophie's room, Jane's attic and – yes – Suzanne's study. 'We found this next door.' A peacock feather.

Suzanne looked at it. 'That's Lucy's,' she said.

Suzanne felt a cold isolation, almost an exhilaration as though she was riding through a storm. The storm howled and crashed but, just for the moment, she was protected from it. Just now, just for the moment, it wasn't touching her. She watched a policewoman talking to the pale, shocked Jane. She listened to the voices around her as they searched Jane's house, the student house, her house. She heard them talking about Joel. No one knew where Joel was.

She thought about Dave. She must have said something, because the policewoman shook her head. 'He was out when we tried to contact him. We've got someone at the house waiting for him, and we've got a call out. We'll tell him as soon as we can.' Suzanne returned to her seat by the window. Steve had gone, and she didn't want to talk to anyone else. She wanted to keep this coldness round her for as long as possible, like the numbness after a physical blow, before the pain hit. Michael would be frightened. If he was still alive, he would be frightened. Her mind split. If he was still alive he would be suffering. If he was dead then it would be over.

Less than two weeks ago, she had run down the stairs from her study, feeling the optimism of the early summer sun and feeling as though, after all, it would all be all right. Her child, her work, her life. And now it was gone, blown away by something that reached out from nowhere and destroyed it. *Michael!*

If – *if* – the children were found, if they were safe, Michael would want Dave. Dave was the one he went to, not her. And Carol, he might want Carol who did eggs with faces on. The police were looking for the children, that was what they were there for, that was what they did. Finding Dave was not their first priority. She could feel the cold barrier start to crumble, and she tried to strengthen it by working out where Dave might be. The pubs would be closing now, though some of the places Dave went were slow about drinking-up time, closed the doors for their regulars, their musicians and stand-up comics and other performers, and let the night go on into the small hours. Where might he go? She looked at Jane, who gave her a washed-out smile. 'Where's . . . ?'

Jane shrugged. 'She's gone to make tea. Oh, Suzanne . . .' There was a blind panic in her eyes that was so unlike Jane, Suzanne couldn't face it. It was like that day, just ten days ago, when Lucy had gone missing and Emma died. Suzanne had run away then, as well.

She couldn't do anything to help Jane. There was only one thing she could do. 'I've got to find Dave,' she said. 'I've got to go and look for him.' She didn't wait for Jane's reply, couldn't even meet her eyes. She needed to get out of there before Hazel came back and stopped her. They didn't understand that Michael would need Dave more than anyone, and this was the only thing left she could do for her son.

She checked her pocket. She had her car keys. She'd go and find Dave, for Michael.

They needed a description of the car that Suzanne had heard in Carleton Road shortly after ten o'clock. House after house was empty, the blight of the student ghetto having hit the area some years ago. Barraclough tried five houses before she found someone in. She was lucky. A disgruntled man not only confirmed Suzanne's story about the car, but had seen someone loading something in the boot. 'Something big, bundles, something like that,' he said. He couldn't describe the man he'd seen, but he was more definite about the car. 'It was a Punto,' he said. 'I used to have one. Red.' He hadn't really seen the number plate, but he thought it was an R registration. 'Drove off like a lunatic,' he said.

She took the information back to McCarthy who was waiting for feedback on any recent information about cars – stolen or driving erratically – in the city that night. He radioed her information through, and the response was almost instant. A red Punto or Corsa, with an R registration, had been reported driving into Bingham Park at ten-forty-two.

284

No one had followed up the call. It had been listed as low priority.

'Shepherd Wheel,' McCarthy said.

19

Suzanne drove away from the city centre. The road was brightly lit, a congested mass of cars and taxis as people spilt out of the pubs looking for the next place to continue their night's entertainment. They walked three and four abreast, wandering onto the roads, laughing, shouting, pushing each other. These were all young, teens, early twenties; these were not the places Dave would go. Suzanne had tried Dave's local pubs, but he hadn't been in. She'd tried two of the town pubs she knew he went to, where he'd played some sessions, and where he met up with friends on his rare free nights. She had hoped that if he wasn't there, someone would say, *Oh, yes, Dave Harrison, he's gone to* . . . But no one had seen him. Maybe he was home already. Maybe he was listening to a police officer and knowing that, despite his best vigilance, she had let Michael down, let the monsters take him.

A taxi blared its horn at her and flashed its lights as it swerved past. She'd let the lights change. She pulled through on red, swerving to avoid a car coming through the junction the other way. Another angry blast and a finger lifted through the open window. She tried to concentrate. She was coming up to the big roundabout now, the one she always felt tense about negotiating. Tonight she didn't care. She pulled out and let the other cars get out of her way. She didn't know what to do. There didn't seem any point in driving aimlessly round places that Dave may or may not have gone to. She didn't know any more of his haunts, not these days. She should be back home, waiting. She was heading towards the bottom of Ecclesall Road, the place where she had had her encounter with Lee.

Her mind was beginning to work more clearly now. The numbness of shock was wearing off, and the pain was starting to gnaw at her. *Michael! I'm coming!* Who had taken the children? Who could want to take Lucy and Michael?

Lucy had gone missing before. Everyone thought that was because Emma had been attacked, but what if whoever had taken Emma had wanted Lucy as well? And Lucy, ever resourceful, had managed to get away. But that person had come back, had watched and waited and chosen the moment. Steve was looking. He must have worked that out as well. And the person who'd taken Michael and Lucy *must* be the same person who'd broken into her house, killed Ashley and nearly killed her as well. The person who'd killed Emma and Sophie. Knives and mud and flames. The car veered as she gripped the wheel against the pictures of Michael, Lucy . . .

Who? The face she had seen in the park that day, the white glimmer, just a glimpse as he turned back, was suddenly clear in her mind. Not Ashley. She had never been wrong about that. It wasn't Ashley. She was driving past the garage now, the garage where she had found Lee, and he had – threatened her? Warned her? What had he said? *It's not Ash you want . . .* Lee knew! Lee knew there was someone else, and knew that that someone was dangerous. *You won't want what you'd find.*

She needed to get back, get to a phone, tell Steve, tell anyone, that Lee Bradley knew something, something about the person who'd taken the children.

And then she saw him on the road. Lee was crossing at the lights, walking fast, his head down, his hands in his pockets, back towards the centre, towards the church where some kind of quasi occult services had taken place a few years ago, the white face of the clock on the tower shining in the moonlight.

She was on a dual carriageway. She could turn back at the next roundabout. He'd probably run if he saw her. He'd made it clear he didn't want to talk to her. What if she phoned the police? They could come and get Lee. But by the time they arrived, he'd be gone. She kept watching him in her mirror, slowing her car as much as she dared. She scouted the landscape. She couldn't see a phone box. She was coming to the lights. She had to make a quick decision. She did an illegal U-turn and followed Lee back down the main road, just in time to see him disappear down the subway that led to the maze of streets below the station. Still no phone box in sight. OK. She could get through the back streets. She turned at the next left, ignored a couple of one-way signs, and saw Lee, again on the other side of the road, turning off again, moving faster now. The end of the road she was on was blocked, and she had to drive across the pavement. Then she was turning left the way Lee had gone, but he'd vanished.

Lucy could feel him standing over her. She wanted him to go away, to go right away so she could call out, struggle her feet out of the stuff that was holding them, run away as fast and as far as she could. Michael was making that snoring noise again, and she could tell it made the Ash Man angry because he muttered again, and then walked across and shoved Michael with his foot.

Then she heard him moving around them in the dark. She heard a sound, a clanging, rattling noise, and then a splashing sound. A heavy smell began to fill the air, a smell like the car, a sweet, sticky smell that made her feel sick and made her chest feel tight. She began to struggle her legs again.

Then he was standing over her. She could see better now, see those feet in muddy trainers. She lay still. She was scared. She was more scared than she'd been in the secret shelves when he'd come looking for her, more scared than she'd been when she'd lost her daddy in London. It was a cold, still kind of scaredness that made everything very slow and very bright. She felt as though she was a long way away, watching, but any minute the scaredness was going to come up close and she would start shouting and screaming and fighting, and then the monster would come and then he would *kill* her like he'd killed Sophie and Emma. She felt the tears on her face again, running down into her nose and into her hair.

'I was going to take you with me, little Luce,' he said. But he wasn't talking to her, he was talking to himself. 'But it's too late for that.' *Tamby!* she said in her mind. But she knew

Tamby wasn't coming. She knew the monster had got him. Tamby would say, *Like a mouse, like a mouse!* She had to keep still, she had to keep quiet, she had to hide herself from the monster. She felt something hard press against her neck. Something cold and sharp. He was whispering again. 'I can't . . .' He was wrapping a blanket round her, gently, like Mum did when she had to go to the hospital with asthma, and for a minute she thought she was having a dream like she did when her asthma was bad and everything got not real. But he was wrapping it round her head and over her mouth and she couldn't breathe.

Then he lifted her up and carried her towards the place where the draught was blowing from. She could feel it, and she could smell the dusty blanket right in her face, and then she was falling and she screamed as she fell, and she heard his voice, 'Luce!' just before the darkness came.

And she was falling into the darkness where no one could find her, the place where the monsters were waiting, the place where Emma was waiting, and Sophie was waiting, who had been dead and cold for days and days and days. And she could hear music and bells, and they wanted her because they were lonely down there in the dark all by themselves, and Lucy had tried, she really had, but the monsters had got her in the end.

Suzanne had waited in the car for a few minutes, trying to think. Where would Lee have been going to, down here? Then she'd remembered the address she'd seen in his file. He used to live in the flats at the top of the hill, the tower blocks that were being demolished, and so had Ashley, once. The lads at the Alpha Centre talked about *the flats*. When she'd gone looking for Ashley, she'd thought that they must mean the flats at the bottom of Ecclesall Road, where Lee now lived, and where there was a convenient garage – *the garage with Lee's name on*, Ashley had said. She'd never sorted that one out. But maybe these were the flats they meant, these derelict blocks where no one came, or no one had any legitimate reason to be. You could do anything in these flats at night. Who was there to stop you? You could imprison two small children here, and no one would know. Go back or go on? There were no phones, no phones. *Michael, I'm coming!* She drew up in the shadow of the towers, and went forward on foot into the maze.

The flats towered above her. The footpath was narrow now, and the walls of the blocks rising on each side of her made it seem narrower still. The lights weren't working, and as she moved away from the road where the street lights – irregular though they were – illuminated the footpath, the darkness closed in. These pathways had been provided to make a pleasant urban ramble, a way through the complex where the walker could avoid the hazard of traffic. She knew there were green slopes on either side of her, but the ground underneath her feet felt slippery, and as she trod and stumbled on things she couldn't see a sour smell rose up.

She looked up. Far above her the sky was clear and she could see the gleam of the moon, illuminating the edge of a cloud just on the limit of her vision. Down here, it was dark. She wasn't sure what she was following any more. She was lost. There was a sense of movement, a feeling of things that rustled and whispered round each corner. Sometimes she thought she could hear the sound of footsteps ahead of her and thought she had caught up with Lee, but each corner she turned surrounded her with empty silence.

She tried to orient herself. She'd come from the road, past two blocks and round the back of a third. As she moved round the corner of the block into the open space, she saw a red car, its wing scraped against one of the heavy pillars that supported the towers. Its doors were open. She touched the bonnet. It was still warm. Joyriders. She looked nervously about her but she couldn't see anyone. They must have run as soon as they'd dumped the car.

She edged past it, and moved into the courtyard, a concrete area surrounded by the towering flats. Rows of garages opened onto it, but, like the flats, they were derelict. The entrance to the stairwell was blocked and chained. The lower windows were boarded up. She looked round, up. There was no sign of life. The garages were deserted, their doors wrenched off, the fronts black rectangles open to the night.

She looked behind her. The garages here still had their doors, one or two of them. A cloud crossed the moon, and the courtyard darkened. There was no one but joyriders here any more. These flats were deserted, sealed up, waiting to be demolished.

She thought about Michael, and about Lucy. She thought, *He is somewhere. My son is somewhere. He is frightened, he is suffering, right now. I need to be with him. I have to be with him.* Maybe she was dreaming, maybe she would wake up soon to the mundane reality of looking after Michael, of providing cheese triangles and strawberry yoghurt, of doing eggs with faces on, of worrying, endlessly worrying, that somehow the black alchemy she worked would begin to affect him, begin to twist and pervert the course of his childhood, until . . . A great wash of coldness swamped her as she realized that it had happened. It had come from a direction she hadn't seen, hadn't expected, hadn't guarded against. It was here, now, and it had carried Lucy away with it too.

She didn't know where she was. She turned round, look-ing for the path that had brought her into this courtyard, the route away from here. Then the moon came out again, and the pale light shone on the garage doors, illuminating the graffiti – the tags, the patterns, the words, the names. And it was there. The red of the paint looked black in the moonlight, but she knew it was red because she had seen it before at the Alpha Centre: the circle, the LB, the slash. Lee's tag. This was the garage with Lee's name on, this was the place Ashley had talked about.

And then she heard the footsteps, soft and quick, echoing from the stairwell of the deserted block.

The intelligent killer. The face of the man they were hunting wavered and changed in front of McCarthy's eyes. First, Joel Severini smiled challengingly at him, then the face became a blur, the face of Simon Walker, sometimes with his father's look of challenge and hostility, sometimes with his brother's wary gaze.

The park was still and dark. They had turned out in force, quick and silent. Whoever waited in the shadows of

Shepherd Wheel, he had killed three times. There was no possibility of a stand-off here. They needed to go in quickly, be in there and in control before he would know or could know what was happening. He had nothing to lose.

Shepherd Wheel was a black shape in the darkness. To McCarthy it looked too lifeless, too still. The park was full of night-time noises. There was the distant rumble of the city traffic. Closer, owls called, the sudden shriek of one answered by the long cry of its mate. The trees whispered and sighed, and the river rushed and tumbled across the stones. The sounds masked each other. McCarthy listened. The traffic. The night-birds. People shouting several streets away. The river. Something else.

Suzanne looked up at the tower of flats in front of her. It would take her a year to look in all these flats. But she remembered the sounds she'd heard ahead of her as she picked her way along the path, and the feet on the stairs. There was something here, something alive and moving. Dogs? Rats? People? Did Lee still come here sometimes looking for – for what? The person who wasn't Ashley. *It's not Ash you want . . . you won't want what you'd find.*

She needed to keep moving. If her momentum stopped, even for a moment, she would fall like a puppet whose strings had been cut, fall onto the ground and never get up again. She'd followed Lee on a gamble, an outside chance, and she had to see it through. She went towards the entrance to the block, the barred and chained stairwell, and looked up into the darkness. She had heard footsteps, and she thought she could see something moving, higher up where the stairs hung out over the shaft. She pulled at the bars, and saw at once that they weren't secure. The chain that was wound round them had been cut and it was possible to pull them back and squeeze through. Easy, in fact.

She felt the surge of adrenalin take her, and she was through and onto the stairway. The stairwell smelt damp, smelt of cats and the musty smell of rodents, and of other things she didn't want to identify. She went up two flights, listening, thankful that she was wearing soft shoes. Then she stopped. Listened. There it was. Maybe just two landings above her, the sound of feet on the stairs, the muffled pad of rubber on concrete. She ran up the next two flights, feeling as light as if she were truly in a dream, flying up the stairs, then stopping again, listening.

Above her again, but closer now. A soft *pad, pad* on the stairs, someone who was getting tired with the climb. Her energy seemed inexhaustible, but she slowed now, so that she wouldn't get too close, wouldn't alarm the climber on the stairs until he had led her to the flat. Another landing. They must be near the top now. And another landing. Her chest felt tight and her legs felt strangely weak, but the energy was still pushing her on. She stopped again to listen. No one climbing above her. He had been just one landing ahead. He must have left the stairs at the next landing. She moved quickly but more carefully now. She kept in the shadows as she looked up towards the top of the next flight. No one.

She went up, keeping close to the wall, and when she got near the top, she crouched down and looked along the walkway. A long, concrete path, a street in the sky, with the doors of the flats on one side, and the drop into space on the other, protected by a waist-high wall and railings. Up here, the boarding on the flats seemed intact, as though the looters couldn't be bothered to climb this high in search of booty. Or maybe they'd been stripped, and then boarded up again, once there was nothing to interest the thief. Vandals would be deterred by the climb.

She needed to find the flat. The walkway stretched behind and in front of her. The person she had been following could have gone either way. She listened again. Just silence now. She hesitated, then decided. If he had turned left, she would probably have seen him from the landing below. She turned right, and crept past the doors of the flats, listening, looking for signs of entry, signs of life in the deserted tower. Each door was boarded up. Each window was a blank sheet of chipboard, solid, unbroken. She was coming to the place where the walkway joined the next block. She reached the end and was faced with bars. She couldn't get any further.

She remembered the bars at the entrance, and shook them, but they seemed solid and immovable.

Then a voice spoke quietly behind her. 'You can't get through there. And you can't go back now.'

Her heart lurched as she spun round. He was there behind her, just a shape in the darkness. She couldn't make out his features, but her eyes were drawn down to his hands. He was holding something that glinted in the moonlight. A knife. 'Lee?' she whispered.

There was a soft laugh. 'No.' Then he took her arm and drew her back along the walkway. 'Don't fight,' he whispered. 'Don't try anything. You won't be the first one I've used this on.'

The children! *Just let me be in time for the children!* It was too late for anything else. She followed.

20

McCarthy tried to keep his mind focused on the now, but his usual detachment had left him. His mind made pictures of Lucy telling him about Tamby and about the monsters, tears trickling down her face and into her hair as she spoke. She'd knuckled them away fiercely, leaving smears of dirt on her cheeks. He thought about skates with wheels in the wrong places and drawings of imaginary dogs and cats, and real brothers and sisters. He thought about Lucy choking in the mud.

There was a flicker of light under the trees and, as they moved forward, the sound that had been there in the background for a while, a sound of running water, a churning sound, suddenly loud as it reflected off the trees, hit him. He remembered that sound, and he was running as he gave the command to go, running towards the yard, running towards the pit where the wheel turned and turned, carrying the water down into darkness.

McCarthy was over the fence into the wheel yard before he'd had time to think about the obstacle. He could hear feet running behind him. He kicked his shoes off and vaulted the low railings round the wheel, stopping himself on the wall to drop as carefully as he could into the pit. The wheel, massive and heavy, was still turning, and if it caught him, it would drag him under and crush him. The water was up to his thighs, and the suction made him stagger. A child couldn't fight against this. He remembered the museums expert, John Draper, telling him about the conduit: fifty metres long, small and narrow. The perfect place to hide small bodies. He knew where it was, the stone tunnel under the water. He was finding it hard to keep his balance. There was no room to move. The wheel turned relentlessly behind him, threatening to pull him under the water and grind him against the wall. He could hear confused shouts, voices from above him, but he didn't see how anyone could help. He ducked down, trying to feel the tunnel entrance, but there was nothing there. He came up, choking, and yelled to Martin and Griffith who were at the railings. 'Get that fucking thing stopped! And get some lights!' and ducked under the water again. This time he was thinking more clearly. He could do nothing if the children had been sucked into the conduit. It was too small to give him access. He came up for air, ducked down again, feeling down the wall, and as he felt the pattern of the stone change he felt something soft and heavy. It was cloth, thick, like a blanket, jammed in the remains of the metal bars that had kept detritus out of the waterway.

It was jammed tight. He reached into the tunnel, got a firm hold of it. It was wrapped round something heavy, something that the current was trying to suck away from him. He pulled hard, then, as it came free of the conduit, he got his arm round it and twisted to free it from the bars. For a moment, he was stuck. He needed to breathe, but he couldn't get his head above the water without letting go, and if he let go now, that would be it. With his lungs in agony, and flashes of light exploding in front of his eyes, he wrenched at the iron, and the blanket came free. He stood up, choking and gasping for air, trying to support himself against the walls as the water swirled and sucked at him. The wheel slowed, slowed and stopped. He lifted the bundle up to the reaching arms, trying not to see the white face and the yellow hair, trying not to feel how cold she was. Lucy. His arms felt heavy as he got hold of the railing to pull himself up, and then he was falling back into the water as there was a soft *whoof* behind him and a blast of heat as the windows of Shepherd Wheel blew out in a sheet of flame.

Barraclough followed Corvin as he ran to the Shepherd Wheel workshops. She could hear the noise from inside, the sound of the grinding wheels. The men were already swinging a ram against the padlock hasps which separated from the wood on the second blow. Barraclough stopped in the entrance to the second workshop, overcome by the chaos of the spinning crown wheel, the spindles driving the belts and pulleys of the grindstones. And the smell of petrol choked and almost overwhelmed her. She heard Corvin shout, 'Back!' as she saw that the light, the intermittent light they had seen from beyond the trees, was sparks jumping from the spinning stones.

She seemed to be aware of everything at once. She could hear voices from behind the workshop, urgent shouts over the sound of the turning wheels. She dithered for a second. The children! In the water or in the workshop? She had her torch in her hand before she knew what she was doing, shining it round the room, gagging on the fumes of the petrol, hearing the lurch and creak of metal on wood. Corvin was talking urgently into his radio, but he gripped her arm as her torch passed across one of the bulky shapes of the grindstones. She swung the torch back.

There was something huddled on the far side, something that was moving or trying to move, flopping like a rag doll tangled up in the web of belts and pulleys that operated the equipment. Its movements seemed random and unco-ordinated, and, as Barraclough watched, the child's head – it was one of the children! – flopped sideways, close, very close to the spinning stone. Then Corvin was past her, inside the fume-filled workshop with the sparks, and Barraclough ran after him, dragging the child away from the wheels as Corvin hacked at the flying belt. He was going to lose his hand if he wasn't careful. Then she pulled the child free and she was running towards the door when something hit her hard in the back and she went sprawling on the gravel of the path as the air above her ignited in a wash of flame.

McCarthy was glad of the warm summer night. One of the paramedics had given him a blanket, and tried to persuade him to come along to the hospital. A heavy smell of smoke and petrol hung in the air. They'd been lucky, the fire officer said. Whoever had set the fire in Shepherd Wheel had been in too much of a hurry. He must have expected the sparks from the grinding wheels to ignite the petrol, and gone, thinking the workshop would become an inferno in seconds: an inferno in which little Michael Harrison was struggling his way out of a drugged stupor. Fire for Michael and water for Lucy.

Or was it, McCarthy wondered, that the desire to kill was not as strong as they had thought? Lucy had been thrown into the mill race to drown, but the killer had not held her under the water as he had apparently held Sophie under the mud. Nor had he killed her before throwing her under the wheel, as he had with Emma. Michael had been dumped like a piece of garbage and left to take his chances with the fire, poor though they would have been, unlike Ashley, who had had the life choked out of him before the fire was set. Maybe the final action of throwing a lighted match onto the petrol had been too much.

McCarthy hadn't wanted, or felt he needed, to go to the hospital. He was cold, frozen in fact, but he was starting to warm up. He'd radioed back to the station for the spare set of clothes he kept in his locker. He was trying to keep his mind on the practicalities. They didn't know yet whether either of the children had survived. They didn't know how long Lucy had been under the water, what drugs had been given to Michael, or what damage the tangling belts of the grinding wheel had done to him. The Punto had been found under the trees close to Shepherd Wheel. The killer must have left the park on foot, through the woods or through the allotments.

McCarthy went back to his car and stripped off his wet clothes. He was buttoning up his shirt when he heard Corvin calling as he came along the path. 'There's been a call from Brooke. We've got to get back to the incident room. Something's happened.'

McCarthy felt the chill of the water round him again. He pulled his shoes on and got into his car. He dialled Brooke's number. He needed to know if the call back meant that Lucy was dead. He needed to know if they had a name for the man they were hunting. He listened to Brooke's terse message, then pulled the car round in a tight turn and floored the accelerator as he headed towards town.

The door closed behind her with a heavy *chunk*. Suzanne stayed where she was. She didn't want to look at him. Her ears were listening for other sounds, the sound of children, frightened, maybe crying, maybe just asleep, just breathing quietly, but there. The flat was cold and dead. It was pitch black, and the silence pressed round her. She heard his voice again, still a whisper. 'They'll be pulling this down soon.' She heard the sound of footsteps, *pad, pad* like the footsteps on the stairs. A dim light came on. She kept her eyes down and the feet came into view, wearing muddy trainers that looked worn and battered. 'Look at me.'

Suzanne kept her gaze lowered for a moment and heard the impatient catch in his breath. She looked at him. The light was faint; it came from a lantern hanging from a hook in the ceiling.

She knew before she looked at him. She knew his voice. His face was shadowed in the lamplight. But she knew it so well. Heavy black hair, dark eyes, pale skin. Only now he made no attempt to disguise the intelligence in those eyes, or the anger. 'Ashley,' she said. And it was unreal, it was a dream. She knew she was going to wake up soon, and she would be in bed, and Michael and Lucy would be in bed upstairs. She looked at him again. He was standing by the doorway, watching her, the way he had that night when . . . *Ashley!*

He seemed to pick up her thoughts. 'I didn't plan it,' he said. 'I got lucky.' He frowned. 'I should have thought of it. Simon looks . . . used to look . . . enough like me.' He lit a candle on the table in front of him and his eyes met hers. 'He followed me. I thought I could keep Simon out of it, but he was starting to get worried. He thought I was going to hurt Luce.' He made a gesture of helplessness. 'I had to . . .' His face was sad. 'He was looking for me and he found me. "It's just a dream, Si," I told him. But he wouldn't listen. He always listened before. They'll find out. They're not as stupid as you'd think.' He was standing close to her, and he touched her hair. 'You came looking for me,' he said.

There was something so familiar about him now, that stance, that gentle, knowing smile. She had felt that flicker of recognition often, felt that she knew him. Jane talking that day in the garden . . . 'He had a child from his marriage.' She looked up at Ashley's face, so close to hers she could feel his breath on her hair. 'Joel,' she said. *Joel!* And that smile . . . But where Joel's smile was empty, Ashley's had been warm and gentle. Not any more. *The children!*

'Phillip Reid,' he said. His voice was calm, but there was something in his eyes that made her stand very still, very quiet. 'He isn't *Joel*. He isn't Severini. He thought he could just forget us if he changed his name. There was only me knew that. I didn't tell the others. Only Simon. Simon doesn't talk.' He smiled at her, holding the knife close against her neck. 'I found him, you see. Our dad. He was stupid. He didn't really change his name. It was on all his business stuff. I told Simon what to look for. Simon found it on the computer. Simon's good at things like that.' Now he was breathing faster, and his eyes were glittering in the candle-light. 'I went to see him. He didn't know me. I'll show him who I am!' His eyes were looking through her, but the knife was level and firm against her.

'Sophie found me. She had a letter. Our mother had writ-ten her a letter. *No letter for me! I couldn't even read it!*' His voice was ragged. His foot lashed out and the table crashed over, sending the candle rolling across the floor. Then, as quickly as it had come, his anger went and his voice was quiet and reflective again. 'I knew about Emma. Uncle Bryan was always talking about Emma. And Sandra. "That poor lass! If you turn out like your dad I'll . . ." Uncle Bryan. I took him a bottle of whisky. He told me where they lived. "You're a good lad, Ashley," he said. "It's all water under the bridge." Under the bridge . . .' He laughed. He looked at the candle on the floor and picked it up. It was still burning.

'Sophie wants us to be a family. It's good, that . . .' He smiled, but his smile was blank and joyless. 'We're going to get a house, all of us. Me, Simon, Sophie, Emma – and Luce. Emma and Sophie, they don't know about Luce. They don't know they've got another sister. It's a surprise. They'll like it. When I tell them. Somewhere by the sea. I've never seen the sea.' His eyes glistened in the light.

'Only Sophie wanted to stop it in the end. She wanted to leave me and go back to her nice, safe family on the farm. I couldn't let her do that.' He held the knife between them, the point just touching her. She stood motionless, her breath tight in her throat. 'I had it all planned. Simon got a room in the house next door, and he got one for So. They always give Simon what he asks for. He didn't want it, but he'd do it for me. He did what I said . . .'

He looked at her to make sure she understood. 'Sophie likes children,' he said. 'I knew she'd make friends with Lucy. But I had to make sure. I said, "Ask if she wants a babysitter." I knew she would. She didn't look after Luce properly. She let him near her.'

'She let him . . . ?'

'Her father. *My* father.' He was breathing fast again, and his eyes that had been unfocused were sharpening again.

She had to keep him calm. 'It's all right, Ashley,' she said. 'Just tell me.' He smiled, and now it was the smile she remembered from the Alpha Centre, from that night at her house.

'You see, Sophie would watch her, keep her safe, while I got rid of him. Emma sold him the pills. She sold her dad the pills, and he didn't even recognize her.' He laughed quietly, then his face changed, grew cold and angry. 'He started hitting on her, *his own daughter*! Buying her things, telling her she could dance in his club. He wanted the pills, see. He wanted to know where she was getting it from. But I've fixed him. "He knows how to make us all rich," Emma said. "Stop pushing me around. I'm going to do what he says and you can't stop me," she said . . .' His eyes were unfocused again. He shook his head. 'I get angry,' he said.

Suzanne asked the question she had dreaded asking, could hardly bring herself to ask, because she knew what the answer would be. 'The children? Michael, and Lucy?' She tried to keep her voice calm, but it shook with the strain. She wanted to scream, beg, *anything*, if he would say that they were safe, they were well.

He frowned in irritation at being interrupted. 'Luce knows. About Em and So. And Simon. Simon told her.' He shook his head. He looked bewildered now, more the Ashley she remembered. 'It was good,' he said. 'When we were all together.'

Her eyes were becoming accustomed to the dim light. All around the walls, from floor to ceiling, there were sheets of paper covered with drawings – people, faces; and paintings – wild patterns, sometimes sprayed over the top of the drawings, all flickering and moving in the light of the candles. Sophie and Emma, alive again in the candlelight. Lucy, over and over again, big-eyed, solemn. 'Please, Ashley,' she said. She could feel the strength draining out of her. She had to know. 'Please, Ashley, tell me what you've done with Lucy. With Michael.' He looked at her, his silence almost an answer. 'Please,' she said.

He looked down, confused. Then he looked back at her again. 'I liked you,' he said. 'I told you what was happening, before Sophie . . . when I didn't know what to do about Sophie, but you didn't listen. You could have stopped it, if you'd listened.' *Listen to me!* He was breathing hard again.

'Please, Ashley. Please tell me. I'm sorry. I know. I did listen, but I thought it was too late.' She tried to keep her voice gentle, tried to keep him calm. *Tell me!*

He seemed to be thinking. 'I don't know,' he said after a moment. 'I left them.' He wouldn't look at her.

'Where? Where did you leave them? Were they hurt? Ashley . . .'

His hand lashed out, hitting her across the mouth. She staggered. 'Shut up!' he said. 'I never wanted to hurt anyone. They just . . . So found out. I had to . . . And Em was going to . . . Stop asking me questions. You always ask me questions.' The dislocated voice of the tape was talking to her now. He grabbed hold of her hair and pulled her head back, holding the knife hard against her neck. 'I get angry,' he said.

There were tears in his eyes, glistening on his lashes in the candlelight. He let go of her hair and put his hand up to her face, running his fingers gently over the swelling that was

302

starting on her lip. 'Sorry,' he said. 'I'm sorry.' Strangely, incongruously, he still made her think of Adam, Adam caught in a trap of his own making, that he could no longer escape. He'd said that he'd left them, Lucy and Michael. Where? He had no reason to hurt them. Maybe it would be all right. Maybe Lucy and Michael would be found, safe and well, come home and . . . and . . . She couldn't think beyond that point.

He was still holding the knife, but away from her now, as though he'd forgotten it was a weapon. It didn't matter. She couldn't run. She couldn't go anywhere until she found out about the children. He ran his finger absently across the edge. 'She didn't want us, my mum. She kept Sophie, but she didn't want us. We went to live with my uncle and aunt. I couldn't understand what they were saying. I cried for my mum. She said she was coming back, but she never did. I didn't know where she'd gone. I didn't know where Simon had gone.' His eyes looked blank. 'I didn't want to hurt him. I hit him and he fell on the bed. Then I . . .' He shook his head as if he was trying to dislodge the images. His eyes came back into focus and he looked at her. 'He was a cunt, my uncle.'

They were operating on McCarthy's hunch, because they didn't have anything else to go on. All they had were the cryptic contents of Ashley's tape, the few bits of information from the case files, and their local knowledge.

The street lighting around the flats was largely gone, vandalized and not repaired by a cash-strapped council. This wasn't an area that was worth canvassing for votes, and now most of the blocks were empty. Barraclough turned her headlights off as she followed McCarthy's car into the central courtyard. Two vans came in behind her.

Simon had made the drugs, Ecstasy and speed. The Alpha Centre had reported a problem with pills about three months ago. Ashley Reid had started at the Alpha Centre then, and his main contact there was Lee Bradley. Lee used to live in these flats, up until six months ago, and in the last months of his being here, most of the flats had been boarded up and abandoned. Ashley Reid, too, had had a flat here, one of the places where flats could be had for the asking. No one wanted to live here through choice. Barraclough knew that the minimal policing of the estate would be wound right down once the flats were empty. What better venue for dealing, and what reason would there be to change? Lee Bradley's old flat was near the top of the block facing Barraclough, and the abandoned Astra in front of the garages, a car that had been reported stolen ten minutes after the fire at Shepherd Wheel, seemed to confirm that McCarthy had been right.

There was the smell of beer and the sound of men laughing. The child tip-toed down the stairs and peered through the kitchen door. The smell of beer was stronger now, and there were people, lots of people, men, sitting round the table. They had glasses in front of them, and they were laughing. One of them looked round and saw him at the door. Uncle Bryan. 'Hey up,' he said, in that loud voice the men sometimes used. 'Who've we got here then?' Uncle Bryan was liking him. He sidled into the room, smiling round his thumb.

'Give over, Bryan.' Aunt Kath's voice, irritable. 'Ashley! Thumb!' Ashley took his thumb out of his mouth and stood by his uncle's solid bulk.

'You fuss too much.' Uncle Bryan was drinking beer. He winked at Ashley. Ashley tried to wink back, but both his eyes closed together. 'Come on, love,' Uncle Bryan said. 'Give us a kiss.' The men laughed. He was confused. 'Come on,' Uncle Bryan said, holding out his arms. Aunt Kath always said, 'Boys don't kiss.' He looked at her. Her back was towards him, stiff and angry. 'Come on,' Uncle Bryan said again, and, shyly, he reached up his arms and kissed his uncle's face.

The blow was so unexpected he couldn't feel it hurting. He was on the floor by the other side of the room, and all the men were laughing, and Uncle Bryan was laughing. 'That's for kissing men,' he said. 'Hey!' He turned to the other men who were laughing and laughing. 'Get it? That's for kissing men!'

He'd cut his finger on the edge of the knife. It was bleeding. He looked at it for a moment, then wiped the blood off on his T-shirt. 'I thought it would be all right after Sophie came.'

His eyes were sad. 'But everything changes. Nothing stays the same. Sometimes there's only one safe place to be.'

He reached out and took her hand. He did it gently, but his grip was firm. 'I'll show you,' he said. He took her across the room to where the window was covered with a heavy blanket. He pulled the blanket away, and they were looking out together across the night sky. The window opened onto a balcony. 'Come on,' he said.

The city lay at their feet. Away in the distance, the lights of houses and roads sparkled on the far hills. Nearer, the lights merged and blazed out in the colour and confusion of the city centre. The glow-worms of the trams wound around their tracks – not glow-worms, Suzanne thought, but dragons, monsters gliding in silent brilliance through the night. The cars made rivers of light; the traffic lights winked red, yellow, green; the street signs and the bars and the clubs flashed out their messages to the watchers in the sky above them. But to Suzanne it was all dead, silent chaos. *Why, this is hell, nor am I out of it.* The words from nowhere formed themselves in her mind.

Ashley let go of her hand, and now he put his arm round her, pulling her close against him, like a lover, and they stood together, watching. Then he directed her attention downwards. There, in front of the block, down at the end of the dizzying drop, a car was drawing up, dark and silent. Ashley pushed her behind him, still holding the knife, and stood in clear view, close to the edge with just a broken railing between him and the drop. *One safe place.* She tried to pull away, but his grip on her wrist was unbreakable. He was so close to the drop, so close . . . She could see figures moving around far below, some apparently milling aimlessly, others moving with intent towards the shadows, round the back of the building.

'They'll already be up here,' Ashley said. 'They've been here for a while.'

McCarthy positioned the team outside the door of the flat. It was quiet now, but a few minutes before, they had heard a voice, the sound of something falling. One of the officers shook his head. No further sound. They'd just heard the one voice, and they knew, now, who that was.

Anne Hays had taken prints from the body removed from Suzanne's house, a standard procedure in the absence of close friends or relatives to make an identification. The formality of linking them up to the prints they had on record for Ashley Reid had been slightly delayed by the urgency of the forensic work from Simon Walker's flat. Only they hadn't matched.

And now Reid was holed up in the flat – on his own, or with Joel Severini, or with Lee Bradley? They needed to know if there was anyone in there with him. McCarthy checked back on his radio. The first confirmation came through. Severini had been found coming out of a pub, apparently ignorant of the events of the night. He'd been arrested. That was for sorting later. Lee Bradley was, according to his mother, out with his mates. She didn't know where, and she didn't seem particularly interested. Someone, presumed to be Ashley Reid, was on the balcony of the flat. He'd seen the cars.

McCarthy cursed and considered the options. He didn't really have any. He gave the signal to the team and spoke quietly into his radio. 'We're going in,' he said.

Barraclough could see the figure clearly from her position by the car. A man standing on the balcony, outlined against the light. Corvin was swearing under his breath. Reid had seen them now. The figure moved backwards, back inside, she thought, then came back to the edge. She heard Corvin on his radio, 'Careful, Steve, hold it, he's on the balcony . . .' and a lot of static and crackling.

'What's he doing?' Corvin was squinting up, his neck at a painful angle.

'I don't know . . . *Shit!* He's going to . . .' They moved back as Ashley Reid came right to the parapet.

'No, he's just standing . . .' Corvin kept moving backwards, away from the danger zone. Barraclough heard the radio crackle, heard voices as an incoherent gabble, and then they were behind the van still looking up at the figure watching them from that precipitous drop.

Quite early in her career, Barraclough had had to help in the aftermath of a jumper. A teacher who had been suffering from depression had jumped from one of the city's tower blocks. She could remember two things that had lodged themselves in her mind. One was the sheer mortality of the human body, its capacity to be smashed to pulp; the other was her conviction that between the leap and the end, there was more than enough time for regret.

Suzanne struggled to free herself from his grip. Relief froze her as he moved away from the drop. She tried to speak, but her voice was gone.

He looked at her. 'It was so good, you see. We all knew it was. It was going to be perfect. It was all going to be new.' He touched her face, gently. 'Why are you crying? I can't stand crying.' Suzanne shook her head. She couldn't explain. He looked into her eyes, running his fingers across her mouth. 'They're outside the door.'

He moved before she could react. He was behind her, pulling her back against him, his arm across her chest. She could feel the cold edge of the knife hard against her neck. He seemed calm, matter of fact. She heard pounding on the door and saw the jamb start to bend and splinter. Then the door was open and they were in. She felt him pulling her back towards the balcony. The knife was digging in now. She closed her eyes. 'Ashley . . .' she said.

She could feel his mouth against her ear. 'Don't worry. I'll keep you safe.' His voice was barely a whisper. Then she looked. There seemed to be hundreds of them, in the room, in the doorway, spreading out, trying to flank Ashley. And in the doorway, Steve, looking at her, and just for a second his face seemed to shatter, then it became a calm, impassive mask. He looked beyond her. 'Ashley! Listen! They're all right. Lucy and Michael. They're all right. Let Suzanne go.'

Ashley's voice, speaking in her ear. Still gentle, quiet. 'Fire and water, *Suzanne*. They're safe now. They're gone.' For a moment, she felt the knowledge open up inside her, a pit she would fall down for ever, but Steve's eyes held hers. He wouldn't lie. Not about this. Not to her. They were at the

307

doors now, and Ashley was inexorably drawing her out onto the balcony.

Then, suddenly, he let her go, and she staggered back against the railing, feeling it start to give. He had swung himself up onto the low parapet, his legs hanging over the drop. 'Suzanne!' Steve was shouting. 'Get away from there! Now! *Now!*'

It was like slow motion, like moving through heavy water. She turned her head, and his eyes, Ashley's eyes, Adam's eyes, looked at her. *No!* But she didn't know if she'd said it out loud or if it just stayed in her head. She reached her hand out to him as he looked from her to the emptiness beside him. *Listen to me!* He smiled slightly, and suddenly he was the Ashley she knew, Ashley saying, *Don't mind them.* Ashley saying, *I'd like to do art at college,* Ashley kissing her with a terrifying desperation. He looked into her eyes. He reached out his hand to her. *Listen to me, Suzanne, listen!* Her hand reached towards his, and he looked into her eyes and smiled. Steve's voice, frantic now, *'Suzanne!'* And she snatched her hand back as Ashley's closed like steel round the empty air.

McCarthy saw it in frozen time, like a stop-go animation, like a scene under a strobe light. Ashley Reid on the balcony rail, silhouetted against the night sky, Suzanne reaching her hand out, taking his hand, and he wasn't going to get there in time, and then she was falling back against the broken rail and Ashley looked across to him and smiled, a wry, regretful smile. And he was gone and it seemed an eternity in the second it took McCarthy to reach Suzanne, to pull her back from the drop, to try to muffle her ears from the crash onto the concrete far, far below.

21

McCarthy brought Suzanne down from the flat, wanting to get her away from the shadows and the pictures that danced and flickered in the candlelight. She was shaking with reaction. Perhaps he should have waited for the paramedics, made sure that she was all right before they attempted the long stairway, but he needed to get away as well.

There was a concrete bench at the bottom of the stairwell. It seemed as good a place to wait as any. They'd find him if they needed him. He put his jacket round Suzanne's shoulders, and then put his arm round her. He looked up at the sky. It was as cloudless as the day he had taken her up on the heather moors. The moon shone clear and cold, making the edges sharp and the shadows black across the courtyard.

'Michael?' she said. 'And Lucy?' She kept asking.

'They're at the hospital,' he said. He couldn't tell her any more.

'I'm sorry,' she said. She had said that over and over.

'Just stop it, OK?' His head was pounding. He didn't want to talk. He didn't know what he wanted to do. He was angry with her, for the way she had run herself – and him – blindly and recklessly into catastrophe. He was angry with her for the way she seemed half seduced by the *one safe place* that Ashley had tried to lead her to. He couldn't handle the way she made her choices, every time, it seemed, for guilt, despair and destruction. He couldn't spend his life in the burial ground, watching her mourn by her brother's grave.

And yet, at the last minute, she had pulled back from the edge.

*   *   *

It was after midnight. Tina Barraclough ran her hands through her hair and tried to focus. She was tired. They were all tired. If she closed her eyes, she could see the figure tumbling through the air above her, floating as if in slow motion, plummeting so fast there was no time for thought or action. She shook her head to clear it. She was dreaming on her feet.

Steve McCarthy came through the door, pulling off his jacket and dumping it on the nearest desk. He'd been at the hospital. He looked terrible. Brooke said, 'We need to know what happened in that last half-hour, what happened in that flat before you went in, Steve.' He paused and took his glasses off to wipe them. 'How did she end up there? What sent her up there after Reid?'

Barraclough saw Corvin start to say something, look at McCarthy and think better of it. After a moment's silence, McCarthy said, 'Silly bitch went off on a wild-goose chase and nearly got herself killed.' He shook his head at Brooke's query. 'I haven't got all the details. They're still patching her up. I'll go back tomorrow and . . .'

Brooke shook his head. 'Not you, Steve.' McCarthy began to protest, shrugged his shoulders and leant back in his chair. He looked exhausted. Brooke allocated tasks for the next day and sent the team home. 'Wait, Steve,' he said. 'I need to talk to you. DC Barraclough, you wait here as well. My office, Steve.'

As the two men disappeared into the tiny room that Brooke had annexed as a temporary office, Barraclough edged round so that she could see through the glass panels of the door. Surely Brooke wasn't going to give McCarthy a bollocking, not about Reid's fall, not about Suzanne Milner. She could see the two men talking but she couldn't make out what they were saying. McCarthy was leaning against the wall, his head bowed.

Brooke reached into the desk and took out a bottle of whisky and a glass. He pushed them across to McCarthy, who poured himself what was probably the largest measure Barraclough had ever seen and knocked it straight back. Brooke nodded at him, and McCarthy poured himself another one and drank it almost as quickly as the first. Brooke stayed where he was for a moment, then came over to the door.

'. . . all right,' he was saying as he opened it. 'You're going home, Steve.' He looked across to the door where Barraclough was standing, discreetly away from her original line of sight. 'DC Barraclough, drive the DI home, and then get off yourself. I want you in again first thing. You all right?'

Like a great bird, dropping out of the sky, dropping, dropping. . . 'Yes, sir,' she said.

Lee Bradley had been picked up, running from the flats after Ashley Reid's fall. A search of his room in his mother's flat revealed a few of the now familiar pills. Faced with this evidence, Bradley told them that he had got them from Ashley Reid, had been, in fact, a regular customer. 'I used to pick up on Saturday nights, but he wasn't there on Saturday, or Sunday.' The news of Reid's 'death' in the fire had been in the local paper that day. It would have been a major topic of discussion at the Alpha Centre. He claimed he had been going back to the flat to look for Ashley, that he had been unable to accept the stories he had heard of his death in the fire, but the flat, with its apparently unguarded supply of drugs, and the possibility of money, must have been an irresistible lure. Only Suzanne had got there first. He had watched her push her way through the bars onto the stairs and had waited at the bottom, knowing that she would have to come back the same way. What he had been waiting for, he was unable, or unwilling, to specify. Trapped by the sudden influx of police officers, he had been making his way to the footpaths through the flats where he hoped to escape unnoticed, when Ashley's fall had panicked him into flight.

The flat itself had supplied evidence that filled in some of the gaps. Ashley Reid had obviously used it as a hiding place after his disappearance, but it showed signs of a longer occupancy. This was where Emma had gone. The flat was minimally furnished – a bed, a table, a Primus stove, a kettle. There were other things – a bag of clothes that Dennis Allan identified as Emma's; and carrier bags with expensive dresses, tops, lingerie, most of which looked as though they had never been worn; more of the pills that had, presumably, come from Simon Walker; a small bag of brown powder that proved to be heroin, some syringes and needles; and nearly three thousand pounds in cash. They found the tape that had disappeared from Suzanne's study the night of the fire, and they'd also found the missing pages from Sophie's diary, tucked carefully away in a drawer in the one remaining kitchen cupboard.

Sophie had traced her brothers. She must have had some recollections of them from her early childhood, and her mother's letter directed her to her uncle in Sheffield. The family had moved, so Sophie had hired a detective to find them. He had traced Ashley, and Ashley had taken her first to Simon, then to Emma. The diary was full of her delight in being reunited with her brothers, and in finding her half-sister as well. The plans that Ashley had told Suzanne of in the abandoned flat were shared by all of them.

She felt guilty that she was the only one who had emerged from their childhood apparently unscathed. She made excuses for her twin. *It's hard for Ash. He's had a terrible time. He'll come round.* She agreed to his insistence on secrecy. And she seemed to accept what Ashley told her without query at this stage. But a darker note began to creep in. The strange withdrawnness of Simon confused her. *He hardly talks. Except to Lucy. Lucy seems to like him.* Sophie was worried about concealing things from her parents, about the taste for destruction that seemed to shroud both Ashley and Emma. *Ash gets so angry sometimes. And Em is angry too. She found a photograph – she showed me – of her mum. Her mum was pregnant, and that was long before Em was born. Em said she didn't care, but I could see she was really upset.*

It was easy to see, between the lines of Sophie's words, the way in which she, loved and stable, was gradually being pushed out of the circle that had existed those first months, pushed out by the two who shared the knowledge of insta-bility and disturbance. Sophie began to realize about the drugs, began to realize that her twin perhaps had another agenda, began to realize that she was out of her depth.

312

I don't like it here any more. I don't know what to do. I'm going to go home. The last entry.

There were still some gaps that they couldn't fill in. Ashley had talked to Suzanne Milner about removing his father from Lucy's life, about revenge. Had he planned to kill Joel Severini? Or had he planned something else? What had he meant when he said to her, *I've fixed him*?

They had arrested Joel Severini on his return to the house, late that Monday night. He'd spent the evening in the pub, he told them; he gave them names of people he'd seen, people he'd spent the evening with, a picture of courtesy and co-operation. Barraclough, interviewing him with Corvin the following morning, felt as though she had wandered into looking-glass land. This man behaved as though he'd been involved in a minor traffic incident. He seemed more concerned with covering his back than anything else. He hadn't left the children, he was insisting. He'd left Suzanne Milner in charge of them. It wasn't his fault if she was unreliable. 'Suzanne's been a bit strange recently,' he said. Barraclough sent up a silent prayer of thanks that McCarthy wasn't there.

He changed as Corvin began to ask about Emma, about Sophie, about Simon. Yes, he readily agreed, he'd left his wife with a young child, and pregnant. 'I couldn't support them,' he'd said. 'Carolyn was going to go and live with her brother.' He'd never seen the children. No, he'd made no attempt to find out what had happened to them. 'Carolyn wanted a clean break,' he said. It had clearly never crossed his mind that Sophie Dutton, the woman he knew as his daughter's childminder, might be one of the children he'd left. He'd had very little to do with her, he said. 'That was Jane's business.' He became more wary, less talkative, as he began to see the direction that Corvin was taking him. 'I didn't know her,' he said. 'And she didn't know me.' *Prove different*, seemed to be his challenge. He shrugged off the meeting with his son that Ashley had talked about to Suzanne. 'How would I have known?' he said. 'He should have told me who he was.'

He agreed that he had a relationship with Sandra Ford in

the early eighties. 'Well, not really,' he said with a deprecating smile. 'It was just an old-times'-sake thing.' Corvin asked him about Emma, and he began to show signs of annoyance. 'I've told you all of this. I hardly knew her.' He seemed to realize that they had more, and shifted his stance slightly. 'She tried to sell me pills. Told me her boyfriend put her onto me.' He shrugged. He hadn't told them before because nothing had come of it and the girl was dead. 'Why cause trouble?' he said. Corvin, playing a hunch, mentioned Peter Greenhead, implying that they had some knowledge of a deal. Severini was unperturbed. Yes, he'd seen Pete. He'd been hoping they could do some business together. He may have mentioned about Emma and the pills – just a story, really.

When Corvin told him whose daughter Emma was and about the doubts surrounding her parentage, for the first time he seemed to show some genuine emotion. The colour left his face and he stumbled over his words. He demanded a break to talk to his solicitor. When the interview was resumed, he had recovered his equilibrium. He didn't think that Emma was his daughter. Sandy had been a very manipulative woman and had probably been spinning her husband a line. There were many men who could have been Emma's father.

'We can do tests if we need to,' Corvin said. Severini remained unmoved. It didn't alter his story. Barraclough felt a weary cynicism. In the end, he would walk away from all of it, leaving other people to bear the brunt of the things he had done. Four people were dead. The Duttons had lost their daughter. Dennis Allan had lost his wife and child. And Catherine Walker, old and confused, had lost the grandson she had been so proud of. Barraclough could remember the woman's face, looking up at her, uncertain; her smile. *He did very well.* And Joel Severini sat in front of them, occasionally conferring with his solicitor, occasionally smiling a slightly puzzled smile, as though he really couldn't understand what all the fuss was about.

In the immediate aftermath, without a role to keep him focused and stable, McCarthy had spun out of control.

314

Brooke had been understanding but firm. 'Go home,' he'd said. 'You're in no fit state . . .' McCarthy hadn't known if he was on the case or off it, if he'd ballsed it up spectacularly, or if he was just reacting to shock. He'd gone home and unplugged the phone. Sleep seemed too dangerous, so he spent the few remaining hours of the night in an armchair in his flat, the whisky bottle beside him, watching the sun rise over the roofs, reliving the scene again and again, sleep relieving him of the sharp knives of responsibility, to leave him trying to run through waist-deep water, jolting awake at the moment of realization that he wasn't going to make it.

There would be an inquest; there was some speculative – and critical – publicity. Brooke had been unmoved. 'He didn't jump as you came through the door,' he'd told McCarthy as he pushed the bottle towards him across the desk. 'We've got that well witnessed. He moved into the flat from the balcony. You got the woman away from the edge. You didn't make him jump.'

And both the children had survived. McCarthy wondered, as the slow night dragged on, why Reid hadn't killed them at once, in the house or, if he was afraid of being interrupted, as soon as he'd got them to Shepherd Wheel. Killed Lucy, presumably, in revenge for his father's abandonment. He had believed the children were dead, and he had said to Suzanne, '*I've fixed him.*' But why would he think that Severini cared? McCarthy remembered the psychologist talking about Simon Walker. *Maybe the only way to stop them from leaving you is to kill them.* Reid had talked to Suzanne about keeping Lucy safe, about the *one safe place*. Would he have wanted to leave Lucy to the mercy of the world as he knew it? McCarthy shook his head impatiently. Reid was a killer, that's what it came down to. The rest was so much bullshit.

He went to the hospital the next day. Jane, sitting by Lucy's bed, jumped up when she saw him and put her arms round him. Her hair smelt of flowers. 'Steve . . .' she said. He held her close for a moment.

Lucy lay on the bed, pale and subdued. She looked at him dubiously, then sketched a smile and reached out her hand to hold his. He stayed with her, giving Jane a chance to get some fresh air and a short break. Lucy fell asleep, and he sat beside the bed, holding her hand, which clutched his tightly, looking out of the window at the bright clear sky, not really thinking, letting his mind drift.

After he left Lucy, he'd gone along the corridor to the ward where Michael Harrison was recovering from shock, injuries to his leg and an overdose of a tranquillizing drug. Reports said that Michael was making a good recovery, and seemed less affected than Lucy by the experience, possibly because he had been in a drugged sleep for most of the time. He had muscle damage to his leg that would take time to heal, but the medics predicted a full recovery. McCarthy hesitated as he approached the ward, and turned back. He was glad that Michael was well, glad to know he was safe and secure, but he wasn't ready for an encounter with Suzanne. Not now. Not yet.

Lucy was discharged from hospital three days later. She was quiet and pale, her calm self-confidence replaced by a tension that McCarthy found painful to see. She was well enough to tell her story, and had agreed to do so if McCarthy could be there with her. 'I'm sorry to involve you again, Steve,' Alicia Hamilton had said. 'I know that this case has been a hard one for you. She's frightened, poor little thing, you can understand it. She wants you.'

Lucy seemed calm and composed when he took her into the interview room, but she ignored the toys and the books and looked round for somewhere to sit where she could have McCarthy next to her. Hamilton was careful and gentle. McCarthy admired her skill as she worked at winning Lucy's confidence and getting the nervous child to relax. She made it clear that they had as much time as Lucy needed, and gradually she moved towards the details that Lucy would find distressing. 'Tell me who this is, Lucy,' she said, showing her the drawing they'd found in Simon Walker's flat – *The Ash Man's brother*.

'That's Tamby,' Lucy said. She looked at McCarthy. 'Can I go home?'

'Soon,' he promised. 'We need you to help us, Lucy. We need to make sure.' She looked at him, and then nodded, slipping her thumb into her mouth, and leaning against his arm.

Hamilton showed her a photograph of Simon Walker. 'And can you tell me who this is?'

Lucy looked at her coldly. 'I told you,' she said. 'It's Tamby.' Then her lip quivered, and she looked down.

'Tamby was your friend, wasn't he?' said Hamilton. Lucy nodded, one jerk of her head. 'Tell me about him.'

He was her friend, Lucy told them, and Sophie's friend. He would sit on the grass with her and they would play games about her family in the park. 'About my dog and my cat,' Lucy said, 'and all my sisters and brothers.'

'Tell me what Tamby did on the day that you got lost, remember?' Hamilton said

Lucy looked at her with exasperation. 'I told you,' she said. 'I told you and I *told* you. He took me to the playground. On his bike,' she added. 'I told him that Emma was chasing monsters. And he said he'd go and find her and then he'd come and get me. Only he couldn't, because I saw the Ash Man in the playground and I ran away.' She looked down again, and then up at McCarthy. 'Can I make the hands go round on your watch?' He extended his arm, and she inspected the watch for a minute, then began turning the winder.

'You pull it out,' he explained.

'I *know*.' She tightened her lips and gave her attention to the watch face. McCarthy and Hamilton exchanged glances. McCarthy shrugged. He couldn't tell how it was going.

'Just a bit more, Lucy,' Hamilton said, gently. Lucy looked at her quickly under her lashes, her attention still ostensibly on McCarthy's watch.

'Look at all the numbers changing,' she said.

He looked. 'You've made it next year,' he said. 'You've missed Christmas.' She smiled at him, and then flashed the same quick glance at Hamilton. The message was clear. He's *my* friend.

'Lucy . . .' Lucy's face went closed and stubborn. She was

317

listening, but she still looked away, playing with the winder on McCarthy's watch. 'Lucy, you know that someone hurt Emma, don't you?' A nod. 'What did Tamby say to you about Emma?'

She checked McCarthy with her eyes, then said, 'Everyone had gone. Tamby said everyone had gone. Sophie had gone and Emma had gone and he didn't know where they were. And he said he was going to watch me and keep me safe.'

'Safe from what, Lucy?'

'From the Ash Man,' she said. 'Only Tamby didn't know it was the Ash Man. But I did. And the monsters.'

'Who told you about the monsters?'

She compressed her lips. 'They didn't tell me. I *heard*.'

'Who did you hear, Lucy?'

'Tamby.' Head down, voice muffled. 'And Sophie.'

'Tell me what they said. What did they say about the monsters?' Hamilton's voice was gentle but firm.

Silence. Then the glance. 'Dragons.' It was a whisper. 'Emma was chasing dragons. But that was *silly*! Dragons don't live in the river.' McCarthy was cursing himself. *Chasing the dragon!* Lucy's monsters hadn't been fantasies at all.

'That's right, Lucy. They don't.' Hamilton paused for a moment, thinking. 'Was there anyone else, Lucy? Anyone else who played with the monsters?'

Lucy's hand dropped from McCarthy's watch onto her lap. Her face was wary. 'It's a secret,' she said after a moment.

'That's all right. You can tell me, Lucy, that's what I'm here for.' Lucy looked up at McCarthy, who nodded a reinforcement of Hamilton's words.

'Once I saw my daddy there, just with Emma. Emma was cross. My daddy said it was a secret. He *always* said it was secret.' She looked at Hamilton, and at McCarthy. 'He was cross because I told you about Emma, but I didn't, I *said*. But he was cross anyway.' Her lip quivered. 'I don't like my daddy.' McCarthy stroked her hair, the way he had seen Jane do at the hospital. 'The Ash Man threw me in the water where the monster is,' she whispered, so quietly he had to strain to hear it. 'Where Emma is, all dead with the monster, and he's all dead with the monster too.' Drowned people

318

and monsters, nightmares and death. McCarthy's eyes met Hamilton's. How did you protect a child from something like this?

The case was closed after the inquest. The verdict on Ashley Reid's death was suicide. There was no question in the mind of the officers who had witnessed the scene in the flat that he had jumped, not fallen, and that he had tried to pull Suzanne Milner off the balcony with him.

The only moment of satisfaction came for Barraclough when the search of Joel Severini's Leeds flat turned up an impressive stash of pills, far more than those found in Carleton Road, far more than those found in the tower, recognizable, both from their purity and their packaging, as coming from the same source. Severini insisted he had no knowledge of them, claimed that someone had planted them. Barraclough found his protestations oddly convincing. But the pills were hard evidence. Severini faced a serious charge.

McCarthy had seemed unmoved by the find. Barraclough had asked him what he thought about it, and he had said, brusquely, that he didn't see how having a father in jail on a dealing conviction was going to do the Fielding child any good. Then he'd given her a hard time about the delay in some paperwork and suggested she keep her mind on matters in hand, rather than waste her time and his speculating about cases that were over. He was back to normal, she decided.

22

It was nearly a fortnight before McCarthy saw Suzanne again. He arranged to meet her at Carleton Road. They were cautious with each other on the phone. It was early Friday evening, and he left his car on the far side of the park, near the house where Simon Walker had lived. He needed to walk, and to think. He didn't know what to do. He had been wrong about her before. He had thought that she had lied to him, once about the sighting in the park, once about Ashley Reid. But the man hurrying from Shepherd Wheel had almost certainly been Simon Walker, looking for Emma, hurrying to get back to Lucy, out of his depth in the world of people rather than the world of things. And though Ashley Reid *had* been in Suzanne's house, in her study, hunting for the tapes that might lead the police to him, Suzanne hadn't known, hadn't known about the route through the roof spaces along the row of terraces from the student house, empty and unused.

He had planned to walk through Endcliffe Park and then on up to Carleton Road. But instead he turned into Bingham Park, towards Shepherd Wheel. A newspaper boy was standing in the entrance, looking up at the noticeboard. A piece of paper with scrawled writing on it was attached to the board. McCarthy read it. TAKE CARE BY ALLOTMENTS! The boy looked round and hunched his shoulders, preparing to leave. 'What is it?' McCarthy said, indicating the note. The boy looked suspicious. McCarthy took out his ID and showed the lad. 'What is it?' he said again.

The boy hoisted the bag of newspapers onto his shoulder. 'It's up in the allotments,' he said. 'There's been a man up there . . .' He made a gesture of opening a raincoat. 'You know.' McCarthy remembered Barraclough saying there'd been reports of a flasher in the park.

'So what's this?' McCarthy said, looking at the notice.

'We leave notes if he's there,' the boy said. 'On our rounds. I take the path through the allotments, see. Only I'll not, today.'

So that was it. McCarthy watched the boy on his way. A warning system used by the newspaper-delivery kids, a self-help group against one of the disturbed misfits who lurked in this piece of urban green. That was what Suzanne had seen, what had made her wary that morning when Emma and Lucy had gone missing. If the note hadn't made her cut her walk short, would she have been there to see Simon walking away from Shepherd Wheel?

He looked up at the trees that were heavy with leaf, casting deep shadows over the path. He went on, crossing the bridge to walk by the narrow channel where the conduit emptied. Shepherd Wheel was ahead of him now, through the trees. Its mossy roof glowed gold in the evening sun. The broken windows were hidden behind tight shutters. It was silent and still. McCarthy walked on up to the dam. The light on the water turned the surface opaque like steel. Leaves were drifting in the gentle current towards the overspill where the water tumbled back to the river. As McCarthy watched, the light faded, and he was looking through the surface· of the water, looking into the depths of a brown mirror where it was dark and cool and fish made dim shadows against the muddy bottom.

One last thing was nagging him. Carolyn Reid's family. Her brother Bryan, the man who had become a bullying disciplinarian, an alcoholic, a man who had lost touch with his family through his drinking – they had never talked to him because they hadn't been able to find him. But, according to Suzanne, Ashley Reid had.

McCarthy remembered the face of the tramp, the unknown man who had been savagely beaten and slashed, and had died with shards from a broken whisky bottle shoved down his throat, choked on his own blood – like Emma.

Bryan Walker had cared for his sister. He had not been able to take his anger out on the man who had abandoned her, and who, for all he knew, had been responsible for her illness. Instead, he had worked to beat the bad blood out of the son. McCarthy knew, now, who the nameless vagrant was and he knew, as well, what had happened to him.

It was seven by the time he reached Suzanne's house, which still showed evidence of the fire. The broken window had been replaced, but the door was smoke-blackened and damaged. The leaves on the cotoneaster were brown and dead where the branches had broken. The flowers had fallen.

He wasn't sure what he expected when she opened the door. 'I saw you coming up the road,' she said as they stood in the front room facing each other, in that first, difficult silence.

'How are you?' he said. It sounded more brusque than he'd intended.

'I'm OK. I'm going to be OK,' she amended. 'How are you?' She bit her lip. 'I've been worried about you.'

He didn't want to pursue that. 'Michael? Is he all right now?' He already knew that Michael had been discharged from hospital, and that he was recovering well.

She nodded. 'Yes. He's back at school. Dave says the important thing is to get everything back to normal as quickly as possible. He's . . . There's still a bit to go, but he's getting there.' She took a breath. 'Michael's lucky. Dave's a good father.'

McCarthy thought of Joel Severini. Severini had been given bail on the plea of his solicitor that his client's traumatized daughter needed her father. He had skipped bail within twenty-four hours of being released. Suzanne picked up his thought. 'Lucy doesn't need Joel,' she said. 'She deserves better.' Her face was serious, sad. She was clearly thinking of her own son, thinking that he, too, deserved better. Maybe she was right. It wasn't a thought to pursue.

'What are you going to do?' As far as he knew, she had no work now. The recent events would hardly get her reinstated at the Alpha Centre.

She shrugged. 'I've got a few weeks' leeway. I'm on leave,

322

and there's still a few months of my grant left to run. I'm not sure what they'll do with a researcher in my position. I can make myself useful – if they'll let me. I'm *persona non grata* at the moment.' She smiled ruefully at him. 'With them as well. But I'm job hunting. When I started my research, I thought I could do something useful, working with young offenders. But I can't. It's too close, too personal. I've got to get away from that.'

So she knew that, at least. He leant his shoulder against the mantelpiece and watched her as she stood looking out of the window. Though the more obvious signs of the fire had gone, there were so many reminders of what had happened here. Could she sit in this room and not remember the night when the smoke had nearly choked her to death? Could she be anywhere in this house and not think of Ashley Reid, the desperate and damaged youth she had tried, however misguidedly, to help? The house was packed with bad memories. He wondered if she would stay. 'What kind of job?'

She moved away from the window to the centre of the room and stood in front of him. 'Anything. Just to keep me going until I've had a chance to think. Maybe I'll apply to join the police.' Her eyes, as they met his, were deadpan, then she started laughing at the expression of horror he hadn't been able to keep off his face.

The laughter brought tears to her eyes, and she brushed them away impatiently. They were both teetering on the edge of emotions that were hard to control. Time to stop talking. Time to move on. He checked his watch. Half past seven. 'Have you eaten?' he said. She shook her head. 'We could go out, go to one of the places down the road.'

She held his eyes. 'What's wrong with dial-a-pizza?' she said. 'No pineapple.'

There were still too many things left unspoken. Any future seemed a distant possibility, a view that was too remote to understand, but here and now was real. He kept his eyes on her as he pushed himself upright. She was looking up at him, trying to read his expression, trying to mask the uncertainty in her face. He could see a faint mark on her lip where the cut had healed. He touched it gently, smiled at her. 'OK,' he said. 'Suits me. But in an hour. Or so.'

Catherine Walker was looking for her garden. She hadn't done anything in the garden for a long time, and now she couldn't find the way. The window, the garden looked all wrong. 'Where is my garden,' she asked the woman whom she didn't know. *What are you doing in my house?*

'Ready for tea, Catherine?'

Or was it one of her dreams? She looked out of the window. It was her garden, and the children were playing there; they'd need their tea soon. She struggled to get out of her chair, but somehow she couldn't, and then she couldn't find the room, it was all wrong, with chairs and people in rows and . . . The TV should be over there and it wasn't, and the table in the window had gone, and the window was – everything was the wrong way round. She struggled in the deep chair and pulled herself forward to stand.

'You don't want to get up now, Catherine, we'll take you through for your tea in a moment.'

A loud voice, and a hand in her chest pushing her back so that her hard fight to leave the depths of the chair was all lost and she wanted to cry out with frustration and fear. *Where am I?*

The children. She looked again. It was all right, they were still in the garden, kneeling on the lawn that had looked like a car park just a moment ago, but she must have been having one of her dreams. She wanted to tell Carolyn. Carolyn would want to know. *Simon's happy.*

But the chair, she couldn't get out of the chair, and Simon was in the garden with another child. Children teased and tormented him. She needed to be there, to mind them. She gripped the arms and began pulling herself up again. Now she could see that the TV and the door and the window were all in the right place. It had just been one of her dreams. And she was walking over to the window and the light was starting to fade. She could open the window and call them in, the two who were looking at her now, two little boys with dark hair and solemn faces. So alike, she couldn't tell one from the other. *You've found a friend, Simon!* She pushed open the door and stepped out into the cool of the evening, only there were voices, and a clattering, and it seemed hard to move forward.

'What are you up to now, Catherine?'

'Simon . . . ?' she said.